D1448456

DAUGHTERS OF EMPIRE

ACKNOWLEDGEMENTS

I would like to thank the following: Sharda Dean for reading the first draft and offering helpful suggestions, Avinash and Rajendra Persaud for reading passages of the novel and Dev Maharaj who readily assisted me with my queries.

Finally, I would like to express my gratitude to Professor Kenneth Ramchand who made some helpful comments, and to Jeremy Poynting who read and reread the novel at different stages, offering valuable advice.

DAUGHTERS OF EMPIRE

LAKSHMI PERSAUD

P E E P A L   T R E E

First published in Great Britain in 2012
Peepal Tree Press Ltd
17 King's Avenue
Leeds LS6 1QS
England

ISBN13: 9781845231873

This is a work of fiction. All characters are imaginary.

In loving memory of
Indra Seeterram,
who enhanced the lives of those she met.

And for
Maharanee Persaud
who brings light to the dark

PART ONE

BEGINNINGS

1

AUTUMN'S ARIA
London 1970s

How I wish I'd been here, Amira is thinking as she and their three young daughters wait for Santosh to open the door. If only I did not have to leave him to choose. She is dreading going in.

The young family stands before the white front door of Number 14 Apple Grove, Mill Hill. Close by, four pairs of eyes are observing them.

Ishani's warnings are tugging at her: *Santosh knows nothing about houses, except that a house is where he expects to find a warm meal and a comfortable bed. It can't be helped, I know, having him choose, so brace yourself for anything.* Her sister, older by several years, and with an eye for business matters, had, as far back as Amira could remember, perceived things accurately more often than most.

Five foot eight, neatly suited, with a full crop of hair that dances with the slightest breeze, Santosh is only too aware of what he refers to as his wife's foibles – regarding what makes a house suitable for a family.

The moment has come; they are before his choice. He senses Amira's mounting tension and the expectation of his eldest daughter, Anjali, just ten. Tall and slender, she carries herself well; two long ponytails in sea-blue ribbons brush her shoulders. Too thoughtful for one so young, he thinks. He winks like a clown, bringing a smile to her face, before inserting the key with a conjuror's panache. He says, 'Cheer up, Amira; I know you'll be pleased. Didn't I tell you I read your list of requirements to the house?'

The two younger girls are nudging the door to open with steely determination; their backs and shoulders have become levers.

'I cannot explain why, Amira,' Santosh says, 'there was a studied silence when it heard your list.'

Perhaps the house, she muses, was too proud to answer in the negative, convinced no building that did not meet her stipulation deserved to be called a house. Instead, she replies, 'Houses take a long time to respond.'

'Whatever the reason, Amira, the windows and doors rattled in affirmation and sunshine burst in. "Thank you," I heard myself say.'

She knows this is his way of explaining that he had tried his best to please her, that what is before her was the pick of the bunch. Even so her shoulders stiffen. Why oh why couldn't she just relax? She had to make the most of what she found. What had she gained from worrying throughout the long plane journey? She'd remembered too late what her father had once taught her at the seaside, when she was small and trusting. He'd told her to jump high, so she wouldn't be swallowed up by huge waves. And when they'd come, she'd been buoyed up, then gently dropped. She'd felt so grown up, exhilarated that her timing was perfect. Be sensible, Amira; he'll have done his best. Just tell him how pleased you are, and do your utmost to ensure our living here is a success.

The contours of her face soften. 'Shhhh Santosh, don't let the neighbours hear. What will they think, you speaking to a house?'

'Turn the key, Daddy! Open up please, Daddy!' Satisha and Vidya cry, their feet impatient for the chase. At almost six, and more than two, they are keen explorers of the unfamiliar.

All this while, they were watched from behind white net curtains. Here was something strange. Mill Hill, though in London NW7, was still just a small town. It was named after the old mill which stands to this day on the Ridgeway. Even devoid of a top half and its sails, the Mill's rotund remains still upheld its identity. The twentieth century had crept slowly on Mill Hill, drifting from its upper terraces to the foot of the Ridgeway, onto grassy plains, interspersed by woodland, farms and country lanes. Cottages were giving way to detached and semi-detached houses constructed along former lanes. Tracks traced by cart wheels and the hooves of horses and cows had become smooth, paved roads connecting Hendon to the north and Edgware to the south.

The residents of Mill Hill, like the generations before them, were content with themselves and the slow pace of change. Even by the 1960s, Mill Hill was such a tranquil, unruffled place that to call it a town was exaggerating in its favour; but it had a railway station, bus stops, a post office, a medical surgery, two banks, a barber's, a hairdresser's, a Woolworths, a Boots the Chemist, a WH Smiths, a Budgens, a butcher's shop, a fishmonger's and greengrocer's all in one – with little to tempt an enterprising cook. There was a police station; few seemed to notice it.

New arrivals were virtually unknown; those watchful eyes saw complexions that did not belong, arriving not only in their green and pleasant land, but coming to live just opposite them. World War II had taught Londoners that the world would be a safer place if foreigners remained in their homes, not marching into other countries in heavy boots. *Let us be!* would have been the motto on any flag raised on the rooftops of Apple Grove.

Amira stepped cautiously over the threshold; her eyes caught the curved arch, quietly gracious above the entrance to the hall. She was surprised to see such circular elegance repeated on the landing. Soft flowing lines conveyed agreeable good taste; the house was built at the beginning of the century to accommodate the aspirations and pockets of southern England's growing middle class. It was rumoured that in those bygone days, these detached houses in Apple Grove were sold for not much over one thousand pounds, with the builders making a decent profit; now they were being sold for more than twenty-five times that sum.

Amira caressed the wall with open palms, giving thanks to the house, to the builders, the architect, to Santosh for choosing it. What little faith Ishani had shown!

She prepared a highly polished brass thali with incense. It looked too bare, but standing in front of the picture window in the kitchen, a solitary rose in the abandoned garden caught her eye. She picked it, held it close, inhaling, but the overpowering, crimson perfume of tropical roses was not there. Memory brought the intense floral fragrances from Tunapuna's shivala, flowing out into the night on Shivratree, filling the open courtyard, enveloping all.

The camphor alight, holding the thali in both hands, Amira slowly traced the edges of each room, leaving wafts of incense behind. When she entered the last room upstairs, she closed the door and there in its bare stillness, with the flickering camphor, addressed the spirit of the house, seeking its permission, as her mother would have done, for her family to share its shelter, promising to keep this place of work, of thought, of rest, of delights, clean and in good repair. Here, in their new home, there would be learning, discovering and embracing only what was good. She could not bring herself to consider life's shadows: sadness, depression, frustration, loneliness and not belonging. Here she made her prayerful request:

'Bring us light and warmth when we are in need. Stand strong when primeval forces threaten, and keep us safe. Our family thanks you for enduring the piercing winter cold, the sun's rays that crack the earth, the howling westerly winds from oceans far. Your sweet wood frames each door and window and welcomes us. We thank you. You who are older than we are, you who have heard, seen, felt much, we ask that you look upon us gently, let your energies and wisdom embrace us.' She bowed, a whispering wind to the unknown, perhaps the unknowable.

Meanwhile, at Number 15, Edward Cohen left the window and turned to Mrs Cohen, 'This is the last thing we need – strong curry smells and what have you driving us out in no time. Sitting in our garden will become intolerable, with their fumes seeping over the garden fence. How do we protect ourselves from that, Janna?'

'Let's wait and see,' soothed Janna Cohen. 'They won't be having curries every day, dear, will they? That would be tedious, don't you think? They aren't in foreign clothes, Edward, that's something. I wonder what language they speak.'

'They come here without English, expecting us to learn their languages, Janna. Such are the times, dear.'

Janna hoped Edward's misgivings wouldn't materialise. The woman and her children were not wearing long costumes, yet they were Asians of some kind. What did that signify? They were not covering their heads either… Maybe they belonged to a sect that had branched out – like the Methodists. Thank goodness they were not wearing those long black gowns and faces masked. Now, that really *would* stir the coffee mornings. She wouldn't be comfortable walking home at night with someone behind her all in black. The men didn't wear black, nor hide themselves in that way. What did it all mean?

She tried to disengage herself from Edward's apprehension, for he tired her with his bleak outlook on things. Nevertheless, reading about foreigners residing somewhere in the Midlands was one thing, having them in your street, right opposite you, was quite another. Oh the comforts of the familiar. She wondered what Alice and Nick were making of them.

Nick Reid, at Number 11, had been complaining for some time that he'd been slowing down. A primary school teacher, perhaps it was time to take early retirement, sell up and move to Devon.

'Look dear,' he said frowning, 'with such people in the neighbourhood, we'll soon be cluttered with vans loaded with goods of every description. What a mess! Apple Grove is not that sort of street. Look, Alice we have a peaceful, orderly place here… Apple Grove will change… but why should it? You know what will follow don't you?'

'What, dear?'

'House prices tumbling! Just our luck, Alice. We've never had these sorts before, not here, not in Mill Hill. There are no jobs here… No cotton mills, no factories. What's happening out there? Why are they coming to a small place like this with no one like themselves? Now that *is* worrying. Maybe there's an overflow from Bradford or Leicester. We'll be in a real pickle if they come here in droves. I heard in the staff room that in Leicester we're already in the minority. Fancy that!'

'What's that, dear?'

'A minority in our own land. Where are we heading, Alice? What will become of us? This is a quiet, English town. It's been like this for as far back as you go. All this around us was once farm land. All those old apple orchards had made way for lawns. Now Apple Grove is an avenue of lime trees – well that's change enough. Acres and acres of green… We want to keep it that way. What's wrong with that? Why can't the government see that? I wonder if they know there are no jobs here… Maybe you could explain to the wife, "No jobs here. No jobs at all." Explain you're thinking of their welfare… Except they may not understand English…'

'It's just one family, Nick. Will one make all that difference?'

'You always hope for the best, Alice, but I know their little ways.'

'What do you mean, Nick?'

'Before you know where you are, these people will be buying up this street. They work in groups. From what one reads in the newspapers, Alice, we have long lost Southall to them, to their shops, their houses, temples and mosques, sounds and smells… This England, Alice, for which our lads fought so bravely in two world wars, is being taken over, before our very eyes, taken from us, Alice, while the government slumbers. We think differently even from our neighbours the French and the Dutch, and of course the Germans… Why can't England remain England? We're unique, Alice. You and I know this. But do they? We just want to be left alone to be ourselves. What is wrong with that? Look at our gates! Wide open, Alice. Anyone can just walk in.'

'Don't fret so, dear. You know it's not good for your blood pressure. Let's just wait and see. Fingers crossed. We might just be lucky Nick, who knows? They might not like it here and their family will not join them. A cuppa dear?'

Mr Reid's troubled eyes pierced the walls of Number 14, but its foundations held firm; the men of England knew how to build.

The Vidhurs had bathed in history's streams, and were inheritors of several sensibilities and ways of thinking. One was from the ancient culture of India that had attracted Columbus to venture forth, the other from the results of his mistake: the potent mixing of the cultures of Caribs and Arawaks; French, Spanish and Dutch colonisers; Africans brought as slaves to work on the sugar plantations, and the Chinese and the Indians who, like the Vidhurs' foreparents, had been brought to work as indentured labourers to ensure the profitability of the West Indian sugar industry after emancipation.

There was the heritage of the language, literature and institutions of Britain – and the seductive modernity blowing in from their large, prosperous American neighbour.

Now, more than a hundred years after the journey their foreparents had made from Calcutta to the Caribbean, the Vidhurs were once again making a long journey: from Trinidad to Apple Grove. They, much more than their foreparents, were full of hope of fulfilling themselves, in search of something not fully articulated, yet felt and in that way understood: 'a good life'.

It was to their inheritance that they looked for direction. It was their predisposition to reflect on what should guide them. Amira grasped the extent to which these new circumstances would bring her daily challenges. She was moving away from the known, from the warmth of family and friendships and her much-loved job as a teacher, all of which had formed her identity. Leaving all behind had caused her anguish. How would she cope with the new, the knowns and unknowns?

Now, as she placed the thali on the window ledge, she caught sight of a face looking curiously at her from a mirror attached to the wall. At first, she did not see what it reflected – electric-clear, listening eyes, fine, silky, long hair held in a neat chignon, a face that beamed with thought, warmth and good will. What she saw was the dullness, the dust of the mirror; she circled it with her forefinger, noting it must be seen to.

The morning sunlight filled the sitting room, and the two side windows of coloured glass sang to her as if a choir of boys were behind them. Their vibrant primary colours would have lost much more of themselves had they not been sheltered from the bleaching summer sun by the shadow of Number 16, the house of Margaret and Jack

Summers, but there remained enough depth of colour to attract Amira's admiration. Were the designs meant to be tulips from Amsterdam or something more exotic from Istanbul? The very fact that 'church windows' – as she thought of them – could be found not only in grand establishments but in their modest house reminded her how far away they were from Trinidad.

Outside, the maple, beech, silver birch and lime trees were still clothed in green, with only hints of the yellow, orange, rust and reds to come. It would be a while yet before the Vidhurs saw them naked, vulnerable – leaves brought low, skating, cartwheeling with the wind.

2

MEETING THE HEADMISTRESS

The morning of her third day came too swiftly for Amira, who was trying to cope with the volatile shifts of temperature, the pavements hard on the soles of her shoes, and the task of discovering where everything was. There, looming before her, was her appointment with the headmistress of St Hilda's school, Miss Williams. She prepared herself and her three daughters as best she could. This was not easy; much was in disarray. Anxiously hurrying from room to room, rummaging in boxes to find the clothes she needed, then ironing them, added to a feeling of inadequacy.

Without the home help she was used to in Trinidad, this domestic environment was new and challenging. Here it was all left to her. Santosh had said airily there was nothing to worry about and left for work.

She dressed the girls with modesty and decorum. All three wore neat dresses with sensible hemlines falling well below the knees – 'little women' of the Victorian age, she thought. Socks that had not lost their elasticity were eventually found. She hoped her own smart shoes with comfortable heels, her straight skirt, matching blouse and cardigan made the right impression.

Shoes had been polished the night before; now nails were examined, hair brushed, unruly strands patted into place, frocks pulled this way and that until their hemlines yielded symmetry. The girls were told to be on their very best behaviour, to be helpful to each other and not to speak when grown-ups were talking. Anjali understood what was at stake; waves of her mother's anxiety had reached her. As first born, she'd been at the centre of her mother's domestic world, absorbing her aspirations, her perceptions of things.

They were all sent to the bathroom, 'just in case'. Vidya did not want 'a just in case'; her mother insisted. Amira had a last quick check to ensure there were no shining spots on her face and that her hair was in place. She made an unsuccessful attempt to smile at the mirror.

St Hilda's was a private school in a detached house about a seven-minute walk from Apple Grove, not far from Mill Hill Broadway. Amira had questioned Santosh about whether they could afford the school fees; she wanted to be sure that they would not be too financially stretched by this choice. He told her there was nothing to worry about. This meant nothing; it was his response to most things that concerned her. Later, he explained that if they'd had boys, he would have risked sending them to the local state school, but for his girls he wanted a smaller, better-regulated environment, one accountable to fee-paying parents.

As Amira approached the school, she began to think the unthinkable. Her empty stomach gurgled; her steps slowed. From the letter they had received, Santosh believed, as did she, that Anjali and Satisha had gained a place.

They were welcomed by a matronly looking woman who was evidently too busy for courteous niceties. She directed them to the office and told Amira to knock 'Just the once and wait', and demonstrated in dumbshow what she meant.

Facing them was the headmistress, Miss Williams – plump, not tall, a daunting ball of confidence behind a substantial oak desk, with glasses through which she gave Amira a penetrating stare. Anjali tried to squeeze out a smile and took Satisha's hand to show she was a responsible sort. She noted that her mother held on firmly to Vidya, in case her sister's curiosity, keenly felt as kittens at play, drew her to select her preferences from a partially opened bookcase.

'I see you applied just six months ago. The children whom I'm enrolling this morning were on my waiting list for a minimum of three years, Mrs Vidhur. Am I pronouncing your name correctly?'

'Yes, you are. You see, Miss Williams, I could not make an application to you before I was sure we would be living in Mill Hill. We wanted to live here, and close to your school too. We were lucky to find a detached house close by, in Apple Grove.' Amira's nervous smile appeared. 'Some might apply to your school, on the off-chance that they'd be here; I did not want to do that. I didn't think it was right or fair to you.'

'Am I to understand you were not sure you'd be living in London?'

'This is connected to my husband's work. He was offered a fine job in the Caribbean, but as he has been promoted to his present position, we've decided to make London our home.'

'I see. When are you likely to be returning to the Caribbean?'

'We are making London our home.'

'Very well. No doubt you are unaware of the predicament you have placed me in, Mrs Vidhur. Were I to take both girls, I would have to say no to others whose parents applied three years ago.'

'I just could not have applied earlier, Miss Williams. I just couldn't.' Amira's stomach fell into cold depths; she made one last plea: 'My circumstances were quite different from those who applied three years ago, Miss Williams.'

'Rules are rules, Mrs Vidhur. This country has got where it is because we keep to the rules.'

Her father's voice comes over clearly. *Take the hits but keep moving forward, my daughter, keep moving forward.* And there was Santosh's *Keep your eyes on the ball, Amira.*

She heard herself saying: 'What is the purpose of rules, Miss Williams? In this particular instance, they are to ensure fair play. Fair play is what guides you.'

'True, Mrs Vidhur.'

'But these rules make an important assumption.'

'Do they?'

Miss Williams took a deep breath, lifted her chest and shoulders, like a bulwark.

'The assumption is that all the players know the rules and their circumstances are similar... My circumstance is entirely different from others', Miss Williams. If... if... let's say you'd been in my position, what then?'

'On being told what the rules were, I would have to abide by them, Mrs Vidhur. It is the way things are done here.' The erect, firm posture became more firm.

'True. But would it have been fair to you? In some situations what is fair to everyone can only be administered with a measure of flexibility.'

'Flexibility, Mrs Vidhur?' Her disdain was quietly reined in, but its presence hovered from the ceiling. 'That is a very slippery road to... to we know not where, Mrs Vidhur.'

'This flexibility I am referring to, Miss Williams, is aware of the dangers you have correctly asserted, so it is rare, and practised only when the arbitrators are given the opportunity to have a larger understanding of the complexity before them.'

Miss Williams was taken aback. That was unexpected – what cricket fans would call a googly. She sensed something relenting within her, a reluctant feeling of admiration for this young woman challenging her on behalf of her daughters, but it held her only for an instant. She'd always used her experience to good advantage. In the past she had relied on common sense topped up by what she called informed intuition. Here was an unknown. She'd observed foreigners in the streets, but today, for the first time, one had entered her school and sat before her.

Amira's fury grew. Miss Williams should have written explaining the rules. True she had not asked for them, but who did that? You were told them. Not knowing the law was no justification for breaking it, but these were just school rules, and if Miss Williams had thought to explain them, she would not be there.

Miss Williams offered a smile of unassailable authority; Amira felt she knew what was coming. Where to turn? She had not made alternative arrangements; what would she say to the children?

Anjali absorbed her mother's wretchedness. She felt like rushing up and putting her arms around her. She, Anjali, would do well no matter which school she was sent to, in fact even if she got into no school at all, she would study hard and do well. Her father's words come to her. *This is nothing to worry about. Life is larger than it.* Daddy was right. Life was larger than this school. Who wanted to come here anyway?

The words sat on her lips, bidding her to end her mother's despair. But she could not do it; she had been trained to do her parents' bidding. She bent her head, stared at the floor with an intensity meant to hold back tears. It brought the desired result. Anjali heard her mother's voice, pleading, desperate. She wanted to stand up and say, 'Excuse me, I do not like you, I do not wish to come here. You're horrid to my mother.' Instead she heard her mother speak again.

Amira wanted to say, *You're not being fair, you should have explained this to me in your letter when I applied. Why didn't you?* But she knew there was nothing to gain by this approach. Instead she asked: 'What am I to do? Is there another school that you could recommend? Is it now too late for any school? St Hilda's is the only school I applied to. I'm now aware I should have applied to others, but coming from far, not knowing this, has placed me and the girls in an impossible position. When we received your letter, we felt that the chances of Anjali and Satisha coming here were good. They are bright girls, attentive in class, very well behaved at all times, and would be a credit to your school. Just look at them, you must see how much they wish to be here. Are you unhappy with their school reports?'

Thus far Miss Williams had paid little attention to the reports; they were from schools of unknown standards. But now as she looked down the subject columns, she noted that the hand was good and the comments thoughtful, neither vague nor generalised. Silence pervaded the room.

Amira's thoughts worked overtime: *I must bring everything I have to this, otherwise when I get home, I'll be saying, if I had said this, or mentioned that, things might have been different. I have nothing to lose. I will inform Miss Williams that I have been treated most unfairly. Why did she ask me for an interview so close to the beginning of term, if the girls had not gained a place? Why? For God's sake!*

'My husband and I will do our utmost to ensure our girls are a credit to your school, Miss Williams... I only wish I'd had some inkling of this, I only wish you'd explained your predicament. It would have been so helpful to know.' There, it had come out, and no sooner had the words left her, than she was penitent. What had she done? Miss Williams' fury was sure to come. She lifted her head, waiting to be dismissed.

The front door-bell rang loudly. Her time was up.

But Miss Williams' thoughts were engaged with the open file before her. This was a decision that could not be revoked. Amira's playing of her last desperate card had escaped her notice – and its tone too subdued to take her away from her concentration.

Satisha wondered what was happening; she looked to Anjali, seeking a clue. Anjali nodded and caressed her hand. Vidya indicated that she wanted to sit on her mother's lap. Anjali took her. A pair of spectacled eyes focused upon them. Innocence and vulnerability – and a thoughtful, articulate mother. Could one lose in opting to take from a home with such a parent?

'They were so looking forward to being at St Hilda's. I brought them here and pointed to your school saying this was where they would be going.'

'That was most unwise.'

'I just could not have applied any earlier. I could not do it.'

'You have made that clear on more than one occasion. I do understand. However, you were foolhardy to build up your own expectations when nothing was confirmed to you. That I consider to be verging on the irresponsible.'

'There are times when one's enthusiasm for having something special takes on a life of its own, Miss Williams. We learnt of your school in Trinidad; the very helpful first secretary at the British High Commission, Mrs Kelly, who knows the girls, recommended St Hilda's, saying that their aspirations were in keeping with those of the school. I applied to no other.'

Simultaneously flattered and pricked, Miss Williams reflected that maybe someone not aware of the procedures might think that an interview was the entrance to acceptance. In practice it was mainly so.

But applications were larger this year than ever before, indeed increasing each year. The task was impossible.

Sparring with parents was her forte; they wanted something from her and were generally prepared to acquiesce to what they perceived as her foibles. This woman sitting before her was not playing by the rules. Yet Miss Williams liked to think her decisions were not influenced by the extraneous.

She too had heard the door-bell; she must make a decision and move on. Something told her that her customary practices had been found wanting. But to be challenged on one's home ground!

She shuffled about, breathed deeply, modulated her voice. 'Having seen your girls, and noted their school reports, having heard your very particular circumstance, I have decided to have both girls. Of course, if anyone asks, you did apply three years ago. You do follow me?'

Amira did not follow fully, but certainly understood the decision. Her own teacher's habit of being a good listener, of nodding sympathetically to parents disclosing discomforts, now appeared of its own accord and reassured Miss Williams.

There were changes in the air, Miss Williams thought. Her school would have to adjust to the times. If she stayed with her present criterion for admission, one hundred percent of the intake would come from one culture or religious group. Perhaps it was in the interests of all that other cultures should contribute to the ethos of the school. Even so, she would continue to be selective, to ensure that the new intake came only from the very best of families – but then, only such families were able to benefit from what the school had to offer.

Miss Williams handed her a sealed envelope. 'What you need to know is there. Fees are paid in advance, school uniforms may be purchased locally here in the Broadway. It is all there. Any questions?'

'As I said in my letter, I would very much like Vidya also to attend school here. She will be three next year; it would be good to have her application confirmed.'

'I have noted it. Of course, her chances of being admitted will improve with the performance of her sisters.'

'I wish to thank you, Miss Williams, for having Anjali and Satisha; they are well-behaved girls and keen to learn. You will have no trouble whatsoever with them.'

'It is what we expect. A very good day to you, Mrs Vidhur.'

Miss Williams got up and shook Amira's hand. 'I shall keep Vidya in mind.' Nothing resembling a smile escaped, but in her eyes a softness shone not visible before.

'Thank you again, Miss Williams, you have been good to the girls.'
The headmistress nodded and rang the bell on her desk.

As they walked back home, Amira slowed her pace. 'You were all so well behaved, and because of that, and your school reports, the headmistress will have you at her school. You're the nicest girls Mummy knows. Nobody fidgeted. You all helped Mummy to concentrate. Now you'll be going to a good school.'

'When will that be?' asked Satisha.

'In a month's time. Very soon,' answered Anjali.

'Soon soon,' repeated Vidya.

'Now let me say this – is everyone listening to Mummy? You all have to work very hard at school. We're newcomers to this country. Newcomers always have to work many, many times harder than those already here. We've only ourselves; this is why you have to learn as much as you can to improve yourselves. It's important to remember this, Anjali. You have only one self; make it a good self. Your mummy and your daddy you will always have. And whenever you think you're walking alone, you will have us beside you – and your good self too. Do you see that, Anjali?'

'Yes Mummy, I understand everything you say,' and she started to cry.

'What's wrong Anjali? You'll be going to a very good school.'

'Miss Williams was not nice to you, Mummy. I don't like her and I don't want to go to her school. I know I have to but I wish I didn't. I want to go to another school. I don't even have to go to a school. I can learn at home.' Amira hugs her and, as she caresses her daughter's back, tears come to her too.

'Headmistresses tend to behave as she did; this is her school and there's only room for a few. She didn't make herself clear in her letters to me but I tried not to say so. It would have made her angry and angry people are not generous people. I had to help her to see our position in a way that was favourable to us but also true. It is a difficult thing to do, to make others walk in your shoes. Do you understand?'

'Yes Mummy.' Anjali nodded, thinking, *I hope I don't grow up quickly because I cannot do the things Mummy does.*

'I understand too,' insisted Satisha, her eyes affirming this assertion, while her open arms ask to be hugged too.

'I too! I unstand too!' shouted two-year-old Vidya, fearing that what she knew was being overlooked. She was also hugged and three heads were caressed in a blessing.

Amira had long been trying to offer her daughters the assurance

22

that the world was full of wonder and beauty. This belief helped her to fight her corner, but it was not easy. Her eyes welled up but did not brim over. Disappointment had come close. Her breathing was still fast; her mind restless.

In Trinidad or Guyana she was at ease with herself. Arrived in London with her young family, facing Immigration, she was a stranger, someone to be questioned. Holding out Santosh's letter of employment, complete with its letterhead from the Commonwealth Secretariat, with a letter from the Secretary General identifying who they were, she had waited as pages were turned, she and the girls looked over. She had brought her marriage certificate, though she did not intend to hand it over without asking why it was required. Then a smile, a nod of affirmation and the word 'Next' came from the voice before her. Next may be an ordinary word, but that day the meaning was large.

As they turned into Apple Grove, Amira thought, 'Next a secondary school.' She knew nothing about which were the better schools or even how to find out; yet within a year Anjali would be leaving St Hilda's for a secondary school.

She wondered too whether it was already too late to apply, or whether she could possibly be lucky a second time. But this was for later. Now, before school term began, while Anjali was at home to help, she had to get as much done as possible in the house.

Tiredness descended abruptly but she made an effort to be cheerful for her daughters' sakes. She knew they had seen her at her most vulnerable. Some things, Anjali saw, were hard and difficult; her younger sisters felt subdued in spirits, but didn't know why.

'Mummy will bake an apple crumble, topped with almond nuts, for the nicest three girls she knows. I wonder who they are.'

'Me and Vidya and Anjali.'

'Me too,' Vidya shouted.

'Shall we have dinner by candlelight and invite all the good fairies who helped us today?'

'Yes, Mummy,' said Satisha.

Vidya nodded her head and asked, 'Fairies coming, Mummy?'

Anjali smiled.

'Daddy said apple crumble with almond nuts is our second name. Is that true, Mummy?' asked Satisha.

'It's a good second name,' Amira replied.

That evening, the aroma of cinnamon, cloves and baked apple topped with almond nuts filled the kitchen; the candlelight flickered and the shadows seemed at play. Fairies? Who can tell?

3

ISHANI'S LETTER ARRIVES AT NUMBER 14

There was something about the spirit of the house that seemed to talk to Amira as she sat in the kitchen, coffee in hand, her thoughts moving from room to room like a walking shadow.

There was at least one thing about her new situation to be welcomed: her actions could no longer be analysed, shown up as mistaken by her so capable elder sister. Then a question came bouncing off the wall: 'Was freedom without knowledge and understanding truly liberating?' Misgivings stirred. Perhaps being alone during the day gave her too much space to think. She missed the bright, engaging youngsters of her classroom, who gave her no such luxury. She shouldn't put off writing to her sister any longer.

Dear Ishani,

You'll be relieved and delighted to know that Santosh found us a house that is comforting to be in. It has pleasant surprises in every corner. Just fancy this: under the stairs there's a cupboard lit with an electric bulb, with shelves too. Such a use of this space, as you well know, has bypassed us at home.

At the bottom of the stairs is a built-in bench for the elderly to rest. Well this is what I thought was its use; you wouldn't guess what it really is. It has a concealed deep recess for newspapers, books and magazines; cleverly camouflaged, a covert place. What a find!

The house is old but with central heating, there's no need for bulky chimneys, so in the beautiful dining room where a coal fire once flickered stands a built-in cabinet with two sturdy wooden shelves; above it, along the cavity of the chimney, there's a curved alcove spanned by two pieces of glass. I guess it's a place to display pieces of pottery or ceramics. However, at present, it will display books and magazines – which are so much easier to come by – and my way of drawing Anjali's attention to them. I do want to help them to develop beautiful minds – thoughtful, compassionate and knowledgeable.

And there's a walk-in pantry off the kitchen with long sturdy wooden shelves spanning almost half the breadth of the house. I doubt you'd see that in newly built London apartments. The pantry is very cool, and you know why? Its window has no glass; instead, there is fine mesh – clever thinking that belongs to a time when home refrigerators were unknown.

You will be pleased to hear, Ishani, that I intend to make my own chilli sauces so this pantry built for jams and marmalade will be welcoming jars of an appetiser from another continent…

She broke off and hurried to the front door. There lay an envelope with Trinidadian stamps. Her sister's bold hand hectored from the floor.

She scanned the first page, noting its big sister's tone, expected in the past and often welcomed; today, it felt unnecessary. There were dos and don'ts regarding where to shop in London; streets to avoid where there were too many of 'all sorts'; nourishing foods to cook for a British winter: *…lentil dhal as a soup; spinach and carrots … and don't forget, a blob of butter before serving will strengthen the stamina and ward off colds.* Her girls should be wearing warm vests, and instructions were given about where to shop for them.

How is your handsome Guyanese husband? Still quiet as ever? He is an enigma. With us, what you see is what is there. Ravi says it is difficult to tell where he stands on anything. Mind you, he listens well, but as to what he is thinking, who knows? I guess you probably do, which means you've developed the skill of mind-reading, Amira.

How are you really managing on your own? Battling with three daughters, no family, no community. It can't be easy. Rest and meditate, or it will take its toll. You must be at your wits' end at times. I would certainly be. You've never had to run a house on your own, so don't hesitate to let me know of any difficulties; it's what big sisters are for. I won't ask about the house, I shall spare you that. Don't be too harsh on Santosh. A man's brain is not like ours. It is something we have to learn to live with.

Amira placed the letter on her lap and smiled.

A scene returns: Her late mother and Ishani are in the sitting room of the family home. Her mother has explained to her that Guyana was, 'behind God's back. Everybody knows obeah is common there; you'll be all alone with no family, so far from us. What if they don't treat you well? Where would you go, Amira? What if he starts to misbehave? What will you do? If that sort of thing starts, you must come home at once. You should think over this move with plenty care, Amira. Your father and I are worried no end that you will be so far from us. It is affecting my sleep.

'We have so many really nice young men here in Trinidad from good, good, families that we know; as a matter of fact, Amira, we have been approached by two very respectable families. Very pleasing young men, good education. Why choose from so far away? Give yourself time to think, Amira; it's a big, big step. Ishani and I are so worried; you are going outside of what we know, people we do not know. Is this safe?'

'But Pa said it was alright, Ma. Pa met the family and he said they were alright.'

'I know he said that, but remember, the family is not as well to do as we are. That means, you'll have to be very careful about everything – things for the house, for yourself. Everything, you will have to consider over and over again. That is taxing.'

'What Ma is trying to say,' Ishani interrupted, 'is that this kind of daily calculation is hard going on the nerves. It will be very difficult for someone, especially from this fortunate house, to manage on an inadequate income. This is a house of plenty. A house of plenty effuses generosity, amiability, Amira.'

It had been so hard to fight on two fronts. She had turned to her mother, who looked forlorn in her old age, and could only guess what she was thinking but not expressing.

'I'll be working too, Ma. His father died when he was a young boy so that made a difference to the family. Santosh has made himself. That is some achievement, Ma.'

'Self-made people tend to be tough,' Ishani again stepped in. 'They often lack a charitable approach to problems. Their mantra is: Pull yourself together; I managed huge difficulties, so why can't you deal with this trifle? Such men are likely to scoff at more liberal, middle-class families like ours, with our flexible outlook. The self-made man is not a relaxed man, Amira. He's oversensitive about his background, constantly searching for opportunities for betterment. Will step on anything and anyone to reach the top. Nothing is sacred before such determination. It's exhausting just looking at him or hearing about his successes.'

'You're lucky, Amira,' Ma said; 'you've a father who is not well, yet flies over to Guyana to see for himself where you'll be going and meet Santosh's family. He spoke to their pundit, he made enquiries from the neighbours about the kind of people they were. Well, it was alright, he said. Your father did his best for you, Amira. But think about it; how much could he do in just a few days and what could he find out by just speaking to strangers, eh? People who don't know him, don't know if they could trust him, what can they tell him eh?'

She had heard their silences. Ma was also saying that she was Pa's favourite, that he was too soft on her to stop her going along with this craziness, marrying someone who came from the outback where obeah was practised. Ma had even repeated this to Santosh when he flew over to meet them.

Santosh had offered his winning smile: 'You're right, Ma. It's true. Obeah *is* practised in Guyana, but it isn't good obeah. It does not do the job because it's too weak. If you want to have strong obeah,' he leant forward, lowering his voice, 'the place to go is Suriname. Not many know this,' he confided.

Ma's face made it clear that obeah was not something she needed, had ever needed or was ever likely to need. But Santosh would not be deterred and continued with his gentle tease, his winning smile. Before he left, even her mother had smiled too, perhaps just out of courtesy. She had lived too long to be won over by charm, and from a young man who wanted the hand of her daughter. But she and Santosh had got married and a year later had moved to Trinidad, which pleased the family.

After her parents died, Santosh had left Trinidad to spend an academic year at Reading University where he completed his PhD and then joined the Commonwealth Secretariat. It was a job there that had brought them all to London.

She lifted the letter from her lap. Ishani's voice rose:

In today's world, Amira, where every man is busy flying his own kite, I don't know where Santosh's reserved approach will get him. Later, when the girls reach marriageable age, his restraint will simply not do. I'm alerting you in good time. I have seen far too many competent and capable young women left on the shelf because fathers were neglectful of their parental duties and mothers at home were cut off from the opportunity to act. Maybe I'm too hard on him; we'll see. Before you blink, Anjali will be a teenager. Ensure she does not keep company with nut heads. Something happens to teenagers' brains that makes even nut heads appear attractive to them. I see this daily in the department store. So please, Amira, keep an eye on the sort of friends they keep. Probe a bit; it is quite an art. I am pretty good at it. If you need me to question the girls at any time just wink. This is why you need to send them to me for their holidays.

Oh! I almost forgot. Avoid English cooking if you can help it. With your sophisticated palate it will disappoint. The scent of boiled cabbage and oily, soggy chips still comes to me when I think of 1950s England. They were far too busy running an empire to think of food. Now that you intend to make London your home, don't be in awe of them. They like to give the impression that they are superhuman, but don't fall for this. With an empire to run, keeping up appearances was vital. They had to play the part, and they did it well, so much so that even today there are many who still believe their make-believe. Yet we know that away from their cooler, ordered environment, their true Darwinian natures rose and they played other games, the outcomes of which are all around us!

The problem is that though they are no longer on a world stage, they are finding it difficult to change their posture, devise a new role for themselves, but given time they will. I admire their chameleon ability when circumstance demands. There is much that we should copy from them and from America too, but much of our own we should hold on to, tightly.

When you get to know them, you will find that they are as human as you and I, with foibles, vulnerabilities and strengths. They can laugh heartily, too – well, not all of them – and they are not much of a people for stirring desire. My three nieces should be quite safe from those stiff bits of cardboard wearing old suits with leather elbow patches I met at university.

You'll find living in London a very different kettle of fish from being a student in that comfortable Protestant hall of residence in Northern Ireland. Actually I'm very fond of the English, you may have gathered. I have a sneaking feeling I may be a little like them myself.

Affectionately,
Your caring elder sister, Ishani.

P.S. Do send the girls to us. It's important that they don't lose their roots.

4

GETTING TO KNOW YOU

Amira was in the midst of sorting the jumble of half-opened boxes, piles of clothes on chairs, when the door-bell rang. A neighbour! She panicked, thinking, *Oh dear! I have to invite her in; if I don't, what will she think?* But not even the sitting room was ready for visitors. Boxes everywhere. First impressions counted. Her mind went into overdrive. The girls had eaten the last of their favourite shortbread – the round ones, the rectangular ones were not half as nice – and for the life of her, she could not remember which box the best crockery was in.

She went to open the door, trying to appear calm, telling herself to smile. She so wanted to do the right thing. She worried that her caller might think people from the Third World lived in such confusion that it was no wonder their countries were too.

It was Janna Cohen from Number 15.

'Just stopping by to say, welcome to Apple Grove. If I can be of help, you know where I am.' Amira tried to smile, thanked her, then simply stood there not knowing what else to say. Only as her visitor was leaving did she manage to blurt out, 'Oh I am Amira, Amira Vidhur.' Janna Cohen turned around and offered a smile which Amira discovered meant, *it's alright*, and she was gone.

The second time the bell rang, it was Alice Reid from Number 11. For a brief moment Amira thought of escaping, but how to do this did not come.

Afterwards she reflected that neither woman had expected to be asked in, but they were friendly gestures all the same. She couldn't pinpoint how it was done – it was all in the body movements and facial expression – but was grateful for the thoughtfulness in not making the situation awkward for her.

She thought about how in her village, where families lived and died in the same house, there was no question about not inviting your neighbours in when they dropped by. They would be offered a seat, a rest from the heat and a glass of cold water before you got round to asking about their welfare. But she was a total stranger to these people.

Her relief over the visits led to such a soaring feeling that she thought she might have lifted off had there been a runway; instead, she wrote to Ishani.

What am I to make of this neighbourliness, Ishani? Isn't it wonderful? We don't call upon foreigners or strangers at home because there aren't any. How would we handle such a situation? People talk of how reserved the English are, but here at Apple Grove it is not so. They didn't have to come over. I am really touched. Mind you, when you consider what happens in other parts of England, my advice to immigrants is, choose where you live and live in the best possible neighbourhood your circumstance allows. What a warm welcome! What a friendly street!

She came down from this flourish of optimism to wonder how she would gather information about a secondary school for Anjali. Boxes were left unsorted; time was running out.

With the reassurance of her offer of help, Amira rang the door-bell of Number 15. Janna Cohen appeared.

'Good morning.'

'Good morning, is everything alright?'

Amira adjusted her face to a smile, realising she must have been showing her anxiety. She asked whether Janna could advise on the good secondary schools within reasonable reach, but Janna said she knew nothing about schools, and advised her to speak to Nick Reid who was a teacher.

At Number 11, Mr Reid answered the door. Amira was not expecting this and his somewhat intimidating presence unsteadied her.

'Good morning, I'm Amira from Number 14.' She pointed to her house and instantly felt foolish.

'Oh yes. So what can I do for you?'

His position a few steps above her made her feel like a child before a headmaster.

'I'm new here and I thought you might be able to help me with the names of good schools for girls.'

'Well, I can't say if they're good or not, you'll need to visit them. There's Mill Hill County High School, Copthall also in Mill Hill. There's Queen Elizabeth's Girls and Henrietta Barnett – both some distance away.'

'Thank you. Of these schools which ones are preferred by parents?'

'I've already said, you'll need to visit them. Schools are up one year down the other. I'm sorry I can't help you further.'

'Thank you, Mr Reid.'

He nodded and closed the door.

Whew! Difficult man! She sensed him reining in his displeasure at seeing her. She wouldn't trouble *him* again. He must have known which schools were preferred by parents and simply did not wish to share this. But he had told her the names of schools and which were far away. It was a beginning.

Undeterred, she walked towards the Broadway. She would take the initiative, too much was at stake. Her father had often said, 'Cast your net far and wide when you need help', so she stopped and questioned several people, men and women, elderly and middle-aged.

'Schools? Now let me see, it's been such a long time since I was there… Neighbourhood schools, you said, is that right? There are a few schools around, you can tell from the uniforms, different you see. Ah yes! Copthall is one, and there's another on the Ridgeway,' and he pointed in the direction. 'I'm sorry I can't recall any more. There… ask that chappie.'

And she did.

'In this country, if you have money, you can go to the best schools.'

'Which ones are those?'

'Do you have money?'

'It depends on how expensive these schools are.'

'Well there's the Mill Hill school on the Ridgeway, but that's for boys. That's no good to you. I'm sorry my wife is not here, she would have been able to help. Don't know much about girls' schools you see.' He smiled mischievously.

Then a slim, serious-looking woman who must have overheard them marched up and said, 'So you're looking for good schools. You mean, I take it, schools that will stretch your daughter?'

'Yes.'

'A middle-class obsession. Would *you* like to be stretched?'

'Living stretches us all. Having to grow stretches us.'

'Precisely. That's enough stretching, don't you think? Let the children be. No stretching please, no stretching. They'll learn a great deal from their elders simply by listening and observing.'

An elderly gentleman advised: 'You should teach them yourself if you can. A sheer waste of time most schools today. The youngsters leave school without any understanding of common courtesy, no manners at all. Can't read. Don't know how to put a decent sentence together. As for a decimal point, they think it is a full stop. You know what the problem is… It's this softly, softly, progressive approach – daft, if you ask me. No punishment for not performing. Let's all be happy, let's all be winners – balderdash!'

'Phone the borough of Barnet and ask them for a list of schools. Tell them you want to know which ones are comprehensive, and which ones are still grammar schools and go for the grammar schools. You'll be on the right track. Good luck.'

'Thank you.'

She had asked about half a dozen people. Despite the range of responses, she'd kept going. This surprised her. Then she wondered whether full-time domesticity had already started to affect her confidence.

A week or two later, a letter came from Ishani:

Simply delighted about the house. Sounds just right for you. Santosh will continue to surprise us all. Steady now, Amira, regarding your neighbours. You've long had a tendency to take people at face value. Those women do not mean what they say. Your neighbours are middle-class English people; coming to your front door and introducing themselves is what they believe they ought to do. It's good manners. But please understand they do not expect you to be knocking at their door asking for help; it's just a way of speaking, like 'How are you?' which you know does not express a concern for a stranger's health or well-being. It's not like here. Only last week I was held captive by dear Miss Fields in the store – by the way, she remembers you well and sends her warm regards. Unaware that she'd had an operation a month ago, I said, 'You're looking well, Grace.' The store was busy; I was two assistants short and my patience did not require further challenges. She replied with the sweet slowness of molasses, 'You think so, Ishani? You really think so? Well Ishani dear, only I know meh perils, what I went through on that operation table. You know what the surgeon saw when he opened me up? He told me he couldn't believe it. The surgeon told me himself that left another day, just one more day mind you, you see me here, I would be a dead woman. I, Grace Fields, dead, just so, with nobody knowing why. Well, you see me here; have a good look. I'm a walking miracle…' I shall spare you the full length of the drama.

But you're in England and the style is somewhat different. Your English neighbours will love you dearly, Amira, if they see little of you and you conduct yourself in such a way that you make it possible for them to forget you're close by.

This was not what Amira wanted to read. Suddenly she had the sensation she was drowning in a sea of difficulties and wished she'd said nothing to Ishani, *the Wise One, the Knower of all things.* So she was a mere child, eh, taking things at face value? Arrogant as ever. Didn't she know that nothing stands still? Time changes everything. Mountains crumble, sea beds become the Himalayas! People change too. Ishani's England was not hers… maybe it was so, it might even be partly so in places now, but entirely so? Well, Apple Grove was different. Amira decided that she had written Ishani her last letter.

When she'd cooled down, she began to suspect that she was taking out her frustrations on her sister.

She had thought of looking for a teaching post, but with so much to attend to, the new home, the girls' schooling, and having time for them, she thought she would not be able to perform to the standards she had set herself in Trinidad. And would Vidya settle into a nearby kindergarten? If not, she would have to teach her. And were she to find a teaching post, could she cope with what she was hearing about the lack of discipline? It did not sound like what she was accustomed to: firm discipline and students who were motivated to join their parents in the upper echelons of society, with learning seen as the means to that end. Then there was Santosh, who needed her support as he tried for promotion. It would take time to get to know her neighbours too, and there was the neglected garden watching her every day. She had to stay at home until the girls found their feet, though it meant that thrift and good household management would have to be her priority. It was the best option, but…

Santosh was happy with this decision. It would be less stressful for her and for the family. In the past she'd just kept taking on things, despite what he said, until she got ill. Her health had suffered again and again, even as she denied the causes. At last, he thought, she was coming to a better assessment of what she could do, realising that she had to temper her expectations of near perfection in all things.

But the loss of the fulfilment her professional career gave her took its toll. She had taught all subjects in a primary school; Latin and Geography in secondary grammar schools; her examination results were among the best. She had worked very hard, often giving extra help to the weaker students free of charge. There had always been piles of work to be corrected, and much to prepare for the next day. She was keen to make a difference, and drove herself relentlessly. It was what gave her life meaning, a quiet, satisfying *joie de vivre* which she had thought could not be taken from her.

Now, plunged into its unending flow, she concluded that there was no such thing as unskilled domestic work. The simplest act needed a skilled hand and thinking through. You cobwebbed, dusted, then vacuumed; any other order would make you weep. You cleaned shelves from the top and worked down, not the other way around. Ironing the shoulder and sleeves of a shirt required expertise, and why had she not learnt to put back everything exactly where it came from and avoid the frustration of looking for things? If only she hadn't kept her head in books and newspapers, but spent some time observing how the helpers gave the house orderliness and cleanliness with such apparent ease and speed.

Each day she saw something saying: *Just you look at me, you must see that I need cleaning*. The refrigerator, the kitchen windows, the kitchen floor. There was the eternal tidying and dusting and wiping over and over again. And each day there were meals – preparation, cooking, cleaning up, and then all over again. Repetitive, dull: she longed for escape.

Amira knew that home was a sanctuary for the human spirit. It held together the essential goodness of living in the minutiae of life. So why was it perceived as insignificant, even by those who laboured at it daily? 'I'm just a housewife,' mothers said when she met them. She had never replied, 'You are the pivot of your family's well-being, a good mother, housewife and neighbour. You are adept at a dozen skills at least.' Why had this not come to her when she was teaching? She knew this, but what she felt came with an intensity that almost smothered her struggling spirit. She was even tempted to phone Ishani.

But waking one morning she smiled to hear her own voice in the classroom. 'Girls, confidence comes from doing, not from wishing it.' She just needed to encourage herself. She sat still, staring at the sunlight streaming in through the window. Toddlers attempt to walk despite the difficulties compared to crawling. They fall over, get bruised, yet in spite of their hurts, they won't sit and see the world walk past them. She would do as toddlers do.

5

SOMETHING STIRS BETWEEN THEM

Arabica coffee, extra fine, dark chocolates and the best of Demerara rums, a gift from Ishani, added to Amira's and Santosh's contentment. Such mingled pleasures of aromas and tastes brought a quiet satisfaction, so much so that Amira felt completely relaxed for the first time for weeks and felt able to tell Santosh what a close thing it had been getting the girls into St Hilda's. She had not mentioned it before because he'd been touchy and irritable. She concluded there were problems at the office he preferred to keep to himself.

At the end of her vivid recollection, she had expected some appreciation of what had been accomplished. Instead, a studied silence. She poured herself a second cup of coffee; in the stillness, the snug sitting room began to feel uncomfortable.

'You shouldn't have argued with Miss Williams, she wouldn't have liked that one bit. You can't appear too knowing here. They resent it; they'd think you were being too clever by half.'

'What a silly thing to say! I wasn't being clever. I was being thoughtful; my circumstance wasn't that of other parents. I had to say so. Why shouldn't I? Who knows what the outcome would have been had I not tried so hard.'

'The outcome was very good. I hesitated to say what I said.'

'Sometimes you should say nothing, Santosh. Maybe you should hesitate more often. I shouldn't have to say this, but you seldom say an appreciative word. It never occurs to you to consider for a moment what I have to cope with. I'm not complaining, but it is all new to me. Getting the girls acclimatised to London, to their school and to much else. I've been battling with getting the house in order, yet there's still a mountain to do. Very soon, I shall have to find a secondary school for Anjali; I've been trying to find out about these schools, but I'm more confused now than ever. You don't seem to understand how everything, the small and the large, is pressing on me and the time I have is never enough.

'There's the garden too; it's neglected, in a near barren state. I'm not complaining, but you assume that I can just move from being who I was, complete with a career and with all the home help I had, to running a home with three daughters, and trying to understand how the education system works. I have to start from scratch on everything. Nothing is simple.

'Take shopping; in Mill Hill, the vegetable shop doesn't have the vegetables we like: channa, sweet potatoes, small leaf chowrai bhajee. I dream of grilled aubergine and ripe tomatoes, with cumin, garlic, onions and sweet peppers; I can't find pumpkins that are ripe or creamy avocados. The girls ask for these daily. Just yesterday Vidya wanted to know when the mango season will come. No sugar apples, star apples, golden apples, Governor plums, pawpaw. I can't find spices, just some dreadful curry powder. Maybe we need to go to Southall one day, Santosh. We need to put aside a Saturday for a trip there.

'Our culture traps women. When a family emigrates, as soon as the man gets a reasonable job, he has nothing more to think about. But the wife is expected to create the same home life for the family, the same foods, the same assurances and loving care they had in the old country. This is crazy. I wouldn't be surprised if many of us suffered mental breakdowns. The expectation is nightmarish! Fortunately, I have the language, but in many instances, Santosh, the woman does not know the language, and even when she does, she hasn't a clue about where to go, who to ask, what there is that may be beneficial to her family. The responsibility is an unbearable burden, yet women silently carry on.

'They don't tell their husbands, whilst they're expected to sit and listen to their husbands' unburdening. Now I'm here, where no one knows me, I intend to create my own individual culture, one that suits my temperament and my present situation. It's so easy to be imprisoned by cultural iron bars closing in on you.'

'But you're an intelligent woman, well equipped to live anywhere. Why should you have problems with domesticity or the garden or food for that matter? Be firm with the girls, let them understand they just have to learn to eat what you find. It hasn't done the natives any harm.'

'I… see… Very well then. I have nothing more to say. Nothing. This matter is now closed.' *My god, is this the man I married? He's so insensitive. I can't bear to think that Ishani and Ma might have been right about him?*

'My reason for saying what I said was to put you on your guard.'

'I do not wish to be put on guard, Santosh. You and Ishani have a lot in common. Far more, believe me, than either of you suspect.'

'Amira, I lived and worked here long before we got married.'

'You said I shouldn't argue with Miss Williams; you weren't there, yet feel competent to tell me what I should have done.'

'I'm sorry. You are right. But just listen for a while. My advice was wrong in this instance, but it has sound roots.'

Silence.

'You were a student, living amongst privileged middle-class girls in Belfast, and then you returned to your home. That's quite different from trying to earn a living and studying; jostling with all classes for a flat or a job. I know how they think; I know what it is to face a landlady, meeting her evasive face when she opens the door and says: "It's taken. Sorry." You look at the next address on your crumpled sheet of paper and cross out the one you've just visited. In the cold damp air your clothes are not warm because you cannot afford better, and you ask yourself why things are as they are, before you take a bus to the next disappointment. Our worlds have been different. It would be negligent of me not to draw your attention to a wider London. That London is not Apple Grove.'

'All that is true, Santosh. I have no quarrel with that.'

'Okay. It was tactless of me. I shall make enquiries at the office about good secondary schools for girls.'

You say that. But I know nothing will come of it. I am in this alone, brother.

'Listen Amira, you say you were being thoughtful and that is right, but it wouldn't be seen like that.'

'How would it be seen?'

'Going over the top. My advice is keep your head down and your opinions to yourself. Be a good listener.'

'Okay, but had I followed your advice on that day, the girls would not be where they are.'

'I said I'm sorry about that. However, as a general rule you should keep your views to yourself. Play it safe even when asked. We foreigners have no choice if we want to survive here. This understanding I have come by the hard way. It works. I live by it.'

'To the neighbours I'm just an ordinary mother with a family; I'd be surprised if anyone was interested in my opinions. Mind you, I have quite a few, but no one has ever asked for them… Pity.'

Silence.

'What about… Should I pretend to be excessively foolish? I'd be pretty good at that.'

'There's no need to feed their prejudices. I'm trying to help you and you think it's a big joke.'

Amira sighed.

'Amira, I know you too well. You can't be a supplicant. You're not the ingratiating type; you'd rather be an outcast than grovel before anyone, or pretend they're right when you believe they're not. Listen to the tone of your conversation with Miss Williams; you don't hear yourself. I wasn't there, but you would have sounded like an advocate. It worked well on that occasion, but I'm merely trying to alert you to what is out there. We were fortunate. Miss Williams was able to appreciate how well you presented your case. But will it always be like that? All I've said is even more applicable outside London. If you want to see England, go to the Cotswolds, to Devon, to Yorkshire.'

'England is all those places including London.'

'Why do you always have to have the last word?'

'Have some more coffee, Santosh.'

Santosh declined and instead refilled his cognac glass with a half measure. He sipped again and again.

'Amira, you seem to forget the reason for this. They had an empire and thought they were superior to us and even to their European neighbours. We were an emotional people who needed a guardian and would only be ready for independence when they thought we were.'

'True, Santosh. Mystical India, certainly not analytical or logical. I wonder if they ever wondered how such people, with nothing but nonviolent resistance, forced them to end their occupation without firing a shot.'

'It's their mind-set, Amira; they are a military people, their culture reflects this. It is quite different from ours. Think of the Mahatma saying, "Britain is not our enemy." Imagine saying that after the Amritsar Massacre and the Bengal famines.'

'That all belongs to the past, Santosh.'

'Yet the thinking that maintained it, Amira, still walks in the corridors of power. Soft slippered, its presence quietly pervades my department.'

'I wasn't aware that you had to cope with that at work. That must be nerve racking. How do you manage? You've never hinted anything was troubling you.'

'I don't want you to worry. I can manage. *Keep your eye on the ball*, I say to the children and I say it to myself... Look at the editorials, Amira: "India must not be allowed to have... China needs to do..." On and on these journalists pontificate, offering advice to men with the acumen and experience of running a country many times the size of their own, with a complexity and diversity that make the whole of the United Kingdom look like one of their duller states.'

'True, Santosh, but the opportunities for the girls, and for us too, are large. That's a blessing. We shouldn't let old attitudes guide our thinking; that would hand our colonial past too great a victory.'

'I've been wondering whether anything ever fades completely, Amira.'

'Time does it, Santosh.'

Silence.

'You're a good woman, Amira.'

'That's kind… We both try… both of us to do the right thing… I just don't find it easy.'

'You do your best.'

'You do, too, all the time, Santosh. You're cautious and that's commendable. And you did such a fine job in choosing this house that I feel the need to thank you again and again. I could not have done better.'

'That sounds reasonable to me. Let's drink to our good judgement and conduct.'

'You're making fun of me.'

'Come on. I'll pour you some. You've had very little.'

'Alright. Not too much now.'

'There, this is called a decent measure by the connoisseurs.'

'That's far too much, Santosh.'

'We both need to loosen up a bit, *lose* ourselves sometimes; enjoy each other's company more. A time will come when we have to leave our children, leave this house, leave the world behind. Let's try not to have too many regrets when we're old and frail. Strength, youth, good health are all temporary, why not enjoy them while they are here? In the long run it's our friendship that matters and doing the best we can all the time.'

'Too many regrets, Santosh?'

'Regrets that we should've done things differently. I want to take you for a walk tomorrow so you can see the larger world. It may help you see our family in perspective. We have a long, complex history. It is how we interpret it that will guide us. Let us see it for what it is, neither something large nor insignificant.'

Silence.

'Thank you, Santosh, but for how long?'

'For how long?'

'For how long do we lose ourselves, Santosh?'

He sipped at his cognac again. 'I'm working on it.'

The cognac warmed Amira, and for a moment a sense of wellbeing enfolded her, thankful to have a husband who spoke his mind before it was too late. Perhaps she had been neglectful of herself of late, become too domesticated. Did danger lurk there?

But she knew she had lost out by their migration, lost the career which gave her self-realisation, while Santosh's power had increased. She sensed that a large part of her misgivings, her low feelings, came from this. But what alternative did she have? Had marriage become too costly for women like herself? Was not a new generation of women fighting bravely for opportunities equal to men's? If everyone in a family couldn't benefit equally, was it inevitable whose well-being would be at the top of the list, and whose at the bottom?

6

SEEING THE LARGER WORLD
WITHIN ONESELF

Santosh was true to his word. He took Amira for lunch in Piccadilly, then they walked to the part of London where he worked.

It appeared grand and complex to Amira, a maze where busy people knew their way around, silently going and coming from enormous buildings; where cars understood the one-way streets, moving in and out without hesitation.

She felt intimidated, overwhelmed by the imposing architecture, the circuses, radiating exits and entrances, a merry-go-round. The self-confidence felt excessive: the grandeur of the Bank of England and Mansion House, the Georgian palace of the Lord Mayor. Santosh showed her St Paul's, Westminster Abbey, Whitehall, the Royal Albert Hall, Parliament and Buckingham Palace. She felt disconnected from them all. They made her feel foreign and small.

However, in the spacious halls of museums and art galleries, she felt more at ease. Here was a purpose to being: to see, to think about what was before her, to learn. She felt delight and thankfulness that these artefacts had been created by men and women from far and wide, all with a vision, wanting those who would see their work to understand from whence it had come, from whence a part of humanity had come.

But this man-made landscape of the metropolis was so unlike the soft textures of the village of her childhood where she could see and feel the earth. Here was the strength of wealth and power: a mass of inner steel covered by a façade, where grand style told a tale.

Here memories were cast in stone memorials, of wars, kings and queens, lords and prime ministers – those chosen to be remembered. There were the grand imperial ideas manifested in India House, South Africa House and Australia House. Though Lancaster House was discreetly tucked away in the West End, its dazzle befitted the rulers of an earlier age; it was there in the 1960s that the Empire had been formally dismantled with signatures and handshakes. How different from the manner in which these lands had been acquired. There was something about the seductive nature of power that seemed to unlock the basest desires for aggrandisement and plunder.

When they walked down Lower Regent Street, there stood, high above all else, the name from one of her nursery rhymes:

> *The grand old Duke of York,*
> *He had ten thousand men.*
> *He marched them up to the top of the hill*
> *And he marched them down again.*
> *And when they were up, they were up;*
> *And when they were down, they were down.*
> *But when they were only halfway up,*
> *They were neither up nor down!*

He stood high on a pinnacle overlooking The Mall, too high for his features to be seen, and so he remained in her nursery. But not far away in Trafalgar Square, there stood that one-eyed, one-armed man who had *chased Villeneuve across the oceans o'er* – the valiant Nelson she'd first learnt about in a poem in the West Indian Reader at her primary school – was it called 'The Legends of the Bocas, Trinidad'? What she had learnt began:

> *'Villeneuve, Villeneuve, why won't you stay, you've crossed*
> *the ocean o'er,*
> *Your cruise has been long, yet you hurry away, when*
> *You're welcome here on shore…'*
> *Villeneuve muttered: 'od-rat, if I can!*
> *It's that little one-eyed, one-armed man!*
>
> *'He followed me to Finisterre; he followed me to Spain;*
> *Round many a reef off Tenerife, and back to France again.*
> *Then westward here to Trinidad, three thousand miles or more;*
> *He haunts me on the open sea, he haunts me by the shore…'*
>
> *When the cliffs of Spain rose up through the rain, then*
> *The fight raged fearfully;*
> *Till England's Pride, heroic died, mid the shout of Victory.*
>
> *And Villeneuve muttered: 'Save who can!*
> *It's that little one-eyed, one-armed man!'*

Here were the deft workings of her colonial education all tucked away in her memory! Who was she? How well they had recited this verse under the spreading mahogany tree at the Tunapuna Government primary school! And there, in the square, in remembrance of that fateful battle, stood England's pride.

In Greenwich, she smiled that London, the great measurer of things, had offered the world a rule: 'Hark ye navigators of seas and skies, henceforth I shall define what is East and what is West.' The mapmakers had listened.

How could one questioning spirit absorb the centuries accumulated in the buildings she saw? There was something fortress-like about them, as if they were protecting themselves against dissenting voices. What of the new buildings of glass? Did that mean an openness, a greater inclusiveness of what could be seen? Did buildings reflect the disposition of their inhabitants?

She still carried a remnant of her younger self, the child growing up in a village; even in Frederick Street in Port of Spain she'd held her mother's skirt. In Regent Street, she felt she was at the bottom of a deep canyon. It was unnerving, claustrophobic. Here the confidence of free enterprise, of capitalism, seemed to have captured even the space high above, which, she believed, belonged to all the city's citizens – like the sky and the air.

Mill Hill, with its large areas of woodland spoke of the pace of the seasons; it was a welcome space to retreat to, to remind herself that she was whole and conscious. It was a place to walk, to reflect upon being, even to hum an English song learnt at school: 'Cherry ripe, cherry ripe/ Ripe I cry/ Full and fair ones /Come and buy.' She would hum, too, the national anthem of India, which she and thousands of Indian Trinidadian school children had sung in 1947, on the open savannah. Hummed, it sounded more like a lullaby to cradle a baby. No pomp, no clashing of cymbals. What would her daughters make of their parents' history and London's offerings?

There was the poem her class recited in the terracotta dust of the school-yard: 'O Mary, go and call the cattle home, across the sands o' Dee.' This would come to her as she walked through the woodlands and parks of Mill Hill. The stillness helped her to think of time past – the Mill's and her own. Standing there, she felt the flow of time, moving her along while she looked back.

7

DISCOVERING BURNT OAK

Winter's long, cold darkness and short days kept my spirits low. There was the dullness that pervaded the greengrocer's in Mill Hill Broadway: carrots, white cabbage; broccoli, cauliflowers, onions, no garlic; in summer peas came in thick pods that were far weightier than their enclosed small, hard green nuggets. The variety of textures and vibrancy of colour in the vegetables I'd grown up with made one sing; sadly they were not here.

Sometimes the voices of my teachers, Lily and Palli, came to me. *Look at the familiar as if they were new. You can do far more than you think; every vegetable has more possibilities than those our mothers and grandmothers knew.* Perhaps I was not looking creatively at carrots; at cabbage, yes, but broccoli was new. I did not know how to prepare it. One day I saw an elderly woman buying some, so I went up to her.

'Can you please tell me how you prepare broccoli?'

'Nothing to it really; just strip off this outer green and chop off the bottom of the stems.'

'Do you steam it?'

'Oh that depends; you can do anything at all really.'

'Like what?'

'Oh just whatever you want to do, dear.'

'A cheese sauce?'

'You could try that. I use a cheese sauce with cauliflower but I haven't tried it with broccoli… I wouldn't curry it if I were you.'

'No. It doesn't look right for currying.'

'It's nothing to fuss about you know.'

'I'll remember that. Nothing to fuss about.'

'Just a light sprinkling of salt and some butter would do nicely.'

'A creamy butter on warm broccoli; I'll try that.'

'That's right. It's a straightforward vegetable, dear.'

I missed the vegetables and the spices so much that I had begun to see them, smell their aromas and recall their taste too vividly and too often when I was alone. The glum greyness and the drip drip of the rain weighed you down. To walk into the house and be greeted by parched cumin or cardamom would lift the spirits.

Hallowe'en reminded me of Cinderella's ball; the greengrocer's was piled high with monumental, watery, tasteless pumpkins that should have been transformed into carriages long long ago. These pumpkins were no good to pumpkin eaters.

I had to take the initiative. So with sketches in my hand I asked my greengrocer whether he recognised a deep mauve, elongated aubergine and sweet red pepper. Even if I say so myself, they were good representations, in shape and colour. He studied them carefully: 'Never seen those, love. No one asks for them. Not here, love. Foreign are they?'

But I was in luck. As I was about to leave with a cauliflower and a white cabbage, a plump middle-aged woman with a walking stick and small, twinkling eyes, to whom the greengrocer had shown the drawings, told me that in the next town – Burnt Oak – I would find what I was asking for, as well as a variety of Indian spices. 'There are a string of Indian shops on the main road. This is a small conservative English town, you won't see them here.' She smiled. I felt like hugging her.

I took the bus to Burnt Oak. Everything I had longed for was there. London had many faces. That day I had discovered a fine one. What a blessed city! I would have sung an aria in the street, were I so talented, in praise of all those who had enabled such a bounty to be there. Trade, trade, glorious trade! What a mingling of colours, sizes, shapes, scents! What a mixture of shoppers and shopkeepers! They'd come from everywhere: Turkey, India, Pakistan and all the countries from the Middle East, the West Indies, parts of Europe, even the Far East. That lady had opened the gates of immeasurable pleasures to me. Some people are walking angels; they help to make this world a fit place for humans.

8

MARGARET SUMMERS AND JILL SHEPHERD

As time went on Amira became close to Margaret Summers of Number 16., Juliet Marsh of Number 2, and forever grateful to Jill Shepherd of Number 17. Like most good things they happened quite by chance.

When Margaret Summers came over, her welcome from the very start was warm and friendly, like apple crumble with delicious custard on a cold night. She had just returned from Yorkshire where she'd spent time with her ailing parents and couldn't stay long. But when she mentioned in passing that she was a librarian, the word alerted Amira to think that she was likely to know about good secondary schools and might have met parents and teachers from the schools. So she hurriedly asked, 'Could we have tea together? What about next Friday?'

'Are you sure? You've just arrived. You must have tons to do. Moving house can be perilous enough, but doing so in a foreign country must be a nightmare. How are you managing?'

What a kind thoughtful woman. 'I would really like it if you could. There are a few things I need to know, being new to the area. I'm sure you'd be able to help me.'

'I'll try. Well if you're sure.'

'Say four o'clock a week from today.'

'That would be nice. Thank you.'

The week went by too quickly; Amira worked hard to put the place in order and on the day asked Anjali to take the girls to the nearby park. A few minutes of being excessively polite went by, but after the third cup of Darjeeling tea, and Margaret declining a second piece of orange cake, 'It's delicious Amira, but I really mustn't,' a pleasant camaraderie gradually sat with them. It was then Amira raised her problem: 'I have the three girls, Margaret, and I need to know about good secondary schools for them. I just managed to get them in at St Hilda's. I learnt I needed to apply well in advance if my eldest daughter Anjali is to stand a chance of getting a place. Can you recommend one or two where she's likely to be happy and receive a decent education?'

'You know there's a private sector as well as a state sector here?'

'Yes.'

'Good. The best schools for girls around here are in the private sector. You should speak to Jill Shepherd, she's a fellow librarian, works in the area, lives close by, opposite me at Number 17. I work outside Barnet.'

'But I don't know her. I don't think I've ever seen her.'

'Oh she'll give you the best advice whether you're stranger or a friend. I'll speak with her and say you'll be contacting her.'

'That is most kind, Margaret. Is she Miss or Mrs?'

'Miss.'

'Thank you again. Let me write it down, I find I get into quite a muddle these days. I'll contact her straight away.'

'Try and do a little each day, Amira. A little a day keeps insanity away.'

They both laughed. 'That's new to me. I shall write that down, too.'

'Oh Amira!'

When the girls returned from the park, all were very upset.

'What happened?' asked Amira.

'We were stoned and told to stay away from the park. "Paki go home, go home Paki!" they shouted at us, Mummy. Then something hit Vidya, Look there.'

'Me too, on my back,' cried Satisha.

'What about you Anjali?'

'On my back too.'

'Let me see your backs.' She lifted their stained blouses.

The bruises were sore, the skin torn but the blood had already begun to congeal. Amira wiped all the hurts with a mix of warm water, a touch of Dettol, a little antiseptic cream, long hugs and wipings of tears. When Amira felt equanimity was restored she said: 'That was not nice. Next time, you'll go with Daddy.'

'They're pigs!' Satisha said with vehemence.

'Pigs! All pigs! Only pigs, Mummy,' emphasised Vidya.

'Well they behaved very badly. You can call them pigs here in the house, but never outside, because they're not really pigs are they?'

Silence.

'What is Paki?' asked Satisha. 'Are we Paki?'

'Paki is a shortening of the word Pakistan. I'll show you where it is on the map. Come.'

'Are we from Pakistan? I mean our great grandparents?' enquired Anjali. 'Aren't we originally from India?'

'Our great grandparents were from India. But there was a time when Pakistan was also part of India.'

'Mummy, in the park, it was Paki they did not like, why?'

'Pigs, pigs, all pigs, Mummy,' repeated Vidya.

'It's not easy to explain why people don't like one another. There can be many, many reasons and when all the reasons come together it becomes something like a traffic jam and everything stands still in one place for years and years. Nothing can move. Living means moving on; moving is not easy.'

'I don't understand what you're saying, Mummy,' said Anjali.

'It's a difficult question and the answer is very long. Sorry, that will have to do for today, I have to prepare the dinner. You know how hungry your daddy is when he comes home.'

'Aunt Ishani wants to know about our experiences here; can we tell her about this?' enquired Anjali.

'Yes.'

'I will draw a pig and send it to Aunt Ishani,' said Satisha. 'I'll tell her what they did to us.'

'Can I draw a pig too, Mummy, with my crayons?' Vidya asked.

'Yes.'

Amira wrote to Miss Shepherd, explaining that she and her husband would gladly consider the private sector if it was very good. She did not say what a sacrifice they would have to make, because she did not want that to influence Miss Shepherd's views.

A week later, Amira received a three-page handwritten letter from Jill Shepherd explaining in detail the strengths of North London Collegiate and Haberdashers' Aske's School for Girls.

'We have not met her, and look at this, Santosh; she gives us so much of her time. Such a fine letter; her hand is crystal clear.'

'True. It is all those things. You wrote asking for help without airs or affectation. No doubt it was a good letter. She must have been stirred by your willingness to approach her, to consider all sectors while desiring the best we can afford. But observe, Amira, observe.'

'What am I to observe now, Santosh?'

'Oh by far the most important thing.'

'And what's that? To me it is her kindness, her readiness to assist us. What can possibly be more important than that, pray?'

'Amira, she tries her best not to choose for you. Doesn't come down one way or the other; yet there's enough information there for you to make a choice. You can tell she is intelligent and has a liberal outlook – the best of the English tribe – her approach, I mean…' He winked. 'She leaves you to choose, not telling you dogmatically, as we West Indians would, if asked.'

'That's true, Santosh, but you didn't have to make a song and dance of it. All that West Indians would be trying to do would be to give a positive direction, and I'd call that helpful. Her letter reflects an old civility, courtesy at its best. We should both bear that in mind.'

Amira was amused by what she had said. When she saw that Santosh was not, she added, 'We've been lucky to choose this street. Imagine if we had a place where filth came through our letter box and our front door was stoned.' She rushed over and kissed his cheek. 'Our street has character, Santosh, but out there, according to the *Evening Standard*, it is not as safe. I feel we are in a small oasis of friendship.'

'You say it's luck, but it is not just luck. It calls for judgement as well, that quality of discernment that for years and years you guided your students to acquire. I have that elixir methinks.'

She smiled. 'I just said that. In fact I've been saying that since we arrived.'

'Have you? I don't recall that at all.'

Silence.

She lifted her shoulders and stared at the ceiling as if pleading for divine assistance.

'Oh! I simply forgot. Nothing alarming is it, to forget? It's a human trait.'

9

THE ALCHEMISTS OF PENAL, SOUTH TRINIDAD

There was a letter from Ishani, carrying the news that her now elderly teachers, Lily and Palli, were thinking of closing down their school courses. Ishani insisted that the girls ought to come before that happened. 'I shall enrol them for the summer,' Amira decided. The news threw her back on her memories of twenty years ago.

She remembered the strained semblances of smiles on the first day the new students had met. She had felt so awkward. The other students came from Penal – a backward, rustic place in south Trinidad compared to Tunapuna in the St Augustine area, up north, where she lived. The smell of mud and farm animals, unpaved roads, open drains, standpipes where men brushed their teeth and bathed openly, rubbing and scrubbing, wearing only loose, worn, short khaki pants, told her she was in another place.

She'd plucked up the nerve to talk to the shy girl standing next to her, who'd been concentrating on some unseen object for quite a while. She'd whispered that their teachers, Lily and Palli, were alchemists. Well, that was what Ishani had told her as the reason for enrolling her on the course. Her companion had looked puzzled. Another girl had pressed her to explain. She'd said that her older sister had told her they would be witnessing transformations of the ordinary into the wonderful. Whether she'd understood what this meant when she said it, she wasn't sure.

This had quickly gone around like Chinese whispers. What she'd kept to herself was a vision of tongues of fire, blue smoke billowing, while the two teachers stared unflappably into the unknown. She hadn't really known the seminal part Ishani had played in the school's opening, or really why she'd been enrolled, and it took a long time for her to comprehend that these alchemists, unlike those of old, were seeking something even more precious than gold – the transformation of their students.

By the time they completed the course, that is what had happened. They were all stronger within, comfortable with themselves, more confident about coping with their home environments and working in the wider world.

Even now she could see the village of Penal: the houses of thatched roofs and whitewashed clay walls; Lily with that twinkle in her eyes and Palli lifting her long skirt over puddles, ornhi in place, a spring in her step, jumping over the hurdles of custom, her face radiant.

The school was an old, rambling, wooden house surrounded by a spacious verandah in a five-acre school-yard of shrubs and grass, shady trees and piercing sunlight. Nearby was a stream, rippling over stones, which she'd loved to listen to.

There they were, the first batch of students, white aproned, hair hidden under white cotton caps, with expectations unhemmed, awaiting the process of transformation.

On the local radio Ishani had promised (and was reported in the newspaper as saying): 'Every girl who attends Palli and Lily's new establishment will leave as an accomplished young woman. They will become better daughters, fine wives, excellent mothers and memorable grandmothers for they will be taught how to live in a way that can change a house of people into a happy home.'

And it had happened, as if a ray of light from above had descended on them. They were taught how to hold the light; they had worked at it for six weeks without being aware it was happening. By the time they left, they had acquired so much. They were conscious of the steps involved in their re-invention because they'd learned to reflect on the process of change.

They knew how to create deliciously healthy meals, food for the spirit and the body, for their families and friends. But they no longer did things because mothers or aunts did them. *We did them based on our knowledge of how and why and when.* They were fully informed about what they were engaged with, and seen how this approach could be transferred to other activities. They learnt about the fibres, textures and flavours of vegetables, meats, fish and spices; they learnt how to hold, touch, smell and taste vegetables and fruits in the raw and in the process of cooking. The structure of the fibres, the strength of the raw materials' natural flavours influenced the choice of spices as well as the methods of cooking: steaming, frying, baking, or the most commonly used method – stir frying. They began to transfer this training to their lives and their dealings with those they encountered.

Methods of cooking became the methods of communicating with others, how to speak to bring understanding – the tone of voice, the pace of speaking, the words chosen and the length of time spent either appealing, enquiring, entreating or requesting. They learnt this from the amount and duration of heat used in cooking. Should the heat be low, moderate or high? The timing of the conversation – the when and where to speak – became related to knowing when to add an ingredient; how much to use was related to discretion.

Addressing people in a non-confrontational way seemed common-sense in some cultures, but Amira had recognised that in hers it was an unknown. If anyone in her community spoke in a considered way, it stood out as the sun in the sky. If there was a disagreement, her people jumped on their high horses, shouting at the tops of their voices. 'Can you tell me if what you're doing is *knowing how*?' Lily had asked one of the students in response to the pugnacious manner in which she responded to a question.

It was only gradually she'd realised how pertinent these lessons were to the problems of families in poor villages. She'd seen this on the day they'd made kachouries with split peas that had been soaked overnight and ground with chopped spinach, onions, sweet peppers and much more. On their own the students came up with the concept of transference. If you could bring together grains and leaves, two entirely different ingredients to form a delicious dish, likewise, with an understanding of the situation, people with varying cultures and backgrounds could also come together to form a strong community. It was a matter of knowing how.

'Ah,' said another, 'you also need to pat the centre a little to flatten it, else the edges will get very brown and the centre remains raw.' That's called *knowing how* someone said, with self-satisfaction. Then there was a whispering amongst three girls before they erupted with the word: 'Potato'. This was followed by laughter and giggling; a few had looked to see how Amira was responding. Earlier, she'd mentioned that her sister Ishani added a grated potato to the kachourie mixture to soften it, so improving the texture and taste. The jeering had come from those who had never added a potato to their kachourie mix and were happy with the results. She suspected they felt that her mention of adding a potato was simply to show off some superior understanding.

Looking back, Amira saw a familiar person, though even then she'd realised that she should have allowed this provocation to pass, but she'd been riled and said with some relish, 'Whenever we bring large differences together, like ground split peas and spinach, we need a go-between, something that will hold dissimilar ingredients together. It could be a little flour which does just that, but a grated potato improves the taste and the texture of the mix as well; it is less doughy. The difference between flour and potato happens to be a well-known fact amongst *experienced* cooks. Why not try it before judging; that would certainly show *good sense* – one of the pillars of *knowing how.'* She had delivered this addition with panache.

There was a hollow silence. She'd been tempted to go further and say there was another lesson to be gleaned: that if we keep thinking imaginatively, and not always traditionally, we can continually make delicious changes. But she hadn't, recognising that the quantity of her input was already excessive for this sizzling hot discussion pot. She knew she was the only one there doing the Higher School Certificate; she was anxious not to appear a Miss Knower-of-all-things. She had failed miserably in the concept of *knowing how* with respect to quantity. What she had also learnt was the extent to which one's personality can be a hindrance or an asset when it came to relationships.

They learnt that if you wanted the benefit of more than one flavour, it was common sense to reduce the quantity of the strong, like cumin, relative to the less strong, like cardamom. And they saw how in a family discussion it was important to ensure the voices of the weak, like children and women, were heard and not drowned out by powerful male voices. Though at that time few of these girls could have brought this particular idea to fruition, Lily and Palli had been content to plant such seeds in their thinking.

Heat was interpreted as passion; a moderate amount was needed. Too much became uncontrolled jealousy or destructive anger, just as too much prolonged heat burnt both meal and pot. Similarly, water added with care to a dish softened it, made it palatable. It was like bringing an emollient, a lubricant to a deadlocked conversation to enable it to move forward. Excess water made things lose their firmness, their character. Using an excess of liquid was interpreted as being impatient, losing concentration, becoming negligent. Such repercussions were familiar.

With hindsight, she saw that Lily and Palli had taken what all their students' mothers did and interpreted it, giving it a profound meaning for their students to use to guide their lives. What Lily and Palli instructed them in was not much different from what their parents did; the difference was their parents did not imbue them with the quality they learnt to call 'a way of thinking'. For Amira's parents, too, cooking was cooking.

She reflected now, that if Lily and Palli had taught them how to make a kitchen garden, there would have been lessons for living there too. It was how they thought. They had been laying the foundations for them to reinvent themselves as well as recipes.

While she'd been there, she'd grasped the purpose of the school, but only later discovered what had triggered the idea for it. Ishani had filled her in: Lily and Palli, with ancestors from different continents, were born in Penal. With the help of scholarships they had been educated abroad and then worked at the Archibald Institute, in St Augustine, for a decade.

On their return to Penal, they'd seen the effects of the slowly retreating Great Depression on the agricultural labourers, the lowest paid in an industry that required, even after independence, Commonwealth Sugar Preferences to survive. They'd decided that something had to be done. What was not available in the sugarcane districts were the opportunities present in the urban areas, of schools, libraries, technical colleges and a wider range of jobs. The effects of endemic poverty made these villages sad, distressing places, where babies died from preventable sicknesses like gastroenteritis; where poor health weakened the strong and took the fragile. With only endurance to hold on to, these were places where regular overflows of intense emotions came with daily hardships and cruel sufferings.

Unwarranted anger flared against those nearest to them, and petty jealousies oozed from the inflamed sores of low self-esteem. Men sought swift, violent redress. The frustrations of meagre wages or joblessness, the crying demands of a large, ever-increasing, family led some men to harbour hurts and resentments that erupted into killings or suicide. Women would sometimes seek escape from miserable lives in the arms of another. Quite frequently, such transfers of affection had violent ends.

It was Lily's and Palli's empathy for these villagers, Ishani told her, and their passion for betterment, that drove them to establish the school in Penal. They used the only leverage available to the women in such frugal circumstances – cooking – and utilised it, not to keep them trapped in permanent domesticity but to give them a ladder to climb out, to other careers if they were so minded.

Amira recalled how she'd learnt that if you gave yourself space to think, you could interpret things in many different ways, for it was your way of thinking about things that gave them meaning. Without your interpretation, it remained simply something that happened.

The majority of the girls she'd met there had only been to primary school; many had left at third, fourth and fifth standard, a few even earlier, to assist their mothers with siblings. The school was well supported by parents and grandparents. It was perceived by even the most conservative families and die-hard traditionalists as an up-to-date way of making their daughters ready for an arranged marriage. What no one thought at the time, except Lily, Palli and Ishani, was that the school was sowing the seeds of a quiet revolution. What they learnt would improve the lives of these women by enhancing their ability to think, solve problems and make their case. But in order to win the blessings of a conservative, paternalistic society, Ishani's recommendation of the school to parents had emphasised the domestic skills that would be acquired. She had played a fruitful part in the venture by enabling it to obtain the finances it needed to get started. Ishani had told Amira that a few of the girls in her year had become caterers, cooking food for pujas and weddings; many encouraged their husbands to make maximum use of the small plot of land they had at the back of the house, growing the higher-priced vegetables for the market.

Many of her fellow students had arrived at the school with a hushed submission to authority. They had learnt to be careful not to give offence at any time. A young woman wishing to marry well had to ensure that her reputation was seen as unsullied by neighbours and even by jealous, distant cousins.

Time had moved on. Past pupils had begun sending their children to the increasing number of secondary schools in the country areas and during the vacation to Lily's and Palli's courses. Women were now far more forthright than they'd ever been. Much remained to be done, for as Amira herself had learnt, no one, including males, gave up power willingly.

She would tell Ishani to enrol Anjali and Satisha for the summer. Perhaps Vidya could accompany them, as an onlooker. She would listen and learn. Children did. She wondered what they would make of it.

Now she asked herself how much of what she'd been taught she really lived by. She tried, but knew there were aspects of herself she was unable to rein in. She thought about the lesson on the application of heat – the when and the where – and wondered whether this was one she had ever really learned.

10

COLLIDING WORLDS

One Thursday evening as Santosh came in he called, 'Here's a letter from Kamla Devi. Where should I put it?'

'Upstairs on my desk, I'll read it later. Dinner is ready. I wonder if she's returning to London. Let's eat now.'

They liked having a vegetarian meal one day of the week; Thursday was the chosen day. On the table were piping hot puris, wrapped in a white linen kitchen towel, fragrant Basmati rice, new potatoes cooked with fenugreek, cumin, a level tablespoon of Amira's massala mix, cherry tomatoes, chopped coriander leaves and olive oil; young beans stir-fried with onions, garlic and sweet peppers; individual bowls of split-pea dhal with turmeric, and long, thin slices of fried hot and sweet peppers with cumin seeds.

Having dined, each retired with coffee to their desks, Santosh to study World Bank reports and company reports on firms he was hoping to invest in when he got the promotion he was anticipating, and to catch up with articles in *Foreign Affairs Journal*, *The Economist* and the *Financial Times*.

Amira picked up Kamla Devi's letter, but found pressing concerns tumbling through her mind. She'd been at Mill Hill's Thames Link railway station that day when her attention had been drawn by a girl, whose parents could have come from Pakistan, Bangladesh or India. The girl was wearing an over-tight blouse and frayed jeans, held together by a row of large safety pins down one leg, purple and gold eye-shadow and a studded belt, an outfit that to Amira looked alarming, but which Anjali had told her was 'Only Punkoid, Mummy'. Half of her head of black hair was spiked in red as if she were a coloured porcupine about to wage war. She was using four letter words loudly and frequently, and speaking some argot that was quite incomprehensible to Amira.

Amira wondered if that 'get up' made the poor child feel 'with it', a young Britisher, on London's front line? It was surreal. What would her cousins in the poor villages from which her parents had probably emigrated think of her appearance? Would they want to make a similar statement? Was that what a young immigrant's newfound freedom in the West offered her? Would Anjali, Satisha or Vidya ever want to dress like that? Was she giving them the best assistance to grow up in this place with bewildering choices? God help parents!

It was the poverty of the girl's vocabulary that depressed her. What kind of an adult would she become? Would she find any place in the labour market? What would happen to her self-esteem? Her parents, thought Amira, would probably be working long hours in factories to pay for food, clothes and rent. How must they feel about their daughter?

She knew that some of the people who arrived from the subcontinent were ill-equipped in education and language. Was this the problem here? What did being British mean to them and to the teenager on the platform? Had parents and child become total strangers to each other, inhabiting quite different worlds, or was the girl more mixed in culture than she appeared – carrying skilfully two separate ways of thinking in one frame. She imagined a scene. There under a street lamp is the girl. On the opposite side of the road are the parents. She is recognised by her voice. The father is overcome by chest pains. Her mother trembles. They continue to stare, unprepared for the shock as they watch from the shadows. This child is theirs and not theirs. They are devastated.

They see their own demise, a loss of face in their community. They know what parents ought to do when children bring shame to their family. They must act swiftly to become parents again, to regain respect. But how, when and where?

Amira imagines a father who has to eat humble pie every day at work, who has to cope with being shouted at, seen as stupid, because he does not understand fully what has been said, or has been deliberately misled by a fellow worker. He absorbs daily the sniggering behind the machines, the jeers behind his back, for he knows it would all be worthwhile, because he had children who, one day, would prove that his sacrifice had a purpose.

For his children there was mobility – upward, ever upward. It was this idea that kept them going. How could they not succeed? This was England. Faraway cousins would be eagerly opening their letters. Full of the possibilities of fulfilling similar large dreams, eager to read the magic words: *We have done well and so have our children. Come now, we will be able to help.*

But to have children who were strangers to you, who saw you as an ill-fitting screw in their scheme of things, who had lost the propelling force you came with – and respect for you and your authority over them. It would be death by a thousand cutting eyes, death by the scurrying downcast looks of the community, death by voices closed to you. The silence would be overwhelming.

But that was not all. They would see age hastening up the path, with its frailties, weakening eyes and hearing, loss of mobility, teeth and appetite. Where would be the grateful, prosperous children to care for them?

They'd ask these questions over and over again. Why did their children not feel propelled to do well? Why couldn't they see the world for what it was – a harsh place for the uneducated and those without money. Why should they, illiterate and unschooled, be more perceptive than their children?

Amira wiped away her tears for she could identify with the consequences. She thinks of the other England she has glimpsed: dark alleys, dirty graffitied walls, broken lights, streets with tins and bottles rolling, soiled paper flying about, broken cardboard boxes and stray dogs. What did the girl on the platform find in these mean streets? Was it the youths on the block who said: 'You don't need parents. Who needs them, when you have your mates eh?' Everyone needed to belong somewhere.

Amira stared at the painting before her of three boys. The light shines brightly on the faces of two of them, one of whom is playing the flute; the third boy, in softer reflected light, looks down at the music sheet he is singing from. The painting held her. She imagined her three daughters playing together in this serene way. *The Concert* by Hendrick ter Brugghen, she noted. She stretched her hands for Kamla Devi's letter.

My dear Amira,

Thank you for your beautiful long letters, they're a treat I look forward to. By now you'll have guessed I'm a poor letter writer, while you transport me to be with you at 14 Apple Grove. But I promise to be a good pal to Anjali, Satisha and Vidya, not an old fashioned, reclusive aunt, when I return to London.

At present I can't give you a date, but when I can I'll certainly let you know. You remind me of our student's years, an age that has left us. You're far too generous in your praises. I swear my head has swollen.

When I come, I shall be returning to my apartment in St John's Wood.

Now that both my parents passed away – within a year of each other – I feel I can leave Maharashtra. London is where I belong. It is the freedom for women, especially single women, that makes it the place for me. Sorry I must close now, I'm on my way to Jaipur to spend time with aunts, uncles and cousins – will post this en route. These relatives of mine are to be cherished, for when they leave me, they can't be replaced. I have the good fortune of realising this before it is too late. My love to the girls and Santosh. I wonder if he understands how very fortunate he is. But you must be on your guard not to be left behind by him, for with his promotions will come greater freedoms – for him. He's a good man, but I've seen too many wives left at home by partners who couldn't resist the temptations around them.

    Working tirelessly at trying to be what you think I am,
Kamla Devi

11

HER PATH TO A GARDEN

Amira felt reluctant to take on the garden, still abandoned and sad looking. She just did not know where to begin. Her sister might have over three acres around her but she had a gardener. Amira had never had to think about gardening. Her students had been her main concerns. Recently the image of a toddler falling over again and again but not giving up had returned – and what would Lily and Palli have made of her failure?

I must make a start; let it be today, let today be special. Look at it; it is feeling neglected, it thinks I have abandoned it. When she went out to hang clothes on the line she heard, 'Look! A few green shrubs, surrounded by a compacted, threadbare lawn. Where is colour?' From the large hollows, now filled with leaves and windswept debris, it was evident that the last owners had taken most of the plants away with them. Look how some people behaved when no one was looking! Her mother used to say God was always looking, but who believed that? Her understanding belonged to another time.

She did not know what to plant, when or how. She had, though, a garden in her head with an abundance of colourful flowering plants and shrubs with varying foliage, swaying in the breeze, with birds and butterflies – and in the damp green-covered corners there were toads, looking askance with bulbous eyes, before disappearing, with one or two hops, into the thick green. But what were the names of such plants? It was time to take the initiative, for God's sake!

She would be sensible. Take it step by step. Go, first, to the garden centre in Daws Lane with a notebook and write down the names of what she liked. But she'd overheard in the Broadway: 'The young people working at the garden centre know absolutely nothing! I had to tell one lad that a rock rose was not a rose found in a rockery. Would you believe it? He hadn't a clue!' Perhaps if she studied the labels tied to the plants… but why was the writing so small?

On her way to the Broadway, she bumped into Janna Cohen and took the opportunity to quiz her about a choice of plants.

'Well,' said Janna, 'I leave that to Edward, I just know what everybody knows.'

'Like what?'

'Daffodils, crocuses, you know, forget-me-nots. Sorry I can't help you more than that.'

'Do you know anyone who could help me a little with suggestions... you know, names of plants so that I can make a start?'

Janna paused. 'I don't... Sorry.'

'Thank you, Janna, so nice to know you're there; someone I can talk to.'

Janna moved on; Amira stood there wondering. When Janna looked back, Amira was still there, lost in a world of her own. She walked back.

'Oh, I've been thinking – perhaps Alice, ask Alice, she's likely to know. She has an allotment, too.'

'How very kind of you, Janna, to be thinking about me.'

Amira walked back to Apple Grove and rang the bell of Alice Reid at Number 11.

'Well, I don't know if *I* can be of much help; have you been to the garden centre? All the help you want is there.'

'I've been thinking of that (*You know that is not true*) but Janna thought that you could give me a little helping hand with the names of plants, as I don't know anything. She thought for a long, long while and suggested that you would be the best person a beginner could come to. You have an allotment too, she told me. How very enterprising! I couldn't possibly have an allotment. All I want is just a little guidance, a little help to start me off. I'm really quite at sea. I need the names of plants suited to Apple Grove. Once I get started with the names, I'll move on from there. I won't bother you after that.' Amira felt like a child pleading to join the game, while others were deliberately ignoring her. She blew her nose. 'Getting a cold,' she said smiling.

'Well, I'm not promising that my advice will work.'

'I understand. But you know what works in this area.'

'What have you in mind?'

'Nothing. I mean I have nothing in mind. It's just a blank.'

'Very well then, let's start at the very beginning. What do you have at present?'

'A bed of old roses which need replacing; there are two evergreen shrubs. No colour at all. Just green, green and still more green.'

'But the Fowlers there before you... Well... well... let me see now. You'll be needing colour all the year round?'

'That would be really nice.'

'Perennials, annuals or both?'

'Perennials. With the girls I don't have too much time. I want hardy

61

plants I can manage.' She brought out her notepad. 'Suggest a few I should keep in mind when I'm at the garden centre.'

'There's no harm beginning the spring with crocuses, daffodils, blue bells, followed by tulips.'

'Yes… And after these spring flowers?'

'Well then azaleas, surely.'

'What would follow these acacias? Did you say acacias? How do you spell it?'

'Give me the note pad.'

'And after azaleas?'

'Rhododendrons perhaps?'

'Yes, let it be rhododendrons and when their petals have fallen, what should we have?'

'Roses are there all the year round; a few hydrangeas, perhaps. I have a white hydrangea, a deep rose pink and another that is an attractive, soft red. They are now well established, their blooms easily fill a vase. Now, before I forget, do not remove their old heads. It's best to leave them until the new buds begin to shoot.'

'Well, that's really good to know. I'm sure I'd have been busy cutting off dead heads! What about aspect, Alice?'

'The aspect of your garden is the same as mine. That's east.'

'I've noticed the sun here is low in the winter sky,' – Amira demonstrates as if in a classroom – 'higher in the summer sky,' – she does not notice Alice looking at her quizzically – 'travelling via the south, to the west until by late evening it disappears.'

'Yes, that's right; note, too, where the shadows fall.'

'The microclimate of my garden?'

'Yes. Knowing where your sunny, warm spots are – and where your cool, shady spots – helps you to grow the plants in places that suit them best.'

'I hadn't thought of that. Thank you, Alice. You've been a Good Samaritan. Have you been to the tropics?'

'Nick and I have not travelled far; he prefers to play it safe.'

'There's comfort in the familiar. I understand that only too well.'

'Do you?' Alice smiles. *What would Nick say if he heard that?*

'Of course. In the Caribbean, no part of our gardens is in permanent shade.'

'Is that so? There must be sheltered places, surely?'

'There's shade at certain times during the day, but never for long. There's a lush profusion everywhere in my sister's garden in Trinidad.'

'Really? How fortunate. No wonder you have such vibrant colours. I've seen your red anthuriums at the Chelsea Flower show. They were outstanding.'

'That's because our sun stays right over our heads, Alice, high in the sky. Its fiery self looks down on the whole island until the evening, when it sinks rapidly beneath the horizon.'

'Well we could do with that here, occasionally.'

They both laughed; then Amira said, 'But there is a down side.'

'Too much heat requiring frequent watering perhaps?'

'That too, but there's another. Our tropical dusk, Alice, is very short; it descends swiftly like a swooping eagle. There's no long, summer twilight, which I find such an enchantment – not having been brought up with it. So much gentle light. It's magical, don't you think? One is tempted to be a painter.'

Alice smiled broadly. 'I haven't ever thought of it like that. I guess we can't have everything, Amira. Sometimes Nick and I forget that. We're not mindful to count our blessings. At our age, rapid changes disorient us.'

'It would me too; which shows we may have some things in common.'

Alice had enjoyed this *tête-à-tête*. She cannot explain why. How very curious!

With her notebook, Amira set off to the garden centre, her footsteps light, her temples throbbing with ideas. A smile must have come to her face of its own volition because she caught a few passers-by smiling at her. Not long after her lawn was also smiling and breathing happily; she had patiently pierced it with a fork and fertilised it.

Two weeks later, she made a cheesecake, and took a substantial piece to Alice and Nick Reid.

'Oh, Amira! How very clever you are. You shouldn't have, really you shouldn't.'

'You're helping me transform my garden, with all that advice.'

'Well, if you say so, but it was nothing really. I enjoyed our little chat. I learnt a lot too… Thank you, Amira; Nick and I love cheese-cake. If you think we can be of help, just come round. Of course, we may not have the answers.'

'I doubt it.'

As Amira learnt, her confidence grew and she began to feel at ease talking about the varieties of daffodils she had a preference for, the wide varieties of tulips, early and late flowering azaleas, rhododendrons, hybrid tea roses, miniature roses, floribundas, lavenders. There were the common poppies and the exotic ones – priced far beyond her reach – and the climbers she loved: the hardy montana clematis with small pink flowers; the deep blue ceanothus she saw in someone's garden that so appealed to her she went straight out to buy one. She recalled the talk about rock roses and found there was quite a variety of cistus – pink ones and white ones with attractive centres; she purchased three.

Mr Fowler had left what she later discovered was a berberis. It was tired. She offered it compost, diluted a little phostrogen in her watering can and fed it. 'Now you can offer us your true self, an outstanding red throughout the summer.' Only its prickly stems prevented her from caressing it.

Her delight with autumn foliage knew no bounds. 'I've found two maples with wondrous colours,' she told Margaret Summers when she came across her in the Broadway. Margaret encouraged her further by saying, 'Let your garden be an extension of your home, Amira.'

'Now that's a grand idea, Margaret. Thank you. Would you have time tomorrow to have afternoon tea with me?'

'That's very kind. It is I who should be inviting you over.'

'Well you're working and I'm at home. I would be really happy if you can make it.'

'You're spoiling me, Amira.'

'About 4 p.m.?'

'Yes. I'll be there.'

She felt drawn to Margaret, and tried to think why this should be. She was so natural, so much herself, but Amira also sensed in her a quiet sadness, even in her smiles and walk. Over tea, Margaret learnt of Amira's other life in Trinidad as a teacher, her affectionate parents and super-competent sister, Ishani. Amira learnt that Margaret was not only busy with her job as a librarian, but had a rapidly declining father and ageing mother whom she tried her best to care for, though they lived far away in Yorkshire. The driving back and forth at weekends was telling on her. Her mother was frail, yet did what she could; her father had cancer and it all weighed upon Margaret because her brother lived in Australia and her sister in the United States. Amira listened quietly. They hugged each other warmly. Before they parted, Amira took her round her garden.

'Any suggestions about what I should add?'

'It depends on what you'd like to have.'

'Perhaps a fruit tree? Plums, cherries, peaches?'

'Mmm, yes. Your garden is small, Amira, and you'll have to imagine a young bush growing, spreading its branches, how it may affect neighbouring plants.'

'I guess like everything else, I have to think ahead.'

'There's a fine nursery that specialises in fruit trees some distance from here, and when next I'm going, I'll let you know; you might consider a Victoria plum.'

'Well that is very kind, Margaret.'

When Margaret took her to the fruit tree specialists, Amira learnt about dwarfing stocks and bought a Victoria plum as well as a cherry. Not long after, she bought two salix Hakuro-Nishiki and placed them at the entrance to the garden where they stood like Japanese sentinels. She cared for them, spoke to them and couldn't help thinking, as she tied them to their supports, that children and sometimes adults also needed a steadying hand when the whirlwinds of life came upon them. Later came a variegated holly and snowdrops.

Amira noticed she was being visited by many more birds: red robins, blackbirds with vicious manners and deep turmeric beaks; the white collar doves were far more amiable as they ambled on the lawn, looking for and finding she knew not what. There were other visitors she did not recognise. They would hop about on her neighbour's tall overhanging giant pink cherry tree, turn this way and that, and descend to peck at her freshly mown lawn.

One summer's day she noticed a large bird with beautiful black and white wings; it was a newcomer and to her surprise it returned the following year and the next. Was this a migrant? Small butterflies and buzzing bees also became regular visitors to her garden – even a damp, greenish-looking toad. Each looked at the other and then it was out of sight hopping swiftly away into the thick patch of overhanging green-ery. She had intended to cut it back, but now considered leaving it.

The one thing that was missing was herbs. Her mother and grandmother had always grown them, Ishani too. At the garden centre, she found a pot of basil, which everyone in her village called tulsi. Her mother had told a story which revealed that the sacred tulsi proffers that most precious of gifts – the gift of life. The fable went like this:

'Once upon a time there lived a woman who could not have a child; with great skill and much patience she created the form of a boy-child with tulsi leaves and stalks upon a home-made altar. Every day she prayed with all her heart, while trying her best to live a good life, sharing what little she had with those around her. At nights she would sit close to the form of tulsi leaves and share her thoughts and feelings. Some time passed until one morning, as dawn came over the eastern range of mountains, covering her hut with its radiance, she was awakened by the cry of a child. She hurried to the source of the sound, and saw a child naked, covered with tulsi leaves, his back to her, attempting to descend from the altar, his legs dangling, unable to reach the earthen floor.'

The scent of the leaves of its cousin born in cooler climes was nothing like as intense as tropical basil, yet it was easily recognisable. In her childhood, tulsi was always present at kathas and pujas, those times of pleasurable offerings of food and gifts to the gods and to neighbours. Even now she could taste in memory channamirit – that delicious sweet milk, flavoured with honey, ghee, cardamom and tulsi leaves; how much she had savoured it. She recalled the pundit's assistant, bringing it to the seated gathering in a polished brass lothar. She received hers in her small cupped palm. It was so delicious that palms were often licked clean rather than washed, and so it was with sticky palms that the guests eagerly awaited the sweet warm parsad parcelled out in brown paper bags, and handed to the invitees, before an appetising vegetarian meal was served. Warmth, food, friendship, nourishment, spices, and herbs – they all came together in the culture of her birth.

It was not long before Amira's garden displayed an uncontrolled growth of herbs: lemon balm, apple mint, chives and peppermint, while sage, thyme and rosemary grew slowly and her pots of basil had to be taken indoors in winter. Now their freshness could be added to her meals.

One day she realised that she'd been so absorbed in creating the garden hidden in her mind that she could scarcely remember how depressed she had once been when she doubted her abilities and thought that she didn't know anything.

AMIRA LISTENS
The End of the Summer Term 1978

'Yes, I've heard you, Mrs Vidhur. I can see your mind is set on one of our top girls' schools…'

'Her sisters are at North London Collegiate…'

'I'm aware of that; much has changed since. Gaining admission to the top schools today is far more difficult than before.' She awaited Mrs Vidhur's protest but nothing came.

Miss Matthew, Vidya's form teacher, smiled. 'Not to put too fine a point on it, the competition is fierce. I could not advise you to apply to North London Collegiate for Vidya. The school best suited to her, where she would be happy, would be one with a somewhat less academic focus; there are fine schools here. I'll enclose a list of these with her school report.'

Amira was sitting calmly. She could have been in a park, observing the swans on a lake. Miss Matthew assumed, correctly, that what she said was being noted. Yet, she was uneasy, sensing passive resistance from this parent.

'You may not be familiar with this, Mrs Vidhur, but schools do have personalities; it is to Vidya's advantage that her personality and that of the school be in harmony. Children from the same home are often very different from their siblings.' Again she smiled. Miss Matthew used her smiles as punctuations, moments in which to pause, so that the parent might reflect upon the import of her words. Amira was attentive; anyone could see that, but Miss Matthew was receiving negative feelings. This, she couldn't abide. Parents must be guided by her, by rationality, not their own rose-tinted sentiments.

'Parents may on occasion find what I'm saying difficult to come to terms with, Mrs Vidhur; it is understandable that they should wish the same for all their children. You will have the summer vacation to consider what I've said.' Miss Matthew was pleased that Mrs Vidhur's expression was now relaxed. She assumed that her arguments had dissolved resistance. 'A visit to one or two schools of your own choosing from the list will enable you to make an informed decision; it is what we both seek.'

Miss Matthew was wrong. Amira had come to very definite

conclusions. She would do what she thought best for Vidya, reflecting, *I happen to know her far better than you. She is just shy; Vidya keeps her thoughts to herself, so unlike Satisha. The appearance of confidence goes a long way in this society. If it does not learn to decipher pretence from reality it will decline.*

But then Miss Matthew wondered if perhaps Mrs Vidhur's stillness and silence might just be detachment from her advice. She felt ignored, bypassed, kept out of reach. This was unsatisfactory. She tried again.

'It would be foolhardy to place Vidya in a school that does not suit her abilities or temperament. I do hope that when you've had time to consider, you will see the matter more clearly.'

'I do appreciate what you're saying, Miss Matthew; I know you have Vidya's interest at heart; my husband and I shall be considering with great care what you've said.'

'I'm pleased to hear this, Mrs Vidhur.'

Miss Matthew halted her flow to look at what she had written on a piece of paper attached to the file.

'Oh yes, there is this other matter.' She straightened herself. 'I'm not sure how I should put this. No offence is meant, Mrs Vidhur; what I'm about to say is simply an observation. As you know, we at St Hilda's do like to bring to the attention of parents what we believe should concern them. For some time now, we have noticed that Vidya behaves as if she were mute.'

'Mute, Miss Matthew? Did you say mute?'

'Yes.'

'She is not mute at home; never has been. Are you sure you're referring to Vidya Vidhur and not another Vidya, perhaps… It can so easily be done.' Amira smiled, a punctuating smile.

'Oh! Of that there is no doubt. We are aware that she isn't, in the way you're thinking; nevertheless, she has shown a marked preference for using body movements to communicate, rather than what is conventional to this country, which is… the spoken word. Perhaps I should clarify further. For example, she engages her head to agree with what has been asked, but that is not all, she also uses the head if she does not wish to accept a proposal. A member of staff has brought a likely explanation to my attention – Indian dance. It could easily be the villain of the piece…'

A smile in the making was halted by the tone of Amira's voice.

'Indian dance?'

'Yes, Mrs Vidhur. I speak of Indian dance. Does she participate in Indian dance?'

'Well, not exactly, but she sees it being practised…'

'Our preference here in England is for speech rather than signs. With language, ambivalences are greatly curtailed… Multiculturalism is all very well, Mrs Vidhur, though I cannot help but get the impression that multiculturalism is about the sensitivities of others, their ways of communicating. Quite often it does not include the English language' – Miss Matthew's rhythm became staccato – 'as it was meant to be spoken.'

'I am baffled, Miss Matthew.'

'I am pleased to hear this, for so are we. However, rest assured, we have observed that she has not yet begun to use eye movements as well. Our member of staff has suggested this may soon follow; it is why we are alerting you early. I gather it plays a crucial part in Indian dance. Perhaps Vidya should stay away from its influence, for a while at least, until she is at ease with our ways of responding. Let me assure you that we have nothing against multiculturalism, though my view is that one should not indulge in it at such an early age; it cannot but lead to muddle. Laying a sound English foundation first, is what I would advise… I cannot think of another language that offers a child better opportunities for life, nationally and internationally, than ours, Mrs Vidhur.'

Amira's thoughts rose rapidly but she reined them in: *Indulge in it! Indulge? Lead to a muddle?* 'Vidya is a shy child, Miss Matthew; she is unlike her sister Satisha who is far more outgoing. She's a very good listener (*not a chatterbox, a Miss Know-it-all*); I'm sure you'd agree that the world has too few of these. Vidya will not speak if she has nothing worthwhile to say. At home we encourage reticence in such situations; it is part of our culture. I do marvel how often people speak when they have nothing to say; it seems like unwarranted arrogance.

'At present Vidya does not attend dance classes, but now that you have mentioned it, she will do soon; both her sisters do. It is possible that she has picked up a few movements from seeing Anjali and Satisha practise at home, but what you have described is only a habit. Habits can be changed. I shall speak to her. Perhaps if I explain our thinking it may help.'

'Please do.'

'You see my husband and I are happy that Anjali and Satisha wanted to attend Indian dance classes; the idea was theirs. It is a source of much enjoyment and harmless fun at home. It enables them to understand and appreciate the movement of the human body, how expressive, how sophisticated it can be in unveiling those fine nuances of thoughts and feelings that are beyond words. Their general posture, I've noticed, has visibly improved in everything they do. Indian dance is about discipline, Miss Matthew, it is about harmonising the rhythm of the human form with the music the dancer hears so that the movements of the music and the dancer become one.'

Mrs Vidhur had completely missed the point, thinks Miss Matthew, who could not permit such an understanding to go unchallenged. 'I will be candid with you, Mrs Vidhur, multiculturalism will confuse the child; Vidya is at a tender, vulnerable age. Encourage her to embrace English culture, Mrs Vidhur, and you'll not regret it.' Her tone was forthright, more than a little peeved at this defiance.

Miss Matthew was not wholly candid, for she was thinking but did not say, *Why does the world want to come here? Millions pushing at our gates to gain entry; yet when they come, they want us to become less of ourselves and more of them. How many countries would have our tolerance, would do as we have done?*

Miss Matthew lifted her head as if from a prayer. 'I have spoken with candour, far more openly than I normally do. No offence is meant. I have done so because I have seen at first hand the slide of several young minds into a thick cultural fog. Young women pulled this way and that and seeing no way out of their dilemma. I do not wish any of our girls to have to face such a predicament. Vidya is well behaved in class, does her work without disrupting others. She concentrates. We had Anjali and Satisha here – such fine girls. We bring our best efforts to prevent the impairment of the young lives in our charge. I do hope you'll accept the staff's observation in the spirit in which it was offered.'

Both women looked at each other, both knew there had been little meeting of minds.

'I am most thankful, Miss Matthew, that you have expressed your fears so openly. Next term, Vidya will not be using head movements at all, or if she does, it will be a rare event.'

'I am delighted to hear this.'

Amira thanked her and was about to rise from her chair when she noticed that Miss Matthew was making eye contact with a teacher who had just come in, the recipient of her message responding with an exquisite eye response.

The English would excel at Indian dance, Amira thought, but resisted saying so. It was not called an eye movement when practised by the English; it became a glance, a studied gaze, or simply a knowing look. The world has always been interpreted by the top dog.

LEARNING A NEW WAY

Her footsteps on the pavement were not hurried. The irritation stirred by Miss Matthew's attitude had quietened. The problem no longer felt as acute, because she had already begun to consider ways of approaching Vidya. Nevertheless, she was annoyed with herself for promising, on the spur of the moment, that next term Vidya would not be using head movements to respond to questions. Why the rush? Now she had to impress this on Vidya, for the girls would soon be leaving to stay with Ishani.

Amira was speaking to herself, trying to work out an approach, and her face had such an attentive expression that some passers-by assumed she was about to address them.

As soon as she arrived home, she called, 'Vidya, come here!'

Her tone conveyed to Vidya that a red flag was flying.

'I want you to listen very carefully.'

Vidya nodded.

'Stop that, Vidya.'

The child jumped, confused. What should she stop?

'Come here.'

Amira led the way so they sat on the sofa facing each other.

'You know I went to the parents and teachers meeting today.'

Vidya nodded.

'Stop that Vidya. Be still. Do not nod, just be still. You understand me?'

Vidya nodded.

'Vidya, is that being still?' Amira demonstrated what stillness was and what it was not as if she were a sergeant major. 'Now listen carefully, Vidya, and do not move your head at all.'

Vidya lifted her shoulders as if she wished to place two bars on either side of her head to control herself.

'Miss Matthew said you do not speak, that you move your head like this and sometimes like this, when she speaks to you. Miss Matthew is English; she does not like her girls to move their heads when they speak or move their heads and not speak, just as you were doing. She wants you to do as she does – speak, speak, speak, Vidya. Only speak.

Nothing! Nothing else! Do not move your head or hands or feet. Never clap when you're speaking.'

'I do not clap when I'm speaking, Mummy. I do not move my hands and feet.'

'I know. That's very good.'

Amira's rage was getting the better of her; she knew she had to unwind. 'Just sit here a while. I'm thirsty.'

Vidya was about to nod in quiet acknowledgement, but in the nick of time lifted both her shoulders to stay her head, while trying to raise her lowered eyes to meet her mother's. Quasimodo, the hunchback of Notre Dame, now sat before Amira.

She went to the kitchen, not knowing whether to laugh or cry; tried to breathe very slowly; drank a glass of cold water; splashed cold water on her face, left it there for a while before she towelled it dry. She must word her sentences in such a way that Vidya would not be tempted to agree or disagree.

She returned to the sitting room.

'Vidya, be absolutely still – like this – while Mummy speaks. Do not move your head at all. What Mummy is asking you to do is very easy, it only seems difficult because you've got into the habit of nodding. There's nothing wrong with nodding, but the teachers at St Hilda's prefer their girls to speak rather than nod. Whenever I say, *Do you understand*, be absolutely still, like this, and speak like this.' Amira demonstrated. 'This is England. We are living in England, so we have to be a little bit like the English, only a little bit, because we are living here. You understand?'

Vidya nodded thoughtfully. Then quickly said, 'I nodded Mummy. I'm sorry Mummy… If I say I'm sorry when I nod, will that count?'

'I will show you how to lose this habit; you will quickly learn this because you're a very bright girl. You are a listener not a talker and that will help you. We will practise a little now. If Mummy says, "Would you like to come to the shops Vidya?" Now tell me, what did Mummy say?'

Silence.

'You forgot?'

'No.'

'Tell me what I just said.'

'Would you like to come to the shops, Vidya?'

'Very good. Now what you say is, "Yes Mummy I would like to come." If you do not want to come, you will say what?'

'No, Mummy.'

'You will say: "I would not like to come, Mummy." But you will not shake your head. You will only speak. When Miss Matthew asks you a question, answer the question but do not move your head or your hands or your feet. Remember she is very unhappy when she does not hear your voice. We must try and make her happy... Alright let's try again.' Amira picked up a magazine. 'Would you like Mummy to read this magazine to you?'

Vidya shook her head.

Amira looked meaningfully at her. 'What should you say?'

'I do not like the magazine.'

'Very well, Vidya.' *I think I have got it now; something has just come to me. Let me try it now.* 'When Miss Matthew speaks to you, first you stand up.'

'I always stand up, Mummy.'

'That is very good, Vidya. After you stand up, remain very still. Don't move your head or your hands. The very first thing you do is say: one, two, three, very quietly to yourself and this gives you time to concentrate, to remember the question, to answer in a sentence and not nod. Saying one, two, three gives you time to be your new self, the Vidya who does not nod. This is a pretend game we're playing.' Amira handed Vidya a Dr Seuss book. 'I am Miss Matthew: "Vidya, would you like to read page two to the class?"... Now what should you say?'

'One, two, three, I would not like to do that, Miss Matthew.'

'I see. Now two things: number one, if Miss Matthew asks you to do something you should do it, even if you do not want to.'

'Why Mummy?'

'Because she is your teacher. And number two, you do not count out loud, you count very quietly inside your head.'

'Why?'

'Because then no one can hear except you.'

'Why should no one hear?'

'Because it is a special thing to do, and special things we do to help us say the right things, we keep to ourselves. It is our little secret. Now everyone has secrets. No one tells a friend or a teacher when they have a secret, for that is what a secret is. It is something no one knows about except your mummy.'

Every day after that, Amira had a session with Vidya, until her five-year-old had got the hang of it. But there was another hurdle Amira knew she must help Vidya to jump clear over. She had to assist Vidya to prepare herself for the coming entrance exams; Amira knew she would have to work hard at it because of the girls' imminent departure for Ishani's.

As she moved about in her kitchen, Amira thought: 'I shall just have to tell Miss Matthew what I think. I've had enough of Santosh's softly softly approach. These people think they are experts at everything – child psychology, Indian dance, what is best for your child. I've had my fill of such arrogance. I shan't let her know that I have every intention of putting Vidya's name down for those academic schools.'

Vidya came into the kitchen and was amazed to hear her mother saying: 'The next time I see Miss Matthew, I shall tell her what I really think of her. She is a goat. I shall say Miss Matthew you are in truth a goat, and this is how you sound: baa, baa, baa. I want to call you a ram with horns but I feel restrained because you are a woman. A goat, a goat you are Miss Matthew.'

Hearing the expressive baa-ing tones of her mother's voice, Vidya began to cry.

'Now what is wrong with you?'

Through her sobs, Amira heard: 'It is not done, Mummy.'

'Who says?'

Vidya's sobs stifled the statement she repeated again and again. 'It is not done, Mummy.'

'Stop it. Go to your room and stay there!'

Vidya held on to Amira's waist and buried her face in her stomach, sobbing uncontrollably. 'It's not done, Mummy; it's not done.'

Amira then grasped the fear she had created in her daughter's mind: that she would have to face an angry Miss Matthew, all day and every day, were her mother to do as she boldly pronounced.

She caressed Vidya's hair. 'I shall say nothing to Miss Matthew. Not a single word. Does that please you?'

Vidya nodded through her tears and running nose. As she wiped her eyes, she stammered: 'I'm sorry, Mummy. I nodded. I should say, I'm glad Mummy.'

'Mummy is very sorry. Mummy was wrong. Vidya is right. You're a beautiful child, Vidya.' She hugged her youngest and tears came. Then she said, 'I'm happy that you'll be having a really nice holiday with your Aunt Ishani. Go along. Here's a tissue.'

God help me! I cannot cope. Sometimes nodding is all one can do when emotions flood the voice and it goes under. I'm going under! I'm losing myself! Why did I say such a foolish, nonsensical thing? Why do I feel so intensely about such arrogance? Why can't I cope? Why can't I keep my eye on the ball. I dare not tell Santosh... I can hear what he'll say...

One of Rembrandt's self-portraits from the National Gallery came to her, how he looked outwards, absorbed in his own thoughts, filled with an understanding of the caprice of the men of his time. Why couldn't she learn that detachment? Why couldn't she just understand and stay as quiet? She knew what course of action made sense, but could not follow it. Why?

She remained still. Nothing stirred. Time passed. Was realising you're separate and alone in the universe, alone in the centre of your own misery, intrinsic to human consciousness? When she was a child she had cried out, *O God where are you?* Now she asked, *Where is the source of the spark that brings human consciousness?*

A VISIT TO THE BARRACKS IN TRINIDAD
Early summer of 1978 at Ishani's

Vidya was not well that day, preferring to read in the garden under the shade of the mango tree. Anjali was to be dropped off at Ishani's department store where she was 'learning the business'; Satisha was accompanying her aunt on a visit to a barracks compound. The prospect of visiting a place where the poor lived had aroused her curiosity, perhaps something to share, with a few embellishments, with her mates at school. Without her sisters, she would be the centre of attention, meeting and greeting with her aunt. The visit was something to do with her aunt's charitable works.

Satisha, now nine, knew from television programmes that the poor would be hungry, so she took two slices of bread, buttered them, divided them into four pieces, lifted her skirt and filled the two heart-shaped pockets of her panties.

On their way to the store, Anjali said she'd observed that 'Everything is more relaxed than in London. People speak more slowly. Urgency is absent. Not a care in the world. It's so different from London where people appear propelled to pack in as much work as they can in a shorter and shorter time... But I think you should encourage queues, Aunt Ishani, because those with loud voices and more body weight push and shove so they get served first, while others who were there long before them have to wait. So do you know what I said? I said, "Now we want to be fair, don't we?", and then I added, "So tell me who was here first, and who came second?"'

'And what happened?'

'There was silence as if I had spoken in another tongue. Then I asked again. Well, a large woman, right up at the front, said, "You see me here, I don't have time for that, serve me and let me run, man, I don't have time to work out that one, oui. That is what I call a complication."'

Ishani laughed; Anjali was trying her best to mimic the woman.

'I see. This is an undisciplined society, Anjali. You can't blame the people, because these same people when they get to London, they queue, wait their turn and see nothing wrong with it. We don't have a culture of discipline, and those who should know better have lost the confidence to say what good behaviour is. What this kind of thinking will do to our society in the long run only God knows.'

'Now when I'm in the store,' Anjali continued, 'I keep an eye out for who approaches first, and I say, you're first and you're second, right? And it's working, but I have to be alert. I overheard somebody say, "Like all yuh have a school mistress here now?" She and those around her laughed. "Like there is no vacancy in schools." It was off-putting, but I held my position. It is better because it is fairer.'

The car descended the cool terraces of the northern hills and entered the Eastern Main Road. Anjali stared at the people going in and out of pharmacies, barbers, jewellers, doctors' and dentists' offices, cafeterias, rum shops, clothes shops opening onto the street, displaying hanging rows of dresses, blouses, T-shirts. Everything along the Tunapuna Eastern Main Road seemed helter-skelter com-pared to the tidy Mill Hill Broadway shops. She saw the vendors overflowing outside the covered market building past the Monarch cinema, spilling onto the surrounding roads, their customers like foraging bachack ants.

Her aunt pointed out the railway station, now defunct. In the distance, she took in the blue-green mountains of the Northern Range, far from this throbbing life, but running almost parallel to the Eastern Main Road, as if not wishing to lose sight of it.

'I like the friendliness and the easy-going way, Aunt Ishani.'

'Very well, Miss Anjali Vidhur, you're getting off here now. Be careful as you cross the road.'

'We have to go through the barracks, Satisha, to get to the compound we're visiting, so hold your nose; the smell is bad.'

Satisha looked down the gravel and dirt track, noticing it was a no-name track. Poor paths cannot afford a name, she concluded. A strong pungent, acrid smell struck her. This was the barracks. On either side were shacks covered with bits of plastic, oil cloth, galvanised sheets, jute bags, oil tins that had been cut open and flattened. There was no plumbing, not even a proper pit-latrine for the four families of squatters.

Ishani walked so fast that Satisha had to run to keep up. She saw how people were cooking on burning wood out in the open, the fire held within a compact enclosure of stones over which an iron grate was placed. Tall tins that once held cooking oil were used for boiling and steaming, the bubbling within held down by square, thick pieces of wood. The smells of fatty meat, salted and tinned fish, boiled yams, half-ripened plantains joined the stink of rotting vegetation and human and animal waste.

A fat woman wearing a plastic apron came out of one of the shacks fanning herself. She smelt, to Satisha, of sweat and burnt popcorn. Seeing Ishani she said, 'Morning Maharajin, how you today? I see it's your day to visit. How charming. I'm visiting too, just visiting. I have a large place in the country, you know. Just come over to help out, you understand.' If Satisha had understood more, she would have seen warmth and endeavour ooze from every pore of this substantial self.

'It is good of you to come and visit, Miss Daisy.'

'Well, with the help of the Almighty, we have to keep trying.'

At last the track opened out to the wide, clean, clay yard of the compound. The houses were either of wood on concrete pillars, or of compacted earth and straw on a skeletal wood frame, the roofs of thatch or galvanised iron. All the front doors looked onto the open yard. Curved striations from a coconut broom were imprinted on the clay, like the movement of waves. Fine dust rose with each passing cart wheel, hooves of cows, bulls and running feet. The wind and the sun cracked it open, and when the rainy season came, the beating rain lashed its loosened crumbs and temporary rivulets carried them away.

Every evening in the dry season, before the coming of carts loaded with bales of grass upon which sat weary men and women, the compound was sprinkled with water to keep the dust down, for it increased the coughing of the elderly. Ishani told Satisha that this place was still like the villages of her childhood.

They had timed their visit well. The women had completed the morning chores of cleaning and washing, tidying and shopping in the open market where vendors from the country came very early. Now was the time to relax, to gossip, to share concerns.

As they walked in, Satisha was struck by the stillness and silence, as if the place had been hastily abandoned. Even the hens hid, crouching under shade. She saw a scene from an old Western film when the hero enters what appears to be a deserted town. *Where will the shots come from?*

But there was life. A boy, dishevelled, trousers fraying, was rolling a truck tyre; a solitary figure with a stick, he came running in their direction, keeping to the circumference of the compound like a performer in a circus. He stopped to stare at Satisha.

She was wearing white socks and fine leather sandals; her flowered cotton frock, lightly starched and neatly ironed, flared to her satisfaction. Her hair was short, professionally cut by Ishani's hairdresser. She wore overly large shades and a pink bandeau partially hidden by her stylishly tilted Panama hat. She had seen him too. Her look asked: *Now what do we have here?*

They stood in the dust and stared.

'Amru, you're playing in this hot sun?' He smiled nervously; his bare feet wanting to shy away as they faced a pair in leather, his toes delved into the earth. Satisha concluded that he was not likely to bite or kick. She had observed children who looked like him fighting in the streets but there was nothing about him that suggested such fierceness.

Amru waited to see if this kind friend of his Ajee had anything more to say. He looked again at this surprising creature in shades, then drove his wheel speedily, expertly, along the dust, leaving the tyre's imprint behind.

In front of one of the doors Ishani called out. 'Bharat Bahin, it is me, Ishani. Anybody home?'

'Coming, coming, Tantie.'

A pink, flowered, cotton curtain was pushed aside, and they entered a dark room. Inside was an ailing, frail old woman. There was the smell of home-made cures: wintergreen, bay rum, castor oil leaves, tiger balm, and oils for massaging the knees. The old lady was asthmatic. Her short breathing tired her. She attempted to get up from her chair to greet Ishani, who came to her aid quickly, insisting that she make herself comfortable. 'Rojani, another pillow please to prop up Nanee's head.'

'Tantie, we don't have another pillow. But I can roll up a towel.'

'That will do for now. I shall send you two pillows today when I get back to the shop. How is she?'

'No improvement, no worse. The same really. The doctor says there is no cure for arthritis, but she gets some relief from the oils and wintergreen; she mix it herself with pounded zaboka seed and the dried rosemary leaves you send. But if you talking about the asthma, if there is improvement… I am no doctor… I don't see it.'

'Is she taking the puffs?'

'Nanee is very stubborn, Tantie.'

'Bahin, you taking the puffs?'

'I take it sometime, I don't always remember.'

'I am telling Rojani to remind you to take the puffs, whenever you need it.'

'Rojani does her best, she has enough to do.'

'Yes. But she wants you to feel better more than anything.'

'Tantie, Nanee knows that.'

'When my time comes na, I will go. When Bhagwan calls, we all have to go. No medicine can stop that.'

'True, but sometimes, Bhagwan needs us to give him a little help. He has given us good sense, he hopes we can give ourselves some comfort, especially when he isn't ready for us. He doesn't like us calling on him to take us away before our time, when he has so many other pressing things to think about.'

'Ishani, you know well good what to say to an old lady.'

'I want to see you take the puff, I have brought a new one for you. I want to see you do it right, Bahin.'

What she saw was ineffective; too much of the medication escaped.

'I will show you and Rojani. Now, first, try to breathe out as much as you can, and when you are about to breathe in, release the puff, so that the breathing in and the puff release go together. Keep your lips tight around it so little of the medicine escapes. I will do it to show you how.'

'Why you taking it? Is that right for you?'

'What is right now is that you do it in the best way. Now look.' Ishani demonstrated it carefully. 'Now Bahin, I want to see you do it, because how you did it just now was not so good, na?'

It was done far better than before, and Ishani praised her warmly. 'Just one small thing, keep your mouth closed longer after the puff is released… Where is Satisha?'

'She is playing with Amru outside.'

'Quiet, shy boy, Ishani,' said the grandmother, struggling with her breathing. 'See what you can do to help him, na. He needs to go to a good school. He needs clothes, books, pencils. He is a bright boy, always finding different different ways to pass the time. He comes to see me. "Nanee, I will be a good doctor and I will cure you." He tells me this. He has set his mind on being a doctor. From the way he speaks I know if we help him on the way, he will. Very sweet child, Bahin. No parents. Ishani, you can be his godmother, na. The Sen family, you know them, they live right here, it is them who gave him his name, na. The pundit's wife, you see, brought him to them.' She stopped to catch her breath and continued, 'I guess the pundit and his wife think of that family because they do not have any children and a son would help them in their old age. The family do their best for him, but how much can they do, na? Two old people struggling too. Amru's father was a young man from India, the mother one of our local girls. She fell pregnant, was turned away by her parents. When she had the baby she leave it at the door of the pundit. We don't know what happen to her or the child's father. Disappear! Gone! But the child is here. His own grandparents do not want to know. We can't judge them. With these things who is to tell what is right what is wrong? What is done is done.'

There was a long pause until she began to breathe more easily: 'Mind you, Bahin, some people want you to believe they are God's secretary, taking shorthand from him, na. They always know what God is saying, what he thinking. Too much foolishness about these days. I getting tired of this world.'

'You should rest now; I shall see what I can do. I just want to show Rojani a few things in the kitchen.'

Meantime, Amru rolled his tyre to the verandah where Satisha stood.

'You want a go?'

'That's silly. Anyone can do that.'

'Show me then.'

She came down stiffly from the top of the stairs. He handed her the stick, the 'driver'. It was sweaty and looked grimy, though its colour came from usage not dirt. She took out a tissue from her pocket, wrapped the end of the stick and with much aplomb attempted to roll the wheel. It moved a yard, turned in on itself, falling with a thud.

'Try again.' This time it was no better; she was enraged. He looked on amazed that she could not do something so simple. Perhaps the tilted hat was in the way.

'I'll help you. Keep near, run with me, then I will pass you the driver. I'll tell you when.'

She was in two minds about this.

'Don't be afraid.'

Who was afraid of an old tyre? Such a silly, stupid boy. 'There is nothing here,' her eyes narrowed, 'to frighten anyone,' said with the assurance of an old colonial speaking to the natives.

Amru's manner accommodated her aloofness with such ease that she took on the challenge. He made it look so simple, the wheel running smoothly, effortlessly, so much so that she felt the thrill of the swift motion and wished control.

'Give it to me now.' The driver was passed, and for a moment the wheel carried its momentum, then seemed to lose its nose for the straight path, became wayward, until gravity held sway.

'That's unfair! Unfair! Unfair! You gave it to me when I had to cross over that tree root,' she shouted.

'Give it to me now, you said.'

'I did not.'

'You said, "Give it to me now".' He mimicked her voice.

'I just said I did not, didn't I? You did not hear me… correctly… This is stupid. Nobody with any sense would want to do this. In London nobody does foolish things like this.'

'You can't do it, but it's easy. I can show you how.'

'I'm not wasting my time over that ugly tyre.'

'Look.'

With the skill of a charioteer he rolled the wheel over roots, boulders, anything at all. She knew it was wrong to have lied, and began to have a sneaking admiration for someone who could do what she couldn't. When the young driver stopped before her, she said, 'I brought something for you.' She lifted her skirt as if she was pulling open a drawer, took the bread and butter from her lily-white panties and handed it to him.

'What is it?' Was this where bread was carried by girls with polished leather sandals, broad hats, dark shades and fine clothes?

'Surely you must have seen bread before? Taste it.'

She had been liberal with the butter and her panty carried two butter marks, and the bread their sweet breath.

'It is good bread and Danish butter. Aunt Ishani buys the best the market has. It is not like the supermarkets in London you know, but it is alright. I can bring you more, next time Aunt Ishani comes and you can show me how to ride over the tree roots and that large boulder clump over there. It is not a very special sandwich. Salmon is my favourite. Do you like granary, wholemeal or rolls with sesame seeds?'

Should he say wholemeal? There was something about *whole* that sounded good. 'I like wholemeal. I like this too.'

'Oh you mustn't say that. This is just plain white; I know you are being polite. But if I do not get wholemeal, I shall bring granary. I can't promise my favourite sandwiches. I don't know if there's any salmon; besides, I don't want to smell of fish.'

He did not want her to smell of fish. 'I like butter… best.'

'You can't. I know you can't. You should not be so polite all the time; you'll never get to taste what you really want if you are so very polite. In London, none of the girls in my class would be so polite; they all say what they really like. Besides, you should make yourself interesting: I do that all the time. Do you find me interesting?'

He nodded.

'You are like my younger sister, Vidya. She used to do this, just as you.' Satisha nodded in an exaggerated, mocking way and laughed. He could not believe that he looked as she said he did. 'Mummy had to work her out of it. "You must have a voice," Mummy said to Vidya. I think everyone should have a voice. Are you of that mind?'

This was an expression he had not heard before, but he nodded.

'Oh dear! You should ask your mummy to help you out of it too. Vidya has a voice now. But sometimes,' Satisha's tone was now confidential, 'it gets in the way of my voice. Vidya's voice is not diplomatic, like mine. One day, it will get her into a lot of trouble if she does not do as I tell her. She's stubborn, you know. Maybe all of us are stubborn, but I don't think so. Anjali isn't. I'm not really stubborn either; I just like to do what I like to do and that's not the same, is it? I'm really trying to help you get your voice.' She shook her head this way and that and said: 'That simply will not do if you want to come to London.'

He would have to look at himself in a mirror. It had never occurred to him that nodding was unacceptable, that it was a source of mockery. How very odd since everyone did it here. He'd been taught to respond with silent respect, to listen carefully. That was the way. Showing that you understood was like breathing; you did it naturally.

London must have its own ways. But what kind of place tells you how you must do simple, everyday things? Did it tell you how to walk, sit, think and sleep? What clothes to wear and how to eat and breathe? No wonder he made her laugh.

'You're coming back?' he asked.

'I don't know when Aunt Ishani is coming again.'

'How I will know?'

'You don't have a telephone, so… there's nothing to be done.'

'But you'll come?'

'I said I will didn't I?'

'Aunty is going now.'

'Oh yes, we're leaving. Until next time. I am Satisha Vidhur. I live in London, but you know that already; I know you are Amru.'

'Amru Sen.'

Ishani approached. 'Come with me Amru. Satisha please bring me my glasses; I left them on the kitchen table.' She took Amru under the spreading branches of the doux-douce mango tree, took out her measuring tape and notebook and measured him so that the shirt and trousers she would send for him would fit. Then she said, 'I shall send you some smart clothes, and see if I can get you in a good school. Can you read?'

He recalled Satisha's mocking manner and said, 'Yes, Aunty.'

'Can you count? Do you know your tables?'

'Yes, Aunty.'

'Very well, I shall come and meet your parents and bring the clothes. I shall speak to the headmaster of a good school for you.'

'Thank you, Aunty… Will Satisha come too?'

'No, not next time, but you can come and visit us; I shall send the car for you.'

'For me, Aunty?'

'Yes. For Dr Amru Sen.'

He blushed. 'Ajee told you na?' He laughed with his eyes, then his whole being lifted itself, trembling with delight. But how should a prospective doctor respond? How could this thing he had kept deep inside his head, and which had no voice, have come to life? Was it because an important person had made it so? There was a lesson here, something to think about, but exactly what, he needed time to consider.

Ishani had long had a liking for the boy, but her life was so full that each time she'd thought of doing something for him, a hundred other pressing things had appeared, but the plea from the old, dying woman was something she would not forget.

As ever, she was as good as her word. His adoptive parents were overcome with happiness that she had taken an interest in the boy. They promised not to take him out of school at any time to help with their vegetable growing for the market. They would encourage him to study and help him as much as they could. 'We will not stand in his way, he can study all day. We are still strong, we will manage.'

'He will help you during school holidays, but not during school time.'

'We know that. He might miss important important things. We have to help him. God has given us strength. You must not worry about us, think only of what is best for Amru. We cannot thank you enough for what you're doing; we will pray for you.'

The headmaster of the chosen school found it difficult to refuse Mrs Ishani Mita, who had never before asked for any favours, though every year she had contributed substantially to their sports day events and Christmas parties. She thanked him so warmly that he sensed that it would be to his and the school's benefit to keep a 'guardian's eye' on the boy's progress.

Before Satisha returned to London, she met Amru Sen several more times in the compound. He showed her again and again how to keep the tyre rolling on, and there were improvements.

JACOB AND AMRU

Jacob, Jack of all trades and master at whatever needed to be done, was one of Ishani's many right hands. She'd asked him to pick up Amru from the compound. This request had nettled him. 'Fancy this little fella, from you know where? The compound if you please. He is to be called for and taken in a BMW; chauffeur driven to boot! And by who no less? Jacob Jeremiah, the best chauffeur for miles if not in the country. And I not boasting. It is not one of my sins.

'Boy, I relieved to see the boy's shoes clean; I was sure I'd have to be cleaning up after him. So that put me in a better frame of mind towards the little fella. He was polite too. "Good morning Mr Jacob, how are you?" he says. "This is a really champion car you have." I said to myself, this little fella here, he has pride in himself, not many people here into self-respect these days. He looked bright, all "put together" for the occasion, his hair neatly combed and his trousers and shirt were new. Well I liked that. I like to see people taking care. Besides, this little fella knows there is something called manners. Some people have forgotten that.

'When I was going for this little fella I really vexed. At my age to have to walk through that trace – no way was I going to drive through that place. Not with this BMW. You think I crazy? You think I don't have anything to do, but wash tyres?

'I don't like to say this, but Miss Ishani doesn't think through this invitation. Can't think of a thousand and one thing at any one time – mind you she does it. But how? Don't ask me. It is not my style. Well fancy inviting this boy over when her nieces are here. You can bet your bottom dollar this meeting will only make this young fella feel how far removed he is from first-class society.

'You know what he say to me when we arrived? "Thank you Mr Jacob for bringing me, you drive really sweet. When I grow up I would like to drive just like you." I like people to come straight to me with the truth.

'You know what I said? "Look Sonny, when you grow up, I, Mr Jacob, will teach you to drive." You shoulda see his face. Like the sun was shining through him… Well who knows? But coming from that compound, you take it from me, he will have a hell of a struggle. How can he fit in with these young ladies? I know how the world works, man. You will be accepted so far and no more.

'And these misses proud for so, they have a way of showing how different they are from you, especially the older one – boy she has airs. Wouldn't I like to see her lose her footing on that pedestal she speaks from. This little Miss said to me one day, in a voice that almost made me jump, "Mr Jeremiah, I can see you are very busy but would you be so kind as to take Vidya and I to Aunty department store. We would be most grateful."

'Boy you shoulda hear she. Accompanying smile and so on. It took me off guard. Well nobody I know speak like that. Anyway, I had me wits 'bout me. I said, "As soon as I finish from here I will drop you." She was not at all pleased. I was waiting for she to say: "How long might that take you, Mr Jeremiah?" Instead, she said, "Thank you, we shall be waiting. I know you'll be doing your very best to assist us." Well fancy that! A real school marm. "We shall be waiting." What does that mean? It means ah better get cracking, oui, and finish off to take she. Look at the psychology, man!'

After that first visit when he was brought by Jacob, Amru visited the house quite a few times. Ishani wanted him to be aware of environments other than his school, the compound and his parents' garden. To him, the house appeared somewhere you could get lost in with its many rooms, and several entrances and exits, though it never felt to him like somewhere to live – big enough to be a hospital, he thought. The garden, too, was grand, neat, orderly. Every blade of grass looked brushed. It made Amru feel small, unsure of himself.

But when he met Ramkisoon, the gardener, he found someone he could talk to, though Ramkisoon tended to say the same thing every time they met. Ramkisoon would tell him what he was doing and how close it was to what Amru's own parents were doing, except that they grew food, while he, Ramkisoon, was doing what?

'Making paradise,' Amru would say.

'You're a very bright boy. How come you know that?'

'You told me. You said, "You see me here, Amru, I'm making this place paradise".'

'Well, that is just between you and me, Okay?'

'Okay. You see I want to know everything. I have to learn and learn every day. And I try to remember what people tell me.'

'You're a bright fella, Amru. Keep what I told you a secret, boy, until everybody else come to realise it on their own, eh.' He winked.

TALKING IT OVER

Whilst the girls were with Ishani, Amira and Santosh spent more time together. It was a good time. On the very day the girls left for Trinidad, Santosh's promotion was being considered by the appointment committee. The long period of waiting had been tense and stressful, affecting the camaraderie among colleagues. Santosh thought the interview went well, but he understood the world. 'You do not know whether they have already made up their minds, Amira, and the interview is merely a charade.'

If the promotion did not come through, their financial strains would worsen. There would be the stress of having to tell Vidya they couldn't afford to send her to a private school, the very school she had heard them say was so good. Amira imagined she could hear Vidya suggesting that perhaps they should send everyone to the same school. Vidya's questions would be theirs and they had no answers they could live with.

They had been trying their best. They had cut back by not having a car, by purchasing second-hand school uniforms, by hunting for bargain fruit and vegetables at Burnt Oak open market, where you could pick out irregular-shaped but fresh and tasty produce much more cheaply than at the supermarket.

The promotion came. They were able to relax, strolling in the nearby St James's Park at the weekends, where Amira noted couples walking hand-in-hand. The touching of hands was giving a little of oneself. It was intimate, to be treated with respect; best left to the privacy of the home. But she looked on and wondered.

They felt younger as they strolled on, pushed like kites by the wind. On their own, they reflected on their relationship, and what got lost in the busyness of work and domestic circumstance. They resolved to be better listeners, more considerate of each other's point of view. It was a time to reminisce, to consider more openly how the children were growing up, what as parents they should be aware of. Amira felt she saw this need far more than Santosh.

On a couple of occasions she prepared a special meal and they both dressed for dinner (something they said they would continue do when the girls returned), and sat by candlelight with the best crockery and cutlery on an embroidered tablecloth. One evening it was tandoori lamb, spinach, yogurt with fresh mint leaves and a few cranberries, stir-fried beans, dhal, basmati rice steamed with a teaspoon of turmeric powder and cumin, warm flaky parathas. Amira said cold water was the best wine with an Indian meal, but Santosh preferred a well- chilled beer; he insisted that Amira be companionable, so she had half a glass, too.

After the meal they set off for her favourite walk – the old Mill Hill village, on the Ridgeway, where William Wilberforce once had a country house and built St Paul's Church in the nineteenth century. Then Mill Hill was described as being 'deep in the country', but even now there were remnants of rustic peace. Here was a past that persisted despite the ravages of time. The Ridgeway comforted Amira in a way she had not stopped to analyse. She felt contentment as they approached the old Mill on the Hill; it was crumbling, defunct, but still held itself proudly upright on the slope that made straining buses change to a lower gear.

Then there were the alms houses, the Old Forge, the pond used as the sheep wash, the railway engineer's abode, the priory, the Post Office cottage, the Mill House, called Sugar and Spice when it became the village grocery shop. But there was also another past, one that was very much alive, one that had travelled to the present, where wealth, learning, status, and sometimes ideas for a better world were reflected in massive structures such as the National Institute for Medical Research, the well-established Mill Hill preparatory and senior public schools, churches and church schools. There were other meeting places that remained foreign to her – the old pubs, complete with their pictorial insignia and names that swayed like hammocks in the Ridgeway's sturdy breeze.

It was after this walk that Amira told Santosh about the incident in the kitchen with an imaginary Miss Matthew.

'How were you to know that Vidya was listening? It must have come as a shock.'

'Vidya was so very English, Santosh. It was the phrase "it's not done, Mummy" that needled me – that very English phrase with all its assumptions; with the tone of voice and body language that once ruled the waves. To hear Vidya expressing it sent me berserk. My response was madness itself.

'You should have heard Miss Matthew on Indian dance. I would have expected some caution – perhaps a few questions – before such pronouncements. Nothing of the sort! I just had to sit there and listen to her exposition of Indian dance and its head movements. Mind you, she would have been pretty good with eye movements. I should have told her so.'

'Tut, tut.'

'It's the tone you know, Santosh, that really gets me. I'm helping out at the school fair, or a second-hand uniform sale, it could be over something as insignificant as pouring the milk in the wrong jug, and I get: "We don't do things like that here, dear", or, "If I were you I wouldn't do that, dear", followed by a patronising smile.'

'Restraint, Amira, why allow a pronouncement on a milk jug to ruffle you?'

'I know, and I do comfort myself with the thought that a culture not informed by knowledge will be a poor one. So I say to myself, leave it to time.'

'You are becoming wiser. So you don't believe in the old adage, "Where ignorance is bliss 'tis folly to be wise"?'

'No. Long ago I learnt from Lily and Palli that how you interpret what is before you guides you; how you interpret anything depends on the level of your understanding. But with Vidya what was hard was to be told the truth, which is what it was, by a mere child…'

'In that assured way too.' Santosh smiled. 'Well not only an assured way but couched in an English assured way. I have a colleague at work from India, he has been here for quite a long time; he tells me that before his daughter got her degree, she listened to him, but since she graduated, he can do nothing right. She was born here. It exasperates him.'

'Yes, born here, but has she picked up the best attitudes of this place? What's a degree worth, if you become pigheaded, lose courtesy and understanding of others? Some of us focus too much on our children's qualifications, on their becoming doctors, lawyers, accountants or the like. We don't spend enough time on helping them with the art of living. We expect them to pick this up on the way, just as we once did, by following our parents' example. But then no one had to tell us to respect our elders. And then some of us keep all the financial problems away from their children, so when they grow up, they think it's all hunky-dory out there, and they're ill fitted for the rough and tumble of the world.'

'I think, in some ways, you've described our family well.'

'How can you say that? I try to widen Anjali's horizons all the time. I show her things in the magazines and newspapers. I've been pointing out the financial constraints we're in. In the kitchen I try to teach them how not to be wasteful – all the things I learnt at Lily and Palli's school, where I intend to send them before it closes.'

'We know that every day our daughters are learning different things from us. But when they leave the house their environment is not ours. They have yet to build up their own frame of reference and while that is in the making, the foundations of their world can be shaken by any whiff of insecurity.'

'You're right, Santosh. Things I wouldn't consider to be of any great importance, such as the colour or shape of what they wear, is to them their entire world. The intensity of their feelings about these things is alarming.'

'Their world is the world of the moment, Amira; next week doesn't count. It's here and now that matters, nothing else.'

'It's about being accepted by friends, not being seen as different; I hope their complexions don't come into it.'

'As you've said, what's important is assisting them to acquire good judgement.'

'And how do we go about that, pray?'

'You know full well, my way is the same as yours. By discussing all manner of things with them – what's in the papers: Ian Smith and black majority rule. What *is* majority rule? Why do they think that it took so long to have that form of government in the first place?'

'That's far too taxing, Santosh.'

'I'm not expecting much; I want them to see how difficult running a country is.'

'Things closer to themselves, Santosh, like would they have preferred to be in a co-ed school.'

'Or what makes people afraid of each other? How best to reduce that mistrust? Just talking things over when we're together at meal times, encouraging them to give their opinion… These conversations will be the nuts and bolts they use to build their own framework of values.'

'What about Vidya? Isn't all this above her head?'

'Oh she'll be listening, she will learn that way. We can make sure that there are topics she can join in.'

'Such as?'

'Are parents always right?'

'Santosh! They're still very young; won't that suggest they have a choice of not complying with what we ask of them? There could be repercussions with that particular topic, especially with Vidya. Being here makes ordinary things complicated. I expected my children would behave towards me as I did to my mother. Whether my mother was right or wrong, we listened respectfully. We might have disagreed with her but we'd never have challenged her. Sometimes I feel I'm losing authority. I don't know any more what I'm meant to do. Where is the boundary line between our guidance and the rights they see their friends demanding as individuals? So much is being asked of us, Santosh.'

Her eyes glistened. Santosh was quiet; he listened to the silence in the room. She, too, sat still, absorbing it for a while. 'I sometimes think Santosh…' She got up hastily and left the room; in the bathroom she cried, then washed her face with splashes of cold water, dried it and returned.

'I want to say this: like so many mothers and grandmothers in London, I'm living outside the culture that formed me. I used to know what good parenting was about; it included guiding one's children to make appropriate choices in their schools, jobs, friends and marriage. Now to be told in a thousand little ways that we must leave such large decisions entirely to them, well Santosh, that seems insane to me. "It's their life, they must be free to choose." I cannot bear to have to listen to such twaddle! At what age: five, six, nine, eleven? And what are they free to choose? Is it their school as well as their clothes? At fourteen should they be free to choose to have a baby? Can genuine freedom of choice be exercised without the tools of discernment? If so, it's the freedom to walk blindfolded on a busy highway. Just the other day, Anjali told me that dark colours and what I would call disorderly hair and heavy eye make-up were the *in things* now. I told her that dark colours did not suit her. Clearly I was missing the point. She said, "Mummy, you're either in or out. You can't be seen to be out. Fashion is like that." I said, "Yes, I know belonging is important." Needless to say she's relieved she can wear whatever, and I'll understand.'

'You have to be more relaxed, Amira, about these things. It's a time when the youth will do their thing. They have the energy, the time and the purchasing power we never had. Combine all these in this tolerant time and you get what you see.'

'It's just the feeling that the world is leaving me behind, Santosh; I'm outside, looking in, not wishing to enter.'

Silence.

'I fear if their lifestyle becomes so different from ours that I shall have to learn to accept it. I don't seem to have the stamina for it.'

'Our children aren't like that, Amira. And even if this were to happen, we will always be far more than whatever the young may think. They may even come round to seeing this. We offer them the best we know. If that fails them, we have nothing to blame ourselves for. Relax; it won't be very long before our children will be thinking that they, too, are "awfully quaint old fogies".' He stood up to mimic the accent and intonation of a teenager, complete with body movements. Amira laughed heartily while he enjoyed his act. They embraced, knowing they had each other and that was precious.

17

A SUMMER ENDEAVOUR

It was agreed that Summer that they'd all return early from Ishani's so Amira could prepare Vidya for the entrance exams of the two schools, one of which her sisters were attending. Bearing in mind that Miss Matthew had emphasised at length that such schools were unsuited to Vidya, Amira gave much thought as to how she should go about it. What motivated her was the desire to offer Vidya a fighting chance to be with her sisters. Why should a shy, soon to be six-year-old, on the basis of her quiet disposition, her artlessness, be judged less intelligent than her more articulate sisters? Such children often had other attributes, other sensitivities that were no less worthwhile. They had to be helped to make their contribution. What effect would being sent to a less academically oriented school have on Vidya's long-term relationship with her sisters?

What was required of a six-year-old? That she did not know. Anjali had entered the school at eleven and when Satisha took the exams, it seemed a more relaxed affair. There was reading, conversation and a little maths. Satisha loved reading and read well. Conversation was her forte, sometimes too much so. This year, things had changed. Intense competition for places meant that the entrance examination was being made more difficult. Miss Matthew had explained that far more would be expected. What was this 'far more'? She needed advice.

Margaret Summers said: 'I really can't say. Fancy having proper examinations for six-year-olds! Keep to the basics, I'd say. Vidya may be asked to write her name, know her address, the name of her parents, her home telephone number, a few multiplication tables – no more than the four or five times tables I would think. Perhaps show she's able to carry on a conversation: Where did you go for your holidays? What did you do? Do you like reading? What is your favourite book? Keep to the basics, Amira.'

'Do you think she could be asked to tell the time?'

'At six, Amira? I wouldn't think so. Well, it's difficult to say; better be safe than sorry. Poor Vidya. In my day children were allowed to be children.'

Better safe than sorry was Amira's thinking too.

Thus began what Vidya called 'Mummy's school'.

Three kilograms of new potatoes were bought, scattered on old newspapers on the sitting-room floor and divided into groups. Soon mother and daughter were looking at groups of two potatoes, placed in a long column as if they were playing some long-lost, rustic game. Then Amira said, 'Let us count how many we have in one group.'

'It is only two Mummy, you only have two here; should I add some more?'

'No Vidya. Now concentrate. Let us see how many there are with these two groups of two.'

'Four, Mummy.'

In this way, Vidya was introduced to the multiplication tables and began to understand the relationship between multiplication and addition. Then came division: 'If we have eight apples and we must divide them equally between two people, how many apples must each have…' So it was that the relationship between division and multiplication was shown. Gradually, multiplication tables were learnt right up to the eleven times table. Then it occurred to Amira that they might ask Vidya to multiply by twelve. Vidya was taught to jump over that hurdle. 'Which two numbers when multiplied do we know are equal to twelve?'

After some time Vidya offered six times two and after some prompting four times three. Amira smiled and hugged her daughter. Were she asked to multiply a number by twelve, Vidya was not to panic. She would first multiply the number by four and then multiply that answer by three.

'So why would you do that if you had to multiply by twelve, Vidya?'

'Because four times three equal twelve.'

'That's right, but this is how to think of it: Since four times three equals twelve, if you multiply by four and then multiply that answer by three, you are multiplying by twelve.'

'That is what I said, Mummy. I know that.'

'You are a bright six-year-old, Vidya. You will pass your exam.'

'Yes, Mummy.'

That night there was prolonged contemplation of how to teach Vidya to tell the time. In her study Amira drew circles, free hand, then armed with coloured pencils, and ruler, and much trial and error she came up with her plan. With the use of pencils and the round rim of a jam jar, she placed before Vidya both a clock and her drawing of the face of a clock, half of which was shaded red, the other blue. Outside the red half was written *past the hour*; the blue *to the hour*. The short hand was pointed out as the hour hand and the long hand as the minute hand. Vidya was asked to show each hour. Then they focused on the long hand and there was a reminder of the five times table. It soon made sense to Vidya that thirty minutes past the hour was half past the hour because the long hand had passed halfway round the circle.

By the second day, Vidya understood that having reached halfway round, the minute hand was now returning to another hour. And then began another chorus, as Amira turned the long hand of the clock this way and that. Mother and daughter sang: five minutes past the hour and five minutes to the hour, ten minutes past the hour and ten minutes to the hour... and so on...

What had been taught was revised over and over again, until Vidya wanted to be the teacher. Occasionally Amira would deliberately get it wrong, and Vidya would gleefully call out, 'Daddy, Daddy, Mummy got it wrong.' Daddy would whisper with a worried face, 'Vidya, you and I will have to help your mummy.'

'Mummy, Mummy, Daddy and I will help you. Don't worry. It's really not hard, Mummy. But you must concentrate, just concentrate Mummy. Please pay attention Mummy.'

Amira was taken aback to hear her own voice so clearly, with the intonation and emphasis too.

18

IN THE SPRING OF 1979

Throughout the first half of the spring term, much attention was given to Vidya's reading and by the time of the entrance examinations Ladybird book ten had been completed. Conversation had been practised: no movement of head; hands to be clasped, brought to the front or kept at the side. Shoulders erect, head held high, chin up; reminders about pleases and thank yous.

Vidya was now polished up and ready. But some things were beyond the abilities of the most caring parents. She developed a chesty cough the day before the exam for North London Collegiate. Linctus and her ventolin inhaler were packed in case her asthma played up.

Before they set off, Santosh said, 'You're a bright girl, Vidya; keep your handkerchief close to you. Cough into it if you need to cough. Stand up and ask for the linctus if you want it. The teachers are there to help you. When you're given the paper, do the sums it asks you to do. You'll have enough time to do everything neatly. Just pretend you and your mummy are sitting at the kitchen table doing the sums, in Mummy's school.'

'Yes Daddy. I know that.'

'This hug that Daddy is giving you is a special good luck hug.'

'Thank you, Daddy.'

In the car Amira said: 'I want you to remember this, Vidya; this exam is not *very very* important. If you pass, it means you can choose to come here, but if you don't pass, your mummy and your daddy will still have the nicest six-year-old in all the land. This is what we want most of all. Remember that always.' Amira turned away as her eyes began to overflow. 'Mummy is getting a cold too.'

'You can have some of my linctus, Mummy.'

When they arrived, Amira pointed out a bench in the school grounds. 'I shall sit and wait for you right there. I'll be here all the time. Now let me give you my good luck hug.'

'Mummy. Like your cold is coming on again.'

'Yes. I need my hanky. Colds are going around today.'

They joined a queue of parents with their well-groomed daughters awaiting their turn to enter. Anxiety showed on thoughtful faces and alert eyes signalled minds ticking over items on their lists. Occasionally a nervous smile was exchanged when eyes met, but mostly they barely acknowledged each other; all were focused on the carriers of their DNA. At the door, a stout, bespectacled middle-aged woman, her dark hair combed back smoothly, spoke firmly: 'Come in, come in, hurry up. Take your coats off, hang them over there, and then wait for me here.'

At the entrance Amira tried to offer a last wave and smile, but Vidya was lost amongst the gathering of girls. She approached the keeper of the gates. 'Would you mind taking this from me.'

'What is it?'

'My daughter Vidya Vidhur – I have her name written on the package – she has a cough and is a little asthmatic; would you please ensure that she has this, just in case she needs it.'

'Very well I shall see that it is in the room she's in.'

'Yes. Please explain to the supervisor that it is her linctus and ventolin inhaler. It is just a precaution.'

'Very well. She will be looked after. Good morning.'

'Thank you. What time will they be finished?'

'About two hours from now. You may prefer to go home and come back if you live nearby.'

Amira was afraid that if Vidya became too anxious, her asthma might come on; it was better for her to stay close by. The sun came out and she decided to sit in the rockery. There she thought of her mother waiting for her on Sunday afternoons to return from a matinee show at the nearby cinema. Her mother was always waiting, waiting to warm her dinner, to serve her, then to wash up after her. Why had she not offered to do it herself? Why at the time had she not appreciated these acts of affection? Why had she taken so much motherly care, so much goodness of spirit, for granted?

Mothers, wives and grandmothers knew all about waiting. They waited for the birth of their children and grandchildren, they waited at schools, at supermarkets, in surgeries with their children, and in some countries they waited in never-ending queues for the basic necessities, or waited all day long with their children for the few available doctors in overcrowded hospitals. She waited. The minute hand moved exceptionally slowly.

Round and round the grounds she walked, stopping to look at trees with an unusual intensity. Had she prepared Vidya adequately? She looked at the fine capillaries of leaves, reflected how, when the roots were unseen, trees looked so top-heavy they must surely topple. She followed the presence of the invisible wind in the movement of the shrubs. She hoped she had done her best. The long hand on her wristwatch would not be hurried. She should have brought something to read.

At last, the sound of children's voices. She hurried to the entrance and there was Vidya, holding the envelope with her medication. Amira smiled. 'How was it?'

'It was alright.'

'Was there anything you couldn't do? Did not understand?'

'No.'

'How are you feeling?'

'Alright. You know something, Mummy?'

'Tell me.'

'You over-prepared me, Mummy.'

'Well that's not a bad thing, Vidya. Do you think it's a bad thing?'

'I don't know. They didn't ask me to tell the time. But at conversation I said that we go to Aunt Ishani in Trinidad for our holidays and that she has a beautiful garden. I said I liked the mountains and the monkeys. I asked the teacher if we were all monkeys, once upon a time.'

'Oh dear! What did she say?'

'She said some things happened so long ago that no one can be sure. I said my daddy was sure and he said many people still behaved like monkeys.'

'Oh! What did she say?'

'She said, "That will do. Next please." And another teacher came and as we left the room the two teachers were looking at each other. I wanted to say more things, Mummy, but she did not want to hear more. She said, "That will do".'

'She has to listen to everyone; so she has to give each girl a little time.'

A week later, Vidya went to take the entrance examination for Haberdashers Aske's. On this occasion she was asked to tell the time. She studied the clock's face on the headmistress's desk for quite a while, and just as the headmistress turned her attention to Amira, she announced the time correctly, to Amira's delight.

This time when asked about her holidays, Vidya was more cautious. She mentioned the monkeys again but only said, 'I like looking at them. They have very sharp teeth. There are no elephants in Trinidad. Mummy says a ride on an elephant is uncomfortable. I like drinking coconut water in the shell. Do you like coconuts? Aunt Ishani can help you choose one with soft sweet jelly.' Satisha had coached her to say many things and she had remembered most of them.

Another wait began.

When the letters arrived, Amira said a prayer before opening them, as if a prayer could transform what was written within. She read. She sat down and read again. It was as she had hoped. She gave thanks. Vidya had been accepted by both schools. Amira's thoughts flitted in one direction, then another. If she had not tried so hard, who knows. Vidya had said she was over-prepared. Was that really so? Surely what Vidya learnt was not a loss?

Vidya was asked which school she preferred: North London or Haberdashers. It was Haberdashers.

'Why?'

'Because it is brighter, Mummy; the light comes into the school. There is more sunshine. North London is dark, the walls are so heavy and thick. The windows are too high and old; there aren't large glass windows, Mummy, and they're the best. Haberdashers has them. You can look outside; I like that.'

Amira regretted she had asked. It was such a silly thing to do. But she was trying to move with the times. She had seen how mothers asked their small children which shoes they preferred when they were in the shops. She had never done that. Her children would wear sensible school shoes; a style of their choice they could have when they were teenagers, not before. She thought Vidya would have wanted to be with her sisters. But no! She was looking at the sunlight.

You were either with modernity or not, there was no halfway house; and so Amira wrote two letters, one accepting Haberdashers Aske's, the other declining North London Collegiate. They were left on the window sill to be posted in the morning. Late that night, Santosh arrived back from Kenya, where he had been on one of many visits to offer technical advice and assistance.

'Have you decided where Vidya will be going?'

'Yes. She wants to go to Habs, and so I have accepted that.'

'Have you posted the letters?'

'No.'

'Well I think you should change it. We will send her to the Collegiate.'

'But I told her already.'

'Leave it to me. I'll sort that out with her in the morning.'

Amira rewrote the letters.

After breakfast, Vidya was told that Daddy wanted to have a little chat with her in the sitting room.

'Your mummy tells me that you not only passed one examination but two.' Hugs followed. 'That is quite an achievement, Vidya. Congratulations on doing so very well.'

'You know what, Daddy?'

'Tell me.'

'Mummy over-prepared me.'

'Your mummy wanted to make sure that if something very difficult came up, you would know how to manage it.'

'Twelve times did not come up, Daddy.'

'I am happy about that. But if it did come, you would know what to do.'

'Yes you have to multiply twice, Daddy.'

'Thanks for reminding me, Vidya. Your mummy and I might need you to remind us sometimes. Is that alright with you?'

'Yes, Daddy. But you should concentrate, Daddy, and try your best to remember. I may not be here.'

'That is very good advice. I shall remember that too. Now I have something to tell you. Your Mummy says that you have a preference to go to Habs because the sunshine comes through the glass windows and the rooms are bright and cheerful.'

'Yes, Daddy. Satisha's school is so cold and dark. Mine is not.'

'Now I want you to know how I am thinking. When you grow a little taller, you'll be able to look through the windows of the Collegiate School, and when it's dark, there will be many lights. But most important of all, Satisha will be able to help you, show you around, tell you which teacher is really good, which one has a short temper, and lots of other things. If you go to Haberdashers you will have no sister there to help you, or to bring you home, if you're not well. We live very close to Collegiate. This means you can be home much earlier and have time to do lots of other things.'

'But I don't like Satisha's school, Daddy.'

'After a time you will grow to like it because you will have two lots of friends: yours and Satisha's too.'

'But I want to go to my own school and not Satisha's.'

'Now Vidya, listen carefully. We know that the Collegiate is a very fine school. We have no experience of Haberdashers. It's a good school, too, Vidya – that's why you did the entrance exam – but parents have to go by what they know from experience, especially on important things. So I told your mummy that you'll be having the same education as Anjali and Satisha.'

'Why did you let me do Habs exams, Daddy? Is that fair?'

'We did not know you would pass both exams. Some girls pass only one.'

'I passed two, Daddy. I don't like Satisha's school and I don't want to go there. I do not want to have Satisha all the time; she is always ordering me about. I want my own school.'

'We will talk about it again tomorrow. We're very proud of you, Vidya; we know you can manage on your own and we'll tell Satisha so too. We'll tell her that you won't be needing her help, that is unless you ask for it, which is unlikely.'

'Satisha won't listen; I know she won't, Daddy. She's bossy, she's always right. I want to be by myself, I want to have my own school... You say we should always try to be fair, but this is not fair, Daddy. I know it isn't. You are not being fair. Is that right, not to be fair?'

Silence.

19

THE SUMMER OF 1981

That summer, two years after their first visit, Satisha and Vidya returned to spend their summer holidays with Aunt Ishani. Anjali said she would prefer to take on a summer job in London and later travel to the Lake District with a group of friends.

The first weekend they were there, Ishani invited Amru to meet her nieces.

A small square table in the large kitchen was set for them. There was pumpkin soup with split peas and a few ochroes. The soup was a little too hot. The girls stirred theirs with their soup spoons and ate by skimming the cooler surface. Amru softly blew on each spoonful first and then a sound of satisfaction came from him. Vidya looked at him, then bent her head low, smiling. Satisha began to communicate with Vidya's left foot. They giggled. Amru suspected he was the source of their amusement, but wasn't sure what was so funny.

'Do you like the soup, Amru?'

'Yes, Aunty, it's very nice. Thank you Aunty. I like it very much.'

'Good.'

Jenny brought dhal, rice, spinach fried in olive oil and small cherry tomatoes that looked like red marbles against the green; chicken bhunjayed in freshly ground massala, beans and paratha rotie. The girls picked up their knives and forks.

Ishani said, 'You don't have to use the knife, the chicken is tender, a fork and a spoon would do.'

'I prefer a knife and fork, Aunt Ishani,' said Vidya.

'That is what we are accustomed to,' Satisha said, lifting her head as if making a pronouncement.

Amru, not wishing to be different, decided to use his knife and fork too. It would be his first time, but the girls made it look easy. Vidya felt the movements of Satisha's feet. They were both stealthily observing him. His way of eating with speed and concentration reminded Satisha of a Charlie Chaplin film. Vidya's urge to comment broke its confines. 'Look how fast he's eating.'

Satisha joined in. 'And he is holding his knife and fork as if they're pens.'

'Nothing is wrong with that,' said Ishani. 'Many people use them that way. And now would you two please behave at table.'

Amru sensed the girls had built a wall around themselves and he was outside it. He must have done something wrong. Was it how he was holding his knife and fork as pens? How could that offend? Aunty said it was not wrong and she knew best. Besides, he had made no spills. Did everyone in England eat the same way then? Was this the first time they'd seen something different? Amru wondered and wondered.

Should he say something? But what? Didn't they want him there? Their averted eyes, the communication under the table made him uncomfortable. The best thing to do was to concentrate on eating his food quickly, then take his leave.

He had so looked forward to this; his parents too. His frail mother had insisted on ironing his clothes that morning, and his father had given an extra rub to his shoes. It had started well but now... He would go home and read. Nothing must stop him becoming a doctor – then everybody would be so pleased to see him. He would be the best doctor ever, make Ajee better. He would learn all that there was to learn and do his very best. Staying here was making them unhappy – and there was so much to read, so much to know.

He said to Ishani, 'Thank you, Aunty, I would like to go home now. I can walk home. I know my way.'

'I will take you myself, Amru; I have a few nice things to say to you. You are looking very smart. The Headmaster said you're among the five brightest boys in the class. Well done, Amru! I am very proud of you, and your Uncle Ravi is too. Have a little walk in the garden, I will not be long.' He looked at the girls to say goodbye, but they averted their eyes.

When he'd climbed down the stairs to the garden, Ishani turned to her nieces. They were about to leave, when she said, 'No! You two, sit down. I have to tell you a thing or two. You made me so ashamed. Amru was our guest. Is that the way you treat someone I've invited to meet you? You did not show him common courtesy. You laughed at him, you did not try to talk with him; instead, you tried your best to humiliate him, to take from him the most precious thing he has. Do you know what that is?'

They understood in part what their Aunt was saying, but as far as they could see, he had nothing precious they could take. He was just an awkward, silly, country boy who did not know the simplest of things. He was comical. If he was with any of their friends, they would have behaved in the same way.

'Answer me. You live in London, you go to the best schools; is this is all you can say? Nothing? I shall sit here and wait.'

Silence distilled to a weight upon them. As the seconds became minutes Vidya said, 'We made him feel badly, and that was not a friendly thing to do.'

'Satisha, what do you have to say?'

'We were laughing at him; it was two against one, which was unfair.'

'Now, you two, listen with care. You never make an invited guest feel uncomfortable in your home. If that's your intent, don't invite him. You have a large advantage over him and you decided to reduce him further, to take away his slowly growing confidence in himself, and kick it about under the table. Finally – and listen very carefully – I cannot think of anything that is of less importance than how you use a knife and a fork. You do not have a clue of what is of lasting value, and what is simply style or habit. I prefer to have around me people who are honest, kind, affectionate, dependable and caring, no matter how he or she eats or dresses, than someone who knows how to wield a knife and fork and is presumptuously ignorant of what is really of worth in life, who selfishly cares only about making an impression on others.

'I'm very very disappointed in you two. You've shown no regard for me whatever. I want you to get this clear in your foolish little heads so that your polished tongues may be better guided in the future. Some things are important because they are intrinsically so. These are things like courtesy, affection, truth, integrity. Only the foolish and the ignorant don't know that. I despair of what education has come to. You are going to the best school in London I am told. Heaven help those who are going to the others! Now both of you go down to the garden and apologise to him.'

Vidya began to move towards the garden; Satisha did not move.

'Satisha, did you hear me?'

'I am thinking of how to say it.'

'Just be honest, it's a good way to start.'

In the garden Satisha said, 'Vidya, you go first, and then I'll come.'

'No, you go first, Satisha.'

'If you go first, you can be quick, because you'll know that I'm waiting.'

They sat for a while, on the steps which led to the garden. When Ramkisoon saw Vidya approaching, her slowness of pace and worried look told him he should get busy with cutting back the hedge somewhere else.

Amru said, 'Wait, I will come with you.'

'No, wait here,' Vidya whispered, her voice about to break. 'I want to say something, Amru.'

He stood there perplexed. *Why was she looking so mournful now?*

'I am very sorry that I joined with Satisha and behaved badly at table. It was wrong. You were our guest, and we behaved badly. I am sorry. Please forgive us.'

He did not know what to say. He just stood there. She turned around, walked hesitantly away, then ran to the house. She sat down, breathed more comfortably and tears of relief came. *He made it easy for me. He just stood there and listened. He was not angry with me at all. Aunt Ishani had got it all wrong. He did not seem to mind.*

Amru began to move in the direction of Ramkisoon when Satisha appeared, she too looking distressed. What was it this time? One moment they were jeering at him and now…?

'I want to say that I behaved appallingly, I am older than Vidya, but on this occasion, I behaved as if I were younger. I did not set a good example to her. We thought certain things were important but they are not. I'm very sorry to behave as I did. I will not do so again. Please forgive Vidya and me. I often do things first and then think about them afterwards. It is not the right way round.' She bent her head, did not look at him. Her contrition touched him.

'I'm going to become a good doctor and I will not charge you nor Vidya, nor Aunty and Uncle.' He smiled to reassure her.

'Thank you, Amru. I must go now.'

As Ishani took Amru home, she talked to him about his class, his teacher, what he liked doing, what he could not do as well as he would have wished. How his parents were.

'My ma and pa are well. I help in the garden during my school holidays. It is hard work in the sun. I wear the hat you sent me.'

'I want you to know that you are carrying very beautiful things inside you. They are the most important things in life. Do you understand what I am saying?'

'I'm not sure, Aunty.'

'Well, let me explain. You want to become a good doctor.'

'A very, very, good doctor, Aunty. I must save Ajee.'

'Yes. And you are working hard at it.'

'I work all the time. If I don't know something, I ask the teacher.'

'Very good, Amru. Now these feelings, these ideas are yours. They will make you a very special person.'

'I want to be a very, very special person. I want to make all the sick people well.'

'You are already a very special person.'

'No Aunty, not yet. When I become a doctor I will be. I will make Ajee better. And if you are sick and Uncle too, I will make you so better that you'll not get sick ever ever again.'

'I know that. Now if something makes you sad, you must come to the store and tell me. I'll drop you off here. Take this bag of gulab jamun for your ma and pa. Tell them I said they have a very special son. Now don't forget.'

'Thank you very, very much, Aunt Ishani. You are the best Aunty in all the wide world.' He and his parents would thank God for their blessings.

20

VIDYA AND KATRINA

It started in the first term of Vidya's second year. The first year passed and it seemed she had settled in nicely. When it started Amira advised Vidya to keep out of Katrina's way, believing that her bullying might stop, but she was wrong. Vidya said that Katrina always looked for her at break time and taunted her, calling her blackie, pelting her with pebbles. She'd managed to recruit two other girls, so there was now a chorus of insults. It was when Vidya came home with scratches on her face, saying she wouldn't go back to school that Amira decided she had to do something.

She phoned Katrina's parents, explaining what had been happening. Mrs Hahn promised that she would ring back, and she did, declaring that she was appalled at what had gone on, and was it possible to come round to see them.

Just after eight the Hahns arrived with Katrina and they all sat down in the sitting room, Vidya close to Santosh. At first Katrina looked an unlikely bully to Amira. She was fair and blonde; her long hair, neatly plaited, crowned her head in a becoming way. Then Amira saw someone determined, strong willed.

Her mother was calm, shook hands and smiled warmly; her husband did the same. Elsa Hahn said, 'Katrina has come to apologise to Vidya; she realises bullying is not the way we would like our daughter to behave. We are sorry that Vidya has had to cope with this from Katrina.'

Mr Hahn said, 'Katrina you may apologise now to Vidya.'

Katrina refused to look at Vidya and said nothing. A minute or more passed by; then Elsa Hahn said, 'Katrina, have you heard your daddy; please apologise to Vidya.'

Katrina did not budge. She sat upright and looked at the door. Minutes passed. Amira said, 'Let's have some tea. I'll put the kettle on.'

Amira went out to the kitchen and returned with a pot of tea and shortbread.

Katrina refused both tea and shortbread; her parents accepted and the Hahns and the Vidhurs chatted pleasantly. It must have been almost forty minutes later when Elsa Hahn winked and said, 'Mrs Vidhur, would you have a spare bed, because it seems that we may have to spend the night with you. We are not leaving here before Katrina apologises.'

'We have a spare bed, and Katrina can share Vidya's room. I'm sure Vidya wouldn't mind,' Amira replied.

Katrina began to sob. 'I want to go home.'

Her father said, 'We can't until you apologise to Vidya.'

She mumbled something. Her mother said, 'Mrs Vidhur, we are so sorry that Katrina has lost her voice. When she regains it and apologises appropriately to Vidya, we may not need the spare bed after all.'

More minutes passed. At last Katrina stood up, dried her tears, looked at Vidya, and said, 'I'm sorry I was bullying you, I shan't do it again.' She turned and hid her face in her mother's warm embrace. Amira saw a performance: an intelligent girl who knew all along what was expected of her and had been using her wits to evade it.

'We are so happy, Katrina,' said her mother, 'that you won't be bullying Vidya again, nor encouraging anyone else to do it. We know you are really a very good girl, and that this won't happen again. We are very proud of you. That was not easy to do.' Both parents then turned to Vidya and said, 'Katrina won't bully you any more, she has just told you so, and Katrina keeps her word; it shows she is growing up.'

When they left, Vidya embraced her parents and went up to bed.

Santosh and Amira had more tea. The empty space left by the Hahns still held a little of their spirit.

'The Hahns knew what was the right thing to do,' Amira said.

Silence.

Katrina kept her word; Vidya was not bullied again.

21

AMIRA FINDS A PLACE IN APPLE GROVE

Who can tell how it happened? How, amongst the twenty residents in Apple Grove, it would be in two very different homes that Amira found a warm and lasting friendship? Over the years, Number 16 and Number 2 embraced her warmly and helped her to understand that she was their good neighbour and, like them, belonged there.

No one would have expected Juliet Marsh of Number 2 to become one of Amira's close friends, for no one else in the street really knew her; one could even say the street did not offer Juliet Marsh much neighbourliness and she couldn't have cared less. She was not one of them. She was a warm, plumpish and fit working-class woman in her early sixties. She had a keen understanding of how to live a good life. Her bachelor son, Michael, who lived with her, enabled her to be financially independent. Amira had first seen her walking briskly, while the wheels of her shopping trolley swayed this way and that behind her, struggling to keep pace.

During the autumn months, she'd try to make sure there wasn't a single leaf on the meticulously clean, wide frontage of her house. Since Apple Grove was lined with deciduous trees – silver birches and lime trees – Juliet's job was a daily one. Whenever Amira passed by she'd stop to say, 'You shouldn't worry if there are a few leaves, leave them until there's a pile, Juliet, before you sweep them up.'

'Oh I couldn't do that.'

'Why?'

'My mother broke her hip, sliding on a single leaf. I wouldn't want that to happen to anyone else.'

'Well, it really is the best-kept frontage.'

'You think so?'

'I know so. When I get my frontage done, Juliet, I'd like to have the brickwork looking just like that. I like the pattern. What is it called?'

'Fish scale, aint it? You'll have to ask Michael; he'll know. Have time for a cuppa?'

'Are you sure?'

'Come in,' she said, with a wave of hand, quickening her steps up to the imposing mahogany front door, with two white pillars standing like Roman sentinels before it and a gleaming brass knocker. Inside, the kitchen was large, fitted in oak; everything was of the best quality: neat, clean, welcoming.

'Sit down Meera.' Fruity biscuits were brought out.

'What large cups, Juliet!'

'You like them?'

'Very nice.'

'Go on, have a biscuit.'

'I shouldn't really; I'm trying to lose weight.'

'Go on, have one, you're just a scrap of a thing.'

'I see you were reading the newspapers.'

'You can have it if you want. I'm done with it.'

'No thanks, we have two papers and I rarely have time to read both… You have a lovely house. I like the wrought ironwork on the balcony. It looks like black lace.'

'Michael designed it.'

'Did he?'

'He does beautiful work. Come let me show you a cake he worked on for a customer; they'll be calling for it today.'

The tissue paper cover was lifted with care. It was magical. Pink roses, rosebuds, leaves and vines looked as if they were freshly cut, with dew drops still resting on them; a few appeared to be rolling off the petals. Amira was astonished.

'Thank you for showing me. It is a fine piece of work; I hope the guests will take photographs of it before it is cut.'

'Well that's my Michael. That's how he works.'

As Michael worked long hours at the National Bakery School of London where he lectured, Juliet was by herself during the day, so she looked forward to having Amira's company over a cuppa. Amira took such a liking to her that when she could not accept Juliet's invitation to join her, she felt genuinely sad, promising that next time she would. She always did, too, even if it was inconvenient.

When winter came, Amira suspected that Juliet kept looking out to see if she was passing. Then there was a knock at the window to attract her attention.

One day, a beaming Juliet tried to convince Amira that she had been the lucky winner of a million pounds, and all she needed to do was to send twenty pounds to sort out the paperwork to have the money transferred to her. She showed Amira the letter.

'Don't believe a word of it, Juliet; they only want your twenty pounds. Your mum would have said what you once told me: "If it's too good to be true, it probably isn't." Keep your money, Juliet. It's a scam. The person who sent this is a criminal. He has no money, he wants yours. Why doesn't he take out the twenty pounds from the one million you've won, and send you the remainder eh?'

'I don't understand this. I've won a million pounds, ain't I? Look Meera, what does the letter say? Read it.' Amira wondered whether she should alert Michael about Juliet being so easily taken in. Santosh agreed that Michael should be told, though he said he'd be surprised if he was not already aware of it. And Santosh was right. Michael knew.

Amira became more concerned when Juliet, who had already shown Amira round her house several times in the past, began to do this even more frequently. Amira's attention would be drawn to the Afghan rugs; the long curtains sweeping the floor; the grand antique pieces like the Queen Anne dining chairs; the tiles around the fireplace that Michael had seen in Italy. 'He fell in love with these Meera,' she remarked. 'You like them?'

'Michael has very fine taste, Juliet.'

One day when Juliet yet again took Amira upstairs to show her the bedrooms, she opened the wardrobe and took out a jewellery box and placed it on the bed. She showed Amira her rings, bracelets, earrings and necklaces – all with precious stones – that Michael had bought for her. 'You should put them away now carefully, Juliet. They are very beautiful.'

Juliet smiled warmly.

As they came down the stairs, Amira said, 'I appreciate your showing me, Juliet, but you should not show your jewellery again to me or to anyone besides Michael and your daughter. You have shown me and I know you have very beautiful things, so I don't need to see them again. You have to be very careful, Juliet. You are too trusting.'

These were the early signs of Alzheimer's disease. One day, when Michael was in the garden, and Amira was about to take her leave, Juliet put on her hat and coat and began searching for her handbag.

'Have you seen my handbag, Meera? It is time for me to get home now; I've been here too long. Michael will be worried. Do you know, my mother moved close by a month ago and no one told me?'

'Oh dear! Oh! I see.'

Amira went out to the garden and called Michael.

He told Amira that Juliet had lost more than a thousand pounds from various scams. If he found such letters he destroyed them, but he was not at home when the post came.

'Mum has left the house several times before, Amira, and I've had

to seek help from the police. She's been found wandering in Edgware.'
It was then that he told Amira that they were selling up and going to
Spain, but because Juliet wouldn't hear of leaving he'd had to tell her
they were just going on a holiday. The property was surrounded by
large grounds with only one gate, which could be kept locked.

'There's so much space for her to walk about in and she'll love
harvesting the orange and lemon trees. Here,' – he showed her a
photograph – 'look at the view, Amira.'

'The grounds are amazing. To have your eyes on this every day,
you'll soon be writing poetry, too. You're doing the right thing, but
I'll miss your mum.'

On the day Michael came to say goodbye, Amira felt she was losing
one of her own. Since she'd become friendly with Juliet, he had given
her so much advice about her garden, helping to give it a form she had
not been able to see herself. 'Your spirit walks in my garden, Michael,
and will always do.' Tears came and she needed a handkerchief.

But what to say to Juliet?

'Have a great holiday, Juliet.'

'When will you be coming, Meera?'

'Soon.'

'Ta ta.'

Juliet smiled; Amira tried but failed to do so as Michael's Volvo
turned out of Apple Grove. She hurried home, a feeling of sadness
over the ephemeral nature of life upon her. It took quite some time
before she could pass by Number 2 Apple Grove and not look
through the windows, expecting Juliet to come out and say, 'Care for
a cuppa?'

The other neighbour who Amira connected with was Margaret
Summers. They were very different in background. Margaret was so
English, with an educated southern accent, yet to Amira she was
'Indian' in her outlook, and she told her so.

Margaret was intrigued. 'In what way, Amira?'

'Oh you worry about everything, you try to do far too much, you
tire yourself out looking after your grown children, worrying about
them and your father in Yorkshire; you are so generous and helpful
to me. Do you remember the day you took me to the nursery to
purchase a Victoria plum tree?'

'Yes, but I was going to Stevenage, the nursery is close by.'

'You also took the trouble to explain what to look for when I
bought it, and then you found me the right spot in the garden to plant

it. I didn't have a clue. And when I found you making your own marmalade it looked very Indian – that day your kitchen smelt like an orange grove at harvest time.'

The scene had reminded her of growing up in the village, when bottling chilli sauces, mango chutneys and achars was so much a part of the cycle of life.

'That was a bit of an indulgence; it's so time-consuming; my days for marmalade-making, I'm afraid, are coming to a close.'

'But home-made marmalade, Margaret, on freshly baked bread, is my idea of a bit of English heaven.'

'It's good isn't it? My mother made chunky marmalade, you know. Baking was something I did more when the children were growing up. But now with Dad not well and Mother so frail, there's much less time.'

'A good Indian daughter.'

'Why Indian, Amira? We English have a heart too, you know.'

'Knowing you, Margaret, I'm now inclined to think there's a strong possibility that this organ may be found amongst a few, if one knows where to look.'

'Amira! You are impossible.'

'You could have put your father in a nursing home; instead, you travel up to Yorkshire at great emotional cost to yourself. I can guess how much you do when you're there, and all that driving back and forth must be exhausting. No doubt a houseful of chores awaits your return. You're certainly an exception.'

'And what about you, Amira? When Vidya left St Hilda's, you gave that friend of mine her school uniforms, all in such good condition. You refused to charge her and said, "I'm happy to let any friend of Margaret's have it as a gift".'

'Oh think nothing of it, Margaret.'

'And then you offered me your prize recipe for that delicious cheesecake; I didn't like to ask; I felt something like that must be a family recipe you'd be reluctant to part with. But no, you gave it to me gladly. You keep spoiling me, inviting me over to delicious lunches, sending over warm kachouries. You spoil me, Amira.'

'Nonsense. You've helped me in every way. You're just a lovely human being.'

'Oh Amira, you'll make me cry, if you go on like this. Let's have some tea.'

PART TWO

22

PROUD PARENTS
Trinidad, June 1984

Ishani Mita was at her desk, studying the results of her stock-take. She was putting together her Christmas orders and needed to know which lines of goods had gone well, which new lines of toys she should try. It was a hit-and-miss thing when wholesale purchases had to be made in July for December. When you got it right you wished you had purchased more and when not, you had to sell at a loss. Public taste was fickle.

The telephone rang.

'How nice to hear from you, Savita.'

'Ishani, I have the best news a waiting mother can have. Our son Praveen is a qualified doctor and is back home.'

'Oh! Congratulations, Savita! You and Haim must be over the moon. What an achievement! You must be very proud of him. What delightful news. Ravi isn't here but as soon as he comes in I'll let him know. We're very very happy for you and Haim. We must celebrate this.'

'Well that's why I'm phoning; tomorrow morning we'll have a little puja, with Pundit Narine, only Praveen, Haim and I will be sitting; but on the following day we're holding a cocktail party for him, to meet our friends. We'd like you and Ravi to be there.'

'Of course we'll be there. What time?'

'Round about 6 p.m.'

'Thank you, Savita. We'll be delighted to meet Dr Mahesh.'

Returning to her list, Ishani decided that she would need to visit the USA herself before ordering any of the new lines of toys. Her thoughts then settled on Savita's good news. It was six years now, or was it more, since she'd last seen Praveen. What was he like now? Her three nieces were with her, attending Lily's and Palli's school, and though custom allowed her to take them along, she knew it would be unwise. Savita and Haim now had the company of their son after so many years. He was their precious pearl. It would be tactful to show no interest; besides, he might have grown into a silly, pretentious fool. She would go about matters with finesse. Even if there were possibilities for Anjali, Savita must not feel threatened.

The following morning, Praveen sat with his parents in the family's shivala. Pundit Narine offered thanks to the Trimurti – Brahma, Vishnu and Shiva – for keeping Praveen out of harm's way in a foreign country and returning him qualified in the art of modern medicine. Saraswatee, goddess of learning, was also thanked for keeping close to Praveen throughout the years of study.

Small offerings of sweetmeats were made to the god Agni, who had already partaken of ghee, incense, grated coconut, sugar, rose petals, and freshly cut pieces of pitch pine. The mingled scents and fragrances circled the four participants, flowing out of the temple, drifting like mist into the neighbourhood, carrying the bouquet of burnt offerings. Delicious pera, ladoo, and gulab jamun, blessed by the pundit, were parcelled out into brown paper bags and offered to family, friends and passers-by.

When Pundit Narine set off to walk home in the early morning sunshine, Praveen accompanied him. On the way, the pundit folded away his priestly manner and placed his arm around the young man's shoulder, for he was also an old family friend.

'Praveen,' he said, 'it's good to have lived to see your return. Are you pleased to be back?'

'I am Punditji.'

'You're looking very well, my son.'

'You have not aged, Pundit; I think your prayers are being answered.'

The pundit's eyes lit up. 'You haven't lost your mischief, I see. But you are a blessing to your parents, Praveen, and to all of us in the neighbourhood. I hope it remains so. In the past we've had too many young people go abroad who, when they return, have airs and manners that are not only superficial, but ugly. I've been asking myself for some time now what leads to this transformation. Maybe they lost self-esteem through the false and careless interpretation of their culture by others; or their ignorance of it. Maybe this meant that they had no sanctuary and they lost themselves to the passionate certainty of others. You've learnt much from the resources that science offered. We give thanks to England for acquiring this understanding and for imparting it to you. This morning, you were offered the spiritual resources of your forefathers. Our beliefs are seldom well understood, so listen carefully, my son, lest what has befallen others befalls you.

'Life in the ancient past was short, difficult and full of perils. Our present understanding of the world and the skills you have acquired were yet to come. But the sages, the gurus, they saw the need for us to have certain human qualities in order to live better lives. Attributes of wisdom, knowledge, compassion, strength of purpose; such qualities enable us to live humane lives.

'There is only one divine form, Praveen, but our imaginations wavered; we could not envisage the creator of all things in one entirety; instead, we gave different names to each of the creator's attributes; the artists gave those characteristics colour and diversity of form.

'If you remember this, you will understand the psyche and culture of your forefathers; you will not lose your esteem for them – nor cease to honour and respect your parents or yourself.'

Praveen was about to bow low before him, but the pundit held him. 'What you're about to honour, you carry within your self, my son,' he said softly. He felt his days were numbered so he'd seize the moment to offer truths he had gathered in his life. With hands clasped, heads gently bowed, they parted graciously at the gates of the pundit's home.

The solemnity of the puja was centuries removed from the celebratory cocktail party Savita and Haim held the following evening. Having a London-qualified doctor in a business family, whose humble beginnings were well known, added significantly to the family's status.

Ishani and Ravi Mita joined the gathering of flowing silk, polyester dresses, colourful and at times daring ties, light suits, colognes and perfumes; the aroma of rum, gin, wines and fruit juices wreathed the laughter and chatter. The gaiety amongst the younger played side by side with the energetic conversations of fathers and uncles, many of whom forgot to congratulate the young doctor or meet his parents, in their closed circles of drink, talk and partisan politics.

'Yu talking rubbish.'

'Some people keep dey head stuck in the sand.'

'Anybody who support a party intending to make them second-class citizens can't have their head in the sand, they have no head.'

Glasses were refilled each time the waiters came their way.

There were a few guarded approaches by young men to young women with 'Enjoying the party?' or 'I think I've seen you before, were you at Amita's wedding?'

But not all had forgotten the focus of the event.

'Have you spoken with him yet?'

'I have, he doesn't have horns you know.'

'Not yet. Horns take time to grow.'

'You wait 'til he gets into the politics of Port of Spain General.'

'Nice house, isn't it?'

'Yes. Who says money isn't everything, or can't buy happiness.'

Enterprising mothers, less subtle than Ishani, had brought their charmingly dressed daughters along, and were urging them to bathe in the disarming smiles of Praveen, who was overcome by the warmth and good will that greeted him.

Those who knew both his parents said that this modest young man, with a good crop of hair, who said little but listened with care, had the temperament of his father, rather than his mother who, in her youth, was known as a 'social butterfly'.

But if that had once been Savita's reputation, marriage into the sedate Mahesh family had gradually transformed her into an astute business woman. When her in-laws died, it was she who led her husband to understand that being in business meant not standing still with what your father left you, but always searching for opportunities. She had played no small part in the expansion of their business in importing building materials.

When Ishani was introduced to the smiling bachelor, her questions were not without purpose.

'Did you enjoy your stay in London, Praveen?'

'London is full of reminders of the past, though I never had time to get to know it intimately. But it is cosmopolitan, very much alive, thrusting forward, challenging old habits and perceptions. A microcosm of the world, really. I shall miss that rich variety. There's an attractive rhythm beating beneath the surface.'

'So you heard its pulse too?'

He nodded and smiled.

She was well pleased with his graciousness and with his response to her gentle probes about his intentions.

'Yes, I shall work in the public sector to begin with. I need to know the doctors, physicians and surgeons in the hospital. I want to see for myself the conditions there. This will help me and my patients later, when I decide to enter private practice. What I have been hearing about the hospital is not encouraging, but first-hand knowledge is always better than hearsay…'

'I understand.'

Combining long-term business interests with a genuine concern for everyone had long been her way. Being a good business woman was a way of life for Ishani, and so she made it her duty to meet as many families as she could at the party. Her empathy was with those mothers who saw it as their duty to be doing whatever they could to have their offspring happily married. It was a formidable task requiring energy, skill and a large measure of luck.

Here in this social gathering she saw the interplay of old and new thinking, an 'arrangement' that Ishani approved. Here, in the presence of parents, uncles and too numerous 'aunties', the young were moving about freely, unchaperoned, seeking out whoever they wished to flirt with or just get to know, as long as they kept within the bounds of good taste. In the meantime, mothers and fathers kept one eye focused on what the person before them was saying, while the other was looking about for possibilities.

She sought out Ravi and whispered, 'Observe the scene; we're in an age of the individual, but the old system of arrangement has not lost favour amongst educated, middle-class parents.'

He gave her a puzzled look. 'I'm not surprised, are you? Look Ishani, these families take seriously what is worth having. It's only common sense that they want to ensure their hard-earned resources are not passed on to the profligate, but to families similar to their own, whom they assume have brought up their children in much the way they've brought up theirs.'

As they drove from the Mahesh's home in Valsayn, Ravi recalled when the place was bush, full of mosquitoes because of its tendency to flood as water flowed from the surrounding Northern Range during the rainy season. It had since been drained and was now a residential area with large houses in substantial grounds.

As they left Valsayn behind, his thoughts went uninterrupted. Ishani was unusually quiet. Normally after a party she shared snippets of conversations, comments on behaviour, manners, attitudes, the catering and much else.

He broke the silence: 'I notice you did not think of taking the girls with you.'

'They are concentrating on Palli's and Lily's homework, the kitchen was in a state of confusion, so I asked them to tidy it all up. I told Jenny to keep an eye on them.'

He knew that wasn't the reason. It was because walking in with three nieces might appear too challenging to Praveen's mother.

'The method has changed,' Ishani said; 'that is what holds it.'

'What are you talking about?'

'I've been thinking that the continued good health of marriage arrangements has come about because parents are less authoritarian and more democratic in their style. The educated, financially independent young person won't abide any other method, Ravi.'

'All that is true, but arranged marriages – they're in the balance, in a precarious position, believe me, Ishani.'

'Why?'

'The individualism we see all around will scorch it.'

'You really think so?'

'I know so. Look at it closely, man. Individualism says, "Listen Mummy, Daddy, Aunty; this is my life, Okay? Get it? My life".'

Silence.

'There's an article in today's paper, Ishani. Apparently, scientists have found that people "in love" lose their faculties for reasoning, for being able to see flaws in their "true love".'

'That's not new. Our grandmothers knew that, Ravi.'

'But wait for it, it's all down to "feel-good" chemicals that rush in and take over the system.'

'So,' continued Ishani, 'the couple find themselves sailing in a hot air balloon, until the reality of life punctures it in mid-air!'

'That is not what the scientist said, Ishani.'

'They don't need to, Ravi. Wake up brother! Get it?'

23

THE REFLECTIONS OF SISTERS

At home, Ishani found a host of appealing ideas moving around in her head. As she stood looking out into the dark, trying to catch the cool mountain breeze, an earlier reflection came through a door she had kept ajar, though she had dismissed it several times as far too optimistic, even foolhardy. The competition was fierce. There were far too many attractive, educated young women from old, wealthy families well known to Savita and Haim. A London girl would probably not wish to live here, and Savita and Hemkish would fight tooth and nail to prevent their son living abroad, though he had enjoyed living in London. But was it possible? Probably not.

By force of habit, she entered the kitchen. Earlier it had resembled a market just before closing time; the girls were each preparing something for Lily's and Palli's school. Now in the silence of the night it felt sad – a kitchen without sounds and aromas, without the thrusting energy of movement. Her nieces had enveloped it with laughter, with lively youthfulness. How much she wished she, too, had been blessed with daughters. It was not to be; yet she cared for them as if they were her own.

As she cupped her hot cocoa, Ishani looked back over the summer. The girls had arrived early, while the school was still closed, and enjoyed being shop assistants. Now they were at the school. She had thought she'd have to make use of Ravi's persuasive diplomacy to encourage Amira to send the girls over for a longer period. But as luck would have it, the suggestion of her having the girls for much of the summer had come from Amira, in the middle of a letter bewailing the state of British society. Divorce rates were rising; excessive drinking and loutish behaviour were too frequently seen; and amongst the young, sex had become as commonplace as shaking hands. Something in the tone of the letter said all was not right. Was Amira hinting at something nearer home? Weren't things bright and beautiful in Apple Grove? Was this just an observation about how things were in Britain, a cry for help with the girls, or something else? Or was it just because this really was the last chance to attend Lily's and Palli's school? She'd decided on a direct response. She telephoned, but Amira was not there; Santosh had answered.

'Nice of you to enquire, Ishani, regarding the girls. We're battling on. Anjali's first year at university will be coming to an end very soon and Satisha will be joining her in seeking work experience this summer. Vidya is still too young, we think.'

'If it's work experience, Santosh, let them come to me. I can put them in the store. Vidya should not be left out; she can work in the hardware section, paints and varnishes, Satisha, in kitchen utensils and crockery while Anjali can stay in soft furnishings or if she prefers fashions, dress materials and haberdashery.'

'Sounds great. But you know it's Amira who looks after these things, Ishani.'

'All I'm saying, Santosh, is if they come to me, they'll be getting ideas about what goes into a successful business, the risks, the planning, marketing and customer relations – a whole new perspective on life for the girls.'

'It sounds good to me, Ishani, but I can't say yes until I've discussed it with Amira and the girls. I'm sorry she isn't here.'

'Where is she by the way?'

'She's either at the British Museum, the National Gallery or the Royal Academy.'

How come he doesn't know exactly? What is going on over there? 'Is she taking an art course or something?'

'Yes, at the Courtauld Institute of Art.'

'On what?'

'Let me see now – architecture, painting and painters, sculpture, photography, that sort of thing...'

'Mmmm... she never showed much interest here in anything outside her girls at school, and of course her family.'

'Amira seems to be enjoying these courses no end.'

'Well, *she's* really organising herself.' *Must have changed too; she used to be afraid of her own shadow.*

'She goes quite frequently to public lectures. She really looks forward to them and sometimes returns home quite exhilarated.'

'Exhilarated eh! I see. Mmmm...' *That looks like something else to me. Far too many classes. My god, just far too many. And he hasn't a clue where she is. Not a good sign at all. Is she avoiding him? Can there be? Maybe there is... Get a grip on yourself, Ishani!*

'It is good for her, good for both of us, when she's on a high with art.'

'On a high?'

'Oh, she returns full of a buzz, almost skips in through the door. It's less expensive than the hard stuff and the after-effects so far have not been injurious to health, though I can't say what the long-term effects are likely to be. Could she become addicted to the stuff, you think?'

I always thought you were a fool. 'When are you expecting her back?'

'She didn't say, but on the whole she tends to be home by six. I shall let her know what you said. It's a very good idea, Ishani, but don't say I said so, just in case you-know-who sees differently.'

'Oh, one more thing. Remind her that Lily's and Palli's school will be closing next year, so it has to be this summer for the girls. They can come early and be in the store before the classes begin and when the classes end they will return to the store.'

Well, it had come about the way she'd planned. Santosh! What a buffoon! How do they manage? Could her sister be attracted by something more than art out there? Trying to get away from him by keeping herself busy? Or could that clown act be a cover-up for something that doesn't bear thinking about. When you marry someone outside your own understanding of life, outside your class, things were more likely to go wrong... Class was more permanent than people liked to think. On the other hand, it could all be above board; at least he was not complaining. Some men want you around all the time, just to pour their tea...

Ishani had begun to perceive in all this Amira's growing independence. Because she lived in London, she imagined she was now the one who was better informed. Once, her opinion had been sought; that had changed. Her sister seemed to be developing opinions – even an arrogant English attitude. That country was changing her and she did not see it. My god! What would she be like as the years rolled by? Still, she supposed she had to accept that Amira was no longer just her little sister, that she should applaud her for getting where she was. But habits die hard and she could not resist writing to Amira with her concerns.

Later, Amira had replied over the nature of her exhilaration.

It was so thoughtful of you to write, Ishani. It's a blessing having a sister, someone to whom you can say things you can't say to anyone else. The truth is I found full-time domesticity was making me afraid of the world outside the house.

The courses you've referred to feed my interests, an aspect of myself that was being starved; they are refreshingly removed from daily household chores and family concerns. I have the opportunity to meet other people too – a younger lot in general; only a few are older. It helps me to regain that aspect of myself that had to prepare work and stand before a class. I was fast losing that, becoming afraid of everything; domesticity hemmed me in. I was losing the art of thinking outside my family and myself.

Now regarding that other matter Santosh suspects you were hinting at, I must say I was flattered that you think your sister has far more daring than she really has. I can see the advantages that go with wanting to look attractive, wanting others besides your husband to find you attractive, but I really don't have the inclination, energy or predisposition. Mind you the opportunities are everywhere.

Are there men anywhere who do not think about sex? If there are, they certainly don't live in London. Anyway, we were well conditioned by our culture and our parents, weren't we? I'm an old-fashioned girl who went against the advice of her parents and sister and married someone I wanted to spend the rest of my life with. You might notice I did not say love, because I no longer know what the word means. Constant usage has given it an elasticity that has stretched it away from my initial understanding.

I prefer to funnel my creative energies into the arts. It forces me to think deeply about what I'm looking at or listening to or reading. I get a real lift doing this. It takes me out of myself. Perhaps an affair does the same for others. I just think how time-consuming all that preparation would be, working at looking your best, being charming and attractive so as to be desired. I just couldn't, Ishani. I just couldn't play games with my affections or those of others. Trust is one of the most valuable things between two people. I hope I shall never give anyone cause to lose their trust in me.

On the other hand, I have of late been wondering about Santosh. I don't know how to express this, especially as it's just a feeling, something I have no words for. I feel foolish and embarrassed as I try to tell you. The truth is there's probably nothing in it, but though it's just an intuition, it's a strong one – there are other minutiae that I can't write about which reinforce these perceptions, but were I to mention them you'd be convinced either that I'm losing it or that I have every reason to be troubled.

When Santosh returned from Malaysia, the moment he arrived, there was something about his smile, his manner; I sensed something furtive about everything he did. Something happened over there. I just knew. I withdrew into a nest of my own making. It was easy, for he, too, seemed to need to have space between us. It has never been so before. Being head of his department, he has a lot of travelling to do. He has to take his secretary and other assistants on his travels – they are mainly women. Recently he has been staying late at work – there are good reasons – a heads of government meeting to prepare for. Intuitively, I just know that something has happened.

I feel better now that I've told you. I have no way of knowing the truth and you and I have never believed in the adage: 'If ignorance is bliss 'tis folly to be wise.' I wish I did. Can you think of an occasion when this is true? I cannot.

Affectionately,

Your sister, still growing, still in the infant class on how to live a good life. I feel so very alone. Ishani, without you I would feel more so. I cannot discuss this with Anjali; she needs, especially at her age, to believe that her father is all she wants him to be – supportive, protective, her daddy, the man in the house, ever upright, loving and wise.

Ishani wiped her eyes, but the tears kept coming. Life and its travails hammered us all. Her protective instinct towards her sister rose: if Santosh had behaved like a fool, she'd certainly let him know to his face that when he was a struggling nobody, his wife had stood by him and helped him all the way. She'd taken her savings to the marriage and lost her career. Not that her saying this would save the marriage. He would just listen and say some clownish thing.

Why were men so bloody foolish? What was in their heads? Or was the problem elsewhere? Where was his brain? The worrying thing was his good looks had become an encumbrance. Why could he not see that Amira was beautiful? He had to set an example to his girls and she would certainly find a way of saying this.

It was time to go to bed; she was tired, her defences down, making her susceptible to every wayward thought that floated by like pollen in the air. She would set Ravi on to do her initial soundings. She was pleased she had not needed him to persuade Amira to let the girls come to her for the summer; he would find it difficult to refuse her now.

24

RAVI AND SANTOSH

As soon as the maid had left the room after breakfast, Ishani said: 'I want your help, Ravi. Amira is worried. Santosh is working far too hard in the office; almost every night he arrives home close to midnight. Then, he's so tired, he's not fit for anything. I don't want to exaggerate, but she can't discuss the girls or the house or the happenings of the day with him – no matter how important or pressing the matter. She's alone, always alone.

'He's developed the infuriating habit of phoning to say he doesn't want dinner, that he'll be having a bite in the office. Well that's crazy. He should be informing her before he leaves for work, not at dinner time. It would be so helpful, Ravi, if you could talk to him, nicely of course, about all this overtime work. She's concerned about his health. He's tense, overwrought. The girls don't see much of him either. It is building up to something very uncomfortable. It's affecting the girls and poor Amira; she just doesn't know what to say to them.'

'Ishani, what's there to worry about? Tell Amira that sometimes I have difficult clients at my office who don't understand the law and being the good chartered accountant I am, I have to bring them round to the fact that I can't change the law to suit their greed. I quite often have to ask Amy to phone you to say I'll be running late.'

'That's true, but you must understand that Amira is beside herself with worry – and she's not really a worrying type. She didn't exactly mention a stroke, but driving yourself like that can lead to who knows what. She doesn't want to be a widow. It's really a cry for help so what will we do? Just ignore her pleas? We'd feel terrible if something did happen and we'd done nothing. Santosh needs waking up, man; how long can he go on like that without collapsing?'

'Do you think I should be doing this? It would be far better coming from you, Ishani – you're her sister. Aren't we interfering more than we should?'

'I don't want him to think that Amira has been complaining to me about him. I just happen to think that it's better to be safe than sorry. She's worried; there must be a reason for it.'

Silence.

'What you're *saying*, Ishani, sounds normal to me.'

'That's because I'm trying not to make too much of it, but I think Amira is not disclosing the whole truth of how unwell this pressure at work is making him.'

'Ishani, Santosh is head of a department; if an important international meeting is a week or so away, he has to get the work done. That's normal in any office.'

'Please, Ravi; just find out why he can't do the work at home.'

'Home? Oh! I see, you think something is going on in the office? Is that really what's behind your concern?'

'Oh! No! Oh not at all, Ravi. You've got the wrong end of the stick. I've just expressed it badly. It's the overwork that is worrying. If he works at home, his family is around him – in case anything happens, that's why I said what I said.'

'He works in the office, Ishani, because he needs his secretary. You know that… Now listen, I shall do it because it seems very important to you. I know if I don't, you'll keep going on and on about it and there'll be no peace in the house. Let me be frank; it's against my better judgement. You can't meddle too much in your sister's affairs; it is not like when you were children.'

My sister has no affairs; it's that chap from behind God's back who may be having a whale of a time. 'Ravi, you're the perfect friend. A friend in need, that's you, Ravi.'

'I hope so, Ishani. Somehow I just don't feel you're being straight with me. But I'll let that go. I don't understand what you're saying, but I have a hunch it's a sex thing.'

'What are you saying?'

'Simple. It's a sex related thing. Women think in a certain incomprehensible way and men don't. They make a much ado about what is just a moment's fancy.'

'Thank you, Ravi. You know Amira and Santosh are very fond of you. This would look so natural.'

'I won't argue with you, Ishani. You protest too much. I'll try not to make an ass of myself.'

Later in the day Ravi telephoned and Santosh answered.

'Who is it?'

'It's me, Ravi.'

'Oh sorry, Ravi, didn't get your voice at first. Good to hear you.'

'How are my nieces?'

'Preparing for school exams; when they're over, the house will

129

return to life. Now everything is on hold. I refer to machines and men.'

'What do you mean?'

'The only sound permitted, Ravi, is Amira's voice – even that tiptoes in a whisper: "Lower the volume of the radio, Santosh," or "Close the door, Santosh, the TV is disturbing the girls." I lower it. Then she returns: "Lower than that, Santosh please."'

'I get the picture. So, besides straining your ears, how are you managing?'

'Well, with these invitations to silence all around me, I've decided to meditate. The only thing about that… well I'll be honest with you, I fall asleep after the first five minutes or so.'

'You must be overworked and tired – or you're onto a good thing, man. Is this the long-awaited cure for insomnia?'

'I empty my mind, relax, then I become too empty, too relaxed. I don't understand how our forefathers made a religion of meditation, man. I recommend it for those with worries, or those who wish to enjoy a quiet sleep.'

'Listen, Santosh, meditation is part of our culture, man, but don't do too much of it. Balance, man. It's a Hindu thing according to Ishani. "Ravi, you must get the balance right. No more late nights at the office." That's Ishani for you. I hope you're not having too many late nights at the office. If you are, your equilibrium won't be in balance.'

'Well, I've had a couple of late nights and more to come, but Amira understands I have to get the work done. I'm not the only one working late. If you're head of a department, you have to set the tone. These Commonwealth heads of government meetings have a way of taking a turn this way or that way at the eleventh hour, and you have to be a bit of a political sage to work out where the twists and turns are likely to occur. You have to back your hunches, and so far, believe it or not, I've been ahead of the game.'

'Well that's something, man, and it's good that Amira is not worried about those late nights, because I couldn't do that; Ishani would put her foot down. She is on to that "balance" thing.'

'Amira appreciates that the work has to be done. It's tiring, but you just have to be philosophical about it or you'll burn yourself out. In the early days I did just that and I was a wreck or close to it. Today I'm a bit wiser.'

'Ishani will be pleased to hear that, unlike me, you're au fait with "balance" and practise it too.'

'Was she concerned about me?'

'I don't know; she hasn't said anything; though it might be in your interest that I don't mention your work-load.'

'Running a department, Ravi, is no easy matter. Take for example the women on the staff.'

'Yeeees.'

'Each one wants you to take them to the conference. It gives them prestige, so they can whisper at coffee time: "I've been asked to go to Malaya, or Kenya." It's a break from the office. They meet people, see places, but you can't take them all, so there's wrangling and jealousy. All have to take their turn, except my secretary; she always comes with me. She's just top class. No matter what I require, she gets it.'

'I see. Top class eh! I have one, she's pretty good too.'

'And that's not all; I have to ensure that those who come with me enjoy a few perks.'

'Perks, eh. That sounds good, man. Between us, man to man, what kind of perks you offer the ladies?'

'Time off to do a little shopping, a little sight-seeing. Occasionally, when things have gone well, offer a treat.'

'You have it all worked out.'

'So, Ravi, don't let Hinduism perplex you, man. As long as neither you nor Ishani is unhappy… It's only when one is unhappy and the other is unaware of it that you have a problem.'

'It would be nice if you sent the girls to us again this summer. We enjoy having them no end. Lily and Palli's school has closed, but they could visit the old ladies; they enjoy getting the news.'

'Leave it to me, Ravi. Tell Ishani she has nothing to worry about; the girls will be with her this summer. When the girls returned last time they were full of their experience in the shop. Amira and I could see the experience was good for them.'

Santosh returned to his favourite chair. He felt relaxed, thinking how much Amira and he benefited from close family ties, and wondering whether this camaraderie would be lost to the next generation. Then snippets of the conversation returned. Working late at nights: how did that come up? Yes it was about getting the balance right. But why the call? Ravi seldom phoned. When did he last do that? It was always Ishani. Why had she asked Ravi? Why had he not asked to speak to Amira? There was something troubling about this conversation, but what? Amira wasn't troubled about anything, was she? But when he'd returned from Malaysia, she'd asked in a particular way whether he'd enjoyed his stay there, and she'd remarked, 'You seem to have had a good time.' Then, when he'd agreed she'd said, 'Well, I hope you showed your appreciation with a gift.'

He'd said he had, because at the time, he'd assumed she was referring to the wife of a friend with whom he often stayed. But had he mentioned anything about not staying with them on this occasion? Why had he agreed that he'd bought a gift? He shifted in his seat.

Since his return, Amira had been unusually quiet, almost invisible, but then he had been coming home late. There'd be a note. *If you still feel like it, dinner is in the fridge* – but he couldn't expect to find her bubbling away or waiting up for him when she's had a long day... He bent his head, closed his eyes, his sigh long. Did one have to accept it as one of life's lost pleasures, the loss of joy in the natural instincts of the body? Was it pain or regret, or both that he felt?

An image came to him of a young, attractive Malaysian woman, and the alluring, overpowering attraction of youth seized him again: the heady tantalising scent; the throbbing warmth of a welcoming body. It had all seemed natural, right at the moment. Some things just couldn't be helped, they had a momentum of their own. Her eyes, her voice had been trained on him; her body opened itself willingly. Soon her impetuosity had become his too. He had been seized by feelings he had thought forgotten.

It was over now, but the remembrance pained and still excited him. Regrets? At first he could not answer this truthfully, or allow himself the evasion of self-deception. Time passed. The room was still. Finally he brought himself before his question. Regrets? The answer came in a form between a thought and a whisper: *If Amira were ever to know.* Some things were not worth it. This was his home – with the photographs of his daughters and his wife beaming at him from the walls. 'It's too foolish to think about. It's closed,' he whispered. The young woman was already forgotten. He wasn't a middle-aged fool... he hoped he was not.

The door-bell rang. It was Amira.

'I left the key in the door, completely forgot,' he said, smiling awkwardly, sheepishly, as if she could see the image of what was recently before him.

'It easily happens.'

He heard a gentle courtesy in her voice; a politeness as if she was speaking to a stranger. It was all in his mind, he told himself.

25

IN A RAINSTORM, A STRANGER KNOCKS
Trinidad, August 1984

It was the eerie stillness of the surrounding forest that alerted her. Hurriedly, Palli hauled herself up on aching knees to close the rattling wooden doors, windows and shutters. Then she remembered the deep trench on the path to her house; it would need its cover. She murmured to herself, 'When the dry season comes, I will get it mended. Age! Age! It takes over.'

Outside, she began to pull at the heavy teak cover, which her students called 'the Bridge'; it barely budged. Fortunately, Taru, a young farmer, was passing in his bullock cart; his attention was drawn down the unpaved track by the signboard for 'The School' which was swaying like a devil's hammock. Seeing Palli, he shouted, 'That's a man's job, Mai,' and with his heavy fork rolled the 'bridge' over and over until it was firmly in place.

As she hastened towards the cottage, the skies opened. She heard the torrential downpour beat heavily upon her roof; outside it carried away anything that was loose. The mist crept down the mountain's slopes, flooding the valleys as the sky disappeared. In the forest, drooping leaves became fast-running channels, little waterfalls tumbling down. Water gushed along the trace as if a dam had broken. A crooked light rent the sky; again and again thunder rolled.

Palli rocked in the old cane chair in the cosy living space which students called 'The Cottage'. It had been a converted part of the rambling school building. Comfort came from a chulha built waist high on a broad rectangular stand; its hot embers kept a pot of kheer warm and the room too. Though she preferred the convenience of her gas stove, there were times when only the chulha would do. Though Malcolm, Lily's brother, had tried his best to reduce some of the dampness and the cold draughts of the old house, its frame creaked and trembled as it was battered by the winds roaring from the forest. It seemed sleeping spirits had been rudely awakened and would not be comforted.

Dusk gave way to night. Between sleep and wakefulness the cane chair rocked.

Along the main paved highway, clumps of tall bamboo danced like witches; tree trunks snapped; cars rolled over and trucks lay on their sides. The mist thickened as it became colder, until visibility was reduced to a few paces. Two barely visible lights left the main road and crept onto the trace, stopping before the street lamp. The driver got out and ran in the direction of the school. All around was tall grass and wild canes. No other dwelling was in sight. Cold and dripping wet, the light of his torch showed him the path to the cottage; he crossed over 'the bridge', and splashed through the shallow pools in the school yard.

Palli heard the knocking, but thought it was part of the primeval forces outside. Yet, this sound had a pattern, was not random. When a voice accompanied it, she stopped the rocker, and listened again. Moments passed; again a call. She peeped through the shutters and saw a shadowy figure in the dark. She heard more clearly, 'Good night, good night, may I shelter here?'

'Coming, coming,' she called.

Soon a warm dressing gown, smelling distinctly of mothballs, was tightly wrapped around an otherwise naked Praveen Mahesh. He sat near the soft warmth from the chulha, a pot, now empty of its kheer, warming his thighs as his garments were dried.

But that was several months ago.

Today sunshine was changing the colour of leaves, creating long shadows near walls and houses. Yet Palli's memory of that cold misty night was kept alive, for whenever Dr Mahesh passed that way, he would drop in to see 'Ajee Palli' with a bunch of coconuts, fresh fish, sea or land crabs or whatever the country folks sold at the roadside. She gathered, in the quiet effortless way of women of her generation, that he was unmarried and working at a private clinic in St Joseph. This got her thinking. *Nice boy, good family, I know them well; he should be married by now, maybe…* It came to her when she was rolling out a paratha rotie – *Why not to one of our girls?* – but then she stopped herself from running with this idea. Who? Would her memory of them and what they now were tally? Yet the faces of a number of girls came to her and she had to remind herself that this was another time – progressive times, people called it. Her students would choose for themselves; in an unexplained way she felt quietly relieved.

Meantime Ishani and her three nieces were on their way to say their goodbyes and thank-yous. They were disappointed that Lily was not there – Palli explained that she was with her family in Port of Spain. The girls had attended the summer course the previous year and were saddened to learn that the school had become too heavy a commitment and was now closed. Vidya recited what she had composed: 'We consider ourselves most fortunate to have attended this establishment. My friends will be green with envy. We thank you warmly.' Anjali kissed Palli and said softly, 'We thank you. You have been good to us. We shall remember you as long as our memory holds. Thank you Palli-ji.' She clasped her hand and bowed. Satisha cleared her throat and stood erect: 'This idea of yours and Miss Lily's was welcomed and grew in strength because it was what the Penal district needed. All good business is based on the principle of demand, as my father would say. It was also a humane thing to do. This we shall not forget. We thank you most sincerely for allowing us to join the class. We shall try our utmost to live by its rules.' She almost bowed, but remembered in the nick of time she was not on a rostrum. Nevertheless, Satisha looked around, hoping that her sisters had appreciated the performance.

Ishani hugged Palli warmly. 'Thank you for making space for them. I know we were privileged. I told them their mother was amongst your first pupils and now they are amongst your last. You have accomplished what you did set out to do. Not many can say that. Remember *that* if you ever feel low, because you'll miss the school, but you'll soon settle into your new life. You're looking well. Are you keeping well?'

'How can Lily and I forget how you advised us when we did not know where to turn, and helped to equip our kitchen? Such foresight on your part over what we were trying to do. Those white cotton caps and aprons you provided helped our pupils to feel professional. Cooking had no status then.'

'Those were small things. Yours was the grand idea and the fulfilment of it was a rare and beautiful accomplishment.'

'Thank you, Ishani, but you always play down your own contribution.'

Palli walked down the path with them. Hugs of farewell were shared; then Vidya said: 'We will visit you whenever we return. You must let us know what you would like us to bring you from London.'

Palli smiled. 'If you bring yourselves that will be more than three vessels of gold. May the good spirits of our school embrace you all.' She lifted her hand in a gesture of blessing. They waved and the car sped away. Silence held them all for some time because they sensed that something important had come to an end. Vidya wished there was a way of stopping time; it was something scientists should work on.

But soon Satisha and Vidya were looking forward to the next day and the next, and the planning of a picnic on the flanks of the Northern Range, not too removed from the St Benedict's Monastery.

26

PICNIC ON THE HILLS
Early September 1984

Vidya and I, Satisha Vidhur, were excited. Anjali was with us, but she was more of a chaperone than an eager participant in this Sunday outing which was Vidya's and my idea; we'd pressed our needs on Aunty Ishani. It was our last day with her and she'd ensured that our picnic would be memorable.

You only had to breathe in slowly, close to the basket, to know it was full of goodies. Of what category, you might venture to ask. I'd say without hesitation: the sublime. My aunt Ishani is simply unable to bring forth anything save the very best.

Puffing and weary, for the ascent was no Sunday stroll, we headed for our 'secret spot', a grassy patch on the forested terrace. Its overhanging branches provided shade. We'd been there before. It offered a view of the wide valley and plains below. We became giants, for the houses, roads and the vehicles on the Eastern Main Road belonged in Lilliput.

There was the mountain range behind us, the plains below and all around us birds, ants, monkeys, buzzing flies, silent butterflies. We felt carefree, hemmed in only by the bluest blue of the sky. We became heady with delight, singing songs our mummy and Aunt Ishani had taught us, as loudly as we could, humming what memory had misplaced. We ran about like frisky squirrels, playing hide and seek, jumping to catch branches that were outside our reach, rolling on the earth, testing our voices to hear if the hills would reverberate them. For a while we amused ourselves with this bouncing game.

When we approached the monastery, we chanted plaintive laments, as if we were monks who'd been thrown out by our superiors, begging to be allowed to return.

Vidya collected leaves and bark for their colour and shape, while I examined their texture and rated their scent. Oh, we loved the earth from which we came. Actually, Daddy says we've come from stardust. This has always made me feel rather special; it means in dark times we'll have the ability to shine forth, bringing light, wherever we are. We both tripped and tumbled several times as we raced over clumps of spreading roots. I wondered whether trees could feel and think and, if they did, how would I discover it. We greeted church-goers with a low bow, a wave of the hand and a broad smile.

Grow-ups are so devoid of imagination, so rigid, so fixed in their ways. They walked briskly past us with eyes straight ahead. I hope I never grow up… well only in a special sort of way.

All this while, Anjali was fretting and fuming like a mother hen, saying, 'Calm yourselves, behave for heaven's sake.' Tired of us, she sat quiet as a church mouse reading her book under a tree. Occasion-ally a buzzing bee, a jumping toad, or our little entertainments drew her attention away from her book; then her near-perfect face would look ruffled. My friends tell me she is ravishingly beautiful. I think she's alright. My friends are at an age when they're apt to exaggerate. I have a maturity beyond my years, of this I'm quite sure. Daddy said this to me on my last birthday.

Vidya and I call Anjali 'Madam Proper'. As she sat there reading, anyone who did not know her could think that she had climbed out of one of the frames of the Indian paintings in Aunt Ishani's sitting room. Uncle Ravi told us that they belonged to the Hindu revival period of the eighteenth to nineteenth century. Well, maybe that is where Anjali belongs.

I saw a grey monkey; he looked at me with inquisitive eyes. I thought there was much good sense in his questioning face. I wondered how old he was, and tried to communicate by telepathy, explaining that we were first cousins and that I felt a close affinity with him. But I could tell I was making no impression, so I decided to change my approach.

'First Cousin,' I shouted over and over again. Even then I don't think he picked up the gist of what I was saying, or preferred not to show it. There was another possibility. Perhaps he preferred not to think he was connected to Vidya and I. While I was pondering such profundities, he sprang effortlessly to another branch and I lost him.

Then Vidya took her coloured pens and decided to write her name on the smooth trunk of a guava tree. She approached it and said, 'Please may I write my name on your trunk?' This was not clever, for how would she know that permission was granted? I went round to the other side of the trunk, caressed the spot I intended to write on, then wrote, 'Hark ye passers-by, there is far more near than ye can spy.'

By now we were really hungry, so weren't we relieved when Anjali looked at her watch, clapped her hands and said, 'Clean hands for Aunt Ishani's delicious offerings.' Vidya washed her hands too eagerly to be effective. I took my time to show her how it should be done. But would she learn? Vidya, you must understand, just cannot say no to food. She only has to have a whiff of it and she becomes impatient. We all have our weaknesses, Mummy says, yet I do not see mine. Maybe I have yet to acquire one, but all in good time. I'm not in a hurry to conform.

We had warm dhal puris bulging with savoury red salmon, tomatoes, thyme and onions, a slice of yummy crumbly fruit cake, and a firm St Julian mango with an overpowering aroma and sweetness that filled the basket. A bottle of water for drinking, and another for washing hands and cooling faces.

As soon as our shadows began to grow tall, Anjali said, 'Time to pack things away, time to leave.' We were hot and sticky, waiting for the cool mountain breezes to descend. The sinking sun was fierce upon us and so was Madam Proper.

Anjali walked ahead of the younger girls. Her fury propelled her steps. Her thighs, knees, feet moved with purpose. She'd had enough. She had outgrown her sisters. Never again would she go on a holiday with them. Once Daddy had said that the three of them formed a bouquet of fragrance, like flowers in an ancient Indian vase. Maybe a long time ago. Now they'd become individuals with tastes, dispositions and thoughts too far removed from each other. She thought she knew how that had come about. Satisha and Vidya had not been brought up under the strict regime that had surrounded her. Before she'd gone to university, she'd been penned in. The thought of this discrepancy expanded her anger. Over the years her parents had become soft, pliant, so that her sisters did exactly as they pleased. She'd asked them to behave, but could have been speaking to the wind. They would not leave the baby monkeys in peace; they'd kept pelting them with pebbles and sticks. They'd put out their tongues, scratched their heads, necks and arms, saying 'We are your first cousins.' Too true. Their silliness had crossed the boundary to extreme tomfoolery. When they'd heard the Gregorian chants coming from the monastery, they'd started singing their own chants. So disrespectful. They'd lifted their skirts, using them as fans, giggling like idiots. It was not surprising that churchgoers had hurried past.

They'd shown no respect for anything. They couldn't be bothered that they'd been asked to behave well, at least in public. She thought of all the things she'd helped them with: Maths, Latin, literature questions. Who'd helped her? She'd had to sit down and work it all out herself.

Who cared about her welfare? Her parents had wound her up tightly in the folds of their culture and expected her to walk the stipulated walk. She'd been born at the wrong moment, lived her formative years when the people around her were apprehensive of the unfamiliar, of changing their ideas. The two behind her didn't know how fortunate they were.

Vidya and Satisha had been allowed to do things they'd never permitted her – like staying over with friends who had brothers, older brothers to boot, and partying. Partying! Nobody asked Satisha and Vidya who would be there. But with her it was, 'Where is it being held? Will there be any parents? Who will be bringing you back… No! No! We can't have that, it wouldn't be right. We shall come for you, Anjali.' On occasion, she'd felt tempted to lie, but was too uncomfortable to do it; afraid that lies would diminish her – or at least afraid of being caught in them. She could not have faced the disappointment in the eyes of her parents. But would her sisters feel the same? Nothing seemed to matter any more. Nothing! Having sex with a mere acquaintance was like trying out a new drink in a pub! At her hall of residence, she'd been amongst the very few who had no boyfriend. Why? Her parents would not have approved. She'd even written a poem:

The Hall and I were shy of lies
And like the sky our thoughts were high
'Twas philosophers of old whose hold
I grasped, too careful to be bold;
My youthful years bear little,
Save striving in a mould.

Anon am I.

She'd told her mother she'd become a whispering willow on the banks of the stream of life, looking at her reflection. She was not to worry, Mummy had said; she was in good company; it was what Rembrandt had done as he'd worked on his self-portraits. 'Contemplation is what thoughtful people do all the time.' Mummy had a way of trying to find something of value in everything, even when you'd tried to tell her something was not working. Maybe she'd been too oblique, not wanting to hurt her mother's feelings. Mummy had given them her best years. She remembered that when they were in Trinidad, Mummy walked with a hop and a skip. She enjoyed her work. In London, the family was her main concern. She was kind to all the neighbours, taking them Indian savouries and home-made sweets. She wanted to belong.

She wanted to be more but was hemmed in by her understanding of her role. Anjali thought she could never knowingly hurt her.

She thought of her year away, of her friends Thyda from Thailand and Ife from Nigeria. No one had asked them out – they'd done nothing to encourage it either. University was not a place to make an ass of yourself, and neither of them could make light of sex, which they saw as too intimate an experience to treat in a casual, offhand manner. Their attitude would not have been lost upon aspiring males.

Thyda and Ife were content to be themselves. They did not wish to be any other. They were scholars, had travelled far to acquire certain skills, not to change themselves. When that was accomplished they would return home.

Once, in order to join in the chatter of those at her table in the hall of residence, Anjali had been on the verge of making up a boyfriend, but decided he would have been too good to be true, or too much of a rascal, and decided life was stressful enough without such imaginative leaps.

Two consecutive years of long dry seasons had cracked the earth and the mountain paths were breaking up in places. Deep in thought, Anjali continued to walk ahead of Satisha and Vidya. She wanted time to herself, to sit on one of the lower terraces where she could unwind, calm herself and await her aunt.

From above, the two sisters trailing behind had a good view of the terrace below; it was Vidya who drew Satisha's attention to a young man strolling there, engaged with his own thoughts. Praveen Mahesh had developed the habit of catching the mountain breeze which descended upon these hills in the evening.

The idea was Vidya's. It was communicated to Satisha with the forward movement of her open palms. It was Satisha's gleeful smile which said that the outcome would be a most satisfying way of striking back at such unwarranted authority. Vidya expressed the wish to be the sole performer of this mischief, but Satisha insisted on playing a part. So together they ran, each trying to be the first to reach the target – two balls of fiery intent aimed at a fast-moving target. On and on they raced.

Anjali caught the full impact of their hands. She tried her best to keep upright, but her feet were slipping, sliding, rushing headlong down. At that very moment the young man, seeing he was in her path, opened his arms to break her fall, to steady her, but the combined force of wilful palms and gravity was too much for him. He was hurled backwards. Instinctively she held on to him.

For a while he was disoriented, numbed. As he recovered his composure, he removed the young woman's hair which was covering his face. She lay upon him motionless, her breathing regular. As he tried to lift himself, Anjali opened her eyes and the indelicacy of her situation came to her. She scrambled to her feet, pressing upon him to lift herself. 'My god!' she whispered, 'how did that happen?'

Praveen got up and said, 'I don't yet reside with the gods, but I'll work on it.'

'I don't know what you're thinking, surely you must see…'

'I heard what you whispered; I was trying my best to respond.'

'This is crazy.'

'I do have my lapses; this might just be one of them.'

'My god! Whatever…'

Anjali was confused, embarrassed, hurt that her sisters could have done this, but Praveen was enjoying himself. 'Oh I see there are two others – guards hurrying to interrogate me.'

'It's not Anjali's fault, it was an accident,' proclaimed Vidya.

'You're not hurt are you?' Satisha asked, in the voice of her headmistress. She studied the young man with quizzical, narrowing eyes.

'I was pinned down, but hurt was not my dominant feeling.'

'What was it then? Can you explain?'

'Vidya! Stop it! You and Satisha have done enough. You can't be trusted to behave.'

'We're sorry, Anjali.'

'You should think first. Mindless! Mindless!'

'Yes, Vidya and I are very sorry. We're relieved, Anjali, that you and this person are not hurt.' Turning to Praveen, she said: 'May I introduce myself? I am Satisha Vidhur, I live in London. This is my sister Vidya, and you have met our sister Anjali in what I suppose is an unconventional manner. It wasn't Anjali's style at all, nor Vidya's; but it could be mine, depending upon… Well, I'd have to give the matter consideration before deciding when and where.'

'I'm disappointed that at least two of you prefer conventional ways of meeting. I'm Dr Praveen Mahesh and I'm very happy to meet you. If you or your sisters need a doctor while you're here, I'd be delighted to meet you again. It might be sudden, but I do really like you all.'

'But doctor, is it advisable to like people you don't know?' Satisha asked.

'I agree with Satisha,' Vidya said. 'Nevertheless we're well pleased that we are liked. I and Satisha, oh, I mean Satisha and I… are pleased to make your acquaintance, Dr Praveen Mahesh. We cannot ask Anjali because she's very upset. But she may like you too, perhaps by tomorrow? You understand we cannot ask her now. The timing would not be right. Our daddy believes in good timing when he speaks to Mummy.'

'Wise man.'

'Oh! Here is our Aunt Ishani. Please excuse us.' The two girls ran to meet her.

Before Anjali could follow them, Praveen said, 'I'm sorry I was in such a light-hearted mood. I should have asked you if you were hurt. What of your neck, is it strained? Can you move it this way and that?' He demonstrated.

'I don't think I've sprained it. I'm sorry, too, for being so cross. I should thank you. You cushioned my fall. My sisters are uncontrollable. My parents have become soft with them, you know. They were not so with me.'

'Your parents are moving with the times. It is to their credit.'

A beaming Aunt Ishani approached. 'Satisha and Vidya have just related the accident. I'm so pleased, Praveen, that you were here to save Anjali. What luck! Fate, you know. We mortals are helpless against it.' She noted that Anjali's dishevelled appearance, the defiance in her eyes, the blush on her skin, the swaying freedom of her hair, gave her a wild, attractive look. Her first impulse was to tidy it, but she stayed her hand.

'It was an accident,' insisted Anjali. 'I'm sure Dr Mahesh has the good sense to see it so.'

'Very well. I'm sorry my nieces are leaving for London tomorrow, Praveen, but the next time they are here, we will invite you over for lunch or dinner, whichever you prefer.'

'Thank you.' He looked at Anjali and offered her such warmth in his smile that she smiled too, albeit with restraint, yet blushing hours after as she remembered it.

27

THE OWL AND THE PANTHER
November 1986

Anjali was writing her dissertation on 'The Citrus Fruit Industry in Trinidad'. At Kings, in North London, a well-researched paper contributed significantly to improving the grade of a degree, so she laboured hard, researching the subject throughout the summer in Trinidad and at London's Institute of Tropical Agriculture.

Students were assigned a tutor to guide them; Anjali's was Dr Marshall. Keen to show how interested she was in her subject, she sent him her plan and a summary of each chapter early. She visited his office three times to receive feedback, but he was never there. She became anxious when friends told her that they were getting good advice from their tutors. Then, one afternoon, she spotted Dr Marshall crossing the courtyard and hurried over to ask whether he approved of her synopsis. It was clear he hadn't read it. He asked why she'd chosen the topic, and whether she was having difficulty getting hold of relevant information – and were her parents from India?

She was devastated. Was her approach correctly focused? Would it have the right balance? These misgivings grew and began to seep into her other studies. Since it was her final year, she knew she had to take a grip on herself, so she went home to discuss the problem.

Satisha and Vidya listened to Anjali's plight, and when Santosh remarked with a resigned weariness that there was not much she could do, Vidya charged in vehemently.

'That can't be true. It means we're not thinking, Daddy. You've often said there's a way out of difficulties if you think hard.'

'Now look here, all of you,' Santosh said. 'It helps if you face the reality of the situation. The staff room is a gentleman's club; your sister's an outsider. The university would close ranks. Dr Marshall is one of their own; Anjali would be seen as a foreigner, someone who doesn't understand what is appropriate behaviour and what is not.'

'That isn't true, Daddy,' Vidya exclaimed.

'Let me finish please. Anjali could also be perceived as a young student with illusions about her own importance.'

'Daddy, please stop that.'

'I expect to be heard; everyone will have their turn… Now where was I? Yes, some may think she's expecting far too much from her tutor, that coming from another culture she is expecting to be spoon fed.'

'Daddy,' said Satisha, 'spoon feeding? How can you think like that when this Marshall hasn't even looked at her plan of work?'

'If that is how universities think,' said Vidya, 'I shall give them a wide berth.'

'Me too. Vidya and I can do without that kind of thinking.'

Nothing more was said for quite a while.

'You're missing the underlying reason for this,' said Santosh.

'No we're not. You said, Daddy, it's because we are foreigners, didn't you?'

'Lewis Carroll said it all, Vidya.'

'Did he, Daddy? How strange! Whatever next!'

'Daddy is thinking,' Anjali said, 'of the Owl and the Panther.'

'Bull's-eye, Anjali. When an owl and a panther sit down to a banquet, the outcome has been vividly described. The observant Lewis Carroll made this abundantly clear.'

'We know, Daddy,' sulked Vidya.

'Were the panther and the owl to participate in a negotiation, anywhere, at anytime, the outcome would be the same.'

'So are we owls then, Daddy? How can I become a panther? I would like to have a substantial growl,' declared Vidya. 'I intend to work at it, and have sharp menacing claws.'

Satisha thought, *Poor Anjali, she's an owl all right; look how she behaved at our picnic on the hills – like an owl she sat on a branch and looked askance at us. I have every intention of being a panther when I need to be; otherwise I shall be a much more flamboyant bird, flapping my wings to draw attention when it suits me… If it is safe of course. If not I shall keep to the highest branches.*

'Look Santosh, is this helping?' Amira asked. 'Can we return to how best to help Anjali with her dissertation?'

'Your mother is right as usual. Yes, Vidya, there is a way out of this difficulty. I'm happy to look at your work, Anjali, and if you feel the need to discuss certain aspects of the citrus fruit industry in greater detail, I can give you contacts to those who can help you. Don't be too self-critical, you have a good sense of what is required from what I have seen. Tutors are often overrated, believe me.'

'Ishani could help her make those contacts in Trinidad, Santosh. Speak to your aunt about what you need to know, Anjali.'

'Thank you, Mummy and Daddy. I feel better already.' Anjali hugged them and left the room. Her sisters followed.

'Dr Marshall doesn't know anything about the subject; he's just trying to prevent you from finding this out, Anjali,' Vidya said.

'It could be to your advantage,' added Satisha, 'not to have him coming up with what he thinks you should also explore, when you know more about your project than he does.'

'What I can't understand,' Vidya said, with a mischievous smile, 'is why he's not always asking you to come to see him to talk about your work? Don't underestimate your quiet charm, Anjali. Satisha and I don't; I'd be surprised if we were the only ones.'

'With such reassurance from my family, I intend to make the most of it.'

'Commendable. That's the Vidhur spirit, girl,' Satisha said.

Much later, when the girls were asleep, Amira said to Santosh, 'I want our girls to believe that this world and its people are just that bit better than they are in reality.'

'As a broad philosophy that may be good for their souls, Amira, but there's danger in bringing them up ignorant of how power behaves behind locked doors. They must be alerted to reality.'

'They are still not much more than children, Santosh.'

'They are fully grown, Amira. Knowing how the world works will keep them on their guard.'

'Look at their energy, Santosh, look at how they apply themselves to their work, their piano and dance lessons and hockey and swimming. Today, they're trying to expand themselves in small things; tomorrow they'll be better prepared for larger things. Satisha and Vidya are giving up some of their Saturdays to help children from the local school to learn to read. They did that on their own. We've tried to encourage their creativity from kindergarten days. Why weigh them down with "the ruthless thrusts of untrammelled power" as you're so fond of saying. We need to protect them from such horrors for a while longer.'

'Which ones precisely?'

'Why do you have to keep telling them about dreadful historical things, Santosh, like the British pushing opium on the Chinese, or the Agent Orange the Americans dropped on the Vietnamese, or Hiroshima and Nagasaki. You've mentioned the Amritsar massacre so many times. There's no end to man's inhumanity, Santosh.'

A silence entered and stayed so long that it began to have its own sound.

'I know you want the girls to be aware of the dark closed cupboards, as well as the fine things in this country, because you believe ugliness is part of human nature, and resides with unaccountable power.'

'And you, Amira, are ensuring that they will be bathed in the best light of this country. With your accommodating, generous ways, you've gathered good things and good people around you.'

Amira's eyes became tearful and she got up to leave the room, but Santosh rose to hold her and hugged her warmly. 'I don't say the things that are really important to me often enough, Amira. We were never taught how to express our feelings. There is so much to learn.'

When he released her he said, 'There is something I need to say to you now.'

Sensing something distressing was close, she said, 'Keep it for tomorrow; I have a lot to do right now.'

'No, Amira. It's very important to me that I speak now. I've kept it away from you for too long. I keep postponing it; the time never seems right. Now is not right, but I need to speak. It is gnawing my insides, wearing away who I think I am.'

His manner, his tone of voice was as gentle as a soft blanket.

'Very well.' She sat down.

'A month ago, when I was in Malaysia… Well, I behaved foolishly there; I had to ensure I wasn't infected in any way; I had two tests in two different centres, to be doubly sure that I was all clear. The second result has just come in and I'm greatly relieved it was as the first. For this reason, I've been keeping my distance. I had to protect you. I could see you suspected something. Your manner was distant, too, but not before the girls. It only showed when we were alone. You've always put them and me before yourself. You've been containing your suspicions, while no doubt smouldering inside. I… I'm hoping, given time, I'll be able to regain your trust. Please Amira, don't give it an importance it does not have; it was an absurd, stupid thing to do. A lapse of judgement. You'll need time. It will take time. I'll always be here always.' He waited to hear her reaction but for a time nothing came.

'Anything else?' she eventually asked, in a calm voice, though a part of her was collapsing.

'No.'

'I must go now.' She squeezed herself together as if struck by a cold blast. She did not look at him as she left the sitting room. He sat still. Mixed feelings of sorrow, guilt and relief surged. Disclosure was over for him; now he must wait for the healing of her feelings. How long would that take?

Her background, her idealism, her limited experience of life as a pupil, a student, a teacher – from school back to school: that, combined with her complete trust in her parents, her sister, was why she had never acquired a hard shell. How would she cope with what he had hurled at her? He realised he did not know his wife sufficiently well to know how she would cope. Would it ever be erased from her memory? He knew the answer to that, but given time, he hoped, it would become a faint trace in the whole scheme of their lives together.

How wide and deep was the separation they'd been living for the past month? All those quiet evenings when she'd returned from her art classes with nothing to say. Or her meetings with Kamla Devi she'd stopped telling him about, their afternoon teas at Fortnum and Mason. Could she have told Kamla Devi about her suspicions? It was her simple, warm way of communicating that had just dissipated before him. Was their companionship so fragile a thing? Had he smashed it for good? He went to his study, closing the door behind him.

Amira felt exhausted. When Anjali had phoned to say she was coming over for supper and would stay the night, she'd left the garden where she'd been weeding, moulding, fertilising, to prepare a delicious evening meal. Now this. She thought how if her parents had been alive she would have returned to the family home, to her own room, to restore herself with a long sleep, a change of scenery, permit time to pass her by. To have had her mother's embrace and her delicious food; a walk on Manzanilla beach just before dawn.

There'd been a time when Santosh and she couldn't have enough of each other, when just seeing him had lifted her spirits. Their skins glowed, their eyes laughed, everything was beautiful, enchanting. Love had lifted them high above the clouds, folded them in each other's embrace for the rest of time. What had happened? Why was it no longer so?

She had lost her status as a teacher, respected and liked by staff, students and parents. She had exchanged that to struggle with domesticity in a new place within a new culture. Motherhood and wifely duties had dominated her thinking. Her creative energies, no doubt depleted, had been channelled into her daily striving with cooking, cleaning, gardening, ironing, participating in school fairs, fighting with teachers for her girls.

But why was she even considering where she had been wanting? Was she responsible for this? Was this a universal female way of thinking? What would Margaret Summers have done in these circumstances? The owl and the panther indeed! What options did she have? If she were on her own, she could go away and knit up her unravelling self. At last he'd been honest with her and he had tried to protect her. Well, that was the least he could do. But he should have told her earlier.

What to do now? She had to be sensible for the sake of her daughters and not be hasty... but if he'd been infected... what would've been the consequences? Would she have got up and left? No! she would have remained and done her best to protect him from the censure of the girls. They needed their parents to be reliable, trustworthy. She must try to heal herself. Would she tell Ishani? She imagined her sister crying out in pain like a trapped animal. Then she would maul him savagely. She would have to shield Ishani from that pain and hurt and he from her anger – say he was going through a bad patch in the office and that her suspicions were wrong. Ishani probably wouldn't believe her; but at least it would rest there.

And yet she felt penned in by this reasonable, sensible way. It was tame, the way of the owl. It was an acceptance of what was. Didn't she have a right to defiance, anger, fury at his conduct? He'd behaved foolishly, no, he'd betrayed her, and there was no cost to him, for she was expected to act wisely. There was something within her that rebelled furiously at this powerlessness.

Yet... was the owl's behaviour unwise when sharing a banquet with a panther? The owl survived. Perhaps she saw the full consequences of each act, and inaction was indeed a wise decision in the presence of the panther.

She had to speak to someone. She would phone Kamla Devi. She was living at the close of the twentieth century and still following her mother's way. But how could you stop the past walking beside you?

28

SAID THE SPIDER TO THE FLY

Anjali accepted the advice of her parents, and though there was still nothing from her tutor, she buckled down to complete a first draft, which she handed to Dr Marshall for his comments.

A month went by and still no response; she decided to make one final approach. If he hadn't read it, she'd just go full speed ahead on her own. But she did nothing until the day she got up from her desk, saying, 'Today has to be the day.' Even then, when she stood before his door, she hesitated, moved away, before she returned to knock firmly.

'Come in.'

'Good morning, Dr Marshall. I wonder if you've been able to look at what I've sent you?'

He looked completely at a loss.

'I'm Anjali Vidhur. The citrus fruit industry in Trinidad. Have you been able to look at it? It's been some time since I handed it in. I'm a bit nervous about it.' She smiled. 'I need to know what you think. Is it possible to discuss the work before Christmas?'

He began searching on a shelf behind him. She felt angry with herself for being so stupid as to ask him again.

'Ah ha! There, there it is… couldn't have lost it, safely ensconced there, you see.' He flicked through the pages. 'Ah yes, it's all coming back now. Yes, yes, I did have a look at it, and will do so again. Not bad, not bad at all. Very promising, I'd say. Good plan. Well thought through.'

She smiled at his complete disarray.

'Now is that all? No? I guessed as much or else you wouldn't be standing there so patiently… What else are you waiting to hear?'

But before she could reply, he said, 'Ah yes, yes, before the Christmas break.' He opened a small battered diary. 'That's not easy.' He flipped a page backwards and forwards. 'Look, I'll call for you this evening at your hall. Which one is it?'

'Magdalena Hall.'

'I shall be at Magdalena Hall round about 8 p.m. and we'll discuss the project at my home. It is the only time I have available before we break off for the Christmas holidays.'

Anjali could not believe her luck; it had been worth a try after all. Her delight was expressed in a warm smile. At first this response seemed to evoke in him a sense of relief, but when he looked at her, she sensed some discomfort, signalled by a trembling in his hands. 'I shall do my utmost to be on time,' he said.

It just shows, Anjali thought, her stride purposeful, one must not write off people. He'd always appeared inscrutable, while all this while he was really trying not to show the world his Dr Jekyll side. Then another thought came from nowhere and touched her. Its hands were cold: *Could it be his Mr Hyde that he's keeping at bay?* What nonsense came into her head.

She was getting the coins together to make a call to her parents with the good news when another thought persuaded her to postpone it. Wouldn't it be far better to wait and then tell them how it had gone? Wouldn't that be more comforting to them?

When she opened her door, she saw a letter lying there and recognised her father's clear, neat hand. She would read it in comfort on her return.

For the rest of the day, Anjali sat at her desk, going over her draft, looking closely at the sections she felt needed a second opinion, or at least confirmation that she was heading in the right direction. There was other work that needed attention, so she was keen to have the dissertation as near completion as possible.

Dr Marshall was punctual. Tall and lean, he looked to Anjali like a dried rod in rough tweeds. Maybe the material of his suit varied with the weather, yet he managed to look the same all year round, irrespective of the seasons. His clothes appeared as irremovable as scales on a fish. The jacket was reinforced at the elbows with brown leather patches. His car smelt musty, like a dark loft, long closed. A folded rug, books and magazines were hastily picked up from the front seat and thrown over to the back as if they had been told repeatedly to keep out of sight.

Anjali had dressed in a new, grey, pure wool skirt, a soft pink merino cardigan and matching blouse. Imitation pearl earrings and a single strand necklace would help her feel gracious and thoughtful.

After fifteen minutes on the road, the weather began to change; fine pellets of hail rained upon the windshield. He asked whether she would like a rug around her legs. She was fine.

'Where are we?'

'This is Radlett. Have you been here before?'

'No. I haven't.'

The side-street off the main road was unusually dark, the street lamps scarcely piercing the leafy branches of mature trees. The houses were large, their grounds spacious. There were black cast-iron gates. From what she could see through the hail, the paths to the shadowy houses were narrow, long and winding. It intrigued her. There was an air of mystery about this private world.

They turned left up a lane, climbing until they arrived at a closed garage. He got out, opened it, put the car in and locked the door behind them.

The sitting room was comfortably warm, but the coal fire was slowly dying. He gave it a new lease of life with the poker and added more coal. 'That will keep you nicely warm,' he remarked and his face attempted a smile. Soon a roaring fire blazed, so much so that Anjali moved away to the furthest end of the sofa. He seemed awkward, confused, like a teenager in a new situation.

He went out and brought back a tray with two glasses and a jug of planter's punch. She took one and sipped; it was surprisingly good. He was drinking his far too quickly, she thought, draining his glass, and replenishing it. She unzipped her briefcase and brought out her copy of the draft. Where was his copy? She sipped slowly, aware that she had not had dinner; she'd have a sandwich on her return. Perhaps he'd made jottings, notes.

Since her arrival, the weather had grown worse. Snow began to fall heavily; a brute wind lashed the branches of trees and shrubs. Dr Marshall stood before the window and invited her to observe the fresh falling snow. Peering through the darkness enveloping the lane, she watched waves of snow drifting in mid-air, whirling and lifting. She shuddered when he placed the palm of his hand and searching fingers on her shoulder.

She was disturbed by it, but said nothing. Perhaps he was just being friendly in an inept kind of way. If she said something, what would he think? That she was objecting because her culture was archaic, backward-looking? Wasn't she supposed to be an educated, sophisticated student who was *au fait* with the flexible boundaries of acceptable Western behaviour?

Whatever his intention, her shudder was noted. Perhaps he had taken her off guard, perhaps she was cold, standing too close to the window. Too much planter's punch on an empty stomach played a part in his interpreting her reserve. Probably just shyness. He noted no rejection, saw no distaste.

Anjali resolved to be practical, use what her mother called common sense. It was better to have the discussion she had come for than to end this opportunity by an act that might seem rude, so she restrained her hand from removing his. Instead, she walked back to the sofa.

'It is getting late, Dr Marshall, the weather is appalling, ought we not to make a start?' He nodded and left the room. As the time passed without his return, she began to feel out of her depth. She sensed, too, that he was not at ease. Perhaps this was not his home? Maybe it belonged to a friend, away on holiday? Where was he? No light was coming from the open door through which he had left. What could he be doing in the dark? Maybe he had forgotten she was there. *Pull yourself together.*

But he came back with his copy of the manuscript and several pages of handwritten comment. Sipping his rum punch occasionally, he gave a careful and thorough review of her dissertation, even appeared to have anticipated her questions. She listened attentively and made notes. She observed how he relaxed when he spoke about his area of expertise; there were even touches of good humour. His face was animated, his eyes alert as he explained that there was one topic that needed further attention. She had examined the difficulties a new agriculture-based manufacturing industry would have; she had noted what the farmers had improved and what was still neglected. He felt that more data was needed on fertilisers, pesticides and fungicides, and if a few photographs could be added to show the citrus groves and the factory, the work, already good, would be further enhanced. Perhaps, too, she needed to consider what alternative enterprise, if any, could have been developed with the resources expended on the production of citrus fruit juices.

These were pertinent and helpful comments. She felt satisfied, relieved.

'Well that's it,' he said, rising. 'The weather seems to be getting worse. Let's have a small drink before we leave.'

'Thank you, but I shan't have any,' she said.

He returned with two glasses of rum punch and handed her one.

'I mustn't really,' she said.

'Well, it's a special pleasure for me not to have to drink alone. Please join me. I'll see you safely back to Magdalena Hall.'

She had been taught by her parents that the willingness to receive graciously enhanced the giving. Gratitude and the warmth of the fire put her at ease. The feeling of being out of her depth gradually loosened its grip.

He began to speak about himself. 'I'm a loner, as you see… Have always been, really. May have stemmed, you know, from losing my mother when I was two. My father worked at agricultural research centres in different parts of the tropics. So I grew up in the company of ayahs in India, just before the years leading to its independence, and servants in Kenya. In my youth, my father took me along with him to the fields where I learnt about the growing of tropical crops – coffee, cotton, tea, sugar-cane and rice.

'I wanted to understand my father because he was all I had, and the environment of my childhood was often unfamiliar and strange. He was a human chameleon, constantly transforming himself into what he felt the company he was in required of him.

'I don't know whether he had difficulty putting down roots, or whether he didn't wish to. This may have played a part in making me who I am. There are comforts, you know, in being a close observer of life. Too large an involvement can have its downsides… I hope I'm not boring you. I can't recall when last I spoke to anyone like this.' He looked at her as if seeking approval.

What he did not tell her, and what came to him insistently now, were his adolescent memories of, on more than one occasion, inadvertently opening a door to witness, unseen, an intimacy between one of the younger maids and his father. He came to see it as a game between a seemingly unwilling young woman, who was in fact privileged to be held so close by his papa. The scenes of his father's overpowering will dominating the struggling, pleading young maids stayed with him. He observed though that no female servant had ever left his father's employment.

As she listened, Anjali felt sorry for him, thinking that she had misjudged him. She smiled.

'Well, I shall now take you back,' he said. 'I don't have to say this, but I'd like you to know that your approach is sound, and with the implementation of the few suggestions I've offered, there's nothing to prevent you from having a fine piece of work.'

She got up to thank him. 'I found this session most helpful; we should leave now please; it's very late.' But why was he still seated, turning away from her, as if there was something he didn't want her to see? Then she noticed his left temple. It had been bleeding and the blood was only just beginning to coagulate.

'You've hurt yourself.'

'It will heal on its own. Please don't fuss.'

'Let me have a look.' As she stretched over to examine the broken

153

skin, her thighs rubbed against his arm, and he felt the warmth of her bosom, neck and face as she leaned over and parted his hair. 'It's not deep, but you need to have it cleaned, put some antiseptic cream on it.' Her voice, the parting of her lips so close to his cheeks and ear, the gentle care she offered, stirred him deeply. As she moved away, again her upper thighs touched against his arm as if caressing it.

Unaware of the intensity of his desire, the tumult in his mind, she smiled and said, 'You should attend to it before we leave.'

'Yes, I will,' he said, and left the room.

When he returned she was making more jottings in the margins. She did not see the way he stared at her. 'Come,' he said. The voice seemed distant. She picked up her bag and briefcase.

He ushered her into another room. It was dark. *Is this where he works? His study?* The light from the hallway barely penetrated. Shadowy forms circled the walls. As she stood there waiting for him to put on the lights, she wondered what he was about to show her. He closed the door behind him.

The curtains were not drawn; a beam of light moved along the wall, only to disappear speedily.

He switched on a lamp but it emitted little light. Anjali looked about, her eyes trying to adjust to the dark. Her pulse quickened. This was a bedroom. Though he was in the shadows, she saw he had drawn the curtains and was beginning to undress.

'Let me out of here. Let me out of here at once, Dr Marshall.'

'You've stirred me up; you can't leave me like this. It really would be more sensible to co-operate with me in this foul weather; later I'll risk it though the gale to take you back.'

'I shall report this, Dr Marshall. Open the door. Take me back to the hall. And I'll put this behind me, I promise.'

'Report me? I'll be retiring this term. Dr Goldberg will be your tutor but I will have to write the assessment of your work. You could have a very good degree, which you deserve. No one need ever know… never from me.' He moved to lock the door and pocketed the key.

His voice was low, sincere, melancholy in the darkness.

'I shall contact Professor McIntyre, as soon as I return to the Hall.'

'The Head of the Department and I are on good terms. Why would he believe you?'

'Let me out of here! Let me out of here, Dr Marshall! I shall find my way back. Just let me out. For God's sake let me out!'

I should've told my parents. No one knows I'm here.

She was in a miserable, ugly room with a man who intended to harm her. The houses were so far apart. He had locked the garage door; screams would reach no one in this blizzard. *A cab. I need a cab. There must be a telephone booth on the main road. I have to get out of here.*

'Let me out of here. Let me out. For God's sake open the door. Please open the door, Dr Marshall.'

The windows are locked. Is there anything to break them with? But what might he do with broken glass? How did he cut himself?

'Be sensible. You'll enjoy this. It can't be your first time. You can't walk far in this weather. It's dangerous.'

Where in Radlett was she? It had been too dark to read the name of the lane. She would have to run all the way to the main road and she could not recall seeing a call box. Could she thumb a lift? Who would stop for a stranger on such a night? And then, should she, alone and distressed, trust a stranger in his car, not knowing where she was, nor the route back to her hall?

He flung the red bedspread to the side. 'I won't hurt you if you co-operate.' He gripped her as she struggled and kicked. Firmly, force-fully, he began to pull her apart, undressing her as if he were removing the skin of a fruit. His hands trembled; her body was stiff as if rigor mortis had set in. *Oh Daddy! Amritsar Massacre, they fell as flies, there was no way out. Pinned against a wall. A firing squad. Where is God?* His fingers began to play upon the soft, firm flesh he had pinned down. Her fear paralysed her.

At length he discovered she was a virgin. This challenge he had half expected. His assault began. He forced apart her legs and the pain intensified. Her mouth opened but her throat held her anguish. A sharp burning within her and blood oozed out as if an underground stream had trickled to the surface. Tears stained her cheeks as he quivered for a moment and let out a guttural cry of release. Her anguish she swallowed. He left the room.

For a moment she curled up, closed in on herself, like a sea anemone. Then she got off the bed and limped forward, feet uncertain, her soreness raw. She took a handkerchief from her bag, bent low to wipe her legs of the blood which was slowly trickling down. She dressed and walked out of the darkness, cradling her dissertation. She stood dazed, looking through the glass, not seeing. She stood. She waited.

'I'll take you back,' he said, and did.

Meantime, Santosh was thinking about Anjali and the letter he'd posted to her. He felt a wave of sorrow for her. Would what he'd written reassure her that it was not wrong to have a positive outlook on the world?

'Although all that I've said in the past is true; what is no less true is that there are still people in this country, not many perhaps, who have beautiful minds, who cannot be bought, who understand right from wrong, who are aware of the strengths and demands of power and who, whatever the cost, will stand upright against power's abuses. The powerful have many masks and they wear them well, nevertheless there are a few who are alert to their craft of camouflage. The example and thinking of George Orwell still lives.' Finally he had added: *'Remember my dear, dear daughter, you are of far greater worth than any examination result, so put your sense of well-being above all else.'*

29

SHE WALKED THE PATH TO CALVARY

It was a bleak December morning. Anjali walked slowly through Regent's Park, her feet directing her down well-trodden paths. It was a place she had long enjoyed. Here the changing seasons sang their songs. The crocuses would ring their low soft peals: 'Spring is here! Look! Spring is here! Will this new world be fair?' She would nod and smile. Later the pink cherries would complain: 'Summer did beat upon my spring from on high; now she's nigh, my petals will fly.' When she had first discovered the park, it was its orderliness, the borders with their colour and variety and the sounds of falling water that held her. She thanked whoever had thought that beauty, form and the hushed embrace of nature should not be lost to the senses in this city of finance.

Today she watched, but did not see. She knew she was pregnant. She had been desperately hoping it would not be so; each day she searched for the sign that would bring relief. That time had passed. She felt as if she were the only sentient being in a cosmic darkness, drifting towards a black hole's open mouth, unable to scream for help, to tear herself from its powerful pull to nothingness. She had to act, to change the direction of her present drifting, or be consumed. There was only one choice. Her stomach ached. She was overwhelmed by thoughts of lost worth, of the vipers' tongues stretched forth to reach her. She'd read too much recently that suggested that reporting rape to the police was the beginning of another ordeal. Who would believe that one so respectable as a distinguished academic would do such a thing unless led on?

She'd spent a week hidden in her room, lying in her bed with feverish dizziness, quivering with fear and loathing as the scene returned, trying to find comfort for her body under the cover of warmth. She wanted to be without form, a floating mist. Sometimes she tried to distract herself in work but failed.

Then she got up, had a shower, coffee, hot toast and cheese, dressed herself and allowed her thoughts to open into the quiet of the room. After a second cup of coffee she found she had become enraged, defiant, and continued to walk up and down, preferring to be in motion. Her

157

parents, her school and university had all helped her to acquire the tools of judgement. She must use them.

What choices do I really have? Will it be a life forever tied to that night? I cannot carry this. It will destroy me. Where and how can I find release from this and not inform my parents? They, at least, must not suffer too.

She had sensed too that her parents were not themselves; something was not right between them. There was an unusual quiet, a restraint, a silence from Mummy. Could she have been told that she was suffering from something and did not wish to alarm them? How could she take her pain to her parents now? Mummy was usually so positive about life. She battled on when most would acknowledge that the dye was cast and nothing could be done to change it. She recalled the interview with Miss Williams at St Hilda's all those years ago. She would try her best to be like her mother. How could she take away her hope and optimism?

She thought of her father's letter which had been waiting for her that night when she returned to the hall. What bullshit, she had thought, crumpling it into the wastepaper basket. The following morning, she'd rescued it, tears trickling, and smoothed the crumples away. A father who was continually thinking of his daughter's welfare, even in the dead of night (it was his habit to write the time and the date of his writing): it was his lullaby, sent to comfort her, an intimate part of him seldom disclosed openly.

Her hurt would cut him deeply, confirming his darkest fears. She could not do it. But what was she to do? What must be done, must be done soon. And what of Satisha and Vidya; were they to know? Might not their natural high-spiritedness turn into withdrawal, shunning contact with others so that such a thing could never happen to them? She had to keep it to herself. Maybe one day she would tell her mother, but not now. She needed to find a place where her anonymity could be guaranteed.

But who could she trust with such a large thing as her family's good name, her own good name? What of her friends? This situation said so much about friendship and its limits. Anything new anyone learned about you either took from your image or enhanced it. It was never neutral. Here in their final year they were competing with each other for better grades, better jobs, for good opinion. She could not afford to lose in this race.

Her thoughts rested on her two closest friends. There was Jennifer with her charisma and good looks (and knowing it), with her confident manner, her ease with the world, flirting with it, sure of her place in it. She would be clear about what Anjali should do: 'Report the cowardly bastard, Anjy, and abort. Who the hell does he think he is? Such a slimy shit. Oh Anjy, a kick in the groin with those boots would have done it.' After warmly embracing her, and visibly upset, the strident suffragette would don her public mask: 'Let's go to that posh place and have tea; it's on me.'

Then there was Maria; just the thought of her was comforting. She was peace itself, so at ease with everyone and with whatever came her way. Always sound, reasoned, reliable. Short, plumpish, with glasses that kept slipping. With quizzical eyes that said she was quietly amused at the so-called intelligent man's ability to make a fool of himself. She listened well, heard the unsaid, understood why it was mute.

Anjali could hear Maria: 'Poor poor thing. How you must feel! Oh, Anjali.' She would stretch out her hands to hold hers. 'What are you thinking of doing? Yes, I think that's wise. You have no choice really, have you? What an abuse of trust. Oh dear me! How brave you are.' Then her voice would give ground to a communication of feelings not requiring words, while their two spirits sit together and their hands channel the flow. 'Yes, Anjali. I think that would be wise. In a matter of days, he will no longer be on the staff, so an accusation would be tricky. We can guess what the fallout could be for you if you report him. You want to get back to your studies and put this behind you. There are some things that cannot be put right and in the circumstance…'

Thinking about what Maria would probably say made Anjali feel that perhaps she should go home and talk to her mother after all. She would tell her what was the best option. Just thinking about doing this made her feel better. Who else could she really trust?

Ishani phoned Mill Hill the following day.

'Amira, it's you. What a surprise! Not at the British Museum looking at the past, when the exciting present is all around you?'

'It's so nice to hear your voice, Ishani.'

'I have a proposal. Is Anjali going anywhere for Christmas?'

'She always comes home for Christmas; she wouldn't want to spend it anywhere else. It's special. You know that.'

'Ravi and I were thinking it would be nice if she could spend it with us. Surely you can spare her just this once? You've three bundles of joy, lend us one this Christmas.'

'What's up, Ishani?'

'Amira, you've a suspicious mind. Whatever you're eating, change your diet.'

159

'We've always been together at Christmas, Ishani. Santosh and I look forward to the gathering of our little tribe more than ever, especially now when we see so little of Anjali; Vidya and Satisha are busy with school exams and their after-school activities. We too rarely sit down as a family.'

'It's a fine tradition, Amira, and the girls are growing fast.'

'It's so nice when we see eye to eye, Ishani.'

'I've been thinking quite lot about what I'm about to tell you… I may be able to help Anjali find a good husband; I may not succeed but it's certainly worth a try. Ravi and I know a most suitable young man; it would be nice to have Anjali meet him.'

'Ishani, she's still a student…'

'True, but youth, like spring, Amira, has its span. Opportunities don't just come when you're ready. Business tells me you have to be always ready for that crucial move…'

'Is life a business, Ishani?'

'Of course it is. I don't underestimate the competition for the young man's hand here in Trinidad; I'm just thinking ahead.'

'You certainly are. You're way way ahead of us here, Ishani… and I'm not sure that Anjali would even consider it. Young people here are looking for their own soul mates.'

'Of course. I know that, Amira. They live in a cloud cuckoo land which says, I shall do my own thing, I shall do as I feel…'

'Anjali has lived almost all her life here…'

'The young are like sheep, Amira. They do what the group wants, what they're made to feel by the advertisements, the magazines and the crowd they hang out with.'

'*They* don't see it like that, Ishani.'

'But let anyone dare to ignore the dress code of the tribe… Over here they can't be seen in Bata shoes – Bata Bullits, they call them. And the lunch bag has to match the book bag, has to match the skirt.'

'They soon grow out of it, Ishani.'

'Amira, you're out of touch. No, it goes on and on. Which wine bar becomes which district to live in, which furniture to have…'

'We don't live like that. Anjali is very far from one of the crowd.'

'Most commendable. There's hope for you yet. Now put it to Anjali, without your hidden directives please. Give her genuine choice, Amira, or better still, let me speak with her.'

'The store must be very busy; how are you coping?'

'Where to begin? The young people know nothing; they can't even pack a shelf. They lean up against the wall with attitude.'

'Wait, Ishani. Anjali's just come through the door. We weren't expecting her. What a pleasant surprise. I'll pass the phone to her. Thanks for phoning, Ishani, and despite what I said, thank you for caring about the girls. You're a true sister.'

'Now there's no need to exaggerate. I'm a busybody. My family and friends tolerate me. I'm blessed.'

'You're a harbour and many find shelter there.'

'Steady on, Amira, as the English would say. Don't overdo it now; it might go to my head.'

Twenty minutes later, Anjali opened the door to the sitting room and said, 'I will go for just a while. It's an opportunity to visit the citrus groves again with a few questions that are troubling me and to spend more time in the factory too. I need to speak to one or two people working in the field. If I put my all into it, I can return before Christmas.'

'No don't do that, Anjali,' Santosh said. 'We'll miss you, but stay even for the New Year if you need time to collect more material. Your aunt Ishani has given a lot of thought and care to your welfare. Understand this and show that you do. We believe she's going to introduce you to a nice young man. Who knows, Anjali, there may be more than one.' He winked mischievously. 'Then you can have your pick.'

'Thank you, Daddy. You've made me feel better about going. I'll pack straight away; she purchased an open ticket and it's on its way, sent it ten days ago, so it may be here tomorrow.'

'Ishani is something else, I tell you. When she mentioned it to me I was not for your going,' Amira said, 'but now I think – here, it's not easy to find a nice group of Indian boys to choose from, I mean from families like ours, because in the long run, knowledge, rational thinking about how a good life can be made, is all there is to fall back on if the personal things don't work out... I worry that some of the Indian people here are looking more for British citizenship than a genuine life partner. Besides, we don't know what their parents will be expecting from their daughters-in-law. I don't want my daughters entering the unknown. The known is trouble enough.'

'Very few people live with their in-laws today, Mummy.'

'I know that; that's not the issue; it's more that their expectations of a daughter-in-law that could be far removed from ours.'

'Your mother is forgetting that while India has remote villages, among the citizens of the cities there are going to be... so many very

very modern people.' Santosh changed his accent in such an exaggerated way that they all laughed. 'In fact, Amira, people like us.'

'Those here at university are not like us. They're weird. Not open; you don't know where you are with them. They're constantly hedging their bets, as if in living one's life every step taken involves making a sound financial investment. It's bizarre.'

'Anjali, you surprise me. A sound investment, bizarre? What better investment than a beautiful, charming, educated, accomplished wife?' Santosh put on his worried look.

'Well, Daddy, those I met at university are so smug and affected. There are a few who stay in the library all day, the first to come, and the last to leave. It's so difficult to find an ordinary guy, you know, someone you can be at ease with, someone interested in what's happening in the world outside their studies. I haven't met one yet. Maybe they are there, but chance, sadly, can seal your fate.' This last observation nearly broke her voice, and though she contained her feelings, they rose to the surface.

'Anjali... You're not yourself,' Amira observed. 'Are you well. Is something troubling you?'

'Just tired, Mummy.'

'I understand. You've a lot on your mind, especially with that tutor letting you down so. You're looking pale, drained. Have things got any worse for you? You must let us know. We're your parents. You are our first born; you have that special place.'

'Don't let him get you down, Anjali,' Santosh said, rising from his chair; 'you will come through. You have what it takes. Come here.' He embraced his daughter and she began to cry.

'Oh Daddy, I'm so worried for myself.'

'Why don't we report him, Santosh? Why should he get away with this?'

'We've gone through all that before, Amira. The situation hasn't changed.'

As Amira hugged Anjali, she said, 'Why not take your manuscript, and make copies of the pages you want to discuss with the varying specialists and ask them to have a look at it. You will feel better, knowing you're on the right track.'

'Good idea, Amira. The change of scenery and Ishani's garden will help you to relax, regain your vitality and see all this in perspective. Don't allow him to destroy your self-confidence, Anjali. You are larger

162

than he can ever be. He's a small, insignificant man. You'll come through. Remember, I'll be only too happy to read your dissertation if that is what you would like… Now, now, I can't have the two ladies in the house so sad; let us go out for dinner tonight so that I can celebrate my family.'

The following morning at breakfast Santosh said: 'Well that's settled then. Go in the store, Anjali, and help your Aunt… If there's someone you think looks alright, exchange addresses and so on. Relax, be yourself. Don't look at him as if he is applying to you for a job.'

'Santosh, this is no time for making light of a serious issue. You don't seem to know what is serious, or what is frivolous. Your timing is unbelievable.'

'I'm not going there to get married, Mummy. I have other important things on my mind.'

'You are not?' Santosh looked at her with a headmaster's mock bearing. 'Why is that? Come, come, Anjali, if you don't manage to get married in – ten days? – your aunt and your mother will be seriously disappointed.'

'You are far more sensible than your father.'

'He's only teasing us, Mummy.'

'Your father thinks life is an unfolding comedy and he's in the stalls.'

'That's not true, Mummy. He knows we take everything seriously. Perhaps too seriously at times. Daddy tries to bring amusement into our conversations.'

'I am relieved to hear this, Anjali. The truth is, I'm trying to save this family from itself.'

'So we're in need of saving, are we?'

'Mummy and Daddy, please behave like grown-ups. I have to go upstairs and start packing.'

30

AMIRA'S TURMOIL

Where and how to bring closure on Santosh's affair? Try as I may, it comes upon me of its own accord and recaptures my thoughts.

As a child I welcomed solitude. I absorbed the sounds of insects at dusk, was intrigued by fireflies with their blinking torches; at sunrise, I listened to the prattle of water, the call of birds. I was at one with the forest, resisting my mother's calls to come home. I felt part of all that was moving there. Now I close the door and in my silent space, I fall apart in anger, disappointment and innocence lost, with nothing to take its place.

When I first saw the Malaysian stamp, my suspicions woke. I behaved as I should. They gave me no rest and later in the day I returned to this stamp. It became a transgressor in the house, needling me. A surge of resolution possessed me. I would never have thought I could open someone else's letter. Actually I got a thrill doing it. I would know what there was to know. But that there could be such a downside – the opening up of vulnerabilities long covered – I had not bargained for.

Hindsight compels me to acknowledge that there are times when ignorance is bliss. The sealed letter proved to be my Pandora's box; frailties I did not know I had flew from it.

I had learnt how to open a letter and reseal it neatly so that no one would suspect anything. This art was demonstrated by a younger member of staff showing off her skill during a lunch break. I saw it as a prank. We all did. Another member of staff said we were acquiring the skill of a secret agent. When I got home that day, I do not know why, but the thought of uncovering the undisclosed, of opening the door of an intimacy, had a frisson of fear and daring. I practised it several times until I was perfect; I demonstrated it to Ishani, wanting to show off before her. She said, 'One day, this might be a valuable asset, dear sister. Let's keep it to ourselves.' We clasped hands in agreement.

That young Malaysian clearly wanted more of him; she was thanking him for the 'dazzling jewellery and the spectacular, tremendous, crazy time' they had together. 'So very unforgettable.' She was ecstatic about him for other things, which should not have been written, and ended with a 'will never be forgotten'. Far too many adjectives and adverbs, though I can't really say whether they are accurate, can I? Certainly too many repetitions – a naivety in expressing herself without restraint. Youth? A desire to keep her memory, and his too, alive? Her hand, I mean her handwriting, needed support; it was not upright.

Fancy my editing the letter! Is it the analyst in me, or am I trying to comfort myself with some feeling of erudite superiority? But he had offered another what I'd thought belonged only to us. Do vows no longer hold, words become whatever the changing wind wills? Where does one turn for meaning? What had given me a purpose had left me and I'd become like motes in the dark, not seen, not known, not felt.

At first it was just in the solitude of my kitchen as I prepared a meal, or in the garden, rooting out ground elder, that I had to struggle to remove from my mind's eye scenes of Santosh caressing another, whispering soft endearments. The more I tried not to think about it, the more intense the imagery became. My God, I really tried to put them out of my mind, but they had a life of their own, outside my control.

I had to find a way to regain myself, to return to the solitude which once energised me, helped me to direct my life. I was losing my ability to concentrate. Is this how insanity begins? Is it a drip-dripping away of oneself until there's nothing left of you? The images began to appear even when I was speaking to a neighbour, to the cashier at the checkout, to the children, and though I knew no one but I saw them, only an iron will enabled me to continue. Would I have them beside me forever? O God I need help. I just can't continue. The images are all around me, they hang everywhere. Their embrace, their suffused faces. I'm going crazy.

I thought of going to my GP but then shrank with shame from the idea. Weeks went by. I'd go on trips to get away from the house, to Oxford Street to see if the change of scenery, the waves of shoppers searching, looking, chatting would distract me. I walked around the sparkling contents in the lighting and glass departments. I waited to see if they would come; and there they were.

My break came when I was returning from the city on the fast train to Mill Hill. I sat down, took out a book on Rilke's letters and tried to focus on it. It deeply engrossed me, a rare moment of release. I looked up for a moment and was taken aback to see that I was sitting opposite a well-known psychiatrist I'd seen talking on television. Fully aware it was not the done thing, but driven by sheer desperation, I turned to him.

'I recognise you, Doctor,' I said. 'I know I shouldn't ask this of you, here and now, but I'm in such a poor state and I know you have the skills to assist me; I've observed how well you help others on the morning programmes.'

'Have you discussed the matter with your GP? If not you should.'

'My GP wouldn't be able to help me.'

'If you haven't approached him, how do you know?'

'He's not qualified to assist me. I'll soon be getting off the train, in fact, at the first stop. Please just listen to what I have to say. It is short.'

He looked at me.

I waited.

He nodded.

I told him about my struggle with the image.

I listened intently to his response and as the train approached Mill Hill Broadway, I told him, 'You've done me a great kindness, Doctor, thank you so very much. May you be blessed. I shall do as you say.' He looked at me, and said: 'You'll do well, you're a brave woman. No image is as strong as you, if you're determined to regain yourself, I know you will succeed.' He smiled for the first time. As I stood on the platform, I repeated his parting words: *No image is as strong as you. I know you will succeed.*

I stood on the platform as each carriage passed by, lifted by his generosity. It is a blessed world.

I began to do as he had advised. The first attempt was not easy, but I persisted, just as he had directed. Gradually the frequency of the images was reduced; until to my surprise they were not there unless I brought them back on my own accord by thinking, wondering, where were they? Where have they gone?

'Let the images come,' he had repeated, peering through his glasses at me. 'Don't struggle against or fight them; whenever you do, you're energising them. Pay no attention whatsoever; just let them come. Don't try to resist them. So they are here; they have come; so what, you won't be bothered. You offer no attention. It's of no importance to you. By not battling with it, you are not energising it and, with time, it should leave you.'

And they faded, as he had predicted – like an unwelcome guest, someone completely ignored, is unlikely to come again. Now more at ease with myself, that maxim – 'Where ignorance is bliss 'tis folly to be wise' – once again crept upon me, like an old woman wagging her finger. I had never envisaged such a situation; on the contrary, I'd seen over and over again the dire cost of being ignorant. But now I began to see that in the whole complexity of life the old adage had its place. And yet it was knowledge, the psychiatrist's knowledge, that healed me. Perhaps it is knowing how to cope with knowing that becomes crucial to understanding life?

With the worst behind me I reflected on how I had come to open that letter. A bunch of letters had been sent by Santosh's secretary and delivered by Mr Rao, who works in his department and lives nearby at Hendon. I wondered whether Rita, his secretary, knew and wanted to alert me. We had been good friends for years and she can't have thought there was anything in a handwritten letter from Malaysia that could be so urgent that it needed to be delivered to Santosh at home.

There was something else. I could have taken the package of letters and just placed them on Santosh's desk. Rita must have thought of that too, because she placed the letter at the top of the pile, all held in place by a ribbon.

If my mother or grandmother had been faced by something like this they would have accepted it calmly, would have gone about their lives as if nothing had taken place. But with the gift of education, they had offered me a choice. I could stay or leave.

Had my parents and Ishani seen something in Santosh that I hadn't, because my head was filled with such deep affection for him? Can I believe him when tells me not to give it an importance it does not deserve? What happens when next he goes to Malaysia? How am I to know she won't write again or he won't be tempted? From her letter it seems to have been quite something. For different reasons I couldn't talk to Margaret Summers or Ishani: I would have to disclose my family's vulnerability to the one, while the other might turn up on our doorstep after Santosh's blood. I had to maintain the pretence of family harmony.

Perhaps I've been lucky in that this happened now and not in the winter of my life. Now I have an energy awakened after being dormant for too long. What happened, too, was that the very process of healing that the psychiatrist recommended placed the affair in perspective. With the images gone, what the affair meant became insignificant.

Then my thoughts rested on Kamla Devi, so unlike me. When she was young she must have been a prize, with all that loveliness and charm. She flirted while talking. Much play with eyes, lips, hands and movements of the body and pregnant pauses. A musical performance. I wonder why she never married. We all have our secrets. I know there are things I could learn from her. For my daughters' sake and my own self-worth, I had to awaken my former self, indeed a self I had never really developed. What I was up against was someone who expressed herself without any restraint, and that must have spoken to something in Santosh. I couldn't let myself be defeated by default.

I phoned Kamla and told her all – except my opening the letter and what I found there – which means I have not told her much. Sheer embarrassment prevented me. We arranged to meet early next week. She listened as if it was one of those slightly worrying things that inevitably comes with living. 'What's important, Amira, is that you make the right response. We'll put our heads together.'

Kamla Devi sighed. This was an old old story. She remembered how fresh and alluring Amira had been when they were at university. Now she'd become gracious, measured, a touch matronly. She needed to recapture that allure. Thank goodness she'd kept her figure… well… not bad at all; a little toning up here and there and she'd be on her way. She needed a change of style to bring out the attractive woman who'd been lost under the years of domesticity. It would be fun doing this together.

Amira had not told her anything about the strength of the affair, and could be keeping the worst from her, but the fact that Santosh had confessed was a good sign. He was not the cavalier type; he enjoyed the pleasures of family life and knew he was fortunate. An intelligent man would do nothing foolish that would lose him his wife and daughters, but she knew that neither rationality nor intelligence had much to do with such matters. She would have to take Amira to a place she had not been before, to start her on a journey she would have to make her own.

SHERLOCK HOLMES PUBLIC HOUSE

Amira wrapped one thought around her on the train from Mill Hill to King's Cross, and continued to hold it firmly when she descended to the Victoria and later Bakerloo lines. She was determined that she would not shed tears.

Kamla Devi had explained that she would meet her at a pub on Northumberland Street. Amira would have preferred their usual choice, Fortnum and Mason, for tea. Images of crowding, noise, loud chatter, warm bodies and the smell of alcohol on the breath filled her head. She had never been in a pub, but had observed them emptying themselves of their motley customers. Kamla must have noted her silence because she added, 'It's a respectable place, Amira. You'll find its ambience pleasing. I know you've never been to a pub. Think of it as a challenge to enter it alone; remember I'll be there waiting.'

She crossed over to Northumberland Street and her steps sounded loud on the pavement. She reminded herself that good advice from Kamla Devi was only possible if she was more open than when they spoke on the telephone. Then she saw 'The Sherlock Holmes'. A horseshoe-shaped bar faced the entrance, but for a moment she wondered whether this was it; its quiet was unexpected. She nodded to the barman who responded warmly, seeing a new face. She looked to the right but there was no one there except an old man. She walked over to the left and there was Kamla Devi looking very much at home. Amira's anxiety evaporated as a warm smile and beaming eyes said *You are here to celebrate life*.

'You're looking swell, Amira.'

'You're just perfect as usual, Kamla Devi. I made an effort, my gesture to our friendship.'

'Well done. Look around. Tell me what you see.'

'I see a row of bottles standing upside down. They look pretty.'

'They contain the different spirits. See the measures attached to them.'

'It's comfortable. I like that. The mahogany varnish on the bar gives the place a rich colour.'

Kamla Devi nods.

Amira observes the upholstered leather seats facing the bar, asks, 'Is the bell part of the décor? Is it rung?'

'Yes, ten minutes before the end.'

'And what do most people drink here?'

'Your favourite, gin and tonic, is still popular; vodka is growing and for those who like beer, Old Speckled Hen, I think.'

Silence

'Let's have half a lager each and just one fish and chips between us. I know you'll have had a sandwich, but the fish is really crisp and fresh here. Besides, you wouldn't want to be staggering when you leave.'

'I'm sure I won't do that! Besides, I trust you not to threaten my equilibrium.'

'Oh child of faith.'

They hugged again. Kamla went to the bar to place the order.

'It's a treat to have you here in a pub, Amira, all to myself, like old times – in our younger, more daring days.'

'You say the kindest things.'

'Not always.'

They laughed.

'Here comes the lager.'

They smiled and clinked their glasses. Kamla Devi said, 'To more pleasurable times.'

'I shall drink to that heartily.'

They sipped and sipped again. Amira felt herself beginning to unwind.

Silence.

'It was well chosen, Kamla Devi, most cosy. If Holmes' spirit sits with us I may detect better insights into my difficulties.'

They laugh.

'Are things mending between you?'

'I haven't resolved it for myself, so that must show.'

'Don't take too long. Begin the healing.'

'I need to find a path that shows I'm greatly disappointed, but at the same time does not harm our marriage.'

'I can't think of a better way to start… Do you know, Amira, what the real reason for the intensity of your hurt is?'

'I told you on the phone.'

'On the phone you said how hurt and angry you were; you felt you had lost all trust in him and wondered whether your marriage could be the same again. Before you got married you were an outgoing, challenging, intelligent young woman with a successful career; you were good at what you did and all acknowledged this. After marriage and before Santosh asked you to emigrate to London, you had that professional you, as well as a happy marriage, three healthy, happy girls, efficient home help and a lot of back-up from Ishani and your parents.

'Here, that support has gone. You've been battling to transform a house into a home. You poured your skills into finding schools for the girls. Often you were made to feel a novice in the ways of this place. Santosh was feeling his way in a new job, and he and the girls became your priority. You offer your demanding family your full attention and care. Disappointments, doubts and anguish roll towards you; you face them alone.'

'Well, there's nothing unusual about that in our family. We were brought up that way. My mother's example still speaks to me.'

'True. For your ma and her generation that's fine. In coming here, Santosh and the girls have benefited, but not you. You sacrificed a career, the part of you that is crying out feels deceived, badly let down. You drank from a bottle labelled Family First and it's made you feel smaller and smaller.'

'I'm not one of those highly organised superwomen. I couldn't manage both. I needed to be there for the girls when they returned from school. I felt inadequate, though I tried hard to overcome it. Santosh had problems too. I wanted him to have an environment at home that would help him succeed. I kept problems to myself. I wanted my family to be accepted; the girls and Santosh did not have time to connect with the street, so I did it for us all.'

'You managed on one salary; that takes skill.'

'You have to do what you have to do, Kamla Devi. But what do I do now? I feel miserable. Lost.'

'You feel cheated.'

Silence.

'Where do I go from here? I am buffeted in all directions.'

'That's normal.'

'Perhaps I need to make a change to cope with my situation. The girls are older, more independent.' She smiled broadly. 'As for Santosh, clearly he is far too well established.'

'Very much so. You know, Amira, our meeting here reminds me of our times together as students. We talked about everything.'

'Of late I hear your voice more often. You were skilled at bringing light to those aspects of life closed to a village girl like me.'

'Learning how to give and take pleasure, Amira – that's what it's

171

about – you have to change your thinking, your orientation. It starts there. It might seem like becoming someone else, but it's only finding parts of yourself that have been hidden. It's not merely a change of lingerie or a different lipstick as the television make-over shows pretend, dear Amira, though every accessory has its function. Let me be candid: someone with your heavy baggage of family obligations cannot possibly perform a pirouette.'

'Unlikely, Kamla Devi.'

'But then pirouettes are inimical to the art of engaging the senses fully to – shall we say? – the heights of unspoken ecstasy.'

The arrival of their order saved Amira's blushes.

'The fish is as excellent as you said.'

Kamla Devi beckoned to the barman who was near by, clearing the tables. 'My guest approves.'

'We never let down the ladies, especially two beautiful ones.'

He smiled at Amira, a fraction too long she felt.

'Sachets of sweet nothings you have not untied for quite a while. I saw how uncomfortable you looked. Learn to accommodate such boldness, see it for what it is: nothing. Our barman's marshmallow style is part of the service. There may be times he reaches someone. Who knows? He has nothing to lose.'

She leant over to Amira and whispered, 'Become a butterfly, Amira. Learn how to flutter about the target; play with your voice. Learn how to rest your hand upon him, to thrill with stillness and with movement; sense when to lift, to pause, to descend on your beautiful wings. Learn how to intoxicate him with the rhythms of your body, a semblance of innocence veiled in gossamer silk.'

They sip and sip again; the glasses are emptying.

'Kamla Devi, you said something similar to me when you heard I was getting married. You were always to the point in your discreet way. When we were students, you were mature even then, and I a mere teenager. You were so very stylish; you walked in a way that made walking one of the fine arts and still do. It was exhilarating to be with you. You knew the workings of the world. I learnt so much. Some things never change.'

'You're a sensible woman, Amira. But you can be too sensible.'

'Now, you're up to mischief, Kamla Devi.'

'You've walked the prescribed paths, Amira, and that's why you are you. I... sometimes. Well sometimes I worry about you. Do you recall my saying this to you?'

'Yes and at the time I said, "Please don't. I couldn't be happier."'

172

'You were as happy as a child playing in her play pen.'

'We are all put into our play pens at birth, Kamla Devi. A few may be larger, more varied perhaps?'

Silence.

'I, too, was once in a play pen, Amira. I know their inadequacy. When the earth shook and the skies burst I was lost. I learnt rapidly that when hard times come, your savings and your acumen are the best friends to have. I do not refer to us. We have had a rich friendship, Amira; difficulties like these strengthen it further.'

'Once you took me to an exclusive place. I couldn't afford anything other than coffee. The atmosphere was too rarefied for me; the people belonged to another world, they dressed expensively, behaved in a manner that matched the clothes. I didn't know why you took me there. You spoke like an Old Testament prophet with an underlying meaning. What I saw were people with a philosophy of life possible only with a large wallet.'

'Do you know why I took you there?'

'No, well except to show me that world.'

'I wanted to show you the competition out there, what housebound wives with young families do not encounter, but their husbands do, especially if well established in their careers. I wanted you to glimpse what circles the outskirts of every marriage.'

'When we were about to leave, I remember an attractive young woman walking in and joining a gentleman sitting alone. You nudged me, then wrote on the paper napkin, *Don't look now. When you get up, try to get a better look without attracting attention.* I placed the napkin in my bag and did as you suggested. Later when we were waiting for the bus outside, I asked what I was supposed to have seen.'

'That young woman was a performing artist, Amira; her *pas de deux* began the moment the cab door opened; every aspect of herself would have been thought through with meticulous care.'

Even now Amira wondered, as she had done at the time, how Kamla came to be so knowledgeable. It was not something she felt she could ever ask.

It was time to go. They embraced – Amira so grateful that Kamla Devi had reminded her of a self she had almost forgotten. Before she left, Kamla gave Amira a card.

'It has an international lingerie collection. Go tomorrow at about 2 p.m.; it's a quiet time. I shall speak to Madame Varekova, the shop manager, and tell her to expect you. She'll be very helpful. Leave it all to her, she'll offer you philosophy, accessories of thought, as well as clothes. Listen well. You don't have to purchase anything. Initially I thought of accompanying you, but that wouldn't offer you the freedom you need. It's got to be something that you're delighted with and not something I like. Move at your own pace, but be imaginative.'

'Thank you, Kamla Devi.'

'Let me warn you, Madame Varekova has her own inimitable manner. She has faith in what she does. One day your daughters or granddaughters might seek your help. No doubt you will assist them in your own way; I doubt it will be Madame Varekova's.'

32

MADAME VAREKOVA

I found the shop, not in a quiet cul-de-sac as I'd anticipated, but in a department store on Oxford Street, and soon I was on my way to the fifth floor. I had been clutching Kamla Devi's written note so tightly that I had to smooth it to read it again, though I knew the directions by heart. I came to a solid door with the sign 'Visits by appointment only'. I rang the bell by the intercom.

'Your name please? With whom do you have a consultation?'

'Madame Varekova.'

As I was about to enter, three ladies left with their purchases; two were wearing burkas and one a hijab. They were giggling.

I walked in, and though I cannot explain why, I felt at ease, even playful. On the wall was a framed sign, in flowing typography, the colour of an ancient manuscript:

'*We offer you the freedom to think imaginatively. We endeavour to enhance the ephemeral quality of the beauty of living, to embrace its inherent mystery.*'

'Good afternoon, I was expecting you; Madame Devi phoned yesterday.'

Madame Varekova was all smiles. 'Please sit down. The beauty of fine art rests within us all. Yes?'

I nod; it is an involuntary action. I have not had time to reflect on what I've been asked.

'How to reach it is our endeavour. Yes?'

'Yes.'

Madame Varekova's accent is unfamiliar – from somewhere between Europe and Asia? It has a melody that holds me.

'Art is alive everywhere in nature; we wonder at the magic of the clouds bringing the first monsoon rains when the earth dances and sings its welcome. We ask how to enfold the beauty of a flight of swallows as their tail streamers and their wings wave to the sunset. Such enchantments we'd wish to have at the fore of our being, where it can be felt by others. Yes?'

It is a rhetorical question; nevertheless I am nodding again like a mare in blinkers. There is only one way to go. I was not expecting a philosopher in a department of intimate wear.

'We do not know what you have in mind, Mrs Vidhur. How can

you tell what you have there, when no one knows how to look into the mind to read its hieroglyphics – all guess-work. Besides, you haven't yet seen what other minds have created for us, yes?'

I nod.

'Remember, you and I wish to breathe that magical quality of light. It is life-giving upon whatever it shines. Our garments will assist you to grasp this knowledge, to carry it within you like a favourite tune. They have the power to lift our inner being above the humdrum. This is what we are about, Mrs Vidhur, colour, light and, of course, movement.' She smiled broadly.

I wondered whether she was playing for time, trying to understand my stillness.

'Old cobwebs are entangling and hampering us, true?' She nods knowingly to all her questions.

I nod too. I have entered her narrative.

'What I'll do now is show you the variety we have and then you can think about it. Are you comfortable with that?'

'I am, thank you.'

'You're a discerning customer, I can see that. Your demeanour says this. You do not open yourself easily. You're watchful. So first let me explain that our intimate garments are grand affairs; if the wearer moves in tune with them they do not fail at their task. Here you see many drawers: "Frills and Thrills" at the top, next is "Wit at Play", then "Fantasies", next is "Provocateur" and we shall stop at "Beaded Sways". There is only so much the mind can attach itself to. Madame Devi suggested I bring to your attention two drawers which I have right here. You see a third one; at the moment it is outside our reach; it is called "Indiscretions", but I can bring it to you if you request it.'

'I understand your approach, Madame.'

'Very good.'

She lifts layers of tissue which pile up like wispy cirrus clouds.

'This is what we call Mystique. As you see,' she puts my hand through an opening in the garment, 'a warm, rich, black lace. It exudes warmth, from the satin beneath; absolutely exquisite, yes?'

'Yes.'

'How does it feel?'

'Welcoming.'

'Bravo!'

'Observe the cut; this flare-cut will caress the legs, keeping to the rhythm of the play. The best accessories are written here to assist the wearer. We suggest that you accompany our costumes with fragrance and jewellery that enhance. Our lingerie is the human voice, the accessories are the accompaniment of violin, oboe or flute; it depends on the circumstance, of course, the place and the feelings flowing yes? This is crucial, Madam. The motivation is everything. We approach the exuberance that produces life with imaginative abaddon.'

'Abandon? abandonment?' It is involuntary; the teacher in me is never far away.

'You're so right. It is such a joyous affair that I forget myself. I am an artist; I was born with an artist's disposition.'

'Of course, Madame.' *What is happening to me? Why am I mimicking her? Has she hypnotised me?*

'You're of a sensitive nature, I see this. I hear this. You understand the meaning of these things; not everyone does. You're fortunate. These costumes require artistry in the wearer. We ask you to create the occasion. Will it be a beautiful Afghan rug, a grand four-poster complete with tassels or... or...'

'Whatever is preferred?'

'How true, Madame Vidhur. But, do not forget, Madame, with mystique, always with mystique, that is the essential. There is no mystique in tiredness, in drabness, in carelessness, in confusion. So bearing this in mind, you could wear accessories such as these: matching masks in satin and lace – and an antique torque, something startling, something arousing curiosity.'

Madame Varekova halted her flow to display a stunningly beautiful Rose Madder shawl. There were two matching lace pieces and an embroidered veil which she opened out on the counter. I realised the shawl was meant to wrap one's nakedness when she placed a pendant on one of the delicate, intimate pieces.

'These evoke the old silk road, when the ancient caravans carried merchandise desired by rulers and their favourite concubines. You hear the wheels of the covered caravan crossing the cool desert night; bolts of silk meticulously wrapped, sealed wooden boxes of tea moving in unison with caskets of cloves and cinnamon. There you are too; you're veiled, your shape wrapped in a shawl of scarlet lake, you are clothed in chosen scents. All this lies far from the consuming challenges of domesticity. Yes?'

'I believe I am moving with the drift, Madame.'

'You have grasped with remarkable speed the essence of what we are about. Now I turn to this drawer labelled Opulence, for that is what it is. Here you see sheer luxury – vermilion silk with gold threads – fragrance, jewellery, perhaps music, a distant flute or nearby harp?

The wearer chooses whether to entrance, intoxicate or bewitch by display or camouflage. Yes?'

The diet had been rich, Madame Varekova's trimmings have been overwhelming. I'd had my fill of this heady stuff – though I had to admire her art.

'I understand, Madame. You have been very good. I have decided on what I shall have.'

'Before you do, would you care perhaps to look at this?'

It is the drawer of Indiscretions. 'Would you have a peep, as the English say? Yes?'

'Well, I'm not sure…' but she looks so disappointed that I agree.

'That's the spirit, Madame. We're young only once; it is the time to be enterprising.'

Indiscretion she opens with care. I would have thought that it was too common a commodity to be concealed in delicate tissue and marketed for a handsome price. What manner of indiscretions could be so finely wrapped?

Much tissue is again removed; each item is attractively folded. Madame handles the pieces as if they were fragile, delicate, gold-filigree creations. She places them on the counter, looks up, a mischievous glint in her eyes; she presses a red button. 'We do not wish to be disturbed at this moment.' A soft blue light is switched on. 'Now I unwrap… There.'

'I see. Well named, Madame, well named indeed.'

'It's beautifully lined. Observe how the light plays on the fabric as sunbeams on a lake; here, the dancing beads unfold, becoming semi-precious stones; I lift my palm and the shadows are alive. The magical quality of light is before us.'

'You have been most helpful, Madame.'

'There are other styles; would you like to see them?'

'You have been very good, Madame, I have decided.'

'There's no need to hurry, Madame Vidhur. Haste is not to be countenanced in these matters.'

'You have enabled me to decide; I shall have this and… this.'

'Tasteful choices, Madame. This way please. Shall I enclose a list of the likely accessories to go with these, yes?'

'Yes, Madame Varekova. Thank you.'

As I leave, I think how much lies within us, how we have the ability to remake ourselves if we so wish; we are born with infinite possibilities, evolution tells us so. I peeped at my purchases and smiled; there was electricity in my steps.

33

FRIENDSHIP
Christmas 1986

Ishani had told Anjali that Jacob would be there to meet her at the airport. He clapped to attract her attention.

'Mr Jacob, so good to see you. I know I'm in safe hands.'

'Miss Anjali, I feel good, too.'

'Thank you, Mr Jacob. I must tell you that you help to make my stays splendid. You drive with care and are so good to all of us.'

'It was the way I was brought up. I can't help it, you know.'

'It is the right way, Mr Jacob.'

'I believe so. But times changing too fast. Look! Look! Look over there at that mad man. You see how dem fellas driving? Like they can't wait to get to the cemetery.'

When they arrived at the Mitas' house, Anjali was reminded again of a luxurious small hotel with well-kept lawns, mango trees, Valencia oranges, grafted pink grapefruit and bulbous juicy limes. She recalled Lily saying: 'A little tight squeeze from the lime, dear, is all the fish asking.'

The vigorous abundance, the nearness of the hills, the steep cliff drop and the plains to the south, the scent of ylang-ylang in the air and the cooling misty sprays of the fountains were helping to temper her anxiety, all the more so as she felt help would now be close at hand. She had wanted to tell her mother, but when this opportunity came out of the blue, she grasped at it hoping it might provide a way out of her difficulties without worrying her parents.

As she strolled down to a lower terrace, with each step her plan moved forward. Rapt in this, she did not see Ramkisoon.

'So you back… I have de place looking real nice eh.'

'Very nice.'

'You can't keep away eh?'

'No.'

'Between me and you, people here don't know how to appreciate these things.' He paused. 'They think gardening is unskilled work. You know what I mean?'

Anjali offered an agreeing nod. 'You do a very good job.'

'Is not for every Tom, Dick and Harry you know.' He came closer. 'You must tell the boss that. Tell him how much you like to walk in the garden.'

Her attention wonders away.

'Is that a humming-bird?'

'Where?'

'There on the tall red hibiscus.'

'Yes. It looking real good eh? Is care, you know, that does bring up these plants fast fast.'

'What amazing colours! Like sunbeams on water. How it hovers in mid-air!'

'You mean what is holding it? Nice eh? Simple, simple; this is God's work, man.'

'The books say it has the fastest wing-beats of any bird. So small, so much energy. She'd need high energy food… so small. Look how hard she works to live.'

'I bet you wouldn't believe this, but she has to visit one thousand flowers every day, drinking nectar. That's what she is doing now. God made her so, she can't help it. But she has brains too, so she know what she doing. All Trinidadian women have brains; they know good good how to trick we poor fellas.'

'Maybe the humming-bird has learnt from Trinidadian women, eh Mr Ramkisoon?'

'Like you beginning to understand this place. You talking good sense, yu know. But let me tell you this, you see that little bird, that bird has more brains than any other bird.'

'You mean its brain is large relative to its size?'

'Well, if you put it so, I don't have trouble with that.'

'I wish I were like that humming-bird…'

'I wouldn't wish that if I were you.'

'No? Why Mr Ramkisoon?'

'Because you not fat. Any good wind could blow you over like a leaf, man.'

'Thank you, Mr Ramkisoon. You're very helpful at encouraging people to think clearly. I must go in now.'

'Anytime Miss. I like to help out people; it is my nature.'

Back in the house, she phoned Ishani.

'So good to hear your voice again, Anjali. How was the flight?'

'Very comfortable, thank you Aunty. You're far too good to me.'

'Nonsense! Travel is hard on the system, so travelling in relative comfort helps; now you must rest for the day, Anjali.'

'I would like to visit Palli and Lily.'

'Good idea, ask Jacob to take you. Tell him to call back for you in two hours, that gives you time to catch up with the old folks. It is nice that you're thinking of visiting them. They'll be overjoyed to see you. You know they've moved over to St Augustine; Jacob knows. They're closer to us now.'

'Yes they told us when we were leaving. And, Aunt Ishani, I also need to make arrangements to meet the managers and workers at the citrus groves and the factory. The earlier the better for me. I have a lot to get through.'

'So my sister and brother-in-law informed me. They want you to gather all you can. You have the telephone numbers of these people?'

'Yes Aunty.'

'Well make the appointments, and give them to me; I'll speak to Jacob.'

'You're an angel.'

'On rare occasions, I do feel my wings opening out.'

Anjali entered the grounds with their high walls of green foliage and walked the path to Lily's and Palli's cottage in St Augustine. Everything was still, including the two hanging baskets of geraniums on each side of the front door. What a contrast to the noisy, vibrant school in Penal. Now that she was here, what would she say, how would she say it? With true friends, you say it all.

Even as she approached the front door, the mask she had worn at home suddenly slipped. She felt weak, feared her legs would give way. When she knocked, it was Lily who came: 'Anjali Vidhur, are you really here? What a delightful Christmas present! Come, come in, you're all mine. Palli has gone out for the day. Boy, she will be sorry.' Lily's warm embrace, her soothing hands caressing her back, released her anguish. Sobs rose to her throat. Her lips trembled. 'Help me, Lily. Help me. I was raped. I'm pregnant. I can't go on. No one knows. Only you.'

'Dear, dear now, my dear girl. My brave Anjali. You're a brave soul. I'll help you. Palli will help you. How far gone?'

'A month.'

'How long are you here for?'

'Two weeks, but it would be nice to get this over soon. Is it possible maybe within a few days?'

'It's not easy, but we'll put you right. I promise that when you get on that return flight to London you'll be as you should be.'

'You're so good, Lily. I thought of you and Palli and this gave me

181

the strength I needed. I didn't want to tell my parents just yet, nor Aunt Ishani. You told our class you were once a nurse.'

'I understand.'

'How will you go about it?'

'Yes. I am a registered nurse; I would have been able to do it, but I don't have the appropriate instruments. Palli knows a good doctor. He works in a private clinic, not far from here. Leave the arrangements to us. I need time to think through everything. We'll have to work out how to ensure absolute anonymity; we have to be cautious. Everybody knows your aunt, and I'd be surprised if she doesn't have enemies – successful people do. Envy you see. This is a small society. People don't mind their own business. Other people's business is more tantalising. But I'd be there with you throughout. It doesn't take long, and we'd bring you back here to rest for a while and take you back.'

'Yes. Then Jacob could call for me. When can it be?'

'When Palli returns tonight, I shall explain all; she'll contact the doctor. He is a nice fella and will want to help her. Some tea is called for and my coconut drops, the best in the land.'

'I know that, Lily… I want to tell you what happened.'

'Only if it would help you.'

During the telling she broke down several times; only Lily's embrace gave Anjali back her voice. Telling of the event, as if she were its observer, began to detach her struggling self from its power.

They sat in silence. Lily's rocking chair hummed an old tune; the clock ticked. Then Lily stopped the rocker: 'When it is all arranged, we will phone you. The code will be: *Palli wants to see you, it's urgent.*'

'Thank you, Lily.'

To fill the time before Jacob's arrival, they talked about the students they both knew, the problems of women in male-dominated cultures.

'You can see the social changes we wished to bring about by comparing the photographs in these two albums,' Lily said. 'This is when we started. Look at their postures; they are tense, held in, waiting for something to happen to them; observe the plain, simple dresses, no individuality here; the girls are withdrawn, fearful, ever watchful of fathers, elder brothers, uncles, not wishing to court disapproval. Now this is the latest album. See, the difference is stark. The girls are posing, they've decided how they want to be seen, they know how to communicate with the camera; they are thrusting forward with self-confidence.'

The albums had captured two distinct worlds. Anjali looked again at a photograph of their first students. Amira was sitting in the front row, smiling. So young, slim, quietly composed, sure even then of what was important, with such attractive eyes. She must have been fun to be with, no wonder Daddy married her. She was so different now. What had happened to those curious, engaging, eager eyes? Now they were gentle, softer, motherly looking. Time, marriage, a husband and the three of them, and everything to do with the house, garden, their education and Daddy's welfare had reshaped her face, her eyes, her body. Anjali felt disquiet at the nature of life's course.

They heard Jacob's walk along the gravel path.

Lily waved as the car began to move slowly away.

Jacob shouted, 'Thank you for the coconut drops.'

Anjali waved, her eyes glistening.

34

THE ARRANGEMENT

Palli and Lily put their heads together. There were long silences. They would stare through the windows, absolutely still while their brains ticked-tocked. Occasionally a thought would burst out of its confines – recognised as 'talking loudly to oneself'.

Two teapots of Red Rose tea consumed, cups washed, Lily rocked in the cane chair her mother had used when there were problems that needed to be rocked away. Palli was in her father's soft, wrinkled leather chair.

At last a plan: Palli would contact Dr Mahesh and explain to him that a young woman had been raped; they needed him to save her from a life of communal shame and dishonour not of her making. He would understand the necessity for concealment and discretion, because compassion towards women was not yet part of the attitudes of many who loved God and honoured men. His assistance would be an act of mercy. Urgency dictated that it be a private job, done out of surgery hours. They'd chosen him because they couldn't think of anyone else as reliable and trustworthy. Palli would explain how the act happened, offering just enough information for him to see that her tutor had abused the power of his office, the trust of his student.

'That sounds about right, Palli. After the operation, I'll bring her back here to recuperate.'

'Imagine, Lily, keeping such a mountain of pain within you, eh, hidden from the world, knowing how the world is.'

'Sheer stamina, Palli. There is no other way to describe it… She's aware of the big big difference between what people say to your face and what they really think, oui. And she came to us.'

'That is trust… But should we inform Dr Mahesh who it is before the day?'

'There's no need, Palli, though he can be trusted completely.'

'I can vouch he'll not tell anyone, Lily, not even his mother… But should we tell her who the doctor is?'

'I don't see any harm in that.'

'Mmmm, it might be better if she doesn't know; it might make her self-conscious if she has to meet him here again.'

'Agreed.'

The following morning, Palli phoned Dr Mahesh at home. As the phone rang, she wondered what to say if his mother answered. She wanted to contact him before he left for work, fearful that there a secretary would be listening in to what was being said. But it was he who answered. He listened carefully. This unfortunate undergraduate was one of her former pupils. The young woman had not informed her parents nor reported the case to the university. Apart from Lily and herself, no one knew of her predicament.

He knew that what Palli was telling him had to be true and he was willing to do what she asked. But, it was not something he wished to be public knowledge; the managers of the clinic would not wish to be associated with it. If those with strong, even fanatical views to the contrary got a whiff of it they might even threaten the existence of the clinic. He had to tread with care.

While Palli waited, her ear was alert to the waves of silence. *If he says no, that he can't do it and recommends someone else, what should I say? I'd have to confide in someone I didn't know...* This possibility had not occurred to her. She heard the rustle of pages.

He was checking his diary carefully; he knew there was little space, but the combination of a request from Palli and the circumstance of that poor girl demanded that it be done. 'You did say it was about a month?'

'Yes. That's right.'

'It would have to be in the private clinic in St Joseph.'

There was another pause. 'If it needs to be done this week, the only time I can just about manage is... let me see... yes, tomorrow at 8 p.m. After that, it would have to be a fortnight later.'

'Tomorrow is right for us.'

'Good. Be there precisely at 8 p.m. I can't keep the non-medical staff hanging around, waiting for us to leave the premises. We mustn't do anything to attract attention, Ajee Palli.'

Then they had to devise a plan to ensure that Anjali could fit into this schedule. They waited for Ishani to leave for work, then Lily alerted Anjali that she would be phoning her about 7 p.m. the following day with the agreed coded message. This would give them ample time for Lily to drive her down to St Joseph.

The following morning, Anjali tried her best to appear as relaxed as she could, though thoughts of snags would not go away. What if Ishani wanted to speak to Palli to find out what it was about? Then, just as Ishani was about to leave for work, she told Anjali that the

Maheshs had just accepted her dinner invitation. Their son Praveen, whom she had met on the lower terrace, or rather had fallen upon, would be there.

'What time are they invited for, Aunty?'

'Six o'clock, but probably around six-thirty. You look worried, is something the matter?'

'Nothing at all. It's just that, well I can't help thinking it's not fair to you. Can it be managed at such short notice? Isn't it somewhat late to let you know? It's common courtesy, surely, to accept earlier. You should postpone it. They're taking advantage of you.'

'Don't concern yourself, Anjali. You take things too much to heart. Everything in the kitchen's been seen to and I've asked my hairdresser to pass by and arrange that beautiful silky hair of yours. Late acceptances happen all the time here. Don't come to the store with me this morning; enjoy the garden, have a swim in the pool. Relax. For your age, you worry far too much. You should go to yoga classes. Something must be worrying you. I hope it's not your final exams. Just keep a level head, Anjali, because you'll need your health to be able to give your best. Remember, if you want to discuss anything that's troubling you, I feel like a mother to you and I'm a good listener. Whatever you share with me will go no further…'

'Thank you so much, Aunty, I feel better now.'

'One thing I should say; you should call the Maheshs Aunty and Uncle; you may prefer Mrs Mahesh and Mr Mahesh, but for us here, it comes across a bit too uppish, too formal.'

Oh God, what do I do? Lily and Palli are trying to help me and now this. What do I say to them? Aunt Ishani should not have friends like the Maheshs.

As soon as Ishani's car left the drive, Anjali phoned Lily and Palli and told them about the problem. How could she now leave at 7 p.m? The Maheshs were her aunty's good friends and were really being invited to meet her. She felt terrible. Aunty had gone all out to make the evening special for her. She didn't know what to do. Could another day be arranged? Tears came and with it a pain in her throat, emptiness in her stomach.

Silence. 'Let me come back to you, Anjali; the situation is not as bad as it looks. I will find a way round it. Don't cry, dear, we're together in this. You, Lily and I will overcome this. You're not alone. I'll phone you back after we've worked out something. Just needs some calm thinking. Are you going out today?'

'No, Palli. I'll be here all the time. Thank you so much. Please thank Lily for me.'

'What has happened?'

'Please Lily, just let me sit down. Don't rush me. It's a lot to sort out. Two things, Lily; first things first. She knows Praveen or will know him and he will know her by the evening. Second, Praveen and his parents have been invited to dinner tonight by Ishani.'

'You think Ishani is trying to arrange something?'

'Think? I know it and you know it too, Lily. Ishani is a first-class woman. If she sees a good thing, she won't wait for it to come to her, not she; no she would just purchase an airline ticket and go out and get it. But now this, Lily – this.'

'Good God! Whatever next is going to come our way. I hope God realises we're not Job.'

'Anjali asked if another day can be arranged. We know the answer to that, and her health has taken a battering for too long.'

Palli clapped her hands, a mannerism she'd picked up from Lily to signify she was about to run with the problem. 'Alright, now where do we start? Let's try and sort it out bit by bit. This problem of recognition; they know each other.'

'I think, Palli, it's preferable that she does not recognise him.'

'Well how to bring that one about is going to be something, I tell you.'

'Leave that to me. I have those eye masks; I shall give her one to wear.'

'But when you're giving her, what will you tell her?'

'I shall think of something, Palli. Look here, we don't have to think through every detail this very minute. Let's get the big thing sorted out first. We're both on edge here.'

'That is true, Lily. I'm sorry.'

'Not to worry. It's age, man, age all the way. And sister, we feeling the heat… Now where did we reach?'

'He would recognise her; there's nothing we can do about that.'

'I really wish it wasn't so.'

'Me too. Especially seeing that Ishani is trying to bring them together.'

'If Anjali had confided in Ishani and not us, I don't think she would have asked Dr Mahesh to perform the operation.'

'No way. We wouldn't have asked him either if we knew how Ishani was thinking. A matter of delicacy.'

'Whew! Don't I know? Who would wish their first intimate encounter to be like this, eh?'

'And if she doesn't know the doctor, while he knows her, how lopsided that relationship would be in the future.'

'But we just can't help it. We can't do any better.'

'We just have to hope that he appreciates she's a victim of circumstance and not hold even a whiff of old-fashioned male thinking.'

'If he does, then he or anyone who thinks like that is not worthy of her.'

'I agree wholeheartedly… But how to get her to leave the party?'

'That's not going to be easy; it means getting her to come here without the guests feeling offended. What can we say?'

'I don't have a clue; but that is only the half of it: how to prevent that clear-thinking aunt of hers asking too many questions?'

'Then coming up with something that would stop her from leaving…'

'I can't see a way out of that one, oui,' Lily said.

Silence.

'Look we have to get serious about this.'

'Come to think of it, there is only one way out of it, Palli.'

'Which way is that?'

'Close off all the likely questions from Ishani at the very start.'

'Close off? How can we do that? Don't ever underestimate that woman; she's sharp as they come. But I know what you mean; I have to give it to you it's casting a light on how we must move.'

'Light? It reminds me of what we're up against. It means the reason we choose to have her come here has to be so good that it stops Ishani's questions in their tracks, so the only response open to her must be to allow Anjali to come… Everybody at the party must see that too, Palli.'

One woman held her head with both hands staring, thinking. The other paced the kitchen floor.

'You know, Lily, sometimes the answer staring you in the face.'

'Palli, if the answer stopped staring at us and spoke out, it would help.'

'Look here,' Lily said, 'we'd better take hold of ourselves or everything will fall apart. Try and keep calm, Palli.'

I wonder who is not keeping calm.

A cup of Lipton's tea helped them to relax. Then Palli burst out, 'Oh my God, we have to change the code for sure.'

'Yes, we don't want Praveen or Ishani, god forbid, calling on you to find out what ails you, Palli.'

'I have a lot of things wrong with me, to choose one wouldn't be a challenge, dear.'

'Let's be serious, Palli.'

'Lily, Dr Mahesh will have to leave the dinner party by 7.30 at the latest to get to the clinic in St Joseph. Is that right?'

'Yes, and she will have to leave at the same time, which is cutting everything too close.'

'The car has petrol?'

'Yes, I filled it up this morning when I went to the market. Now the code, Palli, the code has to be something that will not encourage him to call in, just in case he is asked to drop her off. It has to be something that causes no anxiety to the others, yet is urgent enough for her to leave before 7.30.'

'The more I look at it, the more I see there's no way out.'

'Your mother and mine would have come up with something. There are lots of ideas out there, floating about. It's a matter of catching the right one.'

'Yes, yes.'

Nothing comes. The silence is empty.

'We can't leave it. Just think of what could happen if we do nothing. Think of her state of mind.'

Silence.

The minute hand moved; the branches outside were still. A duck plopped into the pond, paddled and dipped for a fish. The sounds of a passing truck crashing gears came over the wall. A tom cat chased through the school yard.

Slowly, almost as if in sleep, Palli moves towards Lily.

'Let me try this out on you. Tell me what you think; it is based on something someone told me when we were in Canada. One of our former students made a late application to where Anjali is – the university in North London – to read what she is reading. She has been offered a place there. She wants to know whether she should accept it, or wait to attend the London School of Economics, where she has also been offered a place, but in a year's time. The student wants to speak to Anjali urgently as she has to let the Registrar's office know by phone. She is only being offered a place because someone has not taken up theirs. She wants to meet Anjali to discuss this tonight, wants to know what she thinks of the course at King's.'

'Anjali had the choice of either university and chose King's, so she's well equipped to assist.'

'That looks really good to me. It rings true, too. But we have to fill it out a bit, Palli – make it Ishani-proof.'

'How?'

'Something like: the young woman is from a disadvantaged home. Think of her name, where she lives etc. Only one thing, Palli, you will have to make the call. The message needs to be: "Your advice to a student is urgently needed. She is here with her family. They very much want to discuss the matter with you."'

'Why the family bit?'

'To avoid Ishani thinking why doesn't Anjali speak on the phone, or why does Anjali have to come here, when the student should be coming over to Anjali. Don't you see?'

'I get it.'

'Very good Lily, very good. I'll speak to Anjali and explain. It will bring her comfort; she needs it I tell you.'

'Remember no codes. We'll simply phone; she'll be expecting the request.'

Dr Mahesh knew he would have to excuse himself by half past seven in order to meet his appointment with Lily at the clinic. The medical staff left by 7.30 p.m. and the non-medical staff put the lights out at 9 p.m. He had to fit in the operation between 8 p.m. and 8.20 p.m, and leave the building by 8.30, to prevent the arousal of suspicion. He imagined the gossip:

Did you hear about that young doctor?

No. What?

Well, it was after hours, child. At some late hour, he took part in you know what…

The word is mouthed.

Unbelievable. That sort of thing is not allowed in this clinic you know.

Surely he knows the rules… In a thousand years I would never have guessed. He looks so nice. It just shows you, doesn't it?

I wonder if they will give him the sack.

These days, my dear, is who you know.

It was always so, dear.

You think he was responsible for the situation and trying to put it right?

That is none of my business.

You know what doctors are like?

Don't we?

Laughter and chuckling along the corridor.

Praveen had seen something, not dissimilar, played out before. His colleague survived – just.

Would he be able to handle the whisperings? He had always played by the rules, never had to face the disapproval of authority. He would be out of his depth, for what could he say in self-defence? But thoughts about the victim and her aged helpers wouldn't leave him. Yes, he had to be prepared to face the consequences of what he believed was right. It was time to take a stand on things, to work on who he was. Time, too, to have a place of his own. His mother wanted to know more about his work, be involved in his decision making. They were loving parents, and he knew he ought to be more interested in their affairs – but his hands were full. Now he was looking forward to meeting the Mitas and their niece; it would be a rare moment of pleasure in a very full day.

35

THE DINNER PARTY

The tangled web of the day was before her; the fear that it could unravel never left her. There was the new problem: if the Maheshs were very late, how could she possibly leave in the middle of a dinner party that was really being held for her? Her hands trembled as she dressed. Half an hour later, from the greetings that drifted up the stairs, she recognised that they were here. At least they were early.

She thought of what her father had said: *Your aunt Ishani has given a lot of thought and care to your welfare.* Yes. She must make an effort, engage with the guests, show her aunt how much she appreciated what she was doing. She mustn't give the impression she was affected, aloof, unfriendly, especially to older people meeting her for the first time.

She smiled at her reflection on the mirror. A three-quarter length, black 'A' line skirt with a rich lace flounce, a light green, round-neck blouse, its soft three-quarter sleeves stylish with covered buttons.

Ravi and Ishani went out to meet their guests, who had arrived in separate cars.

'So the young doctor,' Ravi said, 'does not travel with his parents?'

Savita frowned; Hemkish, said, 'A doctor has no life of his own these days. Praveen is permanently on call. I told him he has to know when to say no.'

Savita said, 'Don't worry with Haim; Praveen is doing the right thing. He has to build up his practice; he's young. Of course it's hard; life is hard work. Tell me one worthy thing that's easy.'

'I agree with Savita,' said Ishani.

When Anjali came out to join them Ishani said, 'You remember my sister, Amira? This is her eldest daughter, Anjali. The family is living in London now.'

An evening raga flowed from the garden where dusk had given way to night, mountain breezes brought coolness and the play of the fountain drowned the rounds of croaking frogs.

'We thought it would be nice to sit out on the verandah, counting the stars,' Ishani said smiling. 'Ravi likes to be close to the warmth of the barbecue. He often stands here you know. Do you know what he tells me?… He tells me that by being quite still, you can tell from the sound alone the fullness of a dew drop and the speed of its fall…'

'How can you do that? I don't believe it,' Savita said.

'The man is becoming a poet,' Haim announced. 'Now *that* is dangerous. Business and poetry don't mix.'

'No, no, not at all, Haim.' Ravi's face was lit with good feeling. 'The one offers the people what they are asking for; the other opens the door to what they need.'

'Bravo! Well, how can I fault that? Especially when I decide which statement refers to business.'

Their laughter travelled far in the stillness of the night. 'I will say this,' Haim added, 'you wriggled out of it well. For a minute there, I thought I had you in a corner.'

Savita got up, looking at the overhanging clematis, searching for something. 'You have a flower with a beautiful scent. It's reaching me. What is it, Ishani?'

'Oh, that's easy; it's my special cologne. Floral and all that.' Ravi opened his eyes wide, smiling, coaxing the guests to join his light-hearted mood.

Ishani turned to Savita, 'I know what you mean; it comes in bursts doesn't it? It's lady of the night. I also have a few highly perfumed roses, and a patch of lavender. I'll let you into a secret, Savita, I have a mint, too, that dances in the night and throws its aroma to the air.'

Savita had not seen her hostess in so light-hearted a mood.

'For some time now I've noticed,' Anjali added, 'that the scents in the tropics are so ripe and heady, compared to those in cooler places. There's the ylang-ylang. The tropical marigolds, too, have a lovely scent.'

Silence.

Praveen said, 'Now that you've mentioned it, I realise how much we take for granted.'

Ravi agreed and said he might consider wearing a mala of marigolds to the office. His remark was ignored by the others, except Praveen and Anjali who looked at each other and smiled.

She took the tray from her aunt, and offered around pieces of warm crumbly fish together with a mix of hot and sweet flavours, topped with diced cucumbers, and a home-made tartare sauce with crushed mint leaves, both in small clay pots. Not long after Jenny tinkled a silver bell to call them to dinner. Ishani left nothing to chance; Anjali was placed between Savita and Praveen.

Hot bowls of freshly cracked crab meat, ochroes, herbs and pureed lentils in coconut milk were brought in red and white bowls, served with bread that was still warm from the oven.

193

Ravi and Hemkish settled to emptying their bowls and talking about Caribbean politics and the world of business. Ishani smiled and nodded to Jacob as if they were conspirators who had planned the outcome of the evening. He was dressed in a long flamboyant hat, a matching scarf and a lily-white apron over a chef's coat. The barbecued chicken was ready; it had been bathed in olive oil, a touch of maple syrup, orange jelly, fresh garden herbs and crimson-red sweet peppers with a dash of home-made pepper sauce, a combination that was his speciality. Being appreciated made him smile with pleasure. He called and the guests formed a queue with their plates, save Savita. For her, basmati rice, string beans, spinach, aubergine, dhal and fried puris had been made, because she preferred a vegetarian meal. They ate in silence for a while, with the soft beat of the raga delighting their ears, the burst of floral scent their noses. Desert was a ras malai, served with a generous sprinkling of pistachio nuts. Everyone had Darjeeling tea.

Praveen turned the face of his wrist-watch towards him under the table. Anjali noted to her embarrassment that her right foot was tapping the floor as if impatient to rise. She too looked at her watch and almost jumped when Savita's bold voice struck her.

'Can you cook?'

Before she could reply, Ishani said, 'She is one of Palli and Lily's former students.'

'Oh,' said Savita, eyebrows raised, 'then you've been here before?'

'Yes. I grew up here, left when I was ten. I enjoy cooking. I learnt much from Lily and Palli. Mummy showed me how she does a few things too and I experiment in the kitchen at home.'

'Anjali learns quickly; within a few days she knew where things are in the store.'

'So you go to the store too.'

'I like the store; I meet people I wouldn't normally meet. I've learnt why business people have to be aware all the time of what is happening in the world outside. Trying to keep up with changing tastes and styles must be a nightmare.'

'True. Business is not easy; that's why its name is busy-ness. Business makes the world tick.'

'Maybe if there was more of it everywhere, if all countries were involved in fair trade, there would be fewer wars.'

'There would only be fewer wars, Anjali, if it suited the powerful. You stay in a hall? Praveen had to because, look where we are.'

'I stay in a hall. I think it's part of growing up.'

'Hall is expensive for parents. I think that good home-cooking and all the comforts of family are better than a hall. You can decide to grow up anytime, really.'

'Young people need to be on their own, Aunty; it's the only way they'll learn to do things for themselves.'

'When you're on your own, Ma,' Praveen said, 'you appreciate more than ever what good parents you have.'

'Aunty Ishani tells me you've travelled to many places. I'm sure you've visited London.'

'Visited London? I can't count how many times we've been there, especially when Praveen was there. Ask Haim. Praveen used to say, "Mummy, come in the summer." Summer? It's not like a Canadian summer. I find the breeze cold in the mornings and in the evenings too. If you're not careful you can get a bad chill in summer in London.'

'It's true. That's one constant about our weather – change; it keeps us on our toes.'

'It may be fun to be on your toes all day, if you're young, but at my age, I want reliable weather. I want to know what to wear. England is for young people.'

Savita's eyes were focused intently on Anjali. 'But let's hear a little bit about you. What you're studying.'

'I am trying to understand the nature of development. I'm hoping to have a better understanding of why some countries are poor and others not.'

'Do you like the course?'

'I am learning a great deal.'

'Look here, Haim knows why countries are poor; you must ask him before you go back to London. I can help you right now. It's not something you need books for. All you have to do is to look around; this tells you more about the country than books. Poor countries don't have good managers. Managing is not easy; most people don't know head or tail about it. Give these politicians a business to run and before you know it, everything would go bust. Haim believes government does not understand the meaning of the saying: there are no free lunches. They tell you that at the university?'

'What you say is true.'

'I know. I live here.'

'Governing a country well, Aunty, is the most difficult thing I can think of. However, what we expect is large…'

'It may be large,' Hemkish interrupted, 'but the ordinary man in the street here sees ordinary chaps of other countries enjoying heaven, while he can't climb out of the hole the government helped him dig.'

Anjali smiled.

'Anjali is taking it all in, Pa,' said Praveen.

'Look here, there's no need to beat around the bush, Anjali; the culture that creates poverty says to the man in the street, if you're clever in the way you steal, you can have anything. If you're caught; it's who you know that matters. Not qualifications, not developing yourself; it's far more lucrative to attach yourself to the boss, the big chief, the ruling party. That, Anjali, is the long and short of the cause of poverty and misery in a nutshell.'

'There's a lot of truth in what you say, Uncle, but is it the whole picture?'

'Okay. Let's hear what the university's take on this is?'

'Universities tend to have more than one view on any issue you can think of, even on a matter that appears straightforward…'

'Typical. And you know why? They have nothing to lose; they can say anything. Unlike a businessman, their income is not tied to coming up with a plan that delivers the goods.'

'Haim,' Ravi called out, 'give the young lady a chance.'

'In view of what's been said,' Anjali resumed, 'I'll offer my own thinking on development, not the university's… Have some more tea.' As she got up she glanced at her watch, hoping that serving more tea might bring the evening closer to its end.

'Is that it?' Everyone laughed. 'Just by drinking more tea eh? That is England for you.'

Praveen glanced at his watch again and said, 'We're all waiting.'

'Now, don't rush my niece, give her space,' Ravi said. 'She's a bright girl, so listen carefully. You tell them, Anjali. Don't hold back. Self-made people, especially when they're successful, tend to think the university has nothing to teach them. So go ahead, take your time.'

'Development should equip people with the information and skills they need to make real choices, so governments need to invest in good schools, technical colleges; there have to be good roads and railways too, so people can travel to find better opportunities for themselves. And the pillars of democracy – the media, the civil service, parliament, the judiciary, the police force – have to be functioning with integrity and within the rule of law. Now that's not easy. Just think how difficult it is to have all these functioning well even in old democracies, still less fledgling ones, with no precedent to go by. This is so important because these institutions are there to ensure that power and privilege are exercised within the framework of the law. Unaccountable power makes mincemeat of the weak, the vulnerable, the powerless.' Her voice softened, her eyes glistened, she smiled nervously.

'Anjali's been working very hard,' said Ishani, 'it's her final year.'

'I'm not at all surprised that she feels strongly about unaccountable power; her father does too,' said Ravi.

'My sister too; it runs in the family.'

'I just wanted to stress that good governance is very difficult to establish, Uncle. It is not just the influence of the powerful that it has to do battle with. There are those primeval bonds that helped us to survive, that existed long before the concept of democracy was born; they are so much a part of us that we call them natural feelings. They will rise up if threatened and happily suffocate the rule of law. For example, if you happen to know that your son steals valuable instruments from hospitals, despite his denial, do you report him? If a close friend of yours is a poor teacher and asks you for a recommendation for a teaching post because he is unemployed, do you give him one? If it is not to be integrity in our dealings or the rule of law, then what?'

'Point taken, Anjali, so where we go from there?' asked Hemkish.

'I think there are some things we just have to keep working at.'

'Changing our commitments to old loyalties,' said Ravi, 'will not be easy. I wonder if it can be done.'

'Yes,' said Praveen. 'Anjali's examples show how difficult it is to get people to change their way of seeing and feeling about things.'

'I hope the old thinking of family first never leaves us, Praveen,' said Savita. 'That would be terrible. Imagine a world where our culture, long, close friendship and family ties have no influence.'

'I agree with, Savita,' said Ishani; 'it would be a cold, bleak place. It would mean we've become another kind of being. Our loyalties, our natural feelings define us.'

'Your father understands the world as it operates out there, Praveen. It's the real world we are talking about, not idealism.'

'That's true, Ma.'

'Aunty, you've brought into the open a very important considera-tion,' said Anjali. 'It shows how difficult it is to implement the rule of law. Would anyone like some more tea?'

'We have a very attentive hostess here,' said Hemkish.

The hush that followed was discomforting; suddenly through the stillness the metallic ringing of the telephone. Anjali jumped.

'Excuse me, Anjali,' said Jenny, her cheeks warm from the kitchen, 'Palli is on the phone to you.' When she left the room, Praveen said,

'I'm sorry I have to leave now; it has been a super evening. Uncle Ravi, you and Aunty Ishani are the perfect hosts. I did explain this to Mummy and Daddy, hence the two cars and our early arrival.'

'Oh ho! I see. A night out, eh?'

Anjali returned and said to Ishani in a whisper that it was Palli on the phone. One of their former students needed some urgent advice that she was well placed to offer. The girl had to make a choice between places offered and wanted to contact the university registration office that night; she was there with her entire family, brothers, sisters, parents and uncles and their wives.

Ishani thought this was all too neat. Instinct told her, though, that she should *let some things be.* So she did not press further, despite her aroused curiosity. Instead, as Praveen rose from his chair, she moved quickly, explaining to Savita and Hemkish why Anjali also had to leave.

Savita also wondered whether this had been planned, though she was sure that no one but she and Haim were aware of Praveen's plans. 'Who is this girl to request such a big favour from Anjali at this hour? How can she do that? She does not know Anjali. She is the one who should be coming here, not Anjali there. Let's have a good look at her. She does not even know that when you're asking a favour, you should make it easy for the person giving it. Do you know the family, Ishani? Not nice behaviour at all I must say.'

'You're right, Savita, she does not know Anjali. But you know Palli and Lily, they will help anyone who comes to them with a problem; their former students know this, often these young people have no one else to turn to, so they go to them. Not everyone is as fortunate as Anjali, who has her parents and us. Of course it would have been far better for her to come here.'

'Yes. I agree. Wait! Anjali, you are far too good natured. Just let me speak to the girl.'

Suddenly Anjali looked despondent, burdened, strained. Something was gnawing the child, Ishani said to herself. She must allow her to go.

'Savita, leave it like that; to have the whole family here would spoil our quiet evening together. Jenny is about to close her kitchen. I would prefer to have the rest of the evening to ourselves.'

'To our older wiser selves,' added Hemkish.

'I shall drink to that,' Ravi said.

'I'm sorry I have to go now, Aunty,' Anjali said to Savita, 'especially as I was enjoying the evening so much. It was good to meet you and Uncle.'

She took her leave of everyone and went to her bedroom.

Ishani said to Praveen, 'Jacob could drop her, but he's had a long day and is having a nap; would you mind taking Anjali? He'll be calling for her later.'

The two young people took their leave.

Savita and Ishani noted that Anjali was carrying a largish bag as she descended the steps.

When the car had gone, Ishani said, 'It's only half past seven, the night is inviting; let's have something a little stronger in the verandah. What about a little of your favourite, Haim; I promise just two sips. I know you're driving. It would be nice to round off the evening with a little fire in our bellies.'

'Let's drink to the good health we enjoy,' Ravi said, 'to the happiness we have been blessed with and to our caring spouses.'

36

THE HUMAN SPIRIT I

There was something seductive about a car that smelled new, moved in the mountain cool of the night as if it were airborne; something reassuring about an amiable, attentive young man at the wheel. Even so, Anjali's anxieties did not leave; she was only too aware that her cover was fragile and any pointed question could pierce it.

Praveen sensed her unease. 'You alright?'

'Yes. I'm fine.'

'Not worried about anything are you?'

'No, I'm Okay.' She laughed. 'Am I looking unwell?'

He smiled. 'A little tense.'

'I'm forgetting how to relax, that's it really. Do you know Lily and Palli? You know where they live?'

'Yes, I knew them when they had the school in Penal, sometime ago. I'll drop you at the right place, don't worry.'

'Did you attend the school?'

'No! I don't know if they would have had me.'

'I'm sure they would have.'

'I had the impression that it was only for young women. Your Aunt Ishani said you were there. How did you find it, I mean coming from London to a school here, deep in the country?'

'They not only taught us good cooking practices, but also how to cope with life.'

'Maybe that's why past students come to them when they need help. I think they're going to be busy tonight, coping with the anxieties of a whole family.'

'Yes, they're all there. When we were leaving school, they told us that if we had a problem they would always be there.'

'Well, I doubt whether you'll need their help; not everyone has the back-up of such a caring, prudent family as yours… Do you know the girl?'

'No. I don't think I was given a name.'

'I guess you haven't had much time to think about it.'

'True. I'm a bit nervous because I don't know what is expected of me.'

'I understand.'

'In a way we have much in common tonight.'

'In what way?'

'We are both going to help someone at about the same time on the same day.'

'A coincidence!'

'Oh I didn't really answer your question about how I found the school. I vividly recall the pots and pans, polished clean, like mirrors. Everything was on open wooden shelves, almost nothing in cupboards. Saves time and you can go directly to what you want. Today, everything is hidden from the eye. There were scrubbed wooden floors and a chulha which was lit occasionally on a cold, rainy day to warm us all up, as well as to show us the thinking of the past. Don't get me wrong, we had cookers and a refrigerator, but we were being reminded that we are part of an unfolding tale.'

The quiet hum of the engine stirred the silence. The road before them was clear.

'How are your sisters? I often recall our first meeting; it was the best unconventional meeting I'm ever likely to have. I remember what they said to me. How are they?'

'Oh! That day was embarrassing. I must have been knocked out for a moment and dizzy for quite some time.'

'It was an accident.'

'My sisters are well, thank you, and better behaved. Do you come up to London?'

'Yes, from time to time, on a refresher course.'

'Well if you ever feel like a nice meal, I know a restaurant which you'd like. It's not far from Marble Arch; just behind Oxford Street.'

'May I have your telephone number, Anjali?'

'I don't have pen or paper with me.'

'Here, have one of my cards; write it on the back. And yes, let me give you another.'

'Do you have many friends in London, Praveen?'

'Not really. I was never a keen partygoer. I knew my course was costing my parents the earth, the exchange rate being what it was; I wanted to be worthy of them, so I buckled down to becoming a good doctor. I also want to give my patients the best treatment available, which is why I try to keep up to date.'

'That is commendable. Thank you, Praveen, here I am. It has been a good night meeting you and your parents.'

'I enjoyed it. We should meet more often.'

'Yes, I'd like that.'

'Don't be too anxious. Just give your best.'

'Thank you, Praveen, you're nice to be with.'

'Pay attention, concentrate, stop dreaming, I was told over and over again from my kindergarten days. Anjali, it is especially difficult when I'm with you. What should I do?'

'Try harder. That's what my kindergarten teacher would say.'

He beamed a contagious smile and flashed the headlights; she waved him on, but he waited for the gate to close behind her, looked at his wrist-watch and drove on; it would be a close thing for him that night. So those elderly ladies were taking on two problems in one night. He'd have to speak to them; it was just too much of a stress and strain at their age.

She ran all the way to the front door.

37

THE HUMAN SPIRIT II

'Oh my dear, you do look lovely,' Lily said, ready to leave in her nurse's uniform.

'I know we're running late. I won't be long. It took a little time to make my exit. I have a change of clothes in this bag.'

When she returned from the bedroom, Anjali was wearing a skirt and blouse, and soft leather sandals.

'You'll be putting your finery back on when we return I assume.' She nodded.

'Now just check everything, Lily,' Palli said softly. 'See you have everything you need.' She kissed Anjali. 'It will soon be over. Remember Lily is a registered nurse; you're in the best hands.' She stroked her arm as she said this in blessing and reassurance.

When they arrived at the clinic, Lily could see Praveen standing at the entrance. Her heart raced as she pulled up the hand brake. It was 8.05 p.m.

'Wait here, Anjali; I just want to check out something, I'll be back in a minute.'

She hurried up the steps to the clinic's entrance. 'I'm so sorry to be late.'

'Where is she?'

'I'll bring her in now. Could you go up and don your cap, gloves, face mask and so on. I don't want her to recognise you. If you need to speak to me, whisper, or better still, use sign language. It will save her embarrassment if she meets you again.'

'Okay, Lily, but hurry; we're running too close to exit time. Take the lift; get off at the second floor. We'll have to leave very soon.'

'I understand. Thank you,' she whispered, wiping her brow.

As Lily and Anjali walked to the lift, one of the cleaners saw them. 'But eh! Eh! Look at this. Eh! Eh! How come that door open. Good night, ladies. You know the hospital closed. You shouldn't be here.' She raised her voice: 'You're not supposed to be in here. You know that? You have to leave. I can't allow this at all, at all; it's against regulations.' The angle of her mop looked more like a lance. 'No one on duty at this hour. Look at the time. Look at the time.' She pointed to the clock with her chin. 'As a matter of fact that door should be closed. How come it open?'

'Shhh. An accident,' Lily whispered, 'an emergency, a hit and run case; I'm a nurse.'

'Eh eh, you think I can't see that?'

'Shhh. God be praised, you're a sensible lady. You're not like some people. You're the understanding sort. We have to give and take in an emergency, sister. God bless you. I need a little help from you, a little understanding just for ten minutes; no more, I promise.'

The woman stared. The intonation, the arresting but gentle eyes, came with a reminder of fellowship. The nurse's uniform commanded respect, and the appeal to her good sense – which she always knew she had, it was just that not everybody could appreciate what she had to offer – convinced her to bend her head and continue mopping. 'This is none of my business, oui. It has nothing to do with me, oui. Nobody paying me to be watchman. I'm a cleaner. I ain't see nothing, oui. As a matter of fact, ah better hurry up and move from this area fast.'

The lift seemed to be taking its time. Then it jerked and stopped on the second floor. Facing them was the sign: OPERATING THEATRE. DO NOT ENTER. They entered.

'I want you to lie down here; that's good, now wear this eye mask Anjali. Those lights are very strong when they are on. It won't be for long. There now. How does it feel?'

'Pitch black.'

'Good. I shall be at your bedside throughout. It will soon be done.' She softly caressed her left hand.

Praveen appeared in his surgeon's gear. He took Lily aside and explained that he would be using the suction method. She rolled up Anjali's sleeves. 'The injection is both a mild sedative and an analgesic,' she said to Anjali, who nodded.

Her legs were drawn up and held by Lily, who was taken aback at the speedy effectiveness of the injection. A dilator was brought. Praveen used one, then another.

He looked at the bare arm, the covered eyes and knew. He looked at Lily for an explanation, but her back was turned to him.

When it was done, both doctor and Lily nodded. Anjali was now free of the consequences of the violent assault she had suffered.

Lily tidied up, leaving the room exactly as they had found it. She thanked Praveen. He called her into another room.

'It's Anjali. You didn't say.'

'We thought it was better that way. Don't you think? I mean under the circumstances.'

He stood there, looking thoroughly perplexed, wanting to be told again how it all happened, though Palli had informed him at the time. Lily repeated the story of broken trust and violation. 'What worries me now,' she said, 'is her emotional adjustment. The violence she suffered could so easily imprison her, affecting her attitude, even within marriage, to any intimacy. She's kept it all to herself; no member of her family knows, not even her mother or Ishani; she did not want to bring them pain. The strain within her has been enormous.'

'I wish to ask a special favour,' he said.

'What is it?'

'Under no circumstance must she know that it was I who performed the operation.'

'We would prefer that too.'

'It will take a little longer for her to recover completely,' he said, 'but since it's closing time, we must leave; I'll carry her to the car.'

As he did, her scent reached him in the cool car park and stayed with him. They strapped her in, 'Drive safely now. All will be well,' he said.

Lily wound the window down and drove slowly, humming the hymn 'Abide With Me'. The cool night breeze washed Anjali's face, coaxing her to return to consciousness.

When they arrived home, Palli hurried out to have confirmed what she had hoped for. It was all questioning eyes, nods and smiles of relief. She returned to the house, laid the table for tea and waited. Twenty minutes later, a fully conscious Anjali knew it was now all behind her.

Relieved and exhausted they sat quietly with their hot brew. After a second cup Anjali went up to change and Jacob was called to come for her. Lily reminded her of the exercises she should do daily to complete her recovery.

As they waited for Jacob, Lily was thinking that though the world had changed, people still carried their culture's sentiments. *I hope, sweet Jesus, she will choose her husband with care, not one still trapped in primeval ways of thinking. Yes there was a time, when one's hymen was tied to one's desirability, to reputation. But no longer, my dear, no longer; not today, not where you're living; nor will it concern any modern, intelligent young men fit to be your partner. The world has moved on.*

Anjali got up and embraced Lily and Palli, who wiped her eyes.

'I forgot to ask, who assisted me?'

'He is a close and dear friend of ours, a fine doctor, a warm-hearted man. You can trust him with this.'

'Does he know me?'

'No.'

'Does he know that I'm related to Aunt Ishani?'

'We explained to him that you wanted complete anonymity, and he understood. He has a younger sister and said under the circumstances, he would have wanted the same for her. You should know that he co-operated fully with us.'

'He must be a fine man. What's his name?'

'Like you, he also wished for anonymity. It will protect him.'

'Thank you, my two teachers and dear friends. I understand.'

There were more hugs and then a quick drying of tears all round, for they heard Jacob's footsteps along the path.

All the way back, Anjali was silent. Jacob drove as if the car was a cradle. He sensed she needed to be alone with herself. It had been a tiring night for him too. When they arrived, the stillness of the garden brought Anjali the memory of the tiny humming-bird working so very hard each day to refill itself with energy to survive.

Suddenly a burst of wind greeted the wind chime, hanging high on the governor-plum tree. It sang of a China long gone, of its lost world of tall upright bamboos, tundra swans and Siberian cranes, peasants in the fields, backs bent to the earth all day. Anjali listened to its tale and tears came again. As she walked up the stairs, Ishani came to meet her. 'I saw you listening to the night.'

'The night is soft and gentle.'

'Were you able to help her?'

'I told her all I knew.'

'What was her name?'

'Nagina?'

'Nagina what?'

'Maharaj.'

'Well everybody is a Maharaj today. That's one advantage to emigrating, Anjali.'

'What is, Aunty?'

'I'm not complaining, Anjali, I'm all for self-betterment, but I like to see a little more imagination at times. The monotonous Maharaj is so dull.'

'Maybe it was the best they could think of at the time.' *Whew! That was close.*

'Another time, I'm not allowing you to go anywhere this late for anybody at such a short notice. You understand?'

'Yes, Aunty.'

'It's not your fault. I hope she thanked you properly... And her family too. What were they like?'

'They wanted the best for her and asked sensible questions.'

'Well, that's good. How was Praveen? Do you like him?'

'Um, yes – he's really very nice.'

'Good.'

'We exchanged telephone numbers.'

'Good move. He asked for it?'

'Yes, Aunty.'

'Very good.'

'His parents like you. We will step carefully. People do not like to feel they are being influenced. Good night; I see you're very tired.'

'Good night, Aunty, you're my guardian angel.'

'My abode from time to time is heavenly, I grant you that.'

They hugged. Anjali cried.

'Now, now. I have no intention of going there just yet.'

Anjali smiled.

'That's my girl.'

The next morning Ishani noticed a marked change in Anjali. She seemed still, yet completely at ease, at peace. Why so? She couldn't really say, though she regularly applauded herself on her psychic powers. Maybe her niece was just starting to recover from jet lag or overwork. Whatever, she insisted that Anjali rest that day.

So Anjali walked the length and breadth of the garden, slept on a blanket in a shady alcove of jasmine, let her body knit up itself, ready to come back to life.

The next day, determined to make a start, she rose early, swam in the pool on the lower terrace, then made appointments to meet the managers of the largest citrus grove and its nearby factory. All that week she worked at getting as much information as she could. Her camera was hard at work trying to capture the fungus affecting the fruit trees, as well as the effect of copper spraying, and the severe loss of blossom when tropical downpours were at their heaviest. She already had photographs of reaping: the use of the mechanical tiller between the rows of young orange stocks; the varying stages in the processing plant from the washing, the de-oiling, the juice extractors, the finishers, the canning, closing, cooling, drying and labelling. All her film had been developed to ensure she had the desired shots. Now she photographed the effects of the windbreaks provided by the galba, pomelo and the pois-doux. She questioned the managers and workers carefully and made notes, anxious not to miss anything, aware that this was her last opportunity. On and on she worked, a new release of energy surging through her.

Ishani was convinced that it was love; she even began to suspect Anjali's tousled hair, which she had noticed on her arrival back on the night of the dinner party, but knew it should not be mentioned. It was the outcome of something; what else could it possibly be? First love has an energy special to itself, she intimated to Ravi, who said that what *he* saw was someone keen to gather as much material as she possibly could in a short time. 'Ishani, some things are so obvious they don't need deciphering. Not everything is controlled by hidden codes, or thought waves from the far beyond.'

But how did he account for her hair so loose? Had he forgotten what it was like to be young? Shame!

A week later, as Anjali was boarding the plane to London, it was the faces and voices of Lily and Palli that were with her. The day before she'd been with them, saying her goodbyes and expressing her deep appreciation of their friendship. It was then that they had shared with her the concerns they had chosen to withhold.

Later, on the flight, her thoughts were on her caring aunt. She would not dissuade Ishani from trying to bring Praveen and herself together. She needed male friends, knew she was not quite herself in male presence... and he was so easy to talk to, so amiable and empathetic.

When she was younger, she had hoped to grow up to be as good as her mother; today she felt spoilt for choice of role models. 'This is indeed a blessing to have,' an inner voice whispered, as sleep cradled her above the clouds.

38

THE YOUNG DOCTOR

Recognition had not come instantly. The barriers in his path were of his memory's making; only a short time before he had dropped her off at the gates in sophisticated clothes and shoes, had listened to her engaging arguments at dinner, her discussion of good governance. These images had stayed with him. The clothes she had worn later, fetching in their simplicity, had made her look younger, more vulnerable. Lily and Palli had told him what to expect: a young woman in distress, one who was so sensitive that she would prefer not to recognise him in future and he, her. This he understood.

Her eyes had been sheltered from his gaze and he had decided to perform the operation without consciously looking at her; even so he'd felt some troubling resemblance he could not quite place. It was after he'd administered the injection that he looked at her steadily for the first time. Before him was a composed face, its anxiety covered with a film of trust and he knew. It all came tumbling upon him. The way she jumped on hearing the telephone, their having to leave at the same time; it all fitted in place.

This must never reach his parents. He'd tried to regain his composure by recalling what Palli had told him about how it happened, but then he had only heard and not listened with the closeness that comes with personal interest. Then he had begun to comprehend what she had borne alone – and the difficulties the old women had struggled to overcome. What else could they have done? It made sense of her nervousness in the car.

As he left the clinic and walked to where his father's Jaguar stood alone, he heard his footsteps and the calls of the night carried by the wind. He heard, too, the judgemental voices, the righteous condemnations of what was outside their understanding, and it enraged him. It was this attitude that had led young women to commit suicide in the past. He imagined the coffee morning ladies, as they sipped their brew from delicate china:

'She should have sensed it; should have had some inkling of how the evening was going, don't you think?'… 'To my mind, common sense would say don't accept an invitation to a bachelor's house, especially so late. What could possibly have been in her mind?'... 'You can't help thinking there was, I don't know what to call it really, a kind of carelessness.'... 'Stupidity, if you ask me.'... 'Are you telling me, she was an innocent at her age?'

'Yes. Yes. In some things yes! We are not all worldly wise. Too protective a home does it,' he protested.

The voices came again: 'It's as clear as day that she brought it upon herself.' He could see the narrowing of the eyes of another and a grim smile stealthily appearing as the lips part and close like a pair of shears. 'Was she not trying to gain her tutor's favour, and he outwitted her at the game they were both playing?'

But didn't we all want to make favourable impressions on our teachers? Did that mean that power had the right to abuse trust?

He thought again about Miss Lily's request. Yes, he preferred it that way. It was kinder for Anjali not to know.

She should have had it done in London, he thought, as he drove through the night. But then he would not have known. Now he was better placed to be more of the kind of friend she needed. This was so important in a case like this – lest she become withered within. It had happened before. Wasn't that what happened in Dickens' *Great Expectations*? A prudent, watchful friend was what she should have now, someone who'd enable her to rebuild her trust in men. But could she, after this, be as she would have been? Would joyful abandonment ever come her way?

He thought about the tradition of chastity in their culture, of Sita standing on the burning pyre to prove to the citizens of Ayodhya that she was chaste, though for ten years she'd dwelt in the house of the wealthy and powerful king Ravana, exposed to his seductive wiles. Hadn't the god Agni then protected her from his fiery tongues? Anjali would undoubtedly know this epic. How would it play in her mind?

Praveen's imagination hovered like a moth, moving from one attracting flame to another, not knowing when to stay for enlightenment or when to leave lest he be consumed. Did the rules permit a tutor to take one of his students home that late? What drove such a man? What a cowardly bastard? What a shit! The cold depravity of it all.

The events of the evening replayed again and again: her controlled anxiety in the car. The way she jumped when the telephone rang. And yet she had held her own that evening and dazzled. Would her inner strength hold in her quiet moments of solitude?

His parents would never be told, but he wondered what their response would have been.

He reached home and put the car away. As he climbed the outer steps, his mother opened the front door.

'Did it go well, Praveen?' she asked. 'Would you like a hot cup of cocoa?'

'I would like that very much,' he said smiling, as he brightened up to please her. 'Yes Ma, everything went very well.'

'That's good,' she said. 'You're a good doctor, Praveen.'

'I try, Ma.'

'It's the best way, son.'

39

SAVITA AND HEMKISH

Savita looked up smiling when Hemkish asked, 'I hope you like them.'

'They're beautiful Haim.' *I'm sure Ishani doesn't have these in her garden and I won't be bringing them to her notice either.*

'Good. I was beginning to wonder; you were so quiet.'

'Just look at them. The colours and the fragrance – simply glorious. They lift the entire room, Haim. You are always generous. Every year you give yourself so much trouble. *I wouldn't like to think how much these cost.*

She smiled. He knew so well how she liked to be petted and pampered. Haim was always what you saw and heard, unlike most people, including herself. It was part of his attraction in those long-gone days when her own emotional life was a complex maze of desires.

'What about some tea?'

'Angela, where is the tea?'

'Coming, Miss. Sorry.'

As Savita poured the tea, he said in a hushed tone, 'I've something important I want to talk about.'

'You have a problem?'

'No. no. Nothing like that.'

'What then? Is something troubling you? Have you been talking to Praveen about your health? What did he say?'

Silence.

'Alright. Tell me what it is, Haim?'

'Stop worrying, Savita. It's about Praveen and ummm… Ishani's niece.'

'Anjali?'

'Yes. He saw her when he went to London. It was soon after her return. Do you think something is going on?'

'No! He sees lots of girls here, or a lot of girls here go out of their way to see him. He's a good catch for anyone fishing. Has he said something?'

'I think it's time for him to settle down.'

'Settle down? He's not in private practice; he's still with the government and you know they don't pay doctors well. Besides, we really haven't had any time to be with him, enjoy his company; he's been away so long, Haim. We used to talk about what we'd do together when he came back. We don't want to lose him just yet. Besides, he is so busy. Tell him he should take a year; get to know a lot of suitable ladies really well. At the end of that time, we'll all get together and decide on the finest of them all.'

'Okay. But what do you think about Ishani's niece?'

'Would she leave her family and come here to live?'

'I don't know.'

'Precisely. He will have to ask her.'

Silence.

'Has he asked her?'

'I don't know.'

'Has he known her long enough?'

'Well, I believe they keep in touch by phone, and when he went to London, they met.'

'I know that, but he didn't give me the impression that anything was on… He's an innocent, Haim. Could he cope with the wiles and cunning of modern, educated, London girls…? Well, to begin with, they speak their mind too freely.'

'What d'you mean?'

'You know what I mean, Haim. Respect for the older generation is not in their thinking. Let me speak my mind for a change. To be really frank, I found she was challenging you a little too much when she was here. To be talking the way she did to a man with so much practical experience and understanding of business… She behaved as if she was not aware of this, or that it didn't matter. What does she know eh? I did not think she accepted gracefully what you were saying.'

'Savita, I was not offended by what she said.'

'I did not say that, Haim. I'm saying pay close attention to her outlook. That is really worrying. Besides, how many nice-looking young ladies offend you, eh?'

'Well…'

'Let me say this, there's a strong will there in Anjali, a strong independent spirit. I can feel it in my bones. Now Haim, too much of that is not good for a happy marriage. You can't speak your mind openly like that all the time. What will happen to our poor son if we're not there to give him moral support? He will just have to give in. I

213

can't have that, and I know you wouldn't like that either, though knowing you, you'd be quiet about it.'

'I understand what you're saying, Savita. I have no problem with that. But listen to this: you and I have people around us who respect us. They do as we tell them because we employ them.'

'And we treat them very well. Compared to other employers we stand out like the morning star.'

'That's true, Savita. We're not disputing that. We're considerate when they or their children are sick; at Christmas time we're generous to all of them. They're happy, we're satisfied that they are happy. How they speak to us reflects all that, don't you see?'

'And so it should, Haim. They know who butters their bread.'

'But it explains how you felt that day. Savita, we saw a quiet, shy girl.' He tried to ignore her look of utter disbelief as he continued. 'I even sensed a sort of sadness there, a wanting to please. Look how often she tried to serve us.'

'Haim, you're so easily taken in by female wiles. You're a real softie, you know. You worry me no end. Gentleness? There was no gentleness there. Believe me, it was all in your good nature.'

'Okay. Let me have another go. Out of the blue we heard a voice speaking to us as if we were old friends, a voice that does not have a trace of obligation to us, or subservience, speaking to us as equals.'

'Well that's the problem, I'm glad you've recognised that at last, Haim. She is not our equal, how can she be? She has yet to make something of her life.'

'Okay. Wrong word. Anyway, let me make my case and no interruptions please, Savita; I lose my trend of thought when I'm interrupted. Age probably.'

'Nonsense. I'm sorry, Haim; perhaps I get carried away.'

'Well, when that voice comes unexpectedly upon us, when it's a young voice, sure of what it believes, our ears may not be happy with that tone. It's a strain because it's unfamiliar. It may even grate on us. Like a piece of foreign music, it takes time to understand; but if we listen closely, we could even grow to like it.'

'You're right, Haim... I think we're both right. Are you thinking she is suitable for Praveen then? Has he said anything to you? Dropped any hint?'

'No. Nothing at all.'

'Well, let's leave it to him, Haim. I myself am quite open about it, though I would have a preference for someone right here.'

'I understand. It's a mother's preference. But time is passing and he is not engaging himself with the nice young ladies we have here.'

'He's still only in his late twenties, Haim.'

'Is he? Looks older than that.'

'Responsibility at the clinic does it. He thinks far too much about everything.'

'Perhaps he just doesn't know how to flirt.'

'You should have taught him a few of your skills. It comes naturally to you, even now. You're quite something with the young ladies – and the not so young.'

'I don't know what you're talking about.'

'Praveen goes about it as if he were a journalist interviewing the girls for the local paper. I've heard him.'

'Clearly he hasn't inherited his mother's skills. Before we got married, Savita, you knew how to turn every head that came your way.'

'That's only in your imagination, Haim.'

Angela poked her head round the door, 'Excuse me, Mr Mahesh, the gardener is here; he wants you to tell him what to do.'

'I'm coming.'

'Bring me a fresh pot of tea, Angela.'

'Coming.'

As she waited for Hemkish to return, Savita's thoughts rambled over his allusion to her younger days. Did she miss those days? Had something – within – withered? She'd never buzzed too close to the leaping tongues of fire, been over-dazzled by its dance, but she'd been close enough to understand the call of ecstasy.

Haim had been safety, comfort, a steady, respectable place in society. Everything else was ancient history. Was she a little jealous of Anjali, her youth, beauty, her better education? Perhaps she would have had the same assertive confidence had she been as well in-formed. But there was one thing no one could take from her: Praveen. She felt deep down that Anjali's family was not as good as hers, but her duty was to assist him to have a happy married life, not get in his way. She wouldn't be able to face her son's sad eyes if she was responsible for his unhappiness. She even admitted to herself that there were times when she disliked Ishani. Was this jealousy, too? Had her view of life become too small?

Hemkish returned. Savita poured him another cup of tea.

'Let us look at other important things, Savita. She is educated, from a very good family, has inherited the family head for business, like her aunt. And though she is almost as beautiful as you were at her age,

Praveen would do well to have someone as sensible as she is as his wife. I have been very lucky. Praveen might be too.'

'You're too generous, Haim. She is very beautiful; they would have beautiful children. But we don't know if she would live here, and even if she has an aptitude for business, that doesn't mean an eagerness for it. We don't know what makes her tick. She may not know herself.'

'That's true, Savita. These things we will leave to Praveen to ask her. We don't even know if our own son is as keen on business as we are. Come to think of it, how can he be? He asked to do something else and we offered him the opportunity.'

'That's true. Not many business families would have done that. You're a splendid father. Most would have used every trick in the book to get him to follow in their footsteps. Sometimes we're too modern, Haim.'

'I don't think young people would see us quite like that.'

'I know. To them we're from the dinosaur period.Anyway point out these things to Praveen when you speak to him next.'

'I shall tell him what we've decided.'

'You mean that we're giving him a year to make up his mind?'
'Yes.'

'Perhaps it's best not to mention a specific period. Just say we're giving him time and a free hand at choosing, Haim. How much more modern can anyone be? Has he met her family?'

'Yes. He says that they are like us in many ways.'

'That is a shorthand to say he likes them. They, no doubt, would have put their best foot forward. After all, he is a well-spoken, handsome young man, good profession, very good family and I'm sure if they asked Ishani about us, she would tell it as it is.'

They sat, each occupied with their own thoughts. Haim stirred first, was about to get up when Savita said: 'I wonder what happened to that girl who wanted to go to the university and had Anjali leaving us so suddenly? There was something about that, I can't explain to you exactly what and why, but I found it very strange, especially as Praveen had to leave at the same time. I had the feeling that things were not what we were told. I still think so. I wonder if it was all arranged so they could be together.'

Hemkish laughed. 'Pure coincidence, Savita. You know Praveen is always helping out people; you know that. He knew he had to go to the hospital long before she knew she had to help out this girl, and no one, only we, knew he was going to leave early.'

'True. And yet Praveen did not tell us where he was going; we assumed it was Port of Spain General. It is just the coincidence of it all – a mystery to unpick if I had time.' *I wonder what part Ishani played?*

'What are you thinking, Savita? What schemes could two decent, elderly ladies be hatching? Palli and Lily are above anything that doesn't add up. You know that… and I hardly think Anjali has any dark secrets, do you Savita?'

'I wouldn't think so.'

The words *dark secret* were not what she had in mind. They were too severe, but Haim's words affected her.

'I could be wrong. I have been wrong before. But I'm amazed that even now, I can recall that at the loud ringing of the telephone, she jumped with fear. That has come back to me vividly. Isn't that odd?'

40

AMIRA'S WARMTH

It was what Amira had long wanted to do, yet somehow never managed. After much thought, she decided it would be on the last day of the summer term when the girls would be able to assist her.

For two full days she laboured so that she could give her friends a dinner that would be an experience to savour. She was not driven by any need to show how well she cooked, but rather sought to offer them her affection in the company of her family. It was how her parent's generation had done it.

Her daughters helped, but the detailed planning of each dish and the brunt of the work fell upon her. She felt like a composer, working at each bar, each phrase, finding the combination of aroma, colour, texture and taste to create a memorable whole.

At last, the bell rang and she opened the front door to jollity outside. All her guests had arrived at the same time: Alice and Nick Reid, Janna and Edward Cohen, Margaret and Jack Summers and Jill Shepherd. Amira thought of Juliet and Michael, now in Spain.

Anjali and Satisha looked after the coats, while Santosh stood in the hall, all smiles, waiting to escort them to the sitting room.

'Quite a night! Look at the moon! It's before your front door.'

'There's a slight nip in the air.'

'Unusual for this time of the year.'

'Well I wouldn't say that. A summer's night can be quite cool.'

'You must enjoy the heat, Amira.'

'Actually I prefer autumn and late spring best. The temperature then is just right for me.'

'Now I wouldn't have thought that at all. I just assumed you would love it very hot.'

'I agree with Amira,' said Jill; 'those are the best times. In spring there is a special delight in finding crocuses and daffodils in unexpected places… like life, isn't it?'

'What do you mean?' Janna asked.

'From time to time we find true gems of humanity in the most unlikely places.'

'True. Very true,' Jack said.

The men were served by Santosh; Anjali served the ladies. Margaret had a glass of sherry and so did Jill. Alice asked for a soft drink and she was offered pineapple juice with a dash of Angostura bitters and crushed ice which she said went nicely together. Janna had a gin and tonic. Jack and Nick had a whisky; Edward said he would try that fine rum that Santosh was recommending.

The large bronze cow in the sitting room drew Jill's attention. 'So lifelike!' Alice whispered, 'I expect it to move away at any time.'

'Actually it does take a stroll at night,' Vidya said, with a judge's seriousness. 'Quite shy during the day and in company much withdrawn and still, so very still that it seems like a statue.'

Smiles and laughter. Vidya looked puzzled. Why the disbelief? Satisha turned to the heavens with a silent prayer: *Dear God, give Vidya a little sense while we have our neighbours with us.*

'What will you girls do when you leave school?' Nick Reid asked. Was anyone thinking of medicine? He had observed it was a profession favoured by Asians.

Vidya said that she believed hospitals should be consigned to the past. But what would she put in their place, Janna wanted to know.

'Well,' said Vidya, 'that is really not difficult to see.' Amira stared at her daughter in disbelief. Satisha looked to the heavens. *Dear God, hurry please. This is an emergency.* Santosh smiled indulgently.

Satisha said, 'Beware one and all; Vidya is in her clownish mode. We are familiar with it.'

'Perhaps I ought to say that about half the people in hospitals could be safely treated in their homes, where they would be more comfortable. Only the severely ill should be kept in a hospital. Consider this: a large number of sick people huddled together in one place becomes a breeding ground for all types of contagious illnesses. Ailing people need to be in healthy environments.'

'I can see there is much good sense in that,' said Nick.

'You must not forget, dear, that many of us are not blessed with relatives close by,' observed Alice. 'I'm not sure if your goal can be met in all circumstances.'

'Only time will tell,' said Edward Cohen, 'if Vidya is right. Predictions are a hazardous business; experience has shown that the future has a way of going where no thought has gone before.'

'I agree. Look at the great Empires of the past. How many of their wise sages could have foreseen their demise?' asked Jill.

'True. But our empire was different,' said Nick, 'our main purpose was to bring democracy and to trade fairly. We brought civilisation to many countries. Whether one admits it or not, we can see that countries are at different levels of advancement.'

'The aroma coming from the kitchen is wonderful,' Janna said hastily.

'So is this rum,' said Edward, his face quite flushed. 'I join with Santosh here and recommend it wholeheartedly.'

Amira brought in a platter of crispy warm kachouries, paper napkins and various chutneys. Jack said he would appreciate it if Amira passed on the 'know how' to Margaret. Alice and Janna said they would like to have it too.

'The aroma from the kitchen, Amira. What is it?'

'Patience Janna,' Amira said, her eyes smiling.

'If you can get Janna to have patience, Amira,' Edward said, 'you will have done what over a lifetime I have utterly failed to do.'

Jack cleared his throat and said that women had to be more patient than men. They were the ones who brought up children. 'It is the natural state.'

'It is not natural,' said Anjali, as she helped Nick to another kachourie. 'Women were without the means to become independent of fathers or husbands. People who are dependent on others have to have more patience, they simply have no choice.'

'There speaks the new woman, tomorrow's ruler,' said Edward.

'Nonsense,' said Jill; 'men are so entrenched in the seats of power that our tomorrow is a long way off.'

'Have you noticed how the Broadway has changed?' Alice asked.

'It's surreal,' Margaret said. 'Do you know what I recently saw there? The choice of a Thoughtful Therapist or a Manual Therapist. What are these?'

'Manual is well – with the hand, by the hand,' Jack explained.

Laughter.

'That was most helpful, Jack,' said Margaret.

'Thoughtful is more difficult to get to,' he added, restraining a smile. 'Is it therapy by mind readers.'

'Who knows,' Margaret replied.

'Can anyone tell me what blow-dry with Sinead means?' queried Jill. 'That service is being offered in the telephone box, too.'

'Well thank goodness,' said Alice, 'that we still have those old-fashioned general stores where we can find tools of all kinds.'

It was time to move to the dining room.

'What a feast! It does so much for a home to dine like this occasionally,' said Jack. Margaret looked uncomfortable.

'Amira, does Santosh dine like this every evening?' asked Edward. 'I notice he's always hurrying home from the station.'

'You should ask him.'

Santosh smiles broadly and nods.

'That explains his fast pace. I would too.'

'So would I,' Jack muttered, as if aggrieved.

An uncomfortable silence entered the room, but the warmth, colour and aroma of the meal absorbed it.

There was butternut squash with fenugreek, butter, onions and sweet peppers; basmati rice with cumin and cardamom; roasted chicken with rosemary, orange jelly and the leaves of lemon balm and thyme; potatoes steamed with coriander leaves then tossed in olive oil and cardamom; lamb marinated overnight in yogurt, cinnamon, garlic, ginger and a mix of sweet peppers, onions, chives, salt and black pepper then slowly baked in a rich massala, olive oil and a bouquet of fresh garden herbs and tomatoes. It was one of Lily's and Palli's recipes. When the dhal puris, which were silky-soft and wrapped in greaseproof paper, were broken they released into the room the warmth of roasted ground cumin. There were beans and spinach and grilled aubergine with tomatoes and garlic, home-made chilli sauce and chutneys. The guests tried a little of all there was.

Silence. Only the comforting sounds of spoons meeting serving dishes.

'This is simply delicious, Amira.'

'I'm overwhelmed, Amira.'

'If food like this is served in heaven, I shall try to live a life that will ensure my admission through those gates.'

The dishes were removed, the table cleared. The ladies offered to help but Anjali assured them that everything was in hand. Fifteen minutes later, Satisha brought in a trifle topped with cream, large juicy cherries, walnuts and blue berries. The light fruit cake had absorbed Madeira, and the layers of pears and peaches were covered by home-made vanilla custard. Jill said that Amira had made the word trifle inappropriate.

Alternatives were suggested.

'Sweet flights of the imagination.'

'Paradise in a bowl.'

'A dance of the senses.'

By the time they retired to the sitting room and had a choice of teas and coffee and cognac, all were feeling like babies who had been fed, bathed and massaged in warm oil.

'I'm so very comfortable here,' Margaret said. 'Jill please give me a hand. It is time I leave for home. I think I speak for all of us when I say you offered us tonight a taste of the most precious things of life.'

'For she's a jolly good fellow, for she's a jolly good fellow,' they sang and clapped. Amira felt overcome but managed to say, 'You are some of the nicest people I know.'

'You offered us a bit of heaven,' Janna said, rising from her seat.

'The delights of your culture you lavished upon us,' Jill Shepherd said. 'We feel honoured to be offered this, Amira. I thank you for thinking of us with so much affection.'

When the last 'good nights' trailed away in the night's air and the door was closed, Anjali said, 'Mummy, you sit down with Daddy; we three will clear up. Let me make you a hot cup of ginger with clove and a dust of cinnamon.'

'Thank you, Anjali, you did very well. You took a weight off my shoulders.'

'We were proud of our daughters,' Santosh said.

'Don't worry with the ginger tea, Anjali, I shall have a little of that Madeira.'

'You did very well, Amira,' Santosh said. 'You surpassed yourself, if that is possible. It certainly was some undertaking.'

'Suddenly, Santosh, I feel so tired.'

'You are always doing the right things, Amira. I pontificate, but you act.'

'We need philosophies to sustain us, Santosh, and you provide them. With you and daughters such as ours I am blessed.'

At breakfast the next morning, Santosh said, 'Your mother and I were very proud of all our girls last night.'

'How can you say that, Daddy? Vidya almost ruined it with her posturing,' Satisha said, glaring at Vidya.

'No, no. Don't think like that,' replied Santosh. 'She raised the temperature a little with her views, but I will tell you what I was most worried about… that one of you was going to take on Nick Reid's belief on the purpose of the British Empire.'

'Daddy, we couldn't do that to Mummy,' Vidya said. 'Listen to this: Civilisation is such a large word, Mr Reid, I don't think you have fully grasped all it encompasses; you might wish to consider that what is truly remarkable is that in large parts of the empire there is a magnanimous forgiveness by the indigenous peoples, despite the savagery they endured. That is a mark of civilisation, Mr Reid. Now, I could have said that, but I didn't.'

'We could all have responded in that way, Vidya,' Satisha said. 'There's no need to make so much of it. You and I were taught a golden rule many years ago by an angry Aunt Ishani. Be courteous at all times, but more especially to your guests. We were beastly to Amru Sen, a quiet, nice boy who wanted to be a doctor. I often wonder what has become of him.'

'Oh, Satisha,' Amira said, 'you've reminded me, some time ago, Ishani told me that you and Vidya might like to know that Amru Sen – she said you both knew him – was doing his pre-medical at Mount Hope in Trinidad. It completely slipped me.'

'Really? So he is pursuing it. Well he was a determined, simple chap.'

'I would really like to meet him when he's qualified, just to see how he's turned out. He was a good-natured quiet sort. Amazing if he can overcome the limitations of his environment. But, he was determined to become a good doctor. Maybe we'll meet him one day.'

41

ANJALI'S SOLILOQUY
Kensington Park

The obscenity I experienced in that cold room made me feel defiled, broken into, crushed. I've worked hard to get rid of those feelings. No more nightmares, fear of sleeping lest they return. What has comforted me is knowing I'm not alone.

Once I dreamt I was drifting through seething rapids when the strong flow brought me close to a huge log spanning the width of the stream. Many hands reached out from it: my Nanee's, Mummy's and Daddy's, Lily's, Palli's and Ishani's. They prevented me from falling and I escaped into the edge of a wood which, as I began to walk, became Regent's Park.

Their hands remind me that I belonged to their fold. When I woke I was determined to live again, even more fully than before, knowing I was nourished by unconditional love. I've passed the weepy stage, the stage of asking why? I've accepted it happened.

It was an experience at close quarters of how power behaves behind locked doors. Daddy spoke vividly of this on several occasions; perhaps to prepare us for its ruthlessness. He feels very strongly about this. Mummy tried to restrain him, but he reminded us of its presence and the devastation it brings.

Mummy believes one should conduct oneself as if the world is a better place than it is. I cannot. My experience has forced me to reflect long and hard. It led me to take up karate and this new-found skill has increased my confidence. Just knowing that I'm more able to defend myself has given me inner strength.

Keeping close to nature has helped, too. I've been embraced by its silences, its sweet rustlings, the conversation of insects when dusk comes. The walks here and in the beautiful Eskdale valley have comforted me. I believe I am quietly regaining myself. The rent is being healed.

A dog races to fetch a stick. Children are running; fathers are pretending to catch up the gleeful winners. I smile, the winner smiles, his parents too; we are at one with the game.

He's so nice to be with. We sat on this very bench. To have

someone as sensible and sensitive as Praveen close to me is a blessing. If he ever asks, and he just might, I would tell him all. Somehow I know it would not be difficult. It is so easy to talk to him. His temperament suits his profession.

I like his attention. He is gentle with me. It's as if somehow he senses I've been hurt and is trying to help me heal. He gives me time to think of what we should do together. Whatever I suggest, he goes along with it. He is a good, intuitive listener. He suits me well. But his mother, she is such a strong, ambitious woman. As her only child, she will want the world for him. She challenges all the time. It is her way of expressing herself. But I'll be guided by my parents and Aunt Ishani, who I'm sure knows her well. Do I suit him as well as he suits me? Perhaps not right now, but I can become so, regain my former self and create pleasure for us both.

I joined the karate class because of the philosophy of its founder, Gichin Funakoshi: *Do not think that you have to win, rather think you do not have to lose.*

It won't be long now before I meet Praveen. Why am I so restless, why can't I think clearly, why the tears? There must be no regrets. What had Lilly and Palli taught? 'Know your ingredients.' Do I know him well enough? Yes we've spent a good deal of time together, but niggling doubts remain. How am I to know if he feels as I do? I so want to be accepted by him, but I could easily be deluding myself. Then again, how will I cope with intimacy? Will past experiences rush in and paralyse me? Only our intuition dares.

ON THE BRIDGE

Anjali and Praveen had arranged to meet at the Embankment tube station and walk over the Old Hungerford Bridge to the South Bank at eleven. Their day was going to be lunch, listening to a solo performance and then the Hayward Gallery.

Hungerford Bridge was one of only three bridges that combined rail and pedestrian use; the pathway had long been dilapidated, was narrow and recognised to be dangerous at nights. But this was a summer's day and mid-morning. Praveen was unmissable in Bermuda shorts, trainers and a flamboyant shirt. He had his camera focused above the safety rail to capture London's riverscape.

Ahead of them they saw a scuffle of boys and a girl laughing and jeering. They did not look closely and did not see a young boy was being beaten. He was writhing on the ground.

Anjali was focused on the girders. 'Isn't this engineering masterly? Can you call this walking on the waters, Praveen?'

'It needs a new pedestrian way,' he observed, 'but what a view.'

'It certainly is,' said an elderly woman, just walking past them. 'If this river could speak, what tales it would tell.'

It was then they heard a desperate cry and saw the boy and the terror he faced.

'Please, please I can't swim. I can't swim. I won't tell. I promise. I promise.'

His tormenters took turns, stepping back and kicking him again and again. The girl, laughing and egging on two youths much older than the boy, was daring them to throw him over the bridge.

'Stop it!' Praveen shouted. The two youths looked up. One swiftly and deftly opened a flick-knife, 'Come. Come. You come,' he sneered.

Anjali threw her handbag at Praveen. As he turned to catch it, she said to the leering face, 'I'm coming.' He was taken aback, but so sure of himself that he turned to grin at his accomplices. At the very moment he turned, Anjali rushed upon him, held the hand with the blade and pulled it down, kicking him in the groin with such force that he reeled back in agony.

The other youth picked up the knife and rushed towards Praveen, aiming for his throat. The girl shouted, 'Give it to him, Carl.' Praveen raised his hand to protect his face and the knife sliced his wrist. Anjali, coming from behind, placed both her hands on the youth's throat and squeezed his windpipe almost too hard. As he dropped the knife, she turned him round and kicked him in the groin. Praveen picked up the knife and threw it in the Thames.

The old woman who had remained there, intent on being a witness, had dialled 999, and then hurried to the boy who was quivering with fear.

The three attackers began to run, but Praveen, squeezing his left wrist tightly, shouted to a group of young men coming from the opposite side of the bridge, 'Hold them. Hold them.' They did, because they had seen the attack.

People began to gather. The police were soon on the scene and the gang of three were handcuffed and led away. An ambulance was called. The old woman gave a statement and said yes she was willing to say what she had witnessed in court.

Anjali removed Praveen's shirt and used it to tie a tourniquet around his wrist, which was still bleeding despite the intense pressure he had put on it. Praveen knew one of the veins had been severed but merely said it would heal when Anjali questioned him about the nature of the slash.

She ran to the boy and caressed his hair, which was sticky with congealing blood. 'We'll take you to the hospital and call your parents. It will be alright now. When we get to the hospital we'll let your parents know where you are.' When she looked at him still trembling and whimpering, tears filled her eyes. His face was bruised and swollen. Praveen took a few photographs of the boy, to give to his parents as evidence of the attack.

At the hospital the doctor attending the boy said, 'These stitches will help his face heal. There'll be some scarring, but in time it will get fainter. Fortunately he protected his eyes. His fingers are broken in several places, one wrist is fractured, but he shouldn't suffer any loss of function.'

Praveen's wrist was cleaned, stitched and tightly bandaged. 'Had you not put that amount of compression on the wrist, you would not be here,' the nurse remarked.

Anjali phoned the boy's parents, describing in some detail what had happened. She promised to stay with their son, Adil, until they arrived.

After Adil's parents arrived, and expressed their gratitude, Anjali and Praveen left the hospital. The day was almost over; they were both tired and hungry.

'Come home with me, Praveen. I have a spare room. You need to rest the arm and relax. I can offer you a Welsh rarebit and coffee, tea or cocoa or whatever. I need to relax too. I don't fancy a busy restaurant. I want a bit of peace and quiet. Come, let's go.'

'You've never said a nicer thing, Anjali.'

'I keep nice things for emergencies.'

Her flat was tidy and welcoming. Her mother had said to her many times: 'Keep your flat in good shape whenever you leave it. You never know whom you may have to invite in.'

She told him to lie on the sofa, while she made a dish with butter and cheese, shredded chicken, mushrooms, sliced tomatoes, topped off with a creamy sauce. He ate heartily.

In the bathroom mirror, Anjali noted the glow exuding from her skin. He was looking so much at home, but what would tomorrow bring?

When she returned, smiling, he said, 'I saw your karate lessons in action today. Your training helped to save our lives and that little boy's. I was wondering whether to restrain you or not, but you were so quick, faster than my thoughts.'

'Speed and surprise are part of it. You're trained to make both work in your favour. I had a very humiliating experience once. Since then, my desire not to be an owl at a banquet has been all-consuming. I decided that just as we use our intelligence to work for us, we should use our limbs to protect us. I knew I could manage those thugs. Anyone who could seize on such a small boy has to be a coward. The knife gave them power. Without it they were lost. The one with the knife was too cocksure, and I used that to my advantage. We practise with plastic knives, so seeing one did not frighten me as it would have done if I'd not practised. It's hard work. You have to practise all the time. Funakoshi, the founder, puts it nicely: karate is like hot water; if you don't give it heat constantly it will become cold.

'We were lucky, too, that the woman stood her ground and had her wits about her. She phoned the police straight away. They arrived quicker than I would have expected. I find there are a good many elderly women in this country who are fearless. They have far more common sense than many half their age. Maybe because they were brought up in tougher times.'

'And those men who held on to them, they were good too, Anjali. They didn't hesitate.'

'London was at its best. Where else can you find such a metropolis?'

'No need to boast. We were just plain lucky, Anjali. The boy and I were fortunate you were there. If you were not so skilled, we could have been in the Thames and then the morgue. Chance worked in our favour. But she's blind, Anjali.'

'True. That poor, poor boy. I felt for him. He energised me. We should help him to knit up his delicate spirit again. Encourage him with the occasional phone call.'

'I shall do anything you say. Come sit with me.'

That night, within the comforts of her flat in St John's Wood, they felt closer than ever. They fell asleep on the sofa.

Next morning, the sun had travelled far into the sky and yet the curtains remained drawn. When the curious light pierced through the chinks in the windows its rays flickered over a spare bed that had not been slept in and another where two persons were still soundly asleep, wrapped in each other's warmth.

43

INHERITORS OF THE SONG OF LIFE

Once Praveen was back in Trinidad, it was not long before his father found the opportunity to take him on one side for a confidential man-to-man talk. Praveen was touched to hear his father struggling to balance his mother's dictat and his own views. He knew he was his mother's top ace, though he did not know that once she had lived life as if it were a game and the need for the exhilaration of play remained with her. She would use her wits to delay parting with her trump. How could she welcome another who threatened her position?

Praveen heard his mother's voice in his father's pauses and almost stammering speech. 'Your mother and I are sure there are young women in London who know when to be in control, when to allow themselves to be led, or when to walk side by side.' His father cleared his throat. 'With a good marriage, two lives and more are enhanced; but where there are two heads, the family is broken. Times have changed, my boy, but that does not mean intelligent, liberal parents are ill equipped to offer advice.' He paused. 'I shall welcome whoever you choose.'

Praveen smiled and wanted to embrace his father. It was a brave effort. Instead he said, 'I understand, Dad. Thank you for your wisdom. I'll take it on board. I promise you this: whoever I marry will have a high regard for my parents, and bring us all much happiness.'

Anjali, meantime, was concentrating on work for her Masters degree. She had matured, gained in confidence, expected little from her new tutor; so when nothing significant was offered, she was not per-turbed. She feared, though, that when negligence became a way of life, the culture was fraying at its edges.

She was often drawn back to the night of the incident on the bridge. The closeness of death, the cold deep river, the child's helpless plead-ing, had been with them. They had simply comforted each other, as two children lost in the woods would curl up together, each absorbing the warmth of the other. Praveen had continued to be the thoughtful, measured friend, drawing back from the moment of intimacy that the special circumstances of that night had led them towards. But she saw that something had changed. They had become wholly relaxed in each other's company. Trust was complete. But imperceptibly, they had begun to lose themselves in deeper feelings; it was not planned, no thought had guided them. It happened in the way that fruit, when ripe, loses its former self by loosening from the strong stem that fed it, ready to contribute to the feast of life.

After he left, it was separation that did it. The world seemed so dull. The surge of energy which had made their strides purposeful was gone. Now whenever she walked past the paths where they had strolled, she would think like a child, hoping that somehow something of him might have lingered on and would reappear on seeing her. What she did not know was that he, too, could see what was opening before him – a life that sustained and encouraged affection. He did not realise that his very restraint was alluring, quietly seductive to her.

44

WHAT THE SQUIRRELS SAW
1988

Hemkish and Savita could see that Praveen had matured rapidly as a doctor at Port of Spain General where he had to cope with almost daily clinical and administrative lapses and manage difficult situations. They were used to his fairly regular visits to London to attend refresher courses, but when one morning, he said he needed to go to London soon after his last visit, Savita's intuition was the same as Hemkish's. Their son had made up his mind. Savita recalled his response to her concerns: 'Living here has many attractions, Ma. Anjali would have reliable home help, which would give her far more time to pursue her career in teaching or administration. In London, she couldn't have that.' Savita conceded this made sense. But would she not miss her parents and her sisters and all that London had to offer? According to Ishani, they were a close-knit family.

'She'll be able to speak to them whenever she wants and her aunt will be nearby. Once she becomes fully involved in her work, she won't know where the time has gone.'

That night Hemkish said, 'The boy is like his father, he knows what he's about. We must leave it to him now, Savita.' Hemkish understood her silence as acceptance.

In London, Praveen telephoned Anjali's flat but there was no answer. He tried her home.

Santosh answered.

'Is Anjali at home?'

'Yes. She's in the garden, weeding.'

'Good. Would it be alright if I were to call in about half an hour?'

'It would be good to see you again.'

'Please let Anjali know.'

'In about thirty minutes, you said?'

'Yes.'

'We'll see you then. Amira is not in but I'm expecting her anytime now. She'd be pleased to know you're here.'

'Thank you, Mr Vidhur.'

The telephone rang again. It was Santosh's secretary, 'That last chapter of your report on the Eastern Caribbean states is missing. If I could have it by Monday morning, I'll be able to send it off.'

Santosh went off to search his desk, tidying it as he went along, repeating over and over again, 'Now where the hell could it be?', as if it were a means of enlightenment. Eventually he sat down to go through a pile of papers that had attained an unstable height. He became more anxious. He turned his attention to his filing cabinet. 'Hell, where could that chapter be? Let me sit down and think. I need to think. Don't panic.'

The door-bell rang. *Who the hell could that be; I don't have time for neighbourly chatter. Where on earth is Amira?* A beaming Praveen stood before him, formally dressed.

'Oh! Oh! You're here. I see.' Santosh quickly collected himself. 'Good to see you. Come in, Praveen. Let me show you where Anjali is; follow me.' While Praveen entered the garden, Santosh returned to his study and resumed his search.

In the meantime Amira arrived home and went upstairs to change her 'going out' clothes for more comfortable trousers and top. She glimpsed Santosh through the partially opened door, and hoped he was doing some long-overdue spring cleaning. It was only when she thought the picture window overlooking the garden needed a bit of wipe that she saw Anjali, her apron on the lawn, hair in a mess, removing her garden gloves, while Praveen, nicely dressed, was embracing her.

'Santosh, come! Come quickly, quickly.' Thinking that the kitchen was on fire or a wasp was entangled in Amira's hair, he rushed in. She indicated the garden.

'What's the matter, Amira?'

'Look, look into the garden. See what's going on there.'

'Yes. They're kissing. Now Amira, don't be alarmed; that's done frequently these days. When young people have any time left over from walking, talking or eating, they hold on to the person nearest to them and start kissing.'

'That is not so with our Anjali, is it?'

'Well her studying is now all out of the way; she has some spare time and is presently filling it in this fashionable way. It's a common pastime. Something we should give serious consideration to. We don't want to be laggards where fashion is involved, Amira. Should we start now? There's no time like the present.'

'I don't think we should be here.'

'You called me here, Amira, and this is our home.'

'I mean we shouldn't be looking at them like this; let's move away quickly,' she whispered, 'before they see us.'

'Actually, why don't you go ahead of me and find a place for us both to hide. I've lost a vital chapter and I must find it or I'll go crazy. I can't come with you just now.'

Amira pushed him out of the kitchen.

'Gently Amira, gently. I'm going.'

'Oh my god! Look at the house, look at me. Santosh, I'm going to change into something more appropriate; in the meantime, get busy: tidy up the coffee table, plump up the cushions, straighten the rug, put the kettle on, oh and bring out your nice sherry and those fine crystal glasses. Hurry Santosh.'

Anjali had been removing the ever-spreading roots of ground elder, thinking about Praveen and wondering what he might be doing. When she saw him standing there, she said, 'Are you real?'

'I believe I am… but I'd like you to remove your gloves, Anjali.'

'Is this a fingernail inspection? We had them at school.'

'Yes it is.'

'Let me remove my apron too. I must look quite a mess. Look at my hair. I mean don't look.'

'Make up your mind, which is it to be?' He tidied her hair, lifting the strands falling on her cheeks and neck, placing them behind her ears. She kissed his fingers. He brought out a small indigo box from his jacket and asked her to open it.

'It's exquisite, Praveen.'

He lifted the ring from the box and whispered, 'You're very special to me. I'm engaging our feelings with this.'

'You haven't asked me to marry you, Praveen.'

'Yes I have, in countless ways. Does the occasion call specially for words?'

She smiled.

'Well then, Anjali Vidhur will you marry me?'

Anjali came closer and wrapped her arms around him.

No one saw this but a small family of grey squirrels. They kept their distance, save the youngest, who hopped to the front and stood on his hind legs to see what the commotion was about. 'This phenomenon in Number 14 is quite quite out of character for the gardener we know,' an older sister said, her nose perked upwards.

'They've never behaved like this before. It's quite extraordinary. Stay where you are until they come apart and leave our patch. What a nuisance!'

When Anjali and Praveen returned to the house, there were hugs, kisses and handshakes all round. Amira insisted that Anjali should run upstairs and dress for the occasion. Meanwhile Santosh, who had eventually found his lost chapter, though he could not understand how it had got where it was, was so relieved that his elation carried over to the happy occasion. He hugged Praveen in unusual high spirits. Together they shared a little of his finest Demerara rum. Amira preferred a sherry.

Anjali called her mother. They sat together on her bed and embraced.

'We're only lending you to him; if he ever misbehaves, Anjali, you know this home remains your first home and your sanctuary. You are our daughter, you are never alone. We'll miss you so very much.'

'I want to say, Mummy, and that's why I called you, that… well… you've been the nicest possible mummy to all of us. Your background was so different from ours; you accommodated so many changes so quickly. New country, new neighbours, new schools, new ways. Later teenage daughters with perceptions of life that must have seemed daring to you, that must have pained you. You bore it all so well, so calmly, so self-contained. You stood up to everything; I've recalled many times since, especially when I've felt low, how you battled with Miss Williams all those years ago for us. I hope I'll be like you. Look at the beautiful garden you have given us. It had no soul when we came; you've made it sing. I once told you that Lily and Palli were full of praise for you; they said you were quick to see what they were getting at, long before most. I know that if things had been different you would have been able to do far more of what you actually wanted to do. No one knows what that is. That alone tells a lot about you.

'You should go to more classes, the Open University, or wherever, throw yourself into whatever interests you. Satisha and Vidya are old enough to look after themselves. I wanted to say this a long time ago, and thought it must be now, especially when you may think you're losing me. We carry you within us, Mummy. You've helped to form us. Never think you've lost any of us. Your voice is in our heads.'

'You're a beautiful, over-generous daughter. I can't believe you are my daughter; you are so much larger than myself.'

They embraced again. The room was still.

Amira said, 'If you and Praveen would like to celebrate together tonight, your Daddy and I will understand; next time Praveen comes, we'll have him home and he'll dine with us.'

'Thank you, Mummy.'

Later, when Anjali and Praveen left, Amira and Santosh remained standing at the door, looking out until the retreating sound of their steps faded in the dusk; they returned to the sitting room and sat in silence. Their children, whose small fingers had once held theirs tightly, had become adults; how had it happened so swiftly? Loss and quiet satisfaction fought for prominence. The house would not be quite the same, neither would they. For Amira, Trinidad, the place of her birth, had become a faraway place.

45

THE PERCEPTIONS OF SISTERS

Amira phoned Ishani who was beside herself with joy; there and then she explained why the wedding had to be at her home, in the garden.

'Why?' asked Amira, taken aback.

'We know it's customary for Hindu weddings to be held at the home of the bride but London is miles away.'

'But London *is* the home of the bride, Ishani.'

'True. But you can't have a proper Hindu wedding in London.'

'Why?'

'Will the guests hear the beat of tassa drums welcoming the bridegroom to Apple Grove?'

'You don't have to have that.'

'My God, I can't believe what I'm hearing, Amira! What would Ma say if she were alive?'

'Ma was sensible. She knew you had to adjust to the times. She was modern in that way, considering her background.'

'True. I agree wholeheartedly.' *But she knew who she was, where she came from and why certain things were important and should not be lost.*

Santosh passed a slip of paper to Amira. It said: *Hear what she has to say; tell her you'll think it over with me. Remember the part she's played in this.*

'Tell me what you have in mind, Ishani; a wedding has so many aspects to it and at present I haven't thought it through.'

'This will be the wedding of the daughter of Mr and Mrs Vidhur. No one can take that from you and Santosh. But Anjali is my niece and the first wedding in our family for years. We have to keep up the family's name. We're a family of substance. We want everyone to know that Anjali, the granddaughter of our parents, Mr and Mrs Pretham, is celebrating her wedding in a way her grandparents would be proud of. Ma and Pa will witness the wedding; they'll be there together with their parents when the pundit calls upon the spirits of the ancestors to be present.'

'I wasn't thinking like that.' *My God, you have to be practical. This is the twentieth century. Where we are, you have to think differently. Why can't you see that? Surely it is how you live that matters, not the ceremony. Come to think of it, you don't need a ceremony at all. Commitment and affection will do.*

'You know, Amira, an idea has just come to me. I can't think of a better occasion to renew an old custom, and breathe life into it again. Oh how lovely that would be, especially if it is written about and people recognise that it was at Anjali's wedding that this beautiful custom was given its rightful place.'

'What are you talking about?'

My God, she is lost. Does she know who she is? It's all very well to lose some of the trimmings of a culture but to start losing its essence is a death sentence. 'It's what we both had at our weddings, Amira, nothing less.'

'We had many things at our weddings. What exactly are you thinking?'

'Can you recall, Amira, that at our weddings the village women sat in a group, close to the pundit? They explained in song to the guests what aspect of the ceremony was taking place and its significance to the bride, bridegroom and their respective families. There was a particular part of the ceremony when told in song that always made Ma cry, not only at our weddings but at the weddings of young girls she knew.'

'Oh Ishani, you mean kanya puja and kanyadana, when the bride's parents sit beside their daughter and say to the bridegroom: "We offer our daughter, who is dear to us, to you to cherish, to love and care for, according to Dharmic principles." I am feeling weepy already.'

'Me too. What I especially like about it, Amira, is the way it is done. Up to that point, the parents' hands support their daughter's; now the bridegroom places his hands beneath the parents' hands and they slowly, reluctantly remove their hands so their daughter's hands rests upon the bridegroom's hands. Oh how beautifully symbolic!'

'Do you remember, Ishani, that before the bride takes her parents' leave, her father asks the bridegroom three times, three times mind you, in the presence of all, to promise him that in the pursuit or attainment of piety, wealth or other desires, his daughter will not be transgressed. And on all three occasions, the bridegroom promises to honour these paternal requests.'

'So beautiful, Amira! We can't lose that. This ceremony was well thought through by our forefathers; it is as relevant today as it was yesterday. Who we are and how we think, Amira, are all there in our ceremonies.'

'Do you remember this – because we don't have brothers – I was asked to pour water with rose petals on your hands, with Ravi's supporting them. It was an act invoking continuous happiness and prosperity.'

'And I did the same for you.'

'Yes, but because I was so much younger than you, the pundit and the guests were taken aback that I was given that part at your wedding.'

'Well, Ma was crossing two barriers; she was offering females an equal place to males, and she was asking youth to show it could be as responsible as older heads. The pundit was not entirely convinced, yet he went along because he respected Ma.'

'Ishani, I thought the chorus at weddings had completely died out, because the women who knew those songs had all died.'

'I think we have to put a halt to losing parts of the ceremony. If we're not careful the symbolic significance of what is taking place will go. For example, the beautiful Bhavar.'

'I don't think the bride and groom circling the sacred fire will ever go. It is pivotal to the wedding. It is symbolic of the joining together of the bride and bridegroom, as well as sharing the role of guiding their steps into the future.'

'You can't have a full Hindu wedding in Apple Grove. And just think, Amira, how different the atmosphere will be here in my garden, in the open, under the blue sky, with the Caroni plain rolling below us. Compare that scene to a rented place. England is not the place for open-air ceremonies. You've been blessed, Amira. It is important that the full worth of our tradition be brought to Anjali and Praveen at their wedding.'

Silence.

'Are you there?'

'You've been very good to Anjali and to all of us. What you're saying has taken me completely by surprise, so let me come back to you on this. Let me talk it over with Santosh.'

'Of course you have to. I'm really over the moon about this as you can see. I must pass on the good news to Ravi. We must get moving at once in all directions, if things are to be just so.'

Santosh was waiting.

Amira sat down.

'Let me pour you a drink.'

'I don't want anything. Ishani means well, but she just doesn't realise that I'm living in London and this is my eldest daughter. All my life, she has upstaged me. And now the package she presents is so well thought through and neat that not to go along with it appears unreasonable and mean-spirited.

'It's always the same. The year Lily and Palli opened their school, she insists that I go. I'm doing my A levels, I want to concentrate on other things, join a group researching sea turtles on Matura beach; I want to visit the turtles at night, meet people who have been researching them for years. I'm fascinated by the turtles coming out of the water to lay their eggs; I want to see this for myself but I can't, because she wants me to go to Lily and Palli's school not next year, or any other time, but to be amongst the first pupils. She wants to be able to say to a reporter that the opening of the school is so important that she'll be sending her sister. I could go on but that will do.'

'What exactly has she just been saying on the phone?'

'Just what you would expect. She wants a traditional Hindu wedding with all the trimmings, even some rites that have been forgotten.'

'Her perception of a Hindu wedding is what she sees around her all the time, Amira. Yours is different, because we are here.'

'Precisely. So why doesn't she see that?'

'There may be other aspects, too, that she has considered but hasn't spelt out: Praveen's parents, Savita and Hemkish Mahesh.'

'What about them?'

'Well they are very well-to-do business people. This is their only son. They may want a style of wedding that reflects their wealth, their position in society and the obvious fact that their son, their only child, is the inheritor of their worldly goods.'

'And what of our daughter, may I ask? What is she the inheritor of? Is her inheritance and her parents' worth any less?'

Santosh could see that Amira was about to explode.

'You know, Santosh; I'm tired of compromising all the time. I've reached the stage where maybe I should just disappear, for I've compromised myself to insignificance. Maybe I'm already invisible. Oh my culture has written the music and my upbringing directs the libretto; I play the part allocated to me. It is called Miss Noddy. I have not been given lines; it is assumed I cannot have anything valuable to say. But I am on stage, oh yes, I am there, ready with my nod, whenever I'm addressed. I think I do it very well... Well, since it appears I don't seem to have any attributes that matter, I shall just step aside.' *As a matter of fact, I may consider going to Alaska for a holiday and let the wedding be according to what I'm told matters to our ancestors, to the Maheshs and to Ishani herself.*

Silence.

Santosh made a pot of tea, and served Amira. She drank in silence, then got up to go to the bathroom where she sobbed her heart out, washed her face, dried it and returned.

'Good tea. Well made,' she said.

Silence.

'You know,' said Santosh, 'on the face of it compromise may appear to be what the weak do. But don't be fooled by that. There is compromise and compromise: the compromise of fools and the compromise of the wise. You can only tell what a compromise really is by its long-term effects. An intelligent, thoughtful decision may today be seen as a backing down by the short-sighted, but this so-called compromise may be a prudent and profound decision, because with time it will provide a doorway to life's beautiful, sustainable worth.'

'The Maheshs and Ishani are not fools, so why would they demand such a compromise?'

'Because their goals, their perceptions are not ours.'

'I see. Very well, what is their goal and what is ours?'

'Their goal is one of display, of grandeur, of a lavish celebration; they have a place in society that demands things be done in a certain way and be seen. Our goal is more long term and lasting, it is not just holding the stage for one day. We're thinking of the future, of laying a sound foundation for our daughter's life with her in-laws.'

'I have no intention of impressing anyone with Anjali's wedding ceremony, Santosh. It should be an intimate family affair at the home of the bride. Ishani is seeking to uphold tradition. Well tradition states the ceremony takes place at the bride's home. This is our daughter's wedding; this is our home.'

'It would be good for us to begin this relationship with Praveen's parents on a note of goodwill and generosity, especially when distance handicaps us from getting to know them better. Our willingness to compromise on something so important to them would help to ensure that there will be much goodwill towards our daughter from the start. Let us think of Anjali's future in this gesture of ours.'

Amira listened.

She was silent.

He asked, 'Is something worrying you that I haven't taken into account?'

'I can't cope with being a guest at my daughter's wedding. I know Ishani too well; she will soon phone to tell me what the plans are, what's on the menu, who the pundit will be, and who it would be nice to invite. And what do I do then?'

'I shall speak to Ishani myself and make a few things quite clear to her. First, the Vidhurs will be meeting the expenses of the wedding.

Secondly, the arrangements will be agreed by Anjali, Praveen and you. I'll explain to her that your involvement with Anjali and Praveen in making the decisions is the best compromise to keeping the tradition of where the wedding should be held. When you three have decided, you'll let Ishani know what has been planned and ask her how best to bring it about. The three of you will take full responsibility for the kind of wedding it is to be and Ishani will play her part in enabling these plans to reach fruition with the minimum of hassle. I, too, don't want your sister to go over the top with an extravagant number of extras and trimmings. I know only too well her way of enlarging everything she touches.'

Amira said nothing.

'You and I want the wedding to reflect the taste of a serious, thinking, professional family, not wealthy business people, many of whom have acquired an inflated taste for the shapely shells of life. Though these beauties may be highly polished, our family has no need of them.'

Gradually Amira regained herself. She said, 'Yes, that makes sense. We know Ishani means well, but she is not aware of how overpowering she comes across. Well, I guess she has had to rise to the requirements of competitive business. Now we have clarified an important thing. The wedding will be ours, but held at Ishani's. Santosh, our eldest daughter is taking leave of us. This is both a happy and a sad occasion for me. It will be our farewell to her before she also belongs to another. The music we choose for the wedding, and everything else for that matter must reflect this. I just couldn't bear it any other way. But I will tell Ishani myself, it is better that I do. I hope you understand.'

Santosh embraced her, saying that he understood and that she had his backing and support all the way.

The telephone rang. It was Anjali.

'Mummy and Daddy, Praveen has spoken to his parents and I have too. They are very happy. I think you should phone them now; you would find them very pleasant and I know they will like you both very much.'

Santosh and Amira took turns to speak to Hemkish and Savita, saying that they were very pleased that their daughter had met such a fine young man and thanked them for their immense contribution towards his upbringing. They were looking forward to meeting them.

Savita and Hemkish were gracious when they heard that the Vidhurs wished to please them, and the wedding would be taking place in Trinidad at Ravi's and Ishani's, in their garden, and not in

London, which might have been inconvenient for their family and business friends. Savita told Amira that she was relieved at their wise decision, for in her experience summers in London were not really summers at all, then – sensing from Haim's expression that she had spoken without consideration – added that now London would become a very special place for her.

The following day when Amira communicated all that she and Santosh had agreed to Ishani, it was received without opposition. Amira suspected that Ravi might have had a hand in her sister's gracious acceptance. Ishani was forced to restrain her true feelings. She was overcome by this rejection of her generosity. Seeing herself sidelined, so neatly, was too much to bear. There was a wealth of her goodwill that was not being acknowledged. Who, other than she, was responsible for the present outcome? Without her would there have been a wedding? Has anyone said this to her. Acknowledged it? What a family!

Tears came to her eyes as she looked down from her terrace onto the Caroni plain. There were the main roads, the moving cars and the occasional aeroplane slowly descending to land at Piarco. All seemed small and insignificant. She had built up the family business, expanded it, encouraged Ravi to purchase this property and it was she who had single-handedly created its enchantment to the senses. She could not understand why Amira should feel threatened. She was not trying to take her sister's place, she who had not been blessed with daughters or sons. Her tears flowed.

As the days became weeks Ishani came to better terms with the reality before her, though she could never see why her ability in making the near impossible happen should have become something threatening to its beneficiaries, especially her sister, who had gained much from decisions she had taken on her behalf.

The wedding took place a month later. The weather was warm with a continuous flow of Atlantic breezes bathing the house and garden. Anjali was relaxed and truly happy. The trust and affection of others and confidence in herself had healed her wounds. That ancient law imposed upon women by men had become redundant. She knew that a woman's dignity, self-esteem and worth could never be taken from her; only she could allow herself to lose them. Reason and compassion had demolished an ossified concept.

Palli and Lily were sitting in the front row. Lily looked charming in a grand hat and stylish jacket sent from London by her sister. A few of their former students who were present at the ceremony joined together and welcomed them with a resounding clapping of hands and stamping of feet as they were ushered to their reserved seats. The two grand dames acknowledged this graciously and with pride. This was a day to celebrate what had been overcome in the past, to welcome the future.

Palli's sari was of soft silk; she looked elegant and gentle. Her expression seemed one of elation as well as sadness at the passing of time and the ephemeral nature of life. She knew that it would be sooner rather than later that she would be leaving this life of consciousness. Today she and Lily could see and hear how confident their past students were. They recalled those early days when, in order to get pupils to their school, she and Lily went from house to house with a basket of opportunities, of new thinking, to the mothers of Penal.

The wedding ceremony was performed by the family pundit, Pundit Narine, who had officiated at the thanksgiving puja on Praveen's return. Today he wore a dazzling angochar, and in his serene posture, head held high, he brought the rites to a close with the final Sanskrit chant asking that God's blessing be showered upon the couple, their parents, teachers, friends, helpers and all those present.

Anjali and Praveen rise from the mandap and take their leave of the pundit, who insists that this is their day and they must walk ahead of him. They bow low, first before their parents and then before their in-laws to ask for their blessings. They are showered with petals of good wishes for their spiritual well-being. Anjali is about to enter the waiting car, when she returns to the tent and bows low before her aunt Ishani, Lily and Palli. They cannot control their tears as they bless her. Many photographs are taken and the following day, under the heading 'Wedding of the Month', the newspapers offer their readers a full page of happy, joyous, tearful faces.

PART THREE

46

THE CITY AND SATISHA
The Mid-1990s

London Moorgate stood in a quiet cul-de-sac, not far from the Bank of England in Threadneedle Street. On its second floor, Satisha Vidhur sat facing three computer screens. It was not where she had hoped to be. The previous week, she had been interviewed by the personnel director, Herbert Montgomery. She had noted how his Saville Row jacket no longer covered his expanding stomach, though firmly tugged to meet it.

He acknowledged that research was her preference, but explained that this post had already been filled, and that were she to accept a post in sales and trading, he'd be happy to transfer her to research as soon as a vacancy arose. The bank was at present short-staffed in sales and she might enjoy the cut and thrust and the attractive bonuses. She let herself be persuaded; her father had said the City was the hub of the economic life of the country, and she shouldn't duck the challenge.

It was not long after when Satisha met the woman who had taken the post in research: Susanna Mayfield. When Miss Mayfield walked into sales, Satisha noted the welcoming eyes lifted above computer screens. Miss Mayfield had been the best salesperson London Moorgate had seen for years. She was shrewd, highly successful but scrupulous in her dealings with clients. Satisha took in her well-shaped, short brown hair – no strands impeded her view of what was ahead. Her round, steel-rimmed spectacles signalled how well she saw into things. No frivolity here. Firm, well-toned legs carried this weight of expertise in their stride. A graduate of Somerville, she'd managed her wealthy clients' portfolios on the same principles as her clothes: hard-wearing, good lengths, classical style, sensible shoes. Don't draw attention to yourself, keep your clients focused on what mattered and show ease in making important decisions. Her mantra was: *What is of substance lasts. Through me, London Moorgate offers you reliability, good value and sound advice.* But it was time to have something less stressful, yet of importance. Her move to R & D in oil and gas had put Montgomery in a difficult position; in recompense he requested that she mentor the new recruit.

She had listened non-committally to the request. How could the know-how gained from almost twenty years of experience be compressed into little pills of wisdom for this young woman of quite a different background?

'Suppose the potential is not there?'

'Miss Vidhur will see that well before we do and move on. In this respect her attitude is close to your own.'

'Well! That's not bad for a beginner, Monty.' Her eyes flashed at the comparison. But if this was the price for confirming her move, she would co-operate.

'Where is this Miss Vidhur?'

'In the middle row, I've placed her close to the traders. She has yet to get, Jack tells me, the assertiveness needed to hold her own, but she's smart. Help her with how to manage things under stress, how to avoid crash and burn.'

Susanna sent an email to Satisha Vidhur.

At lunch the two women chatted. Susanna seemed to want to tell Satisha that working for London Moorgate was such an impossible task that few stayed. At first, Satisha gave her the benefit of the doubt. Her warnings were no doubt well meant. Then she began to suspect other motivations.

Susanna Mayfield had been the only woman in the upper echelons of a man's world. Her bonuses, the largest in sales, had come from a combination of luck, experience and financial sophistication. She had won grudging esteem, but who had made it easier for her? Had she not struggled on alone? Monty really had a nerve. She wasn't going to make it easy for anyone else. This young woman would have to stand on her own two feet.

Satisha, now twenty-five, with a good honours degree and a masters from LSE, was keen to become a daughter of the metropolis. It was not the big bonuses that attracted her, but gaining an understanding of how the system worked. It was the dynamics of power that fascinated her. She wanted to see how banks grew, how they created their own high tides by pulling the waters in their direction, how they dealt with obstacles. In an effort to survive in sales, Satisha had tried to wear the hard city enamel that neither scratches nor flakes. She wasn't entirely successful; Susanna was quick to see this. The gratuitously sexist jokes and rough teasing of her male colleagues would become too much. She would suggest to Monty that Satisha might be best employed in asset management.

What Satisha did learn very quickly was how to cope with unpredictable fluctuations of the market, whose dance defied reason, even seasoned expectations. She had to take uncertainty in her stride, even when other people's millions were at stake. She saw that concentration at work had to be total – and that she had to leave such concerns behind when she headed home. The bank required another philosophy, another personality. The daily volatility in the market engaged her instinct for risk-taking, but she could not be deaf to the inner voice that said: *We do not understand the workings of much that we do, yet we never admit this to our clients. We move confidently; we offer the knowledge of hindsight when we observe a significant drift in any direction; we offer plausible explanations to those who need to believe in us.* She felt she was fast becoming a dissembler.

She tapped into Santosh's long experience in acquiring a significant portfolio of shares. He encouraged her to be cautious but not risk averse. 'Don't stay on the sidelines too long. Jump in. Enjoy being on the inside of the cut and thrust; go with your hunches. You might not be comfortable with all the means used to keep the City's engine running – its gambling, daredevilish play – but it's what makes the world go round, so give it your all. You can leave it behind whenever you wish.'

At one of their meetings, Miss Mayfield found her own approach opened to closer inspection.

'The approach you suggest works, don't you think, Miss Mayfield, when you know the portfolio and temperament of the client. But what happens if this is a new client? Or you are taking over from another colleague? Your approach favours the seasoned investor; but what of advising the financially unsophisticated, what then?'

Miss Mayfield was not used to having her expertise scrutinised by a mere novice. She had been challenged, her eyes narrowed and before she could check herself she poured forth examples of when and where her rules applied, as well as the exceptions. Satisha was impressed and learnt a great deal.

When Satisha told her mother about these encounters, Amira reminded her that it was in her best interests to be courteous and even generous. 'She is older than you, has acquired much experience; she has made a success of her life and may have helped many to invest wisely. You ought to respect this, Satisha, and show her that you do. You're not in competition with her.'

By following her mother's advice, trust between the two women grew. Miss Mayfield began to appreciate Satisha's mix of boldness, wit and ability to grasp the new. She was flattered by Satisha's public gratitude to her as her 'City guru'. Satisha admired how well she had managed in a man's world. Her explanation was simple. 'Like you I was focused. I knew this was what I had always wanted and therefore worked tirelessly at it. I had no life but this. I wanted to be at the top of the pyramid, knew what I had to do to get there. No regrets, Satisha, though for my parents, especially my mother, grandchildren and a lesser job would have been her preference. I wanted to leave a name that would be acknowledged and respected. I wanted esteem; when it happened, I knew I had arrived at the pinnacle of my world. It was exhilarating. I've also paid a price.'

Meanwhile a madness yet unknown to the city was galloping ever nearer.

47

SOMETHING NEW IS IN THE AIR

Satisha couldn't help thinking that something bizarre had penetrated the minds of many of those who stared at screens all day. The young were the most affected. Their fervour for rising markets drove them to embrace the new internet businesses. At first, her male colleagues on the trading floor were like cowboys on the track of the herd of dotcom shares. Gradually the herd developed its own pace and an increasing momentum became a stampede. The cowboys lost control of the herd and became a part of it; it was not clear who was driving whom.

In public, traders pretended they knew where they were going. They were on a high and neither the young nor the not-so-young, who should have known better, could believe their luck. Satisha preferred to be amongst a small group of 'odd-balls' who dared to express the view that the herd was driving itself. The excitement and energy was as contagious as a virus, multiplying itself rapidly. The newspapers caught it and passed on the infection. Santosh said, 'It cannot go on indefinitely. All markets depend on confidence but who knows here what has value and what hasn't?'

Even Miss Mayfield felt out of her depth and was relieved to be in R&D as an observer of this brave new world. All she offered Satisha was a sigh: 'Beware. A strange beast is here.'

It was undoubtedly stimulating. The City had become a place where everyone had a tale to tell but no one an answer. Those who claimed to be experts on these shares tended to be the young analysts who skipped steps when climbing the stairs. Some of the grey-haired (and those with thinning hair) looked askance, took the lift and retired, to shake their heads and watch. These dotcom shares were an intoxication. How else to explain why so many had laid aside established wisdom on how a market moves?

Satisha got out her compass – a return to the fundamentals of secure investing – and gave it pride of place on her desk. The spirits of Benjamin Graham and David Dodd rose from their resting places and walked beside her. What they clarified was common sense: that buying into companies with undervalued assets, where the price of the stock was undervalued relative to earnings, was the golden rule. What was going on before her was the very opposite: almost the less the earnings, the greater the imagined value. She listened closely to these forgotten mentors. It was a reflective, lonely time.

Large egos, greed, leaping ambitions and, in a few instances, the temptation to deceit, sidestepped the directives of Graham and Dodd. Accounting became ever more 'creative' so that it became harder and harder to see what a business was really worth. Graham and Dodd were declared to be 'old hat' as the hypnotic, soaring strains of an over-optimistic human nature led an exuberant dance. Was this hysteria? It was tempting to see it this way, but intent on understanding the phenomenon, Satisha refused to give way to bemused bafflement.

'These dotcom shares are man-made, not alien to us,' she said. Her training had told her to keep an eye on all the financial indicators such as the price-earnings ratio, the net assets of the companies and their cash flows. But how could this be done when there were only prices and no earnings, nor cash flows? Wouldn't these companies exhaust themselves? How many were there with a sound business model and the capacity to develop? How was one to know without the relevant data? She would not get on the merry-go-round, and whilst the rules of London Moorgate helped her by forbidding her from personally investing in shares, she saw others carried away by the continued buoyancy of the market and the bonuses that went with it.

She wanted to earn a reputation for being discerning in a volatile market and reflected on how difficult it evidently was for City men to see their activities objectively. Hadn't Kant written something pertinent about that?

At about this time, the bank was contacted by Mr Edward Huntington. His great grandfather had been one of its first and most important customers and the Huntington family and Moorgate had remained loyal to each other ever since. Edward's uncle, George Huntington, had managed the wealth of the current generation of Huntingtons, but he was recovering from an operation in hospital and had given his nephew Edward, instructions to purchase a significant parcel of dotcom shares. He had not so far invested in these equities, but had begun to think that he had been unduly cautious. Edward was advised to seek advice from the reliable Mr Robinson before committing himself. Mr Robinson had, however, retired.

So it was that Satisha was given the task of meeting and advising Edward Huntington. She studied the portfolio; it was easy to see that the family were of substantial means and George Huntington had been a financially sophisticated and safe player. Mr Montgomery had informed Satisha that Edward Huntington needed to hear what the bank thought of the new high-tech shares, 'At present he holds none and wishes to be advised. Ten-thirty tomorrow morning, at Chester Terrace, overlooking Regent's Park.'

She was flattered to be given the file.

Mr Montgomery knew it would reveal to Miss Vidhur that this was one of their vintage customers; what it would not show was that Edward Huntington, unlike his uncle, was not *au fait* with the stock market. His interests in life lay with the liberal arts, not finance. She would be cautious, show herself as a serious, intelligent asset manager, as good as the next man, or even Susanna Mayfield.

48

EDWARD HUNTINGTON

By ten o'clock, Satisha stood on the north side of Threadneedle Street, hailing a cab. She had given herself less than half an hour to reach her client and was becoming anxious that it was not enough. Noise was all around – horns, bells, sudden braking, curt exchanges about the sanity or intelligence of drivers, the cries of the newspaper vendor on the corner. At last, cocooned in a cab, she looked at her notes again as it wound its way northwards, slowly along Moorgate, but then more quickly as the traffic thinned; up City Road to Pentonville, past St Pancras, then Euston, pausing with the lights at the right feeder lane into York Gate, right into the outer circle and eventually right again into Chester Terrace. Here the scene was tranquil, as if she was in another period, another world. Now the hurly-burly she'd left behind seemed reassuring in its familiarity; it was the hush of Chester Terrace that unnerved her.

She stood facing the terrace. This was the place; its name was written large, in white against Wedgwood blue, on the tall arch spanning the road. A neat line of period street lamps faced the terrace, which in turn looked towards magnificent copper beech trees partially shielding the green expanse of Regent's Park. She was just on time. She glanced down at herself, hoping her neat, soft, blue jacket with matching mid-length, straight skirt of fine linen, and black court shoes with medium heels accorded with the landscape.

Within a few seconds of ringing the bell, a male voice said, 'Yeeees?' She noted the tone and the lengthening of the syllable. She was in the right place. 'Satisha Vidhur, London Moorgate.'

There was a pause. 'One moment please.'

The large white door opened. Satisha's dark smiling eyes met James's grey, surprised ones. He could not recall ever opening the door to such a female representative of the bank before. Had he heard correctly? Surely London Moorgate... He wondered what his employer would make of it. It was only last night that Sir Mathew Goring had been there, and James recalled snippets of a conversation that turned on the prevalence of illegal immigration and an alarming case where a woman had died as the police had tried to arrest and deport her. Sir Mathew had been as forthright as ever on the need for firmness – and voluble on the threat of immigration, legal or illegal, to the English character – not forgetting to lambast the failure of the colonies after independence. And though his employer had taken a characteristically softer view, his attitudes, James suspected, were not that different. 'Give me the quiet life in West Sussex,' Edward Huntingdon had said. What would he make of this young woman?

'This way please. Would you care to take the lift, Madam?'

'How many floors up?'

'The drawing room is on the first floor, Madam.'

'I shall take the stairs. Thank you.'

On the thick carpet, her heels were hushed. The graceful sweep of the wide stairway curved like a dancer's hip, its ironwork imbued with motion. It was a sinuous flowing stream, bursting, in places, into flowers and foliage. Satisha could hear in it the sound of a sitar.

At the top of the stairs, Mr Huntington stood and watched her movement. Was she meant to be with another client and had been given the wrong address? Too young. Could she be a broker? Nevertheless somewhat pleasing to look at from this height. Those thighs… well… he could see her at the ballet accomplishing the most satisfactory pirouettes. He cleared his throat.

She looked up.

'Mr Huntington?'

'Yes.'

'Satisha Vidhur; I'm pleased to meet you; such a beautiful stairway.'

He saw eyes that were clear, sparkling.

They sat in a drawing room that Satisha saw as a gracious, grand dame. It intrigued and welcomed; held itself aloof. She heard Mozart. The balcony outside was conservative, masculine – columnar. Beyond it was a view of the park. The decorative architraves around the internal doors served as malas honouring those who entered. The morning sunlight directed her attention to the rugs, the large pink marble vases, the paintings of family members, some engaged in the chase on magnificent, striding horses. Two cupboards displayed pieces from ancient India and China.

She took in Mr Huntington's lean, tall, well-proportioned frame, his floppy hair escaping onto his forehead; his V-necked royal-blue jumper over a checked shirt; deep fuchsia corduroy touching his brown suede shoes.

He was anxious to hold up his end for his uncle's sake. Thank goodness the old chap had phoned him last night, filled him in on a number of things which he should consider. Nevertheless, as was his habit, he felt reluctant to go straight to the point. He smiled nervously and began with a question he immediately regretted.

'You are new at the bank?'

'I haven't been there as long as Mr Robinson.'

'From India?'

'No.'

'From where?'

'London Moorgate, and before that Mill Hill.'

Hadn't expected that. A feisty one this, but a contagious smile.

'I came to London at the age of six; I was born in Trinidad. Mr Montgomery informed me that you are interested in the possibility of buying some high-tech shares and would like to be briefed on them before you invest.'

'That is so.'

'I must commend you, Mr Huntington; your portfolio could serve as a textbook called *Guide to Investors*.'

'I see.' *'I must commend you.' Indeed! Must she? Thank heavens the old boy is not here.*

'Your portfolio reflects the cardinal rules of sound investment.'

'Which are?'

'To spread money as widely as possible into different types of investment and not fall in love with any in particular. Falling in love has its hazards but falling in love with one's investments can spell financial ruin. Don't you agree?' *You look so solemn, Mr Huntington. I'm merely trying to enable you to relax a little. You're as stiff as cardboard… bottled up. Perhaps this portfolio was put together by someone more familiar with the art of investing than you seem to be…*

Well… what has Monty sent me? A young woman, an Indian but not from India, with a voice which carries too much authority for her years. Not like any of the women I met there in the fifties… but she wears a suit well…

'You have every reason to consider these new high-tech shares; at present they are bringing good returns. Have you had time to look at them? Do you have any preferences? Are there particular ones you would like to discuss?'

'Which would you recommend and why?'

He doesn't know anything about these shares. Why not just say so. He's not even good at bluffing. He really needles me. Satisha, be diplomatic just this once!

'As this is our first meeting, and I'm aware you've had a long and fruitful relationship with our bank, I want you to know that at all times I'll be frank and honest with you. When I'm not sure, I'll say so; when

I'm as certain as it's possible to be, I'll say so. I'll offer you my reasons for the advice I give; ultimately you decide, Mr Huntington.'

Thoughtful silence.

'Do you have any questions?'

'You are plain speaking I see, Miss Vidhur. I need to know which shares you recommend.'

Satisha sighed inwardly.

'I'll clarify a few things that might be helpful. Though they are all known as dotcom shares, they are not all alike. There are two broad categories. The first is the more vulnerable. I would be troubled to recommend them to you. They enable you to purchase the kind of items you would find in a good supermarket or high street shop from the comfort of your home, and have them delivered. Food, cosmetics, gardening products, even pet requisites.'

'Why are you not favourably disposed to them? Is the demand not there? Most people would like shops to come to their homes.'

'At present, there are far too many of them providing the same services; in the absence of reliable information, we can't predict which ones will survive, which will go under. We don't know a great deal about who is managing them, what previous experience they have had. In the main, they appear to be run by young men full of charisma and self-promotion. It is certainly true that the internet is opening up new ways of doing things, but we don't know yet what the internet can do well, very well, only satisfactorily or poorly. At this stage we are learning.'

'At present, Miss Vidhur, the shares of these companies are doing exceptionally well.' He glanced at his notes. 'The banks and venture capitalists are backing them.'

'I am aware of this, and that a number of these dotcom companies raised substantial amounts of money when they offered their stocks. All this is happening even though investors know that many of these companies have yet to make a profit. It's a new phenomenon. The thinking is that at this stage, what is required is growth, not profits. When you remove the spin, what is actually being proposed is: "Keep going, though we see no profits – none of the customary indicators are there – nevertheless it's a good investment, because we say it is, though when a return will materialise, we don't know and at present do not care." I'm surprised that a number of big names in traditional businesses in the United States are backing these dotcom companies.'

'They can't all be wrong, Miss Vidhur.'

'Neither can the fundamentals of economic thinking, Mr

Huntington. As I said, there are too many of them doing the same thing, vying with each other, spending far too much on advertisements rather than on the business itself. Too much supply for an unproven demand. Adam Smith would be chuckling to himself.'

Her style amused, yet he was miffed by it.

'Do you really think so?'

'I am sure of it. My view rests on sound economic principles, not wishful thinking… woolly ideas, or the folly of those old enough to know better.' She paused, annoyed that she has allowed his tone to rile her, her control to falter, and hurried to make amends. 'Mr Huntington, we're in danger of forgetting what Graham and Dodd and now Warren Buffet have taught us. If we follow their guidance, we'll be doing better than average in the long run. Your portfolio reflects that thinking.'

'It is good of you to remind me, Miss Vidhur.' It was never like this with Mr Robinson. Yet the cut and thrust of their meeting stirred him. Making judgements about these stocks was well outside his parameters. She was evidently well informed and her vibrancy and perkiness attracted him, but she was thrusting forward just too confidently and freely. He knew he was not on his best manners, relieved that his uncle was not there, and yet who knows, the old boy might have found her engaging. He knew he was dependent on her advice and that this was part of his niggling resentment. Why had she not yet told him which shares to purchase? Mr Robinson would have done so, would have known this was his preferred approach. Instead she was making a mountain out of a molehill by continually saying the decision must be his. That was a given, for heaven's sake.

He had been prepared to be obliging when he saw her coming up the stairs. She had somehow been welcomed by the stairway. What a crazy thing to think; yet that was what he saw. She was professional and yet he was uncomfortable with her. Why? Because it was not what he had expected from someone of her complexion? Those eyes seemed to be reading him.

Hold steady. Perhaps it was too much of that Pomerol Mathew brought last night that has got you out of sorts. What did she say? 'The folly of those old enough to know better?' You're becoming soft in the head, Edward, as mother often says. For heaven's sake pull yourself together.

Something was changing out there. Whatever it was, it accounted for her being here. It was not something he sensed at his club, or read in the pages of the *Daily Telegraph*. His colleagues grumbled about immigration when they met, but it was not something that really changed their world. This was different; it was here in his drawing room, demanding not merely his attention but his concentration too. Robinson would have known this was not one of his mornings, but she…

'It is the second category of dotcom shares that I have a preference for. They provide a service of a different order, Mr Huntington.' She smiled in much the way Miss Matthew had done all those years ago at St Hilda's. 'They do not simply replicate the service in the supermarket or the high street shops. These service providers enable us to use the worldwide network to reach a vast range of information. This is unprecedented. I would recommend the search engine Apollo, and maybe Phoebus, too; they provide a global internet service for both consumers and businesses. You can see that, unlike the first category, their services really make use of the global network. You do not have to make up your mind now, but it would be a cautious, sensible way to enter into dotcom share ownership.'

'What would you recommend? How much should I allocate to each?'

'Enter with caution and, as you begin to get the feel of things, add to them, if you are so inclined.'

'I need something more precise, Miss Vidhur. Five million pounds? Ten million?'

'Shall we start more cautiously, Mr Huntington? Apollo I have a preference for, so I suggest five million pounds there and Phoebus, let us say two million pounds. This gives you a comfortable entrée into dotcom shares.' She smiled. 'If they are really going to take over the world these sums will grow quickly and we can always add to them later. It is a conservative suggestion.' Her eyes teased. 'I recommend this approach when dealing with an unknown. If you agree, give me a call at the bank and I will arrange the trades and send you the confirmations.' She rose, picked up her briefcase. He stretched forth his hand; hers was small, lost in his. Holding it firmly, he said, 'Thank you, I will reflect on what you have recommended. James will see you out.'

'Beautiful stairway isn't it?' she said to James.

He nodded. This appeared to require much effort.

'Such an elegant Georgian terrace. We're fortunate that Nash was not a successful investor and so had to return to architecture. Chester Terrace is a monument to his return.'

'Of course… Of course. Good morning, Miss Video.'

The following day a call came from Mr Huntington; he wished to purchase the shares she recommended as well as another of his own choosing. His uncle had been pleased, adding that he knew Robinson was reliable. This misunderstanding his nephew kept to himself.

49

A BARREN DREAM

Even asset management was taking its toll. Satisha tried, but could not see it as a job in which you offered the best possible advice to your clients. The market was not an exact science; it was in constant flux, pulled this way and that by factors that no one fully grasped. Information could not always be had, and what was known changed moment by moment according to what was fed into the market and taken out by thousands of players. Life was a gamble, but this daily drama in which fortunes could be made or lost with the click of a mouse did not suit her temperament. A decisions made could not be cancelled or left in limbo. Once made, it could not be revoked. You had to be the first on the rise or the first to leave before the beginning of the fall.

It was the speed at which traders played that was disquieting. Colleagues accepted the badge of 'expert' when in truth their decisions were made on a hunch topped with a dollop of wishful thinking. It was the thinness of the information they were skating on while gambling with other people's savings and their hopes that unnerved her.

When her advice lost her clients money it depressed her, and she could rarely feel justified in congratulating herself even when they gained substantially. She lost weight, withdrew from the City's social life, neglected her Indian dance classes, phoning home and her chats with Susanna Mayfield.

There were nightmares; a few lingered into her waking life, like the one in which she found herself in an ancient village high on a plateau. She rides a donkey, seeking a way down to the green plains and streams beyond. On the windswept terrain, a hardy, silent peasantry are standing or walking along the single yellow clay road. Some distance from the road, but facing it, a line of vacant pueblos look like monuments to the dead. The living find no shelter there from the burning sun, because their flat roofs have no overhang. There is no resting place.

Her desperation grows but escape eludes her. Why did she not leave a marker on entering? Then she cannot recall entering. The language is foreign to her. No one seems interested in her plight. Everyone goes about their business as if she is not there; they won't stop long enough to try to understand what she is saying. When she asks how to leave, they look at her, then slowly walk away, as if not understanding her predicament. They never speak.

Then a man comes who appears to understand her plight, but he takes her along a route she knows cannot be right. It is far too long and the scenery unfamiliar. She is convinced he is taking her further into the interior. Tall, eroded rocks, like totem poles with the eyes of ancient gods, are watching her. This is a landscape barren of human connections, though there are people moving about. Are they all imprisoned on the plateau? Its sides are sheer. Her eyes keep scouring the landscape, yet no exit is found.

Are these sentient beings or programmed mannequins? They either watch her or watch the sun, saying nothing. Are their batteries charged by the sun? Their actions are identical. Being trapped there with these automatons is terrifying.

When she woke, she was relieved to be in her own bed. This recurring dream forced her to recognise that the City had fractured her. Its philosophy was depleting what made her who she was. She had to leave it immediately if she was to hold on to her diminishing self. So in September 2000, when the late-flowering clematis brought forth another flush of colour, she handed in her resignation to Mr Montgomery. She had applied for the post of economist in the research department at the Commonwealth Secretariat and was successful. Here she felt she could regain her equilibrium.

Before she left, Satisha phoned her clients. She wanted to unburden herself of an alarm that had grown ever more insistent, her conviction that a correction in share values would have to take place, and with a vengeance, since the world could not stay mad. She knew that the minority of pessimists were ignored in the City's thinking. Traders, bankers with large bonuses, would look at the rising graphs, and say to their clients, 'What profits would we have foregone had we followed the pessimists and sold at this point or this or this?'

After she'd made the round of calls she allowed herself a glass of red wine and mused that the very names of these dotcom companies did not inspire confidence; they had become sillier by the day – boxman, mango, ibelieve, bagsoftime, thestreet, unwired. The very names reflected the high-spirited lightness of their being, like beaten egg whites. Three years in the City was quite enough. Whilst the salary at the Commonwealth Secretariat was significantly less, it gave her the chance to regain herself. There were the hints from home, too, on the topic of marriage. But where to look? A lot of old fogies at the Secretariat; nothing there, that much was clear.

50

THE CHASE
2001

On a mild January afternoon, Mr Huntington closed his front door and headed for his favourite bower – the long, rectangular enclosure spanning the houses of Chester Terrace and overlooking Regent's Park. As he was about to open its gate, he stalled when he heard small, intrepid feet running helter skelter, screams of delight, cries and quarrelling voices, followed by reprimands. Darkening clouds hovered above him; there was dampness in the air. He pondered awhile, then, umbrella in hand, walked briskly away from Chester Terrace to Regent's Park. Here there was hush. The fountains were silent, their basins dry, but there was something comforting to his spirit in this absence of nature's thrust.

He had been schooled from kindergarten to swim with the currents of tradition. His childhood, his public school, then university had been laid out for him, and he had donned the costume and played his part on these stages, content to please his parents and his uncle. Of late, a restless need for inner release not sensed before had taken over his life. This brought a nervous spring to his feet.

The mood of the season turned his thoughts to the frailty of his dear mother and uncle. It was his turn to take responsibility for them, attend to what they needed. Though it was kindly put, when he had last visited his mother he could sense her anxiety for him had grown.

'I'm getting on, Edward, as you must see, and your uncle George no longer has quite so much *joie de vivre*. Since your father was so suddenly taken from us, George has been like a father to you. I sometimes think you were the son he never had.'

A long silence. The hooting of owls, the flapping wings of a night hunter, the conversation of insects, the sounds of the night, were lost to mother and son staring at the dying coal fire in the hearth.

'You may feel, my dear, that the time for having children has already been closed to you; yet there are many who would gladly share your comfortable life. You have much to offer the more discerning female members of our acquaintance.'

Silence.

'You've often reminded me that you have a fulfilled life with the

262

ENO. Under your chairmanship it has become a much more dynamic opera house. Few are privy to the source of this development, and George tells me this is the way you wish it to remain. I know you enjoy the work, feel a duty to be useful, but there are occasions, Edward, when even the best plans need to be revised.' She sighed. 'Much as we don't wish to admit it, change is taking place as never before. Your father, and then you, left the family finances entirely to George, yet when he asked you to attend to them recently, you managed a remarkable job in the most volatile of times, your uncle tells me. So please, Edward, for my sake at least, do consider taking over the family's portfolio and think about that other matter too. Edward, forgive me if I've spoken out of turn.' He came to her assistance as she attempted to rise from her chair.

His thoughts returned to the present when a group of chattering girls in salwar kameez passed by. They glanced at him and moved on. As their voices faded, memory of another came.

He had not expected her call and, hearing the urgency of her tone, had asked anxiously if she had changed her recommendation. He was nervous, and his hopes that his uncle would have recovered enough to take over the family stocks looked less and less likely. He was pleased she had contacted him.

'I'm sorry, Mr Huntington, to call at this time, but I won't be in the bank most of next week. I recommend you give your dotcom shares serious consideration. You may have been observing the upward trend in the market, but I think it would be worth your while to consider selling now.'

'All?'

'Yes. A correction has to take place. The dizzying growth of their values has run ahead of actual performance. There's a natural bias to buoyancy in the City, not unconnected with bonuses and large egos. There may be one or two businesses that in the long run may regain their current valuation and develop further, but a number of them will soon begin to fall, and others will rapidly follow. Then there could be a stampede of investors to get out. Sell while there is still time, Mr Huntington. My reason for phoning so late is that I have had to reach other clients as well. I recall that, at the time, you wished to be advised, and I note you have since added substantially to that initial purchase. Sell when you can. Please think about it.'

The park was empty. The wind rose and it began to drizzle. Three weeks after that call, the shares had fallen, though not as much as she had anticipated. In fact all those to whom he had spoken were saying they had fallen enough and would now begin yet another rise. He had asked her: 'Have you changed your recommendation?' The reply was no.

She had steel in that conviction and he doubted whether Robinson would have held so firm, particularly under pressure from his own anxious calls, surrounded as they were by the contagious feeling of recovery. The crash came a couple of months later. It was exactly as she said. He had been tempted to repurchase on several occasions. What a close call. He congratulated himself on holding his nerve. Uncle George had been most satisfied by the substantial gains made over that short period of time, and relieved he had sold in good time.

Miss Vidhur had saved them from incurring heavy losses. She had then disappeared like a firefly in the night. He had wished to thank her, but had received a letter from Monty informing him that she had left the bank.

The wind and rain increased its strength; leaves skated past as if chased. Trees swayed, intent on wrenching free from the earth's tenacious grasp. Then a young woman speaking on a mobile phone ran past him; he thought he recognised the voice. With her silver earrings swaying wildly and her soft dupatta outstretched like wings, Edward thought of a lithe spirit of the woodland, a daughter of Pan. She headed for the only shelter, a small alcove, near the exit of the park, at Gloucester Gate.

Acting on impulse, he opened his umbrella, walking swiftly towards the alcove. Satisha heard the quick, determined steps coming towards her in the mist. Knowing she was alone, her heartbeat quickened. The hurrying steps were closing in. For a moment she was as still as a doe who smells a hunter. Then panic seized her and she made a dash for the gates. She did not look in his direction, but from the shape of her head, neck, limbs, from the very way she ran, he knew it was Miss Vidhur. He called out to her but the wind returned his voice. He tried to catch up with her, but though very fit, he caught only her dupatta. It had become unmoored, snagged on the branch of a tree. With care, he unwrapped it and walked out of the park.

Meanwhile Satisha had bolted through the gate into the Outer Circle. Street lamps, people walking briskly, the headlights of cars glimmering on the wet road, the swishing of tyres on water confused her fleeing senses, making her dizzy; she tried to slow down, but could not stop. A cab was approaching; she hailed it. Her dupatta has gone, but she was safe. The cab sped away.

A middle-aged woman walking her dog noticed the young woman running out of the park; then she saw the figure following her. What she thought was not favourable to Edward. He walked up to her, conscious of how it might appear.

'I was hoping to reach her. I saw this floating away from her.' His accent, his bearing gave credibility to what he said. Smiling she said, 'I saw her take a cab; she was in a great hurry.'

James was surprised to see Edward so wet, though holding an umbrella. It was a conundrum which no doubt might be explained in good time. When, however, he was handed the dupatta and told it should be dry cleaned, he concluded that here was behaviour quite without precedent. Meanwhile, Edward Huntington contemplated a bold, and tempting, idea.

Satisha had hurried back to her flat, thinking better safe than sorry and glad that she kept fit. She had just showered when the telephone rang. It was her mother.

'Guess what,' she said. 'I've good news for you, Satisha. Ishani phoned; she wanted you and Vidya to know that Amru Sen is now a qualified doctor and working at Edgeware Hospital. She says he's living not far from us on Hale Drive.'

'Well, he did it. Good for him.'

'His parents are here too. Do you know them?'

'No Mummy, I've never met them.'

'Ishani says we should arrange to meet them. They are quite elderly and haven't been here long. It must be lonely for them living amongst strangers.'

The following day Amira went over to Hale Drive, hoping to meet Dr Sen's parents and introduce herself, but they were not there. Two days later she did the same, but again no one was there. Seeing Amira at the door, the next-door neighbour explained that the family was away and wouldn't be back for a while. When Amira phoned Satisha to tell her this, she said, 'Thank you, Mummy. It was good of you to try and get in touch, but there's no need to try again; if they're living so close, we'll meet them sometime. Let's play it cool.'

51

AN AGE-OLD CUSTOM
January 2001

James rang her bell. 'Good morning, Miss Vidoo,' he said, handing her a large envelope.

'Oh thank you, James… You're looking very well.'

'Thank you, Miss Vidoo.' He nodded and was gone.

The size of the envelope intrigued her. She hurriedly pulled apart the gummed flap and eased out a neatly folded dupatta. How on earth had he come by it? There was a letter.

Edward Huntingdon had been in the park that afternoon, just happened to be behind her, saw when the scarf floated away with the wind. Her eyes moved rapidly down the page. There was an invitation.

His handwriting was well formed. His letter expressed concern for her welfare. Satisha was not to know this was a part of him that was closed to all except his mother and James. His voice rose from the page. 'I would like to invite you to dinner at my club. I would be on my own and I'm hoping you will accept. I would like that very much for I have not had the opportunity to thank you appropriately for your financial acumen. Your company would immeasurably enhance the evening for me.'

Not having a good reason to decline without giving offence, and curious to know what he would be like in such an environment, the invitation became an intriguing adventure. Satisha picked up the phone. But as soon as it was agreed that he would call for her the next evening, she began to wonder whether she had acted too hastily. To be seen with an older man at his club? How should she dress for the occasion?

She called Kamla Devi.

'Now do you wish your evening wear to be Indian or English?'

'Both.'

'Typical, typical. You Vidhurs want everything.'

'Anjali managed it, why not me?'

'Well…' *You're not Anjali, you're a daring butterfly*. 'How is she?'

'Happy, I think. She's really busy with the boys; she's started teaching again and worries about giving them enough quality time, but she's well-organised. We speak to them on the phone. I love hearing Ishan, Sachin and Vish speak – quite the little Trinidadians.'

'That's good to hear. Now, Satisha, whatever you decide to wear, you must let the gentleman feel comfortable with you, let your elegance be pleasurable to him. You have to decide of course. Ultimately it comes down to how you're feeling. A full skirt with its extra bounce, I'm not sure about, certainly not that cocktail frock that says you want to give god-alone-knows-what vibes to those spoilt city brats. I don't know what anyone would make of your wardrobe. The variety is mind-boggling. From the sophisticated to just about any-thing that takes your fancy. Perhaps the one common thread is: Here I am chaps!'

'That's a sign of youth, Kamla Devi, though I'm getting heavy hints from home about its passing.'

'The evening requires a touch of sophistication. Now let's see, mid-calf skirt, that matching blouse in white satin you haven't worn for a while; it is not transparent, yet subtly draws attention. Sleeves just below the elbow, not too much bare arms, not at this stage anyway.'

'What do you mean?'

'I don't know what you have in mind, Satisha, nor am I asking. I'm merely ensuring that what you wear will be right for the occasion. Now for the Indian bit. Wear the necklace with that fine filigree work, the matching earrings and a fine tiki. I like that piece of opal you have. I leave the rest to you. Whatever, make sure it's something you're comfortable with and remember to enjoy the evening…' She cleared her throat.

'What is it Kamla?'

'I know you Vidhur girls and I know I do not have to say this, but just in case restraint is lost, something erupts within…'

'Well, I'll call for a doctor; surely the bursting of a blood vessel, especially in the brain, is a serious matter.'

'You know full well what I mean! What I'm saying is – please stop interrupting and be sensible, Satisha – just in case a surge of fine natural feelings overcome you, don't agree to be taken to Chester Terrace for coffee or another drink. Just you return to your flat, insist on it if you must. Let him drop you off first and then take himself home.'

'Of course, Kamla Devi.'

'I know I sound too much of an old-fashioned mother hen.'

'You're wonderful, Kamla Devi.'

'Glad to hear it. You Vidhur girls want to carry your parents' wisdom in your youthful bodies. It does not always mix well, you know – oil on water.'

'I can't envisage any surge of feeling that would be strong enough to drown your voice and Mummy's and Daddy's. It would have to be of tsunamic proportions.'

When the door-bell rang, she was ready.

'Good evening, James.'

'Good evening, Miss Vidoo.'

'How are you?'

'I'm very well, thank you.' For the first time she sensed he was welcoming her in his own understated way and he led her to the car most graciously.

Mr Huntington was meticulously dressed for the evening. Here was a detail historians had overlooked, she thought. Perhaps it had been the fine tailors and shoemakers of London who had won the Empire. Something about the suit – the lapels, buttons, seams, the very fabric – gave the wearer an imposing presence.

They exchanged smiles. 'What a pleasant night.'

'Refreshing,' he said, looking at her. His eyes, seldom so engaged at such close quarters, had not learnt the art of camouflage.

London was throbbing with movement. Rain had fallen, tyres splashing and spraying, and the play of diffused yellow light onto the wet pavement had transformed Piccadilly into a Disneyland representation of itself. In the quiet of the car, Satisha listened to her thoughts.

Would they be fencing tonight as they'd done at their first meeting? They'd acknowledged each other with a mutual bow when she'd entered the car. But what was the object of fencing? Attempting to protect yourself from an opponent while at the same time trying to find an opening in his defence? Was this not life, politics, competitive business? Weren't all people fencers? The answers would have to wait; they had reached Pall Mall.

'Here will do, James.'

He helped her out of the car. He was both a princess's father and an admirer, though restrained by place and the moment.

The large room was already half full, a quiet sociability flowing amongst the tables. A huge chandelier and a painting of large crowds at a fair – an original Stubbs? – attracted her attention. They were taken to their table – one no doubt coveted – in a quiet corner; cosy, intimate, removed from the pathway of comings and goings.

'Goodnight, ma'm, good night, sir. What would the lady be having?'

'Gin and tonic, thank you.'

'The usual, sir?'

Mr Huntington acknowledged a few nods without appearing to look.

'How have you been, Mr Huntington?'

'Fine, thank you. And you?'

'Reclaiming myself. I stayed too long in the City.'

'I never thanked you properly for such sound advice. You were firm all the way in your belief that it could not last.'

'It wasn't difficult. I could be more objective than most, for though we're not allowed to invest in shares, I didn't invest my emotions either. The expectation of large bonuses overexcited some.'

'You are quite unusual.'

'What I will say is that it lasted far longer than I envisaged. I had to believe that the law of gravity would in time come into play.'

'Where are you now? Are you happy there?'

She nodded and they toasted each other's good health and friendship. She sipped her drink and said, 'I need to dilute this, or I'll be leaving horizontally, and you might have to carry me.'

'I would be envied, Miss Vidhur.' He beamed. 'Let me help you.' He poured more tonic.

They ate halibut with herb and lemon sauce served with apricots and walnuts, beans, butternut squash and new potatoes, accompanied by a light German Riesling. Satisha had said that strong wines did not agree with her.

'Are your parents alive?'

'My father died ten years ago; my mother lives in West Sussex, not far from Wilton Park. Do you know it?'

'I'm embarrassed to say that I really haven't seen much of England, except for the Lake District. Do you visit her or does she come up to London?'

'My mother used to enjoy being in London, but now travelling tires her. She's becoming frail – though not her mind. I go down to see her once a fortnight and sometimes spend a night there. If you're ever down there and the opportunity comes to see the place, it's well worth a visit. You can go back in time effortlessly. The grounds are beautiful. You feel like swimming in the wind with the green below.'

'I shall remember that… No brothers and sisters?'

'No. I'm an only child.'

'I have two sisters: Anjali who is older than I – she's married and living in Trinidad – and Vidya who is the youngest. I don't know how I'd feel if I were an only child.'

'What one misses most, Miss Vidhur, is unconditional trust between people. What you did for your clients was exceptional.'

'It has to do with the way we were brought up. Once you are clear about what's unfair, unkind, unjust, you really have no choice. I couldn't just leave you like that.'

'Did you feel this way about all your clients?'

'Yes, I did.'

'It must be emotionally draining.'

'That's why I had to leave.'

'You said you are happy at the Commonwealth Secretariat, but did not appear too sure.'

'I'm not sure what happiness is.'

'I am very happy in your company, Miss Vidhur.'

'I enjoy your presence too, and I like being here.'

'When I say I'm happy in your company, Miss Vidhur, I'm not explaining myself adequately. What I mean is that being with you is like the moment I heard Beethoven's "Ode to Joy" coming to me through an open window as I sat on a wooden bench on a late summer's evening in the grounds of Wilton Park.'

'You express yourself beautifully, Mr Huntington. I am greatly touched.' The urge to touch his hand was intense, but she feared where that would lead. She could not look at him. He saw she was uncomfortable. Perhaps he had shown his hand too soon, but he also felt relieved that he had, that she knew how he felt.

'It's a beautiful night for this time of year.' Her tone tried to nudge his declaration, still circling them, to recede.

'Yes. It's not as cold as it could be.' Nothing further was said for a while and then he asked, 'Do you think it's possible for people of differing backgrounds to trust each other completely?'

'Of course, though I suspect complete trust is uncommon even amongst men and women from similar backgrounds.'

'It's a pleasure being with you, Miss Vidhur.'

'I feel the same, but that's not the same as complete trust. Pleasure and trust may walk hand in hand but it's not often they're lasting.'

Her observation, from one so young, amused him. She felt generosity in his laughter.

'You know, I visited India with my uncle as a young man only a decade or so after Independence, and what impressed me was how welcoming people were, when you might have expected some bitter-ness.'

'So what did you make of it?'

'How old it was, how complex – the variety was mind-boggling. All humanity there, so to speak. Poor, vulnerable, but able to cope with such extremes.'

'I've never been, but I'd very much like to one day.' She looked down to avoid his gaze of overwhelming earnestness.

'I see cherry pie on the menu. If it's freshly baked and warm and packed with luscious cherries, it's a delight; if we have it with custard or vanilla ice-cream or even with both, it will be an experience to savour again and again. Sometimes a little excess is in order.'

She smiled and so does he, but she feels uncomfortable. 'Perhaps we should have a more measured delight.'

'You are more English than you think or may wish to think.'

'It only appears so, Mr Huntington.'

'I knew you would disagree. Why can't you embrace us?'

'I don't think England wants to be embraced. She prefers to be admired. She has much to her credit in her long history and is keen to remind herself and the world of this. She finds it difficult to embrace another whose history is unknown, or who has still to prove herself by England's criteria.'

He is thoughtful. 'But an individual is not England.'

'True. But her milk runs through their veins. England is not alone in such a stance; other countries in her position would do the same as she does. It is a characteristic of power.'

'Do you think that?'

'All old cultures are conservative and proud. The West dismisses this at its peril.' The way he looked at her made her uneasy, he was saying without words that she was wrong, or that he didn't really understand what she was saying. She wished she could unsay it. She would put his mind at ease.

'I believe as you do, Mr Huntington. Individuals are unique and when their minds are beautiful, they are precious. We can embrace our common humanity and our common values, whatever the differences in the costumes we wear.'

He nodded in agreement.

'You're looking very well indeed. Your friends, if asked, would agree. I can see there are some here tonight, for several pairs of eyes have turned towards our table.'

'I was hoping you wouldn't have noticed.'

'Perhaps a few years ago, I wouldn't have, but I'm slowly learning to read the Englishman's ways.'

'Why must you be so refreshingly candid all the time?'

'Just trying not to be like the natives.'

He laughed. 'I am enjoying myself. I hope you are.'

'It is clear that I am, Mr Huntington.'

They had the cherry pie.

'A fitting way to close our evening,' she said.

'Would you not care for a cognac? Please have one. The evening is still young. James is not expected for quite a while.'

Satisha looked about her. What harm would there be in that? The cognacs were brought.

'I've been reading about the Battle of the River Plate, in 1939. Do you know of it, Mr Huntington?'

'Yes. I know we used bluff and superior intelligence to force the German captain to disengage from battle and scuttle his battleship, the *Graf Spee*. It was a great victory for us and helped to turn the war to our advantage.'

'I found myself absorbed with the moral dilemma Captain Langsdorf had to face and was moved by the choice he made. He forced me to think of where I stood on loyalty to individual or nation, and to have a strong preference for the former.'

'He could have made a run for it to the open ocean, as only one heavy cruiser was near by. Of course he was not to know that, or that it was no match for the *Graf Spee*. He could have escaped and continued to wreak havoc on our merchant ships.'

'Yes, and this is where the fine mettle of the man showed through. Believing what he did, he offered himself two choices when most naval officers could only have perceived the one. He could either save the lives of over one thousand men, prisoners of war taken from British merchant ships, as well as his own crew, or take them all with him to his death, like a Pharaoh, through a suicidal blaze of fire. He chose the former. He allowed them all, prisoners and crew to disembark. His last act was to write to his wife, a most beautiful letter, explaining his predicament, his love for Germany, his family and ship and the choice he had made. Then he scuttled his ship. Later he shot himself. What would you have done, Mr Huntington?'

He thought for a while then said, 'One never knows what one would do under such circumstances. I hope I would have had the courage to do the same, though I don't really know.'

'Such men should not be forgotten. They have much to contribute. We need Captain Langsdorf's kind of thinking when we feel cornered, and can think only of annihilating the other.'

'I can see you are moved by his decision. War is a barbaric way to solve what I often think is solvable with a combination of patience, truth, reason and honest negotiations.'

'It was an individual's values, not those of the nation. Perhaps Captain Langsdorf knew Wilfred Owen's profound words: "The old lie: Dulce et decorum est pro patria mori". So, to come back to your question: complete and genuine trust doesn't depend on our backgrounds, but on the thinking of the individuals involved. So there is hope for us all.' *I must change the subject. He appears too vulnerable; the cognac is acting upon me too. I feel like embracing him. The amount of cognac in this glass makes me wonder if the waiters are in league with him.*

'A penny for your thoughts, Mr Huntington.'

'They are worth far more, Miss Vidhur.'

As James stopped before her apartment, she put out her hand and said, 'Good night, Mr Huntington, thank you for such a fine evening. I enjoyed myself immensely.' He held her hand and she leaned over and kissed him on his cheek. She could feel his tremor and knew it was time to leave. He allowed her hands to leave his.

'Good night James.'

'Good night, Miss Vidoo.'

The car waited until light came to her apartment; then slowly, almost reluctantly, its wheels turned away. She lay in bed and hugged her pillow tightly. The effect of the cognac, Mr Huntington's feelings and the comfort of blankets accompanied her sleep.

52

ON THE WAY TO A WEDDING
May 2001

Vidya was in two minds about what to wear to Sonia's wedding; there was her dark-blue silk jacket and mid-length skirt with scarlet satin lining, and deep crimson lace top – an outfit that had a special appeal since it would offend the die-hard traditionalists – but she opted for a rich sari with an aanchal. Not having one that was sufficiently eye-catching, she borrowed one of Satisha's, a warm, creamy-yellow and gold, designed to enhance the female form.

She turned to Kamla Devi for help. She wanted her sari draped in the classical Indian style to impress those men with dour, grave faces who would probably think she had become too Western. Indo Caribbean women tended to wear Western style dresses, wearing only the salwar kameez or the sari on special occasions. Vidya had not worn a sari for quite a while so with an old sari she practised climbing the stairs, gathering and lifting the sari folds with one hand, and an aarti plate with the other. She looked at herself in a mirror, turning her head this way and that, trying out various facial expressions, winking, pouting, and making head, eye, hand and shoulder movements for some invisible observer. She was aloof, questioning, unamused, disdainful. For the *finale* she put her palms together, bowed her head and whispered 'Namaste' to her mirrored self. She was in the mood for having fun at the wedding.

Kamla Devi arrived half an hour early, knowing that anxiety charac-terised the Vidhurs, well, all except Anjali; she considered carefully what she said and did before acting; the younger two rather lacked their older sister's reflectiveness. She'd learnt from Amira that Anjali had settled in nicely to her new life, was enjoying her three children and getting along well with her in-laws too. It showed Anjali had acquired the art of how to live. As for Satisha and Vidya, well, time would tell.

'This choli is far too close fitting; I'd prefer the other one; it's a little looser.'

'Nonsense, you're only young once; a beautifully shaped bosom like that was not created by the maker to be hidden beneath a chaddar.'

'You have a direct line to Him, have you?'

'When you've been a student of philosophy, a classical dancer, and once even a courtesan in the best traditions of that ancient art, you know the purpose of the female form.'

'And I can't wear these earrings though they're stunning; I love the gold bangles, but I can't wear the earrings. My ears become red and they hurt.'

'I'll place just a whiff of soft cotton between your ear and the screw; leave it to me. Why you refused to have your ears pierced, I don't know; your mother tells me you call it primitive. Pierced ears would be better than tight screws surely.'

'I don't hanker after wearing them, Kamla Devi.'

She set off from her flat in Satisha's Toyota. All seemed well until she realised she had a flat tyre. Keep calm, she told herself, get to a telephone booth and call a cab. Her mobile she had lent to Satisha. Then she made the mobile users' discovery that call-boxes were no longer plentiful. She walked slowly along Avenue Road wondering what to do, fearful, on what was a warm May day, she would look hot and flushed, like a long-distance runner. On both sides, the houses were large and imposing. The idea of walking up to such front doors and explaining her plight was daunting. She walked for fifteen minutes, but it seemed an hour.

An idea she had been resisting returned. She would thumb a lift to the nearest telephone booth – but wearing such finery? She would wave down cars with female drivers. Time ticked by; no female drivers. Then she saw a buttery yellow Nissan Micra approaching at a comfortable speed; it looked as if it was smiling warmly. She held out her hand and kept it firmly outstretched. As the car began to slow, she saw the driver was a well-dressed young man. When he popped his head out of the window, there seemed something decent and reassuring about him; besides, she was desperate.

'Is this a damsel in distress?'

'I have a flat tyre; I'm on my way to a wedding in Hertfordshire. Would you mind taking me to the nearest telephone box so I can call a cab? It'd be such a great help.'

He looked at his watch. 'I'd gladly have changed the tyre for you, but I'm running late. I'm happy to take you to the wedding, though.'

'Oh I couldn't possibly ask you to do that; I'll telephone my sister when I arrive and she'll see to the car.'

'Does she have keys?'

'Yes. It's really her car.'

'Good. Now, I shall take you to the wedding.'

'Oh no! I couldn't allow you to go all the way there. It wouldn't be right. I'll get a cab.'

'Are you by any chance going to the wedding of Kumar Sharma and Sonia Rao in Arkley?'

'Are you going there?'

'I had every intention until you told me I mustn't take you there.'

'Well, I'm delighted to accept your charming offer. I'm Vidya Vidhur, and you?'

'I'm Mark Baverstock.'

'Sonia and I were at LSE; after graduation, she went into the City and I decided I'd teach. My sister Satisha was in the City, too, until recently; I didn't want to be doing the same things as she. Of course the bonuses were just fantastic, but from what Satisha said it was very stressful. Of course, so is teaching – and without the bonuses. I teach at St Thomas Girls' and you?'

'Kumar Sharma and I are on the staff of St George's College. He teaches physics and maths in the upper school; I teach maths to form one and English in the upper school. Our schools use the same car park, but I've never seen you there.'

'I don't own a car. I use the school bus. I borrow my sister's sometimes. Satisha and I live close to each other; she has an apartment on the first floor; mine is at the other end of the building.'

'What a coincidence to have met now.'

'True. But how did Kumar and Sonia meet? Their paths seem unlikely to have crossed.'

'Kumar said it was arranged.'

'There's something to be said for arrangements, even today.'

'Kumar told me what his father said: Respectable good family, educated nice girl.'

'Very, very good job, big bonus, caste not important, but all the same, right caste.' Vidya mimicked the accents she heard on comedy shows.

'I didn't think that caste mattered any more.'

'I'm being mischievous; education and professional status mostly take its place today. They offer social mobility. There's no mobility with caste. With good qualifications, good luck and good looks the sky's the limit we're told.'

'You said there was something to be said for arrangements. I wouldn't think that any young woman today would be saying that.'

'Well, arrangements have their place. We have a good example here. If it had not been arranged, how would they have met? They were working in very different fields, unaware of each other's existence. The economic viability of any venture is important, and from what we know, they stand a better than average chance of succeeding. I say better than average because we don't have the input of the compatibility of their personalities, their respective goals in life.'

'You make it sound like a business.'

'The best business strategies are really common sense. Were you to hear my aunt Ishani on this topic, you'd be convinced.'

Silence.

'Would you have an arrangement for yourself?'

'That depends on so many things. My parents are sensible, they would never force me to marry against my will. So if I had an arranged marriage it would be something the young man and I would be happy with.'

'What about love? What part does that play?'

'Oh that's just a word so worn out that even those who use it aren't sure what it means.'

'I thought it meant deep affection for… caring.'

'Could do. Though, observation tells me it's used far more frequently as an expression of biological need or when a socially acceptable proposition is before the players.'

Silence.

'Are you a mind reader, a feminist or both?'

'Suffice to say, I've been proved right far too often; nevertheless, as you see, I don't have a swollen head.'

He looked at her head supported by a very kissable neck.

'You should keep your eyes on the road; concentrate on what is before you, despite temptations elsewhere. It may save you from an accident, Mark.'

'I need a notebook to jot down these recommendations.'

'I'm sure your mother would approve of them.'

'I'm sure of it too. What a relief we can agree on something.'

'Don't be too hard on yourself. But to return to the point in question: in a way, marriage is a business.'

'You really think so?'

'I know so. It's the business of living, of how to live a good life with another, how to live it so that both of you develop and grow, respecting and caring for one another.'

'So… um… now how should I put this: has lusting no place in this business arrangement? What is politely referred to as "chemistry".'

'Well, you may think as you please, Mark Baverstock, but some people have evolved a sophisticated brain. It's what lifted us out of a primeval state. Lusting does not need a developed brain; a visit to a farm confirms this.'

'It's all in the brain, Vidya Vidhur.'

'Balderdash! Though I know what you're thinking.'

'The mind reader is at work.'

'You're thinking that you need a brain to achieve the end of lust.'

'You're intelligent.'

'You probably are too, Mark.'

He laughed so heartily that he had to wipe his eyes. Vidya handed him her tissue. He looked at his watch. 'We're making good time. I told you what Kumar's father said; what d'you think Sonia's parents would say to her?'

'I don't know, Mark. I know Sonia, but not her family. I'd be guessing. If you had a sister who was considering marrying him, what would your feelings be?'

'I don't have sisters, and that puts me at a disadvantage.'

'For heaven's sake! Marriage is about human relations, compatibility, remember? You're in a staff room with Kumar, you know him. What would you say to a dear sister?'

Silence.

'I'd say that he's easy to get along with, has a good sense of humour, responsible, thoughtful, well mannered. However, I'd have to add that his parents might not like the idea of them marrying, may even have arranged for him to marry someone whose culture is similar to their own. Since he has a deep affection and respect for his parents' views, I'd ask her to consider the pain that their marriage might bring and the possible repercussions. Marriage is not to be rushed into.'

'What a thoughtful reply. You could work in a marriage guidance bureau.'

'That would be presumptuous, not being married.'

'True, but you'd listen well, and any advice would have been thought through. Well, that's what I see.'

Mark smiled. Not bad for a first meeting. Would there be another?

When they arrived, Mark saw his colleagues gathered together as if they were planning a staff meeting. He said, 'Why don't they move about, get to know the people here better? We keep to our clan, they to theirs.'

Vidya phoned Satisha who advised: 'Enjoy the wedding, meet the eligible young men, leave the flat tyre to me. Just relax. Not every occasion is a fencing match. Do the small talk. You have the skill, Vidya. Use it before it becomes rusty.'

Vidya spotted a group of young women whose body language had constructed an impregnable wall around them. Those forming the enclosure were mostly in their mid-twenties to early thirties. All were dressed in exquisitely fine saris. Vidya was thankful she'd had the good sense to borrow Satisha's and not wear one of her own.

Undeterred by the signals – the averted eyes, the tightening of lips – Vidya entered the enclosure and smiled. The lively conversation ended abruptly. But why? She wouldn't be shunned like this.

'The garden is so well kept. I wonder if there's a keen gardener in the family?' No response. She tried again: 'The weather is perfect, must have been specially ordered for the day, don't you think?' Again: 'Nice spacious tents, though. Someone was taking no chances.'

A young lady in gold and blue who stood opposite her in the circle turned her head and spoke in Gujarati to the three closest to her. They glanced fleetingly at Vidya and smiled with disdain.

Vidya was about to move away when one of the Gujarati speakers addressed her: 'We see you walked in with an English fella.' The voice, its tone and the stare that accompanied it indicated that this was not just a statement of fact.

'Yes, I did. There are so many English people in this country, you just can't help bumping into them. I don't understand how it came about. How did they manage to get in?' She wanted to say a good deal more, but heard an inner warning voice that sounded like her mother's.

The sisterhood look confounded by her impertinence. 'How indeed, I wonder?' This came in an accent aspiring to be English upper middle class, but the emphases, the pauses had not quite arrived; a few more elocution lessons were needed, Vidya thought.

A young woman, just outside the circumference of the circle, gave her a sympathetic nod. Good for you, it said as she approached.

'I'm Taru.'

'I'm Vidya.'

As they walked away, Taru whispered, 'Those people are so false, so class-conscious. Posturing, striking an attitude… You've more courage than I, Vidya.'

'Their affectations are wound around them so tightly that I really felt like unravelling a few layers, but this is not really the place or time.'

'They must have a deep sense of insecurity, don't you think?'

'Well, probably, if they need to display that kind of feeling of superiority. I'm sure they think people like me are very inferior kinds of Indians. By the way, where are you from?'

'I'm from Fiji. I guessed you're from the Caribbean by the way you carry yourself. Caribbean people tend to be outspoken, but I did not think there were many Indo-Caribbean people here in London. They certainly keep out of the news.'

'Well, we ex-indentured people should stick together. "You walked in with an English fella." What was that supposed to mean? It was that smirk that got me. Did you see the way they looked at my sari, my hairstyle. Okay. I'm not on the pinnacle of high fashion, but is that what we should be focusing on? Shit! All the time they're calculating who is more important than whom, and trying to manoeuvre themselves accordingly. They really piss me off.'

'You're right, Vidya. Deep down they see us as second-class Indians, or not really Indians, a people who've lost themselves. I met a chap who told me that once you've left India and crossed the kala pani, you've lost the hearth and that can never be replaced.'

'Nonsense! We've lost the language – and granted that's a large loss I sorely regret – but we've also lost much baggage which has proved to be an advantage. So many restrictive customs – what day is best to cut your nails, to open a business, to move to a new house... These are things, like caste, that we freed ourselves from.'

As they walked back towards the house, Vidya said, 'Excuse me Taru, the ceremony is about to begin, I need to find someone. It was nice meeting you.'

They parted with a hug.

Vidya went to look for Mark. He was engaged with a beautiful female butterfly in a dazzling sari. *Look at how she's flapping her eyelids like a bird's wings in a courtship dance.* Mark looked quite taken by the performance. A surge of energy came to Vidya's steps.

'Please excuse me. Mark, I came to say that if you haven't been to an Indian wedding before, I'll gladly do some explaining.'

'Oh, I wasn't aware that this is your first, Mark,' the young woman said softly. 'Do forgive me. Sonia and I are first cousins, and I've two seats reserved for me at the front; from there you'll be able to see the ceremony at close quarters.'

'A front seat is what you need, Mark.' Vidya smiled, graciously she hoped. 'It'll be nice to hear what you make of the *Vivaha Samskara* on our way back.'

'What's that?'

'Sonia's cousin will explain.'

★

On their way home, Mark was on the verge of asking Vidya to explain what the *Vivaha Samskara* was, but sensed that the time to ask was not right. She looked out of sorts, preoccupied.

She was still going over the encounter with the superior Indian ladies and wishing she'd said what was on her mind, admitting to herself that she'd felt wounded by their unspoken but sneering contempt. Why had they come to England when they evidently felt they had nothing to learn from the place? They picked up the trivialities of consumer trappings and ignored the worthy core. How did they define civilisation? Didn't they hear the first two syllables? They were all Indians, but she hoped she had nothing in common with them.

But why was she bothered by their opinion? Why was she so vulnerable? Why did she feel the need to speak her mind all the time? Why couldn't she be like her father? Just listen, don't speak, keep smiling at sheer idiocy. When would she acquire the wisdom to change, to stop feeling things so strongly she was always going over the top? Why the need to put down the butterfly cousin?

Mark noticed that she was wiping a tear. He stopped the car.

'Is something wrong? Can I help?'

'My earrings are paining me; can you help me remove them please.'

Mark leaned over, her hair silky to the touch; he parted the fine strands over her right ear; her ear-lobe felt hot and tender. His hands were so gentle and her scent and warmth registered on his face and in his brain, especially when she turned to let him reach her left ear.

'Thank you, Mark.'

As he dropped her in front of her apartment, he said, 'I hope we meet again in the car park before the school bus arrives.'

'We will, I think, and thank you.' She noticed that he was hesitating, then he said, 'I want you to know that in future, anything to unscrew, unzip or undo, I am at your service.'

'I'll store that information in case of an emergency, Mark. Thank you again. You were nice to be with; forget everything I said in the car, I talk far too much.'

'I found you a delight to be with... It would be nice to meet again.'

'You say the right things all the time. How is that?' *Why can't I?*

'A mind reader should be able to tell me.'

They laughed and parted.

Later, he found the tissue she had used and her scent came back to him.

53

THE HICKORY TREE

Satisha thought the beautiful countryside of West Sussex ought to have been conducive to new reflections. It was there at Wiston House in Steyning that the two-day conference of Commonwealth ministers on the economic development of small states was taking place. The focus was on the challenge of free world trade and lowering of tariffs.

From the very first day, however, Satisha thought it was a meeting of people in denial. The world had moved on since 1968, when the Commonwealth Sugar Agreement had ensured favourable sugar prices (and with them political stability) to states where sugar was the monoculture.

Now, almost half a century later, British and other European taxpayers could not see the logic of subsidising the sugar and banana exports of former colonies, whose products could be had at a significantly lower price from the much larger and more intensively run estates in Latin America and elsewhere.

The response of the small states was very clear. Caribbean ministers argued that in a situation of rising populations and increasing demands for a better quality of life, the solution lay in bilateral agreements on even more favourable terms. There was no alternative. The problem was located in a world that had lost its values, and not, as was being hinted, in their stubborn holding on to the ideas of yesteryear. A prominent Caribbean minister asked, 'All yuh want we dead?' His colleagues applauded his courage and acumen. Others pointed out that the past was being conveniently forgotten. They reminded the conference that they had assisted Britain during two world wars, and after, by supplying metropolitan sugar needs at reasonable prices when world prices were astronomical. 'I never envisaged this day would come, brothers and sisters; you live and learn.'

When Satisha spoke, she agreed that for such small island economies changes were never going to be easy. It meant acquiring new skills; finding niches in the world market and exporting viable products to them. The full potential of tourism with its many ancillary industries was another path that had to be explored. Governments had no choice but to move on to new ventures; the old ones were unsustainable. The young in the Caribbean would leave rapidly for more developed societies if they saw there was no future for them at home. The losers would be Caribbean taxpayers who had financed their education.

After her speech she was given a wide birth by those convinced that her heart and head had been truly colonised by the free market gurus. Long residence in Britain, they murmured, had brought this about. She was no longer one of them, had lost her identity.

Feeling suffocated by such sentiments, she sought release by leaving Wiston House to walk in its rolling fields. Now, as the conference neared its end, it seemed even clearer that it was going nowhere. Too many ministers seemed happy to remain cradled in illusions.

On the last evening, Satisha left her colleagues soon after dinner, feeling that there was little to be gained from their coffee conversations. Instead, she prepared herself for an early departure in the morning and went to bed. If men in the City were far too daring, recklessly so, here there was such a reluctance to move that she wondered just what it would take to wake these ministers to the changed world around them.

The next day she rose before the rising sun, the morning mist heavy in the air. A stillness and hush enveloped the rolling grounds. Something about the place spoke of the beginning of time.

Satisha tiptoed down the elaborately carved stairway, trying to prevent it creaking. She opened the heavy entrance door and was caught in the sweep of the wind blowing over the grounds. As she walked away from Wiston House, she turned around to see its many chimney stacks like sentinels staring solemnly into the distance.

Far away on higher ground, a flock of sheep had crouched close together like emperor penguins for the night. Not feeling the sun's presence, they did not stir themselves. For a moment she embraced the fancy that they were pieces of cloud broken off from the sky by the wind. As the sun rose, the dew caught its first moving rays of light; it blinked and dazzled.

Her boots left imprints on the damp lawn. She pulled her scarf tighter and looked around. A giant tree stood apart. It called out to her. Hesitating at first, for it was a good walk away, she was drawn towards it. Closer up, she saw a severely storm-damaged hickory tree holding tenaciously to life.

Its trunk had been struck by lightning, gutting its stratified entrails. Softer lines and curves, once bark-protected, were the colour of charcoal. The image of a critically wounded soldier came to her. The tree had been exposed too long to the harsh elements. What a survival instinct it had. It lived. It grew. It thrived! Of course, it no longer had its former symmetry; destructive storms had hurled themselves with savage thrusts; the tree had been diminished. But even with half its trunk gone, leaning low, the hickory still survived in splendid style, like a few elderly folks she knew. Perhaps the branches, now unable to lift themselves to wave to the clouds, took pleasure in listening to the whispering blades of grass.

The rising sun was still hidden. She caressed the bark with the palms of her hands and stood beside it smiling. 'You're magnificent,' she whispered.

Someone from the house was entering the grounds and, without thinking, she moved to share her perception, hailing out to the lone figure: 'Hello there, hello.' She waved and clapped. The man turned, saw the waving hand, hesitated, then walked briskly towards her.

Though the morning mist was lifting, it took her a while – and even then she was not sure – to see something in the stride – straight, purposeful, erect – that seemed familiar. How well he carried himself; then reality unveiled. No! My God, what on earth was he doing here? She couldn't say she didn't realise who it was. What should she do? Play it cool.

'Oh! Miss Vidhur? It is Miss Vidhur isn't it?'

'It's only her ghost. I roam the grounds on certain mornings, but leave before the sun shows its face, before I am dazzled into nothingness. I return to the past from whence I came. What brings you here?'

He recognised in the childlike play an act of embarrassment, suspecting that had she recognised him she would not have hailed out. How much like us she had become. An enigma. She had learnt to keep her feelings to herself and show only what she intended. He could not read her well. He wondered how people like himself were really perceived by those who had once been colonised. Was she a daughter of the Empire, its ghost?

'The ghost of Satisha Vidhur.' His eyes sparkled. He looked so gentle, so vulnerable.

'What are you doing here, Mr Huntington?'

'I'm a trustee of Wiston House; any ghost that roams this park would know me well.'

'No doubt the ghost of Isabella Thomas knows you well, since these are her grounds. Today she sleeps soundly and I was asked by the spirits of Pan to help her carry out her promise.'

'What's that?'

'To guard these grounds from those who wish to destroy their soul.'

'Is it threatened?'

'That I can't say. I'll show you where she rests; tomorrow you may ask her; I'm leaving today.'

'So am I. Are you returning to London?'

'Yes, I'm with a group from the Commonwealth Secretariat. We had a conference on small states. It concluded last night. After breakfast, we leave. You told me about this place, so when the opportunity came, I thought I'd come and see for myself.'

'Are you disappointed?'

'Oh no! Mr Huntington, it is truly beautiful and so moving. Thank you.'

It was not to be, he saw. It was not only in Britain that culture, values, history and tradition mattered; it was the same with her and her family. What ideas beat within her bosom? What ideas did she have of us? She was British but came from another vine. She made him think that England had to move on from a period when not rocking the boat was the watchword, back to another self. Maybe it would become again the place where the Rights of Man – and women – were held aloft, for that was surely part of its history, too.

'It's a special pleasure, Miss Vidhur, to meet you here.'

'It was so unexpected. Come, you must know it well, but let me take you to where Isabella rests.'

How she stirred him! The folly of those old enough to know better.

She led him to the churchyard and there, at the side of the church, read what was written on the gravestone:

'I will lead them in paths that they have not known, I will make darkness light before them and crooked things straight, these things will I do unto them and not forsake them.'

Isaiah XL11:16.

In the silence of the place her voice seemed to be coming from within the locked church. Both stood there saying nothing, the stillness uncomfortable. Satisha was thinking that though she was an agnostic most days, she found the old church comforting; it moved her. She also knew that when the sun showed itself and removed the long shadows from the grass and from the crumbling church walls, she would see it with different eyes.

She looked at her watch and said, 'I must leave now.'

He put an arm out to restrain her, saying, 'May I kiss you?'

It was so easy to say yes, but she was afraid of where it might lead, and the moment was surrounded by the other world to which she belonged. Yet, she cared for him. Not wishing to offend him, and wishing it to be perfect, she drew close to him and whispered, 'Be still, I shall kiss you.' This was a moment she would offer him. Before he could regain his composure sufficiently to reply, she caressed his forehead, temples and cheeks with her lips and the softness of her fingers. He closed his eyes. Then she caressed his entire face with the palms of both hands saying, 'Goodbye Mr Huntington. We shall always be good friends and I shall think of you with affection always.'

He held her hands and kissed them both gently, releasing them as a child would his favourite bird to the woods.

They walked in opposite directions, she, hurrying back to the house and he, moving out of the churchyard in the direction of the rising sun.

54

AT THE SURGERY
June 2001

Satisha was amongst those waiting patiently at Mill Hill Surgery, when she was drawn to a baby's cry. It was the loud and recurring whimpering that alerted her. The young mother was trying her best to comfort him. Satisha asked how long the baby had been unwell.

'A day or two. It was cold his father saying. Now… I think no cold, something not good. So I come.'

'You did the right thing.'

The woman, Mrs Ali, explained that both she and the baby had a fever; she had a sore throat and a stiff neck too and her head was aching. 'But I have to look after baby and house.' When Satisha saw the rash on the baby and the young mother, and the baby vomiting on the mother's shoulder, she was convinced that both mother and baby had meningitis.

The waiting room was bursting full, but it seemed no doctor had arrived. Mrs Ali began to walk the length of the room, cradling her child. The baby's body was in perpetual motion, turning this way and that, all the while whimpering.

The receptionist explained, again and again to those whose patience had run out, that one of the doctors had suddenly taken ill, another was on sick leave and still another was on a well-earned holiday, long postponed. Help, though, was on its way. A doctor from another surgery was coming to assist them.

When the doctor arrived, Satisha's back was turned to him. She was at the far end of the waiting room trying to rock the baby to sleep in his pram. The young mother cried, 'The doctor! The doctor!' Satisha hastened towards the receptionist who was saying something to the doctor as he was leaving the room. 'This baby needs to be looked at immediately, I think he has meningitis.'

'Are you a doctor?'

'No.'

'How do you know? You're not a doctor and I won't be spoken to in this way. Will you please take a seat?' A few of the patients looked at Satisha as if she were trying to jump the queue. 'We're all unwell here,' one complained. The receptionist said, 'Everyone will be seen to in good time. Thank goodness we don't all see our own case as an emergency. An appointment has been allocated to every patient here and I will keep to that.'

'I am saying this loud and clear so that everyone can hear me. If this baby is not attended to immediately, he could die. I know meningitis when I see it.'

'There's no need to take that stance here; we have procedures in place. You will just have to wait your turn. Now please sit down and don't make a scene. I don't have a magic wand.'

'This sick baby has been here well over an hour and a half. For God's sake, his life depends on your acting now.'

The doctor was still within ear's reach and when he heard a clear voice propelling itself with firm authority, his memory was stirred. Something about its pace, its colour, opened within him a file long stored: *That is silly. Anyone can do that... You must have seen bread before... Do you find me interesting?... Please forgive Vidya and me. I often do things and then think about them. It is not the right way.* He turned around. The mother's eyes were beseeching him; beside her, he was sure, was Satisha Vidhur. She, too, could not believe her eyes, but she contained herself, knowing it was best to take her cue from him.

He returned to the receptionist. 'I shall have a look at the child, now.' He lowered his voice. 'If the child has meningitis, it becomes an emergency; you will need to get an ambulance. It is contagious and I can see there are other babies here. So send them in.'

The mother turned to Satisha and said, 'Come. Please come.'

'No. She waits her turn. She does not have meningitis.'

'She tells doctor everything. My English, no good.'

The receptionist looked exasperated and said, 'Very well. Go on... Dr Sen, a moment please.' She whispers: 'I shall allow this young woman to accompany the mother and child, but a little warning. She is very highly strung. I thought I should warn you. I shall send her file in to you. It is preferable that she leaves the surgery early. I would be more comfortable and so would the patients here. She tried to order me about, Dr Sen. I am not used to this.'

'Thank you, Ann.' He offered her a warm smile that said you and I are on the same side.

As the doctor and his patients climbed the stairs, the disquiet in the waiting room stirred by Satisha's refusal to take a seat began to revive.

'What did she say?'

'I didn't hear really.'

'Meningitis.'

'Who has it?'

'The baby.'

'How does she know?'

'Sometimes these people will use any trick to jump the queue.'

'I think she must have said something that made sense to the doctor.'

'If she is right, the baby should be seen to first.'

'I believe it is contagious.'

'The mother may have it too.'

'Oh dear, I hope not.'

'That young woman was right. It can be fatal. She was right to say what she said. She was acting responsibly.'

'Well we hope you're right. We have been here for two hours.'

Silence.

Dr Sen examined the baby. 'Mrs Ali, I can tell from the rashes that you and the baby have meningitis. Though I suspect it is viral and not bacterial, both forms are serious and you need to be in hospital.' He picked up the phone. 'Ann, Dr Sen here. It is meningitis; I'd like you to call for an ambulance immediately. They should be taken to the Royal Free hospital. Thank you.'

He explained to the mother what would happen and told her to return downstairs to the receptionist.

Mrs Ali thanked the doctor and Satisha. Dr Sen handed her a letter which she was to give to the receptionist at the paediatrics department immediately on arrival. He wrote the word URGENT in large letters on the envelope and signed his name.

As Mrs Ali left, a nurse entered with Satisha's file. Dr Sen opened it.

'Well what can I do for you?'

'Will she be alright?'

'I think she and the baby stand a very good chance of recovering. They need the best care.'

'You handled that so well, Dr Sen – I'm so happy to see you here. My goodness, for years we met at Aunt Ishani's and then you were at medical school. We were children growing, becoming teenagers. I was a prig. I recall apologising to you. It is so good to see you. You were always so kind, gentle and forgiving. I have often thought of you and what became of you. Your parents must be very proud. My mother told me that they are with you and living near by.'

'They are. You must meet them. We're renting a house in Hale Drive.'

'My aunt Ishani must be over the moon. She was so very fond of you. You were the son she would have loved to have.'

'Your aunt has been very good to me. I've been very fortunate.'

'You must come home and meet my parents. Oh it's really lovely to have you here. You are like, like, well, family. We met you so often when we were young, younger I mean. I'm so happy for you.' She leapt out of her chair and kissed him on the cheek.

He was not less pleased at meeting her again, but not given to expressing his feelings as readily or openly. 'You have to be very careful here, Miss Vidhur. There are strict rules about patients' behaviour towards the doctor.' His eyes, though, smiled.

'Dr Sen is right as usual. Are there cameras here, in this room? Have I got you into trouble?'

'I don't think so, but if there were and I knew of them, I would turn them off when I saw it was you.'

'You're teasing me. How nice. Why should you be proper all the time? Life is short, Dr Sen.'

'I'm sorry. I have to get down to business. You've seen the waiting room. What brought you here?'

'It's my blood pressure; my father thinks it's high. He insisted that I come. He's been taking readings and is not happy with them. My doctor, Dr Davenport, is not on duty today.'

'How are you feeling?'

'Oh, just fine. Only an occasional feeling of dizziness. It was my father's insistence that brought me here.'

'Let me take your blood pressure.'

She removed her cardigan, and rolled up the sleeve of her silky white blouse. 'Just relax,' he said. Her sleeve kept unrolling and Amru refolded it carefully. He was surprised at how soft the material was. As he took her pressure, he looked at her outstretched hand, the hand that could not roll a tyre on compacted clay. She looked at his buttoned shirt – so neat – and listened to his regular breathing.

'I'm afraid it's 163/95. This is high. But it has been an unusual morning for you. The dizziness…'

'It's very rare for me to have such a high reading. Only twice before I think. I'm sure it's a rogue reading.'

'Hmm. I suggest that you take your blood pressure readings for about a month, make a note of them and bring them in. Then Dr Davenport can decide what to do. A single reading on a morning such as this is not what I should go on. Walk as much as you can. Exercise helps. But if the dizziness returns, see your doctor at once.'

'Thank you, Dr Sen.'

'One other thing; it may be important to have medication. A long period of high blood pressure can lead to a stroke.'

'You sound like my father.'

'I am pleased about that. If you behave like a child, you need a father. I am saying this because you're giving me the impression that it's not something you consider important. I'm not sure how well you're listening to what I am saying. Persistent high blood pressure is very serious. The consequences can be grave. I have chosen my words with care, Satisha; I need to emphasise this.'

Why do you have to be so professional? 'I'm sorry. You're right.'

'How is Vidya? And Anjali? I haven't been in touch with her and Dr Mahesh for quite some time.'

'They are all well. Anjali writes how she is just about managing her teaching and her boys. They would be very happy to know that I have met you. Are you able to have tea with us this evening? My parents would love to meet you.'

'I think today will be a long day.'

'Well, why not phone us on your way out. My parents would be really happy to meet you, even if it is for a short time.'

'I will do.'

'Ooh! Are you married?'

'Why do you ask?'

'Well, it would be right to invite your wife too, if not today, certainly another day.'

'I am not. But I am being pressed to think about it. It's been my parents' concern for some time now.'

'Well. My parents may be able to help, even Vidya or Anjali. I shall ask around for you too. You deserve someone really nice.'

'You are as interesting as you always were, Satisha… I'm sorry but I have to be firm with you on your health.'

'I have no intention of contradicting the doctor.'

'I shall see how long that lasts, Miss Vidhur.'

Her scent, her warmth, her impetuosity, were such a delight, but he did not have her middle-class confidence; his upbringing, together with his personality, had made him reserved, cautious, thoughtful. What was important was that success in his profession would ensure a comfortable old age for his parents and bring them and Mrs Mita much happiness. It was the least he could do for those who had invested in him. His ajee had died before he started medical school and that had further motivated him to learn well.

★

Santosh was reading the *Financial Times* in his study. Amira had been in the garden gathering rosemary for the small vase on the kitchen table. When Satisha returned from the surgery, they joined her in the sitting room.

'Why were you so long?'

'Is something wrong?'

'What did the doctor say?'

Satisha explained all that had happened.

'I'm not surprised,' Santosh said; 'the Health Service as we knew it can't last long. Someone on the train told me that she had to wait three hours in the accident and emergency department of the hospital nearest to her. And waiting two hours or more at our surgery – it's unacceptable.'

'Why must you say such a thing, Santosh? This was an unusual morning. Satisha said so. With three doctors absent what would you expect? No system can cater for that. Be fair for heaven's sake.'

'Amira, forget about this morning. Let me explain: people are making greater and greater demands on the health service. No matter how much money the government puts in, the cost of the NHS will grow because demands are never-ending. New medicines, expensive new cures and a society that says me, me, me. I deserve the best, just like the adverts for hair colour tell us.'

'Your father and Mr Doom are Siamese twins. Tell us more about this nice Dr Amru Sen. Was he pleased to see you?'

'Yes, Mummy. I think so. But he would be pleased to see anyone. He is just well mannered and big hearted. I was very happy to see him, too. He hasn't really changed, or what drives him hasn't changed. We recognised each other instantly.'

'I'm pleased. Do you like him, you know, really like him? He sounds very nice from what you say, Satisha.'

'You and Daddy would like him. Vidya and Anjali know him too. Aunty Ishani likes him very much.'

'Well, we should invite the whole family over, don't you think?'

'I asked him to drop by for tea; I didn't think you would mind.'

'What should I prepare, Satisha; what do you think he'd like?'

'Oh Mummy, don't do anything.'

'Why, Satisha?'

'The surgery is full. He may not be able to come. Even if he comes, he'll be on his way home to have his evening meal with his parents. The most he will have, if he does come, is tea.'

Even so, the sitting room was tidied, and the garden raided for flowers. All three returned to their tasks, though mother and daughter were alert to every passing car. When at half past five Dr Sen did call, a palpable tension was released.

Satisha opened the door.

'I won't be able to stay long.'

'I understand, Dr Sen.'

'Amru, please.'

'Mummy, Daddy, come and meet Dr Sen.'

'Come in, Dr Sen. Satisha told me that you know my sister Ishani.'

'I can see the resemblance.'

'I take that as a compliment.'

'Amru, this is my father, Santosh Vidhur.'

'I'm pleased to meet you, Dr Sen. How long have you been here in London?'

'This is our second year.'

'Have some tea, Dr Sen. I know it's close to your dinner time, but I have a few kachouries. Home-made. Just the one, eh?'

'That's tempting, I'll try one. Thank you, Mrs Vidhur.'

'I have made a little chutney with Granny Smith apples. No green mangoes here. We all have to make adjustments.'

'You have long hours. Is the work satisfying?' Santosh asked.

'It's becoming more difficult to give each patient the best attention. The system works when they are articulate and knowledgeable, but the shy, the inarticulate, those with little English – well they require more time than the system was devised for. More often than not, though, it works remarkably well. The NHS is a noble concept; it's important to remember that.'

Amira looked meaningfully at Santosh.

'We would like to invite your parents over, perhaps Sunday afternoon?' Amira wondered.

'Would you prefer us to write to them?' Santosh asked.

'I shall let them know.'

'Sunday afternoon. Perhaps half past four? Is that convenient?'

Santosh and Amru exchanged cards.

As Amru was about to leave Santosh said, 'Dr Sen, do discuss our invitation with your parents and if this Sunday isn't suitable, perhaps the following Sunday or another day that suits them best. Thank you for calling.'

'I'm pleased to have met you, my parents will be too. Sorry I'm rushing in this way. I must make a house call.'

Afterwards, Santosh said, 'He looks a fine young man. This meeting may yet bloom, Satisha.' He winked.

'Daddy, it's bad enough having Mummy and Ishani getting us all married, not you too. Give me a break, I'm getting tired of it.'

'So where did you meet him first?' Amira asked.

'At Aunt Ishani's.'

'Well then, I shall ask her about him.'

'Oh she likes him very much.'

'How do you know? Did she say so?'

'No. But when we were there, she treated him like family.'

'Well I can't go by that. I shall ask her myself.'

'Mummy, I hope you're not thinking what I suspect you're thinking. He is just a very nice person I knew when I was young. We have grown up. We're different people from when we were children. His parents are thinking of getting him married, but he's not thinking about it.'

'You should be thinking about it, Satisha.'

'I have not yet met anyone suitable.'

'Dr Sen is very suitable. Your daddy and I think so.'

'Mummy, you've only just met him.'

'True, but we can tell he's a responsible, serious sort of person. Parents know these things.'

'Mummy, give me a break.'

'Wouldn't you like to meet his family?'

'I would like to meet them. I've never met them.'

Amira was as good as her word. 'If I were you,' Ishani said, 'I'd do my utmost to bring them together. I can't think of two personalities better suited to each other. They need each other. He's so thoughtful and gentle. She can be impetuous. He'll keep her to the rational side of a discussion. Amru is shy, and Satisha has the vibrancy and wit he needs to have around him. She's socially adept, she'll give him the confidence he needs, stir him to get that promotion he knows he's the best qualified for but could lose because he doesn't put himself forward. He needs to have someone who has faith in him and will nudge him on from time to time. He doesn't have the competitive drive that London requires.

'This is not important, but you ought to know the Sens are not his parents. They died in a most unfortunate accident. Now don't mention it to the Sens, their memory of the accident is too painful. If they say he is their adopted son, just say you know.'

Santosh wrote a letter to Mr and Mrs Sen inviting them and Amru to have lunch with them the following Sunday. He added that Amira had spoken to Ishani and she had asked after their health and hoped that life in London was agreeable to them.

Two days later the Sens' acceptance came and Amira got into action. Ishani had pointed out that though the Sens were in the main vegetarians, they would be happy to eat a little fish. Amru, though, was carnivorous.

'What's the matter with Ishani? We're thinking of him marrying our daughter and she tells me he is carnivorous? What is happening around me? Why are people no longer gracious in expression?' She would have accepted non-vegetarian as a description, but to describe a man as carnivorous who might marry her daughter was unseemly. She said, 'You know, Santosh, I don't fit in anywhere. Not even my sister understands me.'

'You won't believe me, Amira, when I say that you're managing much better than most and far far better than you think.'

'Santosh, you must speak seriously to Satisha.'

'I will, in good time.'

'I'd really like her to settle down; the years are passing; the trouble is, she doesn't see this. Just childhood friends meeting together after a long time – that's what she keeps saying.'

'I suspect Satisha likes him, but she has such a strong, independent spirit; she thinks that falling in love would compromise her independence – and it will. But a time will come, Amira, when she'll be happy to forego some independence for a suitable life companion.'

'I hope you're right, Santosh. I can't wait for her to come to her senses.'

'I am behind you, Amira. We have to help her see what she refuses to acknowledge.'

'When Amru comes, Santosh, please talk to him, not as an inspector of the NHS, but as a favourite uncle. With his parents, make yourself active, see what is needed. Make an effort, try and be likeable. So far you've done very well. A good father, looking after his daughter's future. Another thing, when they come, we mustn't swamp them. There are four of us and all of us like talking. We want to know more about them, so we must encourage them to tell us about themselves, how they have settled in and so on.'

'I promise to follow what you've said to the letter, and if after all my efforts Dr Sen cannot see that Satisha would make him a good wife, I'll be forced to say, let us forget him; he doesn't have sufficient intelligence to join our family. After all, I have to consider the IQ of my grandchildren. Let it not be said that I was negligent in that regard.'

55

KEEP ON THE LINE
July 2001

It had been a long day; the school year had come to a close and Vidya Vidhur was so tired that she felt like sitting right there at her desk for the rest of the afternoon.

Her class of six-year-olds had become her little dears. Their handwriting exercise books showed that they had improved slowly at first and then, when she least expected it, by leaps and bounds. Her cry, 'Keep on the line', had been picked up by the girls themselves. Jennifer had given it a tune: 'Keep on the line. Keep on the line, on the line, on the line.'

Vidya had learnt that it made sense to bring together subjects that had common fundamentals, such as handwriting and geometry. With new concepts came new words. The letters with straight lines above, such as b and d, had similarities with pillars and standing walls. The meaning of new words such as horizontal, vertical and right-angled was seen and felt by small palms on the classroom walls. In the same way, letters with curves and partial curves were shown to have similarities with numbers such as 3 and 2 – and to the shapes of the moon and arches. The characteristics of squares, rectangles and the equidistance of parallel lines were discovered by measuring their tissue boxes brought from home.

Now she reflected with amusement on those few occasions when choosing a poor example had thrown the class into a commotion. *If there are five birds on a branch and I throw a stone and three fly away, how many are left?* Several in the class said none, their reasoning being that all the birds would fly away. Then there was the incident with Geeta Pande, a shy little girl who insisted in putting out her left hand when asked to shake hands with the Headmistress. Ms Mayhew had said to Vidya, 'Please see what you can do with that child. We shouldn't have our girls failing at such a common courtesy.' At break, Vidya spoke to Geeta.

'Which hand do you use to hold your spoon, Geeta?'

'My right hand, Miss.'

'Now listen, when anyone comes up to shake hands with you, you must put out your spoon hand.' Geeta bent her head and shook it from side to side. 'Alright, now don't be upset, you don't have to use your spoon hand… but tell me, Geeta, why you don't like to shake hands with your right hand?'

'It's my eating hand. We say *Namaste ji*, Miss. I don't like touching hands not even with my left hand. I like to keep my hands clean. Mummy says my body is a beautiful temple, and I must keep it free from germs, Miss. We always say *Namaste ji*, Miss.'

Later that day she had entered the Headmistress's office.

'Well, Miss Vidhur, how did you manage with that child? For some reason, she was oddly stubborn. Nice child in every other way.'

Vidya explained what Geeta said.

'What a foolish idea! We wash hands before eating, don't we? Is the child unaware of this?'

'Perhaps I should explain what Namaste means. When we meet a stranger, or a member of one's family, we bring the palms together and say *Namaste* with a gentle bow. There's no need to shake hands. It's a pleasing custom I think – and no risk.'

'What risk is there when we shake hands?'

'Well, you don't know whether the hands you clasp are washed hands, or for that matter where they were before you saw them.'

Miss Mayhew's eyes took on a puzzled look.

'But when you say Namaste, you do not take that risk, and the word accompanied by the gesture says: "The good that is within me recognises that which is good within you and salutes it." '

'Well, whatever next, Miss Vidhur. Such a strange thing to say to someone you may not have met before. Isn't that a misplaced faith in strangers. Seems like making heavy work of what should be lightly skipped over. Isn't a handshake or a "how do you do" quite enough?'

'Will *Namaste* harm anyone, Miss Mayhew?'

'I'm not saying that, Miss Vidhur. I just think it is taking this multiculturalism somewhat too far. In a school, one should begin to inculcate a feeling of community, of well, fellowship one with another. A certain amount of conformity is necessary for this; we show at this early stage in their education how much we have in common. But to bring forth such a salutation, a philosophy, Miss Vidhur… in everyday encounters, is surely going over the top.'

'I believe the angel Gabriel brought salutations to Mary, the mother of Jesus Christ…'

'This is precisely what I mean. That was a very special meeting, Miss Vidhur, the message was sacred. It was the only time such an announcement occurred in the history of the world.'

'Perhaps at St Thomas's we could consider that if a certain way of doing something is neither ugly nor harmful, nor puts anyone at a disadvantage, we should not discourage it. This would make us a forward-looking school in multicultural Britain.'

'Well I guess we'll just leave that Pande girl to her little ways. But I do have my reservations. Setting precedents. Move with extreme caution when the path is unknown, Miss Vidhur.'

With memories of this conversation, Vidya stirred herself and rose. Time to say farewell for the summer to Miss Mayhew.

She was thanked for her good wishes, and thanked for doing a fine job.

'We are fortunate to have you. Have you plans for the holidays?'

'I may be going to Trinidad or the Lake District. I'd also like to say you run a very good school and that you are open to new ideas. It is an exceptionally difficult thing to do, Miss Mayhew. Some immigrants have these very problems. They are unable to adjust rapidly to new ways of thinking. It creates anguish and pain.'

'Well one does try. As you say it is not easy. I am fortunate in my staff, Miss Vidhur.'

'Namaste,' and Vidya clasped her hands and bowed her head in such a gentle way that Miss Mayhew felt somehow… well… honoured.

Miss Mayhew bowed her head in acknowledgement. Vidya saw the guarded beginning of a coming together.

She walked around the empty classroom and saw again the bright eager faces of her six-year-olds. They were moving up the school. Next term there would be new faces, new personalities, each with unique possibilities, but letting the familar faces go saddened her no end.

Seeing the school bus was about to leave, she ran the length of the yard; the driver spotted her and waited.

'Oh thank you so very much, Mr Abbot.'

'Oh! Someone else is running for the bus; I think he's from St George's. Never had him on my bus before.'

Mr Abbot opened the door and Mark climbed on board. Vidya knew he was looking for her but looked outside, pretending to be oblivious of the commotion at the front of the bus.

He saw her and said, 'My car can take one more.'

'Are you sure?' she replied.

He nodded.

As they left the bus, there was stamping of feet from more knowing pupils and one cried, 'He's a jolly good fellow, ho! ho!' And the whole bus replied 'For so say all of us. Ho! Ho!'

'Phew that was close,' said Mark when they were in his car.

'Thank you, Mark. I have a special affection for this Micra.'

'And for the driver?'

'Well, I didn't see the driver when I saw the Micra. It smiled at me, the moment our eyes met. This colour is comforting when you're distressed. Are you going anywhere this summer, Mark?'

'I may go to the South of France with my parents. I'd also like to go to the Lake District. And you?'

'I may go to Trinidad. My aunt Ishani lives there. She's an aunt with a difference. There is nothing she can't do. For example, if you were to go to her and say you'd like her to help you choose a wife, she'd do a superb job for you.'

'Sounds like a superwoman… Is she arranging someone for you?'

'If she is, she hasn't told me. When I'm ready, I'll ask her to find me the perfect partner.'

'What is he like?'

'Who?'

'The perfect partner.'

'I'll have to give it some thought. Besides I may just change my mind before the month's out. So it's best to wait until I'm ready and then I'll send round a questionnaire to all those who may have shown an interest.'

'How many have expressed this wish to you?'

'No one. Mummy says that my body language tells any eligible young man: "Beware, here stands a Rottweiler!"'

'That's not what comes over.'

'I worry about bringing children into this world. Just look at it, Mark: the bombing of Air India off the coast of Ireland, then the bombing above Lockerbie. The murder of that toddler James Bulger by two ten-year-olds. I became afraid of children, too. When we saw on TV the plastic toys floating off the coast of Ireland, Anjali and I wept. I felt I was with them in the cabin as mothers clutched crying infants and fathers despaired. When I saw a photograph of little James, I was with him on the railway line. There are paedophiles amongst our priests, our relatives and trusted friends. I've been thinking that life in a nunnery might have much to recommend it. When I look at the world, I wonder if civilisation isn't just a veneer, an attractive cloak which men in powerful democracies wear on stage. But in the privacy of their homes, they remove it and dance naked, barking, snarling, grunting, howling, growling and roaring, satisfied with their place in the animal kingdom.'

'You can't carry the world's hell within you, Vidya. Live as good a life as you possibly can. What other choice is there?'

'I think I should invite you to lunch with us one Sunday, perhaps before you go off to France.'

'Are you serious?'

'Eating, Mark Baverstock, is a serious business at our home.'

He laughed.

'I mean what I say. Let me ask Mummy which Sunday you can join us. My parents would like to meet a nice young man. They have daughters, so I would advise you not to be *too* nicely behaved.'

'I would be on my best behaviour.'

'Relax, Mark. Just don't mention the British Empire.'

'I had no intention of doing so.'

'Though if you did say something outrageous, there'd be no harm done. There'd be a sudden silence. My parents would quickly recover and my mother would assume that the reason for your views comes solely from your want of better foods, by which she means good Indian foods. She'd feel you had not been looking after yourself and this neglect was reflected in your thinking. My father would say you had the right to express your understanding of the Empire but that it was not the complete picture. All the while he would be thinking: "Why has education failed this young man?" They would be amiable and try their best to make you feel at ease; genuinely interested in your welfare, they'd offer you sound advice regarding your career, without your having to ask for it, such is their generosity. But when you leave and I had to face them, my judgement would become a family discussion. It would be seen that I was excessively tired, overwrought and in need of a long restful holiday.'

'The Empire is a closed subject to me… I have been thinking… Why not come to the Lake District with me.'

'Are you crazy? I couldn't do that?'

'Why?'

'My parents would have heart attacks.'

'I'm not that bad looking am I?'

'I don't think you understand or you're pretending not to.'

'We would be staying in separate rooms.'

'That simply will not do, is what Aunt Ishani would say.'

Silence.

'As long as my parents can visualise you tiptoeing into my room…' – she winked mischievously – 'then, surely, you must see that it won't do, Mark Baverstock.'

'Well, we can stay in separate hotels.'

'Look, we live in different worlds. Put simply, my parents would not like me to share a holiday with a young man before marriage. Even if we were engaged, it would be a touch-and-go thing with my mother. If she allowed me, then it would remain a family secret; she couldn't tell Aunt Ishani, for example, and I'd have to promise to conduct myself appropriately. If I felt myself wavering, not up to the task of self-discipline, I'd have to promise to come home immediately.'

'Absolute truth is not required in all aspects of one's life, Vidya.'

'I agree. But this is about trust.'

Mark said nothing.

'You wouldn't want… um, say, your wife to abuse your trust would you?'

'I'm sorry.'

'For my parents, marriage is a *Vivaha*. It is one of the more important Samskaras.'

'Oh yes, I remember now. Those *Samskaras!*'

'I'm surprised that Sonia's first cousin – remember the brilliant butterfly fluttering around you? – didn't explain it all.'

Mark blushed. 'I don't remember any fluttering butterfly… Am I going to learn what these *Samskaras* are?'

'They're ceremonial rites, purificatory rites. They're performed to sanctify the mind and the body too, to prepare the individual for the stage reached in his or her life.'

'Oh, how could I have forgotten.'

'The *Vivaha Samskara* stipulates that you devote your life to loving your wife, Mark.'

'Oh I would eagerly perform that duty daily, maybe twice a day, if circumstances permit. I have the potential for being a good Hindu. Should I mention this when I meet your parents?'

'Both my parents are university graduates, well educated; they take very seriously the skills of living a good life, a considered life. My parents have their own study spaces. They try their best to understand the drift of current thinking, how to live well in this environment. They get high on knowledge, on reason, on discovery, on enlightenment. They talk endlessly, are able to explain themselves rationally and coolly most of the time. They made it possible for us to conduct ourselves reasonably well, because we saw in their behaviour models of courtesy, thoughtfulness, forgiveness, empathy and patience. The last I find the most difficult. They discuss with us any topic we bring to them – lesbians, gays, arranged marriages.

'They would never force me to marry anyone. If I wished to marry someone they didn't believe was suitable, there would be no attempt to browbeat or use moral blackmail. They would talk to me quietly, earnestly. If after their best efforts I were so stupid as to say that I could not live without this person or that person – and I am not that foolish yet, mind you – my parents would attend the wedding, though with very heavy hearts.

'My mother would weep in the bedroom; she would lose weight and look miserable and keep asking where she had gone wrong. My father would be asking himself the same question, but on the day he would put on his best suit, look the fine gentleman he is and they would give me their blessings in a quiet restrained way. And if time were to show that they were right all along, they would not say, "I told you so." Oh they would think it, say it between themselves, but before me, they would be silent on the matter. That would devastate me. Their forgiveness would humble me no end. They would think that the difficulties I'd created for myself – if there were children involved and their father a scoundrel – would be punishment enough. They'd be concerned with damage limitation. Now when you have parents like those, why would you want to lose their trust?'

'Your parents are exceptional.'

'Maybe. What I do know is they worked hard at it. It was not easy for them; they too struggled with the new and the old. From the very start it was Dr Spock and Dr Seuss for Anjali. My mother has Bowlby amongst her books. Why? She does not believe that all good ideas are the new ones. She likes to go back and forth all the time. But she has her firm ways, her no-go areas. She wants us to love this country; my father is trying to ensure that our affection for it will not be offered unconditionally, that we approach it with an awareness of past history.'

'The world is an unjust place, Vidya. You just have to conserve yourself to live as best you can. Roll with the punches.'

'You sound like my mother, Mark.'

'I'm only too aware that I sound like my own parents at times, especially when I'm in the classroom.'

Vidya laughed.

'We have to be thankful, Vidya. We have caring parents. A number of boys in my classes are not so fortunate… Anyway, now that you've told me how to impress your parents, when will I be invited to this serious lunch?'

'I shall let you know. It may not be for a while. The timing has to be right, Mark.'

56

TWO FAMILIES ENGAGE
Late summer 2001

Amira realised that most of the music she had collected over the years tended to an underlying pathos. Eventually she found an engaging light classical piece of Indian music suitable for Sunday lunch with the Sen family – a raga, played by Pundit Shivkumar Sharma, santur music to meditate upon, but with cheer; a composition that brought a smile. She had also taped another recording from the radio of the last movement of a raga, to be played just before her guests thought about leaving. It had movement and richness, a farewell caress.

The guests were punctual. Mrs Sen handed Amira an arrangement of lisianthus, carnations and pale yellow roses. Amira was touched. Satisha put the flowers in a blue vase near the blue curtains.

Mrs Sen said, 'Very nice room, sunny. Must be warm all year round, na?'

'A very good cow you have. Does it moo?' Mr Sen queried, bending low to have a better look.

'Only when Satisha enters the room,' Vidya said.

They all laughed. Satisha looked self-consciously at Amru, who, like his father, was also examining the cow. Santosh asked whether they found living in London stressful. Adapting was never easy.

'The problem is,' said Mr Sen, 'back home, everybody knows you and you know everybody; here it is totally different. People live their own lives. They keep to themselves, na.'

'Here na,' added Mrs Sen, 'people live tight lives; no room for anything outside house and garden. Have you noticed how they sit and walk?'

'Is it different?' asked Vidya.

'Have you not noticed? Here, they only take up the room they need.'

'Yes,' Santosh agreed. 'West Indians spread themselves out when they sit, when they walk, when they talk. We like opening up. Maybe we all suffer from claustrophobia.'

Vidya and Satisha looked at each other. Amira smiled. But Amru did not seem to be following the light chatter. Unexpressed thoughts appeared to engage him.

'Just undisciplined,' Vidya remarked; 'if they'd had to fight a war or two, they would be far more disciplined.'

'The British were in many wars,' observed Mr Sen. 'We wouldn't know how to fight a war. This alone trains people to concentrate on what they have to do.'

'Do you mean,' Santosh asked, 'it conditioned them to be upright, to hold themselves together?'

'Yes. Older people here think like military people all the time. I heard somebody on the bus say they will keep their powder dry.'

'I agree,' said Santosh. 'So many phrases like that: bite the bullet, draw a line in the sand, the die is cast, a feather in your cap, a flash in the pan. As you said, military thinking circles them. It must have an effect on their character.'

'That is not true with young people,' observed Mrs Sen.

'Today all young people are alike,' Vidya affirmed. 'There is a youth culture out there; you can't miss it.'

'That is so true,' Mrs Sen said. 'I have noticed rings.'

Puzzled silence.

'Rings seem very much in fashion. Rings are everywhere – ears, many, many times, from here to there.' Mrs Sen demonstrated with her hand on her right ear. 'Also, I have seen, on lips, navel, even tongue too. I couldn't look. Can you imagine that?'

Apparently her audience had already done so. No one responded. She continued: 'I don't know what is happening today. And when they're outside, they're not really outside; they're shut in with their music. If you want to talk to them, you have to tap on the shoulder na, smile and use signs.' Once more she demonstrated. 'They return to this world and say, "What's up?"' She mimed the abruptness very well. 'It is as if they're in a different country from you and me.'

'There's another thing,' Mr Sen said, turning his attention to the ladies. 'When you go out, you get the feeling you have to hurry.'

'Yes, simple, simple things, like packing your groceries in the supermarket,' added Mrs Sen, 'and getting into a cab or even getting out; you can't get out fast enough. The driver is tapping the steering wheel with his fingers, counting the seconds he's losing.'

'Yes,' Mr Sen agreed. 'Hurry up is what they're thinking all the time, even if they're not saying so.'

'They talk a lot with their eyes and face. After a time you begin to sense what a look means.'

'I think some are embarrassed to look directly at you, na?'

'Deep down they don't like a row...'

305

'They call it a scene,' Vidya interrupted.

'We don't really know the English,' observed Mr Sen, 'and they don't know us at all.'

'But they think they know us,' Mrs Sen said. She turned to Amira. 'It's hard work when you come to a new place at our age. We couldn't live here without Amru. A very kind immigration official stamped our passport so we can come and go. Amru talked to him; I don't know what he said. We're not working, Amru has a good job, and we're not here for medical help. The immigration chap listened to what Amru was saying.'

'An immigration officer can use his discretion,' Amru said. 'We were lucky that day; I don't know whether the officer being young helped. All my parents have to do is to show any immigration officer the stamp: "Indefinite stay permitted". Their passports are new, so we shouldn't have a problem for quite a while.'

'We're only here because of Amru,' Mr Sen confirmed. 'It's no use he is here, we're there. It doesn't make sense. If you're young, looking for work, it's a different matter, na?'

'I miss my neighbours too bad.'

'But we're getting used to everything bit by bit.'

'And there's so much to see. Amru took us to the British Museum; so many things there. I like the Indian, Egyptian and Mexican sections. How did they bring all those heavy statues over here, eh? A lot of work to bring all that from so far away and then to set them up for us. Very nice. Very nice idea. Except for the winter, this is a very good place.'

'The Victoria and Albert museum has carpets; you have seen them already, na?'

Santosh nodded enthusiastically, though he hadn't a clue what they were talking about.

'Those with difficult designs, I couldn't describe them, very complicated, na?'

Santosh again agreed, his nod set on automatic.

'Jewellery also we saw, na. Very fine filigree work. My eyes are not so good now. But the workmanship? Excellent quality.'

'That is a good place too, but you know that already.'

'It is a very good place,' said Santosh. Amira wondered if he had ever been there.

Lunch brought relief.

Mrs Sen said, 'You cook a lot of vegetables, I see; are you also vegetarians?'

'No, we are like Amru.'

'Amru likes vegetables but he also likes lamb and fish.'

'Ishani was very pleased that we were at last meeting you. She told us that you were primarily vegetarians, but from time to time you'd have a little fish.'

'That's good.'

'But we should've told you,' Mr Sen said with unexpected firmness. 'I don't like to give people trouble to do something special for me. I know there'll always be something I could have, so I keep quiet.'

'I just said so, na.'

Satisha helped them to spinach with cherry tomatoes and fenu-greek. There was grilled aubergine, cut open, flesh scooped out to which warm olive oil, sweet peppers, onion and roasted garlic, cumin and a single hot chilli had been added – bygan chokha – and fried ochroes, channa dhal, the flakiest paratha rotie possible with ajwain seeds, and basmati rice with ginger and cardamom. Amira had grilled three salmon steaks for the Sens. The rest of the table was treated to her rosemary lamb in a tandoori massala with sweet peppers.

Mrs Sen said the food was very very good. Mr Sen agreed whole-heartedly. He asked whether the girls could cook. Mrs Sen wanted to know whether Satisha could cook like this and whether there was any dish she had prepared by herself. Having noticed that Mrs Sen was enjoying the chokha, Amira said that this was what Satisha had made – and that she had helped her with the parathas. This was partly true for the chokha and wholly true for parathas.

'You know I sent all the girls to Lily and Palli's school.'

'Oh then they could cook very well.'

'I went, too, you know,' Amira added. 'I was amongst the first group of students. My sister Ishani sent me.'

'Oh well, it explains why the food is so good. That was the best school for girls.'

After a dessert of lightly chilled Alphonso mangoes, they returned to the sitting room to have Darjeeling tea.

Santosh said, 'Amru has been quiet.'

'Amru does not talk much while he is eating,' Mr Sen said. 'Especially when the food is so good. He believes that talking too much shows disrespect to the food.'

'I agree entirely. Now that is a profound statement. You have struck the right chord there, Mr Sen.'

'I think so too,' Mr Sen continued. 'To eat well requires peace of mind, a little concentration on the food na. Some people eat and don't

know what they've eaten, how it tasted. So I say give time to the food.'
He was very earnest.

They were all amused. Vidya said, 'I haven't ever given this matter any thought. I hope I'm not losing out.'

Amira looked at Santosh, signalling that he was doing fine and should keep going.

'These days,' Mrs Sen added, 'Amru is very tired, too many long hours, so he eats very quietly, doesn't talk too much. Talking takes effort; you have to pay attention to what people are saying, and he must do that all day. He has a lot on his mind.'

'Amru, have you something particular on your mind that's troubling you?' asked Vidya.

Amira gave Vidya a warning glance.

'I have many things on my mind, Vidya.' Amru smiled.

'Something troubling perhaps?'

'Vidya, please,' Santosh scolded.

'No. I'm fine, just a bit tired.'

'Satisha, take Amru to your daddy's study and show him those photographs Ishani sent you.' Then she said hastily, 'Vidya would you pour us some more tea? And please play the tape of the raga I put on the coffee table. Don't rewind it; I want the last movement.'

Vidya did as she was told, sensing what lay behind the instructions. The uplifting beat of the raga filled the room.

There were photographs of the barracks, its large central compound circled by mud walls and thatched roofs. There was the tree with its roots above the ground, the spot where you had to be skilled to roll a tyre, and there was the massive pile of flat boulders that had daunted her, but which Amru had climbed with agility. There were photographs of Ishani's garden and Amru, aged nine, in his new school uniform, hair brushed and smiling engagingly.

'This is a beautiful photograph of you. Aunt Ishani sent us the negative; I think you should consider enlarging it. Would you like me to do that?'

'I think my parents would like it. It would give them much pleasure…'

'Of course. I shall ask Mummy to offer the negative to them.'

'Are you engaged?… I mean emotionally… to anyone?'

'No.'

'That's good. I didn't want to put you in an awkward position. I'd like us to have dinner together, somewhere nice. You choose the place. Let it be either Tuesday or Friday. The other days are impossible and I like to give the weekend or part of it to my parents.' He opened his diary and said, 'I'm afraid, it will have to be some time from now. What about three weeks from now, then we could have a really good evening and not feel rushed.'

'You haven't changed. You're one of the nicest persons I know. You shouldn't be in a hurry to get married. Make sure that the young lady is special. You should have the best.'

'I just might.'

'Do you have someone in mind?'

'Yes.'

'You shouldn't be in a hurry you know.'

'I will consult you.'

'Oh no! Supposing you like her very much and I didn't. You should marry someone you feel you can't live without. That's what I'll do and you should too. Here's my telephone number and my St John's Wood address. Any time after eight is good for me.'

The Friday of the third week was chosen and a table was booked at Satisha's favourite restaurant. But on the following Monday, quite by chance, they met again as they got off the train at Mill Hill Broadway station. He waited for her. He explained that he was standing in again at the Mill Hill surgery.

'I didn't know you were on the train,' she said. 'I've come to spend the night with my parents.'

'So where will you be on Friday?'

'At my apartment in St John's Wood.'

'Would you like me to call for you there?'

'That would be nice.'

As they climbed down the stairs and walked together under the bridge, Mrs Ali, mother of the baby who'd had meningitis, came up to them.

'Good afternoon, doctor, I want you to meet Ali, my husband.'

'Happy to meet you, Doctor.'

'How is baby Hassan?'

'Very well. Thank you, Doctor.'

She beamed at Satisha, her face lit up with pleasure. Then she spoke to her husband in Urdu. He looked uncomfortable. He spoke slowly: 'My wife knows this young lady here; she tells me you and she make a good team at surgery. If you will marry, because you look good together, she wants to know.'

'I leave you to answer that, Satisha.'

'No, I think you ought to.'

'Yes. We're both thinking of getting married,' Amru said.

Mrs Ali beamed even more, but when she spoke again to Mr Ali, he could not be persuaded to translate what he heard. Mrs Ali was not deterred. 'I,' pointing to herself, 'made doctor and you come... Yes?' In an attempt to make clear what she had in mind, she brought the palms of her hands together and clapped.

'Yes, you did a very good job,' Satisha said. 'Thank you.'

Mrs Ali's beam was recharged and she spoke again to her husband who looked even more uncomfortable.

'My wife, please excuse; she thinks different from how this country thinks. She brings other thinking with her. She likes weddings too much. Thank you. We leave now.'

They were both thoughtful as they walked on. Then Amru said, 'That was something coming from Mrs Ali.'

'Her husband was so embarrassed; did you see his face? He couldn't translate the last request.'

'Who says Eastern women are subdued?'

'I'm not going to have an argument with you now, Amru, I'm too tired, but give me your telephone number and when I'm up to it I'll call you.'

'After nine, use my mobile; I'm in my study and my parents won't be disturbed.'

At Number 14, dinner was full of pleasantries; after cups of tea Amira said she had to sew on a few buttons and do some mending. Satisha was left with Santosh in the sitting room.

'I've been neglecting my duty as a father, Satisha, I haven't been asking you about your work, how you're managing and whether I can assist in any way.'

'It is better, Daddy, that the staff aren't reminded of our connection. I might be seen as having "contacts". It's better for me to manage on my own.'

'Very well. Nevertheless, if you think I can be of help...'

A shuffling silence sits with them.

'There's also the matter of marriage. You're now in your late twenties or is it early thirties? It may appear too early to you, but you should be thinking about it, particularly if someone suitable appears on the scene. Good people are rare, and good people who are likely to make suitable life partners are rarer still. You've worked in the City.

You know a worthwhile opportunity in the market doesn't remain unnoticed for long. You may not want to accept this, but your mother and I have more experience of what living a good life requires and the qualities that are likely to sustain it. We find these qualities in Dr Sen. Your aunt Ishani has further reinforced our thinking.'

Santosh sits tall, as erect as a sentry at attention.

'Satisha, consider this: if tomorrow you received an invitation to Amru's wedding, how would you feel to see him circling the flames of Agni with his bride? I don't want you to give me an answer, just to think how you're likely to feel. Look around you and see if there's anyone where you work or amongst your acquaintances that you would like to marry. Other families will see the benefits of their daughter marrying a fine man like Amru. I'd have failed in my duty as a father, if I were not to bring this to your attention.

'We've seen you grow up, we understand your love of a challenge. Your desire for freedom, guided by responsible behaviour, is admirable. On the other hand, to have lost the opportunity of a lifetime is no small matter, especially when you can do something about it. I have nothing more to say… Well, there is just one more thing. You were always drawn to the exciting, the alluring, the matadors. Amru doesn't have that type of flare, the charisma that attracts public applause, which you may prefer. He's sensible, quiet, thoughtful, considerate, guided by a sense of duty and responsibility. These attributes may seem dull, but believe me, effervescence just fizzles out, while what Amru has will develop further and mature with time.'

He waited, but she did not respond. How did her father know her so well? Things must be serious if he felt the need to talk to her in this way. He had telephoned and asked her to come.

'Do you want to say anything?'

'No, Daddy. I shall think about what you've said.'

'Good. Come here.'

Father and daughter embraced. 'You're a lovely daughter and a very fine young woman. My daughter and Amru deserve the best.' He gave her his mischievous wink, because she appeared concerned, thoughtful.

Amira came in and said, 'It's time for a hot cocoa drink with a touch of Demerara sugar.'

After cocoa with her parents, Satisha kissed them goodnight and went up for the night.

'I said all that you had suggested.'

'What about her preferences? Did you…?'

'I brought it up. She may suspect that you filled me in; a number of the phrases were not mine.'

'I wanted you to be alone with her. With the two of us, the girls become defensive. I've spoken to her about this before, so it becomes the same old thing her mummy is repeating, yet again. Your quiet way gives her time and space to reflect.'

What her father said stayed with her. She thought of the elation she felt when she saw Amru, how contented she was when he was near. Images of him smiling, listening, speaking came to her. His caring warmth she had begun to take for granted. To lose him to another, as her father had warned, did not seem right.

But what of the person he says he has in mind? She should have told her father that. All that week she'd wondered how she could find out. Was it too late to tell him that her feelings towards him had changed from a warm friendship to... what? The Kama Sutra? O God help, she needed a clear mind to sort this out. She would discuss it with Kamla Devi.

There had been several nights when she had gone to the phone intent on speaking to Amru, but not wanting to be a nuisance did not make the call. Then the urge to speak to him became too great.

'Amru, it's Satisha. I hope I'm not disturbing you.'

'No, I'm here in my study reading and I was just thinking of you. Telepathy is at work. How are you?'

'I am well, I believe.'

'Tell me.'

'I want to discuss a matter with you. It is nothing life-threatening, but I'd like to meet up sooner than our restaurant date. I want a second opinion.'

'Is it a medical matter?'

'Yes and no.'

'I see.'

'You did say that Tuesdays and Fridays aren't too bad for you.'

'Just let me double-check; I'm sure it should be alright... Yes, tomorrow would be fine. What time?'

'Why not come and have dinner at my place, say eight?'

'Done. See you at eight, Satisha. Thank you.'

Next she phoned Kamla Devi and explained all.

'What's your problem? He sounds a really nice fellow, but it's difficult to advise you about someone I haven't met, so I'm inviting myself to dinner. Chill that Sauvignon Blanc I love so much. Soon after dinner I'll leave and you'll play your hand. Now if after observing him throughout the meal I think he is all that you say, what you should do is…'

Kamla Devi was elegant in a sari while Satisha dressed simply in a gathered, deep-lilac skirt and matching soft lilac shirt. She served crispy prawn spring rolls with her mother's tamarind and pepper sauce, followed by pumpkin soup. The main meal was fried rice with green peas and very thin slices of carrots, cabbage, leeks, cauliflowers, sweet and hot peppers – and a fragrant herb-roasted chicken. Dessert was Belgian chocolate ice-cream topped with walnuts. Amru was animated and charming.

One bottle of wine was now empty and another was half empty. Kamla Devi had just replenished Satisha's glass and was about to do the same for Amru when he said, 'Thank you, Kamla Devi, but I mustn't have any more. It is very good, but I have to work in the morning and I'll need my car. I think I ought to have a strong coffee. Satisha, I'm delighted that though you cannot roll a tyre, you can prepare such a delicious meal.'

'I am pleased that Dr Sen approves,' Satisha said.

Kamla Devi got up and said she must leave. At the front door she whispered, 'If you don't propose to him, I will.' As Satisha climbed the stairs she began to feel dizzy. The stairs could not possibly be moving. Kamla Devi had ensured that Amru and Satisha had drunk most of the wine, while she simply cradled hers saying, 'Doctor's orders.'

Amru had removed his jacket and was making the coffee. 'You had everything there, Satisha, so I decided to be useful.'

'Amru, the room is spinning.'

'The earth is rotating. You may be feeling its effects or it could be the wine. I had too much myself.'

'I have entered the world of Bacchus, Amru.'

'Where Bacchantes await with open arms. Don't lose yourself there. Have this coffee. Here, have it black.'

'Thank you.'

'Amru, I need to say something.'

He sat next to her on the sofa. 'Have a little of the coffee first.'

'I need to say something, Amru.'

'I'm listening, Satisha.'

'I want you to marry me.'

He was taken aback. Was it the wine? He was not sure whether to pretend nothing had been said or to make light of it.

'You need to rest a while.'

'I'm serious.'

'Of course you are.'

'I want you to marry me.'

'A delightful suggestion.'

'Do you approve? Say you will.'

'I will, Satisha.'

Then she fell asleep. He watched over her and used his jacket to cover her. Forty minutes later, she stirred and he brought a glass of water.

'That should help. Stay put for a while longer, I can't leave you while you're still feeling the effects of the earth's rotation.'

She sat up and said, 'I'm feeling much better now.' And then after a moment, 'I want you… I can't remember. Am I going to marry you, Amru? Did I ask you? I wanted to ask you. Did you ask me?'

'Yes I did. We will get married, Satisha.'

'Are you sure? I want you to be sure, Amru. I'm sure.'

'I have no choice. I wish it very much, you wish it, both our families wish it; we have no choice.'

They embraced and she wept. It was such a relief. She had not lost him after all. Later, they were convinced that the hands of their watches were in error.

Their formal engagement took place at the Sens' home. Both Amira and Mrs Sen cried. Santosh and Mr Sen embraced. Each said how privileged his family was to be joining the other. Vidya kissed everyone and announced that she was very happy and that if Satisha ever gave Amru any trouble, complaints should be sent to her and she would straighten the matter out; since becoming a teacher she had acquired the skills of a counsellor.

Two months later, a small family wedding was held at the Vidhurs' home. Ishani and Ravi Mita made the journey; Anjali and Praveen came over too, with their three sons in long trousers – Ishan, Sachin and Vish. Kamla Devi was there. When the ceremony was over, Satisha bowed low before her parents and her in-laws, and before Ishani too, to receive their blessings.

Anjali welcomed Amru to the family, pleased that Satisha had not succumbed to marrying outside the preferred choices; she knew too well how impulsive both her younger sisters could be.

The following day a reception was held in a hotel not far from

Westminster Cathedral. Amru had a few of his medical colleagues and Satisha had invited friends from the Commonwealth Secretariat and the City. Susanna Mayfield was there as was Edward Huntington. Satisha had him seated next to Kamla Devi.

Vidya was allowed to invite three of her friends to the wedding reception but said she only wished to invite one, and there he was, a young Englishman, Mark Baverstock. She introduced Mark to her mother who was only able to offer a preoccupied greeting and smile before she hurried off to attend to something that Vidya was sure could have waited. She could not help feeling disappointed, for she had wanted to bring up what she had long delayed – having Mark home to lunch. Her father, though, went out of his way to welcome Mark warmly and to talk to him. Santosh hinted to Vidya that it would be courteous to introduce her guest to all the family, and then leave him a little with the other guests.

'You need not be so protective of him, Vidya; he is safe in our hands. The hazards of your profession have taken their toll. He doesn't need a chaperone like the children in your class.' He winked.

Just as Kamla Devi and Mr Huntington had introduced themselves and had taken their seats, Anjali came up to them looking embarrassed.

'Satisha would like you, Kamla Devi, to promise her on this special day that you'll make one of your delectable cherry pies for Mr Huntington. She asked that it be served either with vanilla ice-cream, your home-made custard or both, if the gentleman so prefers. Satisha says she would like you to favour her with this request.'

The immaculately dressed gentleman blushed too and looked uncomfortable. When she left, he turned to Kamla Devi. 'I will not hold you to this. Please, it is far too large an imposition. Let's hear no more of it.'

'Satisha wishes to please. We both know her. This is her motive. So, let me say that I'd be happy to bake a cherry pie for you. No trouble at all. Satisha will soon be off on her honeymoon and her apartment would be the right place to do this; it's her idea, and my apartment is being renovated at present.'

'I couldn't possibly impose upon you. Think no more of it.'

'Here's my telephone number. Let me see, would next Saturday be suitable? Do not make up your mind now. Let me know later.'

They were surprised at how much they had in common. Edward told Kamla that he had recently been reading a good deal about India and its arts, that his memories of his visit in the 1950s were still fresh in his mind.

'I saw that our years in India,' said Edward, 'were at best a very mixed blessing for that country; I was horrified when I discovered that we used India's ancient sculptures in the Elephanta Caves for shooting practice – such arrogance in treating a culture more ancient than England's in the way we did.'

'It's the nature of absolute power, Mr Huntington. It always overleaps itself.'

'You were fortunate in having men such as Mr Gandhi and Mr Nehru to set the foundations for a democratic secular state. I think those two men enabled the country to move forward. That was admirable.'

'It was farsighted, Mr Huntington. But the Satyagraha philosophy was not new; its origins go back over five thousand years. In Harappa, none of the art or sculpture glorifies warfare or the conquering of enemies. So what did you make of the Ajanta caves.'

'They filled me with wonder… Those paintings are so lifelike; one can only imagine what they would have looked like when new – the colour, the movement, the facial expressions. What seemed uniquely Indian is that these were secluded retreats for Buddhist monks. Now, other religions would have chosen caves with bare cold walls so there were no earthly diversions. You have the most seductive female forms I have ever seen carved in stone.'

'Yes, in India the sacred and the sensuous are woven together. India respects the spirit that abstains from sensuous pleasures, but her arts also celebrate the raptures of the sensuous.'

'What do you think helped to bring this about?'

'The answer may be lost in time, but the erotic was always a joyous aspect of life. Within two well-defined parameters there's no "Thou Shalt Not". Nothing's explicit, but from the epics, the tales, the sculptures you have mentioned, the custom of daily massages, the draping of soft folds of silk around the female form, you can deduce a culture that is sensuously informed.'

'How very interesting. I don't know how I came to believe asceticism and abstinence defined India.'

'I think our Mahatma may have nudged you in that direction.'

He laughed. 'It's seldom just the one thing, or in this instance the one person, don't you think?'

'True. India produced the Mahatma, but it also offered the world the *Kama Sutra*.'

He blushed. 'You're right, of course. I think foreigners tend to take a single aspect of another's culture and believe it is the whole.'

'It's far less taxing to believe that other cultures are easy to read.'

'Especially if you have an empire to consider. I don't know if what I'm thinking is a polite question, and I hesitate to ask, but I'd very much like to know.'

'I'll try my best; go on.'

'Earlier you mentioned that within certain parameters... What are they?'

'Well, the first is within marriage; this is why an Indian bride is prepared mentally and physically for that experience with massages of oils, herbs and saffron – the very poor who can't afford saffron use turmeric instead, but all are conscious of the need to delight the body, to receive and to offer pleasure as well as to enhance the mind. The second is where two unattached persons, of their own accord, without any duress, mental or social, wish to share an experience of the erotic. They must know that in so doing no third party is being cheated, hurt or offended.'

'Your parameters sound like common sense to me, Kamla Devi,' he said. But Edward Huntingdon also reflected that common sense could rarely offer such a prospect of enchantment. What would a cherry pie, put together by Kamla Devi, be like? Had he protested too much?

57

THE COLOUR-HARMONY OF LOVE
December 2001

There was a tactile softness to the night. Rain had fallen and the amber lights of Apple Grove made everything hazy; nothing seemed solid, nothing had form. The rain and the light seemed to have swallowed what was there.

Amira and Santosh were in the sitting room, enjoying the peace, the quiet satisfaction that comes from a wedding reception well done. From the many thank-you cards they received, they knew it had been an enjoyable occasion for all.

Suddenly, the turning of a key at their front door; then the doorbell rang.

'Who could that be?'

'Has to be Vidya,' Santosh said, getting up. 'I must have left the key in the door… It is Vidya.'

'Would you like some dinner?' asked Amira.

'No I've eaten. How are you?'

'We are well and you, Vidya?'

'I've come to tell you I'm engaged to Mark.'

'What? What did you say?'

'I said I'm engaged to Mark.'

'To whom?'

'Mark Baverstock.'

'Who is he? Do we know him?'

'I introduced him to you and Daddy at Satisha's reception.'

'I cannot recall that. But even if you did, is this the way you tell us? We are your parents, Vidya. What is the matter? I can't believe this. I have no recall of meeting this… this Mark.'

'Yes, she did introduce him, Amira. I remember Mark Baverstock. I spoke to him at some length.'

'But is this the way we should be told, Santosh?'

'I'm glad somebody has not forgotten, completely lost it.'

'That's uncalled for, Vidya,' Santosh said.

'I shall ignore that. That day I met well over fifty people I'd never met before. And yes, my memory is not what it used to be. I don't need to be reminded, Vidya. That day, I had so much on my mind. I was overseeing everything; I had to ensure that nothing went amiss. Yes, come to think of it my memory is different from yours in an essential way. It remembers the things that matter, like common courtesy. You inform us that you're engaged to Mark Baverstock in this brusque way and I suppose you're thinking of marriage, yet he is someone we've never really met. As far as I'm concerned, I would not call what you have described as meeting him… Is he English?'

'I'm not going to apologise. With a name like that he's certainly not from Pakistan.'

'Unlikely. I'm relieved for you. I believe they are allowed four wives if the fancy takes them and they can afford it. I just can't see you with three other women in a house. However, from your behaviour, the way you now think, your disposition may have changed.'

Vidya said nothing, but seethed.

Amira felt exhausted, but she was going to stand her ground; she'd had enough of giving precedence to everyone else's feelings.

'The very least we could have expected is that you would pay us the courtesy of bringing him here to meet us, to get to know him a little.'

'I wanted to do that. I waited and waited to tell you, to bring him here, but the time was never right – there was Satisha's engagement and getting to know Amru's family, Satisha's wedding, Satisha's reception. It was all Satisha's something or other; her concerns were always before mine. I couldn't move; I was hemmed in. Before that it was Anjali. I realised I was on my own. No one was thinking of me. You gave me no choice; I had to make my decision this way.

'Mark wanted to meet you; he asked me several times. I promised him that I would, but the time was never right. Everyone was so happy for Satisha and I knew why. Those very reasons would be up against Mark. No one paid much attention to him at the reception although he was obviously with me.'

'I think we should have had a better opportunity to meet him. Was Satisha's reception the place for an important first meeting, with so many people around and so much going on?'

'You never gave me any time. I know how you both think. He doesn't have the kind of job with great prospects like Amru and Praveen; he has not been to one of the elite universities you approve. His parents are just another middle-class English family. He's not one of us.'

'But what is he like? Is he multicultural in his tastes? What sort of food does he like?'

'Food, food, food. It's all you ever think of, Mummy. You're such an ogre. I dislike this house, I can't bear you. I knew you wouldn't approve of him. I've never met anyone you would like. You make my life hell with constant questions, filling me with doubts and anxieties. You have answers to everything. I knew I shouldn't have bothered to come here to tell you.'

'If my knees weren't failing me, I would slap you.'

'Now please, both of you, just stop it.'

'No Santosh, you are partly responsible for this nonsense. You offered her far too much freedom and now we see the result. I warned you. Her head is full of values that are as light as puffs of air. I wouldn't be surprised if it lifts her out of this room… Now Miss… I can't bring myself to call you a Vidhur.' She bent her head, her throat hurting. 'You, you who are engaged to a Mr Baverstock, I wish to give you choice, something you never gave us. You don't have to invite us to your wedding. You don't have to tell us anything further about this Mr Baverstock. It would be very foolish to communicate with an ogress on such matters. However, you need to get at least one thing clear…'

'I hope this isn't going to take long. I don't have much time.'

'If you don't hear me out and you leave now, I'll find it difficult to welcome you here, though no doubt your liberal father will still do so. I, you see, expect a minimum of courtesy.'

Vidya picked up her handbag.

'Vidya, please stay and listen to your mother, then leave if you must.'

'I am only doing this for you, Daddy.'

'Sit down, Vidya.'

'I prefer to stand, Daddy.'

'That's the new way, Santosh. Her standing must be higher than her parents'.'

'Amira, please.'

'I'll wait until she's finished, Daddy, but I'm not sitting down.'

'When I asked what sort of food he liked, I was trying, in a discreet way, to get to know at least a little about him, his thinking. Food preferences can reflect one's wider tastes, disclose misgivings we do not wish to express openly. I know people who just hate curries and they also despise things Indian. An international taste in food can reflect an open disposition, a personality at ease with others. I have nothing more to say.'

Vidya sighed and left the room in haste. She closed the front door gently behind her and walked away briskly, her eyes glistening, her lips tightly compressed.

★

'Pass me the dictionary, Santosh.'

'What are you checking?'

'Ogre. She should have said ogress, but I plainly didn't manage to teach her everything. I've failed miserably where it mattered most – common courtesy. How could I have missed that? She's right; I am losing it. I don't need pity from others, Santosh; I'm wondering how long I've had this decline, when did it begin? I obviously need to monitor myself with greater care; I intend to miss nothing. From now on I shall monitor myself closely, observe where I'm drifting to.'

'Amira, for god's sake!'

'I will get the dictionary myself… Hmm. A terrifying person.'

'You know she doesn't mean that.'

'When I require assistance in deciphering what Vidya means, Santosh, I shall ask for it. I wish to close the matter now.'

She left the room and took refuge in the comfort of a warm shower. Her tears streamed and she sobbed like a child of three. Were her struggles on her daughters' behalf so terrifying? Perhaps they all thought she was terrifying, but only Vidya had the boldness to speak her mind. Well, she would spend her time in the garden, see more plays, start going to the cinema more often, learn to make beautiful pots, vases. Pottery would absorb her.

Perhaps even Santosh felt the same. And what did her neighbours really think? She wouldn't be asking them. Had she really filled Vidya with doubts and anxieties? When had that been? She had spoken to her from time to time about the need to reflect, to consider until she was sure about her decisions. Amira felt battered.

So had her entire life been a terrifying act and she not aware of it? Was senility closing in upon her? She would have to get in the habit of saying very little, simply listening, having no opinions. Talk only to herself. That would, at least, be safe. An ogress: well, well. What a transformation from being a fine teacher. Once upon a time, parents, students and colleagues had respected her for what she'd had to offer. That was another world, or was it a dream, only in her imagination? How had she become what she was?

She was about to put on one of the beautiful nightgowns Santosh had bought her. But she returned it to the drawer, where it lay beside the fine pieces from Madame Varekova's caravan on the old silk road. She closed the drawer gently, her eyes streaming. Of all her daughters, only Anjali really understood her. They'd been so close. Oh how she missed her.

Drying her eyes, she sought the monastic comfort of soft white cotton with a high collar and long sleeves, donned her crimson dressing gown, went downstairs and poured herself a glass of Madeira. Normally she would have asked Santosh, who was now in his study, whether he would join her, but she didn't, and he knew too well it was not the right moment to say anything to her. He would give her time, space to reflect, to communicate with her inner self, before joining her.

Time moved slowly. When her silence began to unnerve him he went to the kitchen cupboard and filled several small ceramic green, white and yellow bowls with cashews, pistachios, walnuts, almonds and Brazils.

'For the lady of our home,' he said.

No reply.

'May I join you with a glass of something stronger?'

Silence.

He poured himself a rum and sat down. She passed him the tray of nuts; he took a few; she helped herself.

'They are excellent,' she said, 'but you always buy the best, Santosh.' He wanted to say that she deserved the best – but he could see how sore her spirits were. With Amira, timing was paramount. If it was ill judged, the best of offerings would be blasted over the boundary with the energy and skill of a maestro at the wicket.

Moments passed before he said, 'You and Kamla Devi were so careful in seeing that everything was in its right place. I saw you moving a vase of flowers just a little more to the left, because you must have felt it offered a better display. The place names, the flowers, the seating arrangements, communication with the management of the hotel: you did not spare yourself. Everything went just as you planned; that is a miracle.

'Well, before we sat down, Vidya brought Mark Baverstock and introduced him to you first. After this, she brought him to me, and I encouraged her to introduce him to Anjali and Satisha, Kamla Devi and Ishani. This she did. Now you're unlikely to remember him for two reasons. You were preoccupied with many things that needed your attention. Besides, Mark was only one of a number of our daughters' friends, young English men, who were brought to meet you.

'Then again, Vidya did not hint in her introduction, or even in what she said later, that there was something more than being fellow teachers between Mark and herself. It would have been awkward for her to say more; the time was inappropriate, as you've said. However, because I had only to ensure that everyone was happily engaged, I was able to observe her. She was reluctant to let him go. She was over-protective of him, overly anxious. Actually quite nervous. I tried to put her at ease. I could see that she felt deeply for him, as I know she does for us, despite her anger. She wants to be able to live happily in three worlds – ours and his and her own.

'She has seen her two elder sisters marry young men whose backgrounds are very close to our own. She has observed the warmth and instant camaraderie with which we embraced their families and they us. Vidya has the good sense to realise that what we share with Amru's and Praveen's families will not be there with an English family, at least not for a while. It may come, but if it does it will take time in the making, while with the Sens and the Maheshs the bond was instant.

'You should forgive her, Amira. She'll need your support, despite what she says. By the way, I see that the other meaning of ogre is a man-eating giant in folklore. A creature of the imagination. Perhaps each tribe had to pretend they had their own ogre to frighten off their enemies and protect themselves. You've had to be especially protective of her. You fought her teachers at St Hilda's tooth and nail and you were with her against that bully she met at high school. You advised her well. She may not know it, but the steps she takes in life, the path she chooses to walk on, will be in a large part designed by you.'

'I'm well aware I was not on my best behaviour. I'm so tired, and I was terribly hurt. What resentment! My god, I was taken aback. I couldn't believe my ears. Just like that, out of the blue. Before she burst in, I was so enjoying the late evening, thinking how fortunate we were with our children. I don't understand why she feels she's in competition with Satisha. But I suppose if you look back it was always there; why she didn't want to go to North London Collegiate; why she didn't think about a job in the City, though I'm sure she would have managed it better than Satisha; she has more steely determination in her, but she wouldn't go where Satisha had already been.

'I'm mentally and physically exhausted. My tiredness reminds me that I am not getting any younger. I am not listening to what my more honest, inner self is saying. I have tried to do too much and have become weary, strained.

'I think there is just one thing in my life I have done that I have no cause to regret and that is marrying you, despite warnings from my family.' She rose from her chair and embraced him.

'I've been thinking, Santosh, that we need to go on a holiday. I feel the need to embrace mountains, breathe pure air, walk miles on a path in a forest where birds and deer look up and question my presence. Not a crowded place. A little solitude somewhere, to knit up the unravelling of my spirit. I want to escape the noise, the crowds, the continuous bombardment of unwholesome, vacuous images everywhere one turns.'

Amira chose the island of Dominica. She had been there once and remembered walking along such a height that the clouds appeared low, giving the impression that with the help of a ladder and a rod she could have touched them. It is said that when Columbus was asked to describe the island, he took a piece of paper and crumpled it to show its rugged mountains, ridges and peaks. She remembered how Dominica had been so quiet, so hushed, that a mother hen with two chicks had crossed the one main road in the capital, Roseau, and passers-by saw nothing daring in that family's waddling stroll.

Three days later Amira received a letter from Vidya. She made herself a coffee and took the letter to the sitting room.

My dearest Mummy,
I hope you can find a little place in your heart to forgive me. I am very sorry for what I said and how I behaved. I am ashamed. I know how hard you tried for me to gain what I have, how you helped me all along the way. I know that I owe so much to you and Daddy. There is such a great deal more to say, but I am overflowing with remorse and can barely think. Please forgive me. A large part of me would wither if I felt that you were unable to forgive me. I must have made Daddy despair of me too.
Your daughter
Vidya Vidhur

The surname Vidhur was underlined three times, with the P.S. *How can I not be? If I am not a Vidhur, who am I? I am nothing.*

Before her parents set off on their holiday to Dominica, Vidya came to see them. She said that she had learnt from her appalling behaviour that she should not do important things when she was tired, angry or frustrated. Ugly, unhappy emotions had a way of taking over uninvited. Having her back in the fold was healing to all.

Their holiday in Dominica was just what they needed. They walked as far as they could through mature rainforest and when their steps were slowed by humidity and heat, they would pause to listen to the forest sounds and absorb the deep vivid greens, observing patterns on the leaves when sunlight pierced the branches above them. They stumbled over roots of trees spreading out like the legs of a tarantula.

Amira's curiosity was captured by the wild species of anthurium. They were pale in comparison with the cultivated ones, yet it was their hardiness, she remarked, that had enabled the propagation of more vulnerable but flaming, vibrant reds.

There, engulfed in clouds of rising steam and sulphurous fumes – becoming invisible to each other – they experienced uncanny sensations. The numerous mountains, radiating ridges, valleys and caves, the hot mineral streams, the fumaroles and boiling lake, were reminders of the volcanic creation of the island. Everywhere along the narrow paths were signs of erosion, as the rain and the strong Atlantic trade winds worked at the slow crumbling of these massive mountains into boulders, stones, pebbles and sand.

That evening, after dinner, sitting in one of the oldest grand hotels in Dominica, they recalled their honeymoon in Grenada and the wonder and awe of the Grand Etang, once a fiery volcanic crater. There too they had listened to the harmonies of the natural world. It had completely absorbed Amira who had to be persuaded to leave. Its violent birth had made her reflect then, as it did again in Dominica that night, on man-made violence, thinking that its outcomes were never beautiful like the lake, Grand Etang, surrounded by tropical life and colour.

The following day they joined others to be transported in a hanging gondola through a mile of protected Montane forest, enveloped by the lush growth, the thick canopy overhead, among colourful butterflies, and the occasional humming-bird. But it was the astonishing variety that stirred them. Wherever light or moisture or exposure to the wind varied, nature brought forth something different. Among the buzzing of insects, the play of the wind over the canopy, the piercing cry of an unseen mountain whistler, the Rufous-throated solitaire, Amira and Santosh felt they were at the beginning of time. London was another world.

They returned to Mill Hill after a fortnight. An invitation from Mark and his parents awaited them, inviting them to Sunday lunch. At their house, Amira was struck by how peaceful and ordered it was. Mark said that he had prepared the bread pudding, which Santosh and Amira agreed was delicious. Mark bowed his head and blushed; he said the crust of his apple pie was just as mouthwatering and hoped, one day soon, to offer it to the Vidhurs. Amira asked his mother, Margaret, whether this was so; she confirmed it was – most times. Each family tried its best to please, and both felt the occasion had gone well.

The Vidhurs entertained the Baverstocks and six months later Mark and Vidya were married. It was a humanist wedding. They vowed to love and cherish each other, but not obey. Amira and Margaret read poems. The second movement of Mozart's 'Concerto for Flute and Harp' brought the ceremony to a close.

Ishani and Ravi invited them to their sea-view cottage in Toco on Trinidad's north-east coast, with its wild cane, tall grasses, rocks, sky and the Atlantic Ocean. There they were well served with a car and a housekeeper trained by Ishani.

Long ago, Ravi and Ishani had brought stones, boulders and pebbles to enclose an inlet that washed the lowest step of their cottage. When Ishani asked the housekeeper whether the couple were enjoying their stay, she said there was much shrieking and yelling, much splashing and spraying of each other with water and sand.

Two weeks later Ishani and Ravi had a full house of guests: Amru and Satisha, who was pregnant with Asha; Santosh and Amira; Vidya and Mark; Anjali and Praveen with their three sons, Ishan, Sachin and Vish, shy boys who introduced themselves with soft sibilants, then ran off to another part of the garden; and Savita and Hemkish. There in the midst of the fragrance of lady of the night, small red roses, mint and thyme, the twittering of birds, the tales of the swaying windchime and soft hiss of the fountains, they rejoiced in each other's company.

Mark was warmly embraced; Ishani said that Vidya was fortunate to have found a fine young man from amongst such a motley crowd of undecipherable people as the English. Mark said he was gratified he had been chosen by Vidya and welcomed by her family. Now that the old dame of Empire was retiring, her place was being taken by a younger generation with another perception of the world. A new, more questioning England was being born.

Ishani said that she had sad news to disclose. Both Palli and Lily had died recently. Palli had died first; three months later, Lily. They visited Lily's grave with flowers and her former pupils offered their silent farewells as they had done many years ago in Penal in that old, wooden schoolhouse with its spacious verandah. They threw flowers into the Caroni River where they were told Palli's ashes had been cast, remaining silent with their thoughts on the passing of time and its rebirth.

Satisha wanted to visit the old barracks; Ishani and Ravi explained that it no longer existed. Miss Daisy and the other squatters had moved on; the compound with its compacted lateritic clay, surrounded by thatched houses, was no more; in its place a shopping mall was being built. Nevertheless Satisha wished to go and Amru held her hand as she crossed over planks and piles of rubble. They received permission from the site manager to enter and were given helmets to wear.

They were astonished to see how completely the past had been erased. Even the large spreading tree with its numerous surface roots, over which Amru had rolled his tyre, had been uprooted. There was no trace of the large pile of stones. Amru was drawn to the spot where he thought it once stood. Affection for the place and the sadness of loss came over him as he remembered the innocence, the pure, unadulterated goodwill of the little boy who had so wished to please, to learn everything there was to learn, to empty the hospitals of the sick, the boy who had been unaware of the complexity of life, its harshness, its ugliness, its frustrations, as well as its beautiful people and its joys.

He left Satisha standing there and walked around the new foundations trying to work out where his family home and his ajee's house had been. He thought of the kind, wrinkled old lady, how helpless he had felt when she died, thinking he could have saved her, if only he had been a doctor. In her sick bed, gasping for air, she had said a few words to Aunty Ishani. That small exchange had changed his life.

He moved to an opening between two concrete pillars reinforced with steel rods. His throat tightened; a childhood prayer returned to him, and he offered it to the living earth that once heard him learning his tables, reading aloud to his parents as if he were a mandarin before a crowd. This was the earth that he had looked after with seeds and plants, water and manure, where he walked barefooted as a boy. This was the nature of time, the character of progress. This was no ground for nostalgia or sentiment; he would have to keep his past in his memory, lest it be irretrievably lost. You had to keep moving on, ever onwards, though where he could not say. There was no time to stand and stare. He swallowed to ease his dry throat, bit his lips and returned to where Satisha was standing.

The baby moved in her womb; she said that little Asha was saying she would have liked to roll a tyre here. She would have to do this in London, Amru said, adding she was likely to be better at it than her mother.

That evening, Satisha received a long-distance call from Kamla Devi. Edward had wished to offer her a more settled position, but she'd declined his thoughtfulness. 'It was better, Satisha, for him to remain free.'

'Why?'

'His friends at the club and his family wouldn't approve. He doesn't see this as fully as I do; but I hear the many things that have no mouth. I, too, have no wish to be constrained on where I go, what I do with my spare time, how I dress and conduct myself. Independence and I have long been one. To be his occasional companion suits me.'

Satisha said she was glad to hear that Kamla Devi would keep close to Mr Huntington, adding that she still had a deep affection for him. Kamla Devi ended the call by saying, 'I would never have thought that miracles could be brought about with a well-baked cherry pie, Satisha.'

When Satisha returned to the gathering, she joined in a chorus of 'For she's a jolly good fellow', holding hands with the family in a circle around Ishani. Gifts were brought to her. Embraces, hugs and tears.

That evening, after dinner, when all the rest had left the garden, some retiring early for the long flight back to London, Santosh and Amira stayed behind. The night sounds of their childhoods could be heard: a crowd of cicadas on the move, the rustling of birds settling themselves between the branches, the whistling wind, croaking frogs in the canal, hooting owls not far away, stray dogs in a chase along the road, a distant crowing, a donkey braying.

EPILOGUE

IN ISHANI'S GARDEN ON THE HILLSIDE
August 2002, Trinidad

They have all left with their laughter and mirth. What rests with me is a solitude I've sought. Our grandchildren filled the day with the buoyancy of youth. Santosh and I remain behind. We sit looking out at Ishani's garden, the flowering ixoras and sweet-scented frangipani. We sit with our silences, comforting, reassuring.

He says, 'It's time to go in now.'

'I will stay a while longer,' I say, sensing the past and present merging within me and the need to reflect upon them. He doesn't try to persuade me to leave. A life together brings a rare understanding at times; we've been lucky. I imply that he understands me, but I mean as much as it is possible to know another, bearing in mind that knowledge of oneself rolls with the throw of the dice.

Now he too walks towards the house. His soft strides gently touch the earth, reflecting his temperament and his journeying with time. He moves without the camouflage of appearances, without their inherent stresses, and the grass, holding the falling night's dew, gladly carries another uncontrived thing, as natural as itself – his walking shadow.

I perceive with clarity tonight, as never before.

After the fullness of the day, there's something about the feel of this place, of this hour, that opens, enlightens, clarifies the hidden.

It was only after their first son was born that Anjali told me all. I wished I had known what I should have done differently, how to have prepared her for this, how to have ensured that I would have been the first to know. I was so ignorant when I needed to know much, was unaware, until recently, of the many demands of our multifaceted selves. I thought of swimming lessons and Indian classical dance and drama and music but not karate classes… yet we were fortunate.

'We are neither panthers nor owls,' I told Anjali when she asked me this at the age of nine. 'We were once stars in the heavens, offering streaks of light to perpetual night, so darkness was halved.'

'Is that true, Mummy? Is it true?'

'It's the truth we know, my beloved daughter. It's the truth we live by.'

Oh how she mirrors me. Like Santosh and I, she came to London already formed, with the energy of the tropical sun, which offers another light, another way of seeing.

Long before her wedding I sensed she was carrying some deep sadness. I saw it in her eyes. We were both blessed to have Lily and Palli teaching us that good living, like great cooking, is an art, with love, understanding and knowing how as important ingredients. They lived as they taught.

I so wished she had shared her anguish with me. I have asked myself over and over again why this did not happen. Why didn't she? Yet I can see why she could not share it with Ishani, preferring Lily and Palli. This was my failing too. Was there a vital ingredient missing in what Santosh and I offered her at home? My being pulls apart, when I consider what she went through alone, because of my not knowing the art of parenthood, its complexities – its how and when in offering compassion, empathy, affection and discipline to my daughters.

I was not sufficiently wise to realise what I did not have and then acquire it. We offered them the best we knew, Santosh would say. He is very good at saying soothing things when my spirit is in turmoil. It may not always have been so, but over the years he, more than I, learnt that exquisite art of how to live.

In some ways I am like Anjali, for I have not told Santosh, not wanting to bring him pain. I hope Anjali knows far more than I did, so her daughters will run to her.

When Santosh was here, the full moon was overhead but now its gaze is before me. The wind rustles as if a flock of birds have descended; the branches vibrate. A shower of light falls. I look within its perimeter.

From the tall shrub that leans upon the massive knobbed tree trunk, a solitary shadow emerges. It seems so alone. I know this form well; it is Margaret Summers. I have her letter here in my handbag. Her husband Jack found a younger woman from South America and has asked for a divorce. The house has been put up for sale; meanwhile she will be living in Yorkshire. There will always be a warm meal and a warm bed for Margaret at 14 Apple Grove. 'You were a light to me and my daughters,' I wrote, and meant it.

When they were all dining with us, I sensed something was not right between them. But couples have their off days. How could anyone leave a warm, caring, affectionate person like Margaret?

It won't be the same in Apple Grove without Margaret. And then both Alice and Nick Reid and Janna and Edward Cohen sold their houses and moved, respectively, to Devon and Dorset. Alice and Janna came to say they were on their way when the removal vans left, just as they came all those years ago to introduce themselves. We will now have lived in Apple Grove longer than anyone else, but I fear we will be returning to an emptiness wrought by time.

The spacious lawn invites the wind which hums, lifts leaves, stems, branches. The bamboo wind-chime is still silent, I await its dance as the wind grows. The darkness listens. My throat constricts.

There are days when my spirit takes refuge in another time, reliving my childhood: there were holidays at Maracas Bay where I was in awe of waves high as mountains, or when, sitting on a huge white marble-like rock stuck in a shallow river bed, I would be engrossed by sunbeams hopping on the water, while parrots squawked deep in the surrounding green forest. Or my running and running round the savannah opposite our home, stopping to catch breath, seeing only the familiar. And there I was, lying on the grass, prickly and tickly on my bare legs, listening to the fast-moving tales of clouds.

From far away a tune comes. I ask why couldn't I have had both, this life with my family and my teaching career? Why am I feeling so inadequate? The tune returns; I hum it. Though I know all the words, only a few sentences now come from across the ocean of my memory.

Some day I'll wish upon a star
And wake up where the clouds are far behind me
Where troubles melt like lemon drops
Away above the chimney pots
That's where you'll find me…

'You've been asleep Amira,' Santosh says when he comes out to look for me. 'Look, the moon has travelled on. Come. You need to rest. It has been a good day with our children and grandchildren. The house is fast asleep. Come, let's go in.' He offers me his hand. 'Tomorrow we leave for London.'

Tomorrow, we will be returning to a house empty of the voices of our daughters. No doubt, soon, there will be the patter of little feet exploring, hands and mouths searching, tasting, pulling and tugging at everything within reach. I've missed out on not knowing Anjali's boys as well as I would have liked, but that cannot be helped.

331

'Now here is an opportunity, Santosh, for us to embrace our remaining time and do those things we often said there was no time for. I would love to be a potter of fine pots. I shall find out how best to prepare myself and make a start.'

'I have beautiful books to read,' he says, rising, 'and I need to recall certain events for our daughters and grandchildren before my memory leaves them behind and they're lost to me.'

'Soon, we'll be alone Santosh; time for another beginning.'

'Look, it's a full moon; let's use its light to find our way to the house. Come Amira.'

I am reluctant to leave. He offers me his hand. 'Come, come now, Amira.' His presence makes the coming silence comforting; the sound of our footsteps is soon lost to the night. Only the wind-chime plays.

ABOUT THE AUTHOR

Lakshmi Persaud was born in 1939 in the small village of Streatham Lodge, later called Pasea Village in what was then still rural Tunapuna, Trinidad. Her father was a shopkeeper and her home was hard-working, secure and increasingly prosperous. It was a devout Hindu home where pujas, kathas and other observances were regularly held. She attended the Tunapuna Government Primary School, St Augustine's Girls' High School and St Joseph's Convent, Port of Spain. She records in *Butterfly in the Wind* the mental conflicts that attending a Catholic school caused for a Hindu girl.

In 1957 she left to study for a BA at Queen's University, Belfast and a postgraduate diploma in Education at Reading University. She draws on this experience in one of the episodes in her second novel *Sastra*. After teaching for several years in the Caribbean she obtained her doctorate in Geography at Queen's University, Belfast. She taught at Queen's College, Guyana; Tunapuna Hindu School, Bishop Anstey and St Augustine Girl's High School in Trinidad and Harrison College and St Michael's Girls' High School in Barbados. After leaving teaching she became a freelance journalist.

Her published fiction includes *Butterfly in the Wind*, *Sastra*, *For the Love of My Name* and *Raise the Lanterns High*.

She has lived mainly in the UK since the 1970s, with a two year spell in Jamaica in the 1990s. She is married with three children and now grandchildren.

Butterfly in the Wind
ISBN: 9780948833366; pp. 200; pub. May 1990; price: £7.99

This fictionalised autobiography gives a richly woven portrait of Kamla's life from early childhood to the point where she leaves her family, Pasea village and Trinidad to attend university in the UK. It gives a vivid and inward picture of a Caribbean community still in touch with its roots, seen from the developing perspective of a young woman at the crossroads of diverse social, cultural and religious influences. The portrait bears witness to the moral strengths of the community as well as showing Kamla's growing awareness of the repressions and hypocrisies of its treatment of women. From early in her life Kamla is surprised by a contrary inner voice which frequently gainsays the wisdom of her elders and betters. But Kamla is growing up in a traditional Hindu community and attending schools in colonial Trinidad where rote learning is still the order of the day. She learns that this voice creates nothing but trouble and silences it. In this book the voice is freed.

Set in the 1940s, *Butterfly in the Wind* was enthusiastically received when it first appeared in 1990. Its portrayal of a passage from childhood to young womanhood was praised by *The Sunday Times* as 'a sweet-natured book which is above all a tremendous celebration of life'. *The Observer* praised it for 'the empathy with which Lakshmi Persaud writes of the natural world... and Hindu customs'.

Sastra
ISBN: 9780948833717; pp. 273; pub. 1993; price: £9.99

The pundit warns Sastra's mother that her daughter's birth signs foretell two possible karmas, one of prosperous security if she keeps to the well-tried path of obedience to tradition, the other of mixed joy and misery if she should attempt to 'fly' and follow her own desires. These are indeed Sastra's choices – between the traditional, collective Hindu society of her parents, and the world of individual destinies and responsibilities to which her generation is increasingly drawn.

Set in Trinidad in the 1950s, *Sastra* is a moving and tender love story, a rich evocation of the village world and a memorable portrayal of a brave young woman who never tries to evade or complain about the consequences of her choice.

'One of the novel's most striking qualities is the assurance with which it registers inner turbulence. It often suggests a web of feeling that trembles within a framework of courtesies.' – Mervyn Morris.

For the Love of My Name
ISBN: 9781900715423; pp. 336; pub. 2000; price: £10.99

Torn between confession and self-justification, President for Life, Robert Augustus Devonish writes his memoirs as his country falls apart around him; Kamilia prepares for a workers' last stand against his regime; Vasu sets off to investigate the rumours of untold horrors in a commune deep in the interior; and Marguerite Devonish has to decide between loyalty to family or country in bringing to an end her brother's crimes.

Through these and many other unforgettable characters Lakshmi Persaud tells of the last days of the Caribbean island of Maya before it sinks beneath the sea. This challenging novel profoundly dramatises the consequences of ethnic prejudice in a culture of masks which gives licence to individuals to abandon moral responsibility for their actions. Its echoes resonate across the killing fields of Bosnia, Kosova, East Timor – or wherever state power gives free rein to the most primal impulses of kith and kin.

Told through multiple voices, whose tones range through the lyrical, the direct and unvarnished, the conversational and the polished, *For the Love of My Name* weaves a striking tapestry of hatreds and loves, duty and the degradation of consciousness, despairs and hopes. Above all the bright threads of human resilience glint in the weave.

Jeremy Taylor writes in *Caribbean Beat*: 'Lakshmi Persaud's third novel is a much more ambitious affair than her first two… It asks the question: why and how do we allow tyranny to take root? As the despot entrenches himself – the violence, the sophistry, the vote-rigging, the power-games, the asset-stripping – why is he not unmasked by other governments, by the intellectual elite, by the churches, by ordinary thinking people? Why is it so easy for him to outsmart us, divide us, manipulate us, until it is too late and there is only ruin and desolation? These are questions which range far beyond the Caribbean, but they are dangerous and uncharted territory for the Caribbean novel (yes, and why is that?), especially when the case study is a barely disguised version of a Caribbean state which will be easily recognised by any Caribbean reader. (And it's not Cuba, either; this is not post-Cold War polemic.) What's more, Persaud suggests a large number of persuasive answers, which do no credit to anyone. The book is adventurous in its structure and its range of narrative voices... an important book...'